Praise for the novels of Elysia Whisler

"Smart, sexy, and full of heart, *Rescue You* is one of those warm and fuzzy books you want to stay up reading all night. Elysia Whisler has crafted an unforgettable story of loss and love and the power of finding your own strength. If you love dogs and a great slow-burn romance, this one is for you!"
—*USA TODAY* bestselling author Sara Ackerman

"Sweet and raw, beautiful and gritty. A heartwarming romance about the power of healing, *Rescue You* was everything I wanted in a story. Elysia Whisler's remarkable debut is sure to earn her many fans."
—Sarah Morgenthaler, *USA TODAY* bestselling author of *The Tourist Attraction*

"Heartfelt... The beauty of this book is in the down-to-earth characters. Whisler's intimate look at the bighearted women's lives makes for a worthy, stirring tale."
—*Publishers Weekly* on *Rescue You*

"A complicated story about tormented people finding and healing each other. The rescued dogs are almost an excuse for the human stories, except for Humphrey, the poor, abused beagle Rhett saves. Whisler is a licensed massage therapist, and her description of Constance's massage practice is fascinating, almost spiritual. An unusual and wonderful story."
—*Booklist*, starred review, on *Rescue You*

Also by Elysia Whisler

Rescue You

Look for Elysia Whisler's next novel
available soon from MIRA.

ELYSIA WHISLER

forever home

mira

ISBN-13: 978-0-7783-1160-7

Forever Home

Recycling programs
for this product may
not exist in your area.

This edition published by arrangement with Harlequin Books S.A.

For questions and comments about the quality of this book, please contact us
at CustomerService@Harlequin.com.

Mira
22 Adelaide St. West, 41st Floor
Toronto, Ontario M5H 4E3, Canada
BookClubbish.com

Printed in U.S.A.

For Mike

Because every girl deserves a dad who shows her how to fly

forever home

one

Three Rebels Street.

Delaney should've known that this was where she'd end up. This was the kind of street a woman went down when all the big changes in her life were happening at once. You simply couldn't hit a retirement ceremony, the road and a funeral all in one week and *not* end up on Three Rebels Street.

"*Small* is not the right word. I prefer *quaint*." The real estate agent, Ronnie, gazed around the studio apartment situated on Three Rebels Street, and nodded her head in approval. "You said it was just for you, right? Which means it's the perfect size."

Stop trying to sell me on the apartment. Ronnie had described it as an "alcove studio"—not just a studio—because even though the living room and kitchen were all in one large space, the bedroom was situated in a little nook, with its own door. Delaney didn't care. The living quarters didn't really matter. Right now the place was dumpy. Dust everywhere, the ceiling fan hanging crooked with exposed wires, and debris in the corners, like the previous tenants hadn't taken care of the place and then left in a hurry.

"We didn't have a chance to get this cleaned before your showing," Ronnie said, following Delaney's gaze. "Remember, I suggested waiting until Friday."

But Delaney hadn't been able to wait.

Ronnie lowered her voice to a near whisper. "They were evicted. But this place cleans up nice, I promise."

"Can we go back down to the shop?" Delaney ran her hands through her hair, rubbing the weariness from her scalp. Ronnie had whisked them through the front bay door and up the stairs, like the apartment was the prize inside the cereal box. And Delaney supposed it was—small, an add-on, not really the point. For Delaney, the shop downstairs was the *entire* point.

"Of course." Ronnie's voice was bright, forced, like she didn't give two shits. This was probably her last showing of the day and she wanted to get home, into a hot bath with a glass of red as soon as possible. She clacked down the stairs in her high heels.

Delaney followed, the earthy clunk of her motorcycle boots the bass drum in the cacophony of their feet.

"The shop." Ronnie swept out her arm. "Look how much space." There was no enthusiasm in her voice. Ronnie, who probably did mostly living spaces, had no idea how to sell the garage.

Didn't matter. Delaney sized up the shop herself: concrete floor, perfect for working on bikes. It was kind of dinged up, but that was okay, she was already envisioning painting it beige with nonslip floor paint. Modern fluorescent lighting. Large bay door, wide-open to the cool air, excellent for ventilation. A countertop with a register. Empty shelves on one side for parts and motor clothes. Showroom space for custom bikes, and enough room for at least two workspaces out front. The rest, Delaney would provide. Hydraulic lifts. Workbench. Parts tank. Tools. Parts. Bikes.

She wanted to pinch herself, but chose a poker face. Ronnie stood in the center of the floor, like she was trying to avoid touching anything, to avoid getting any grease or oil on her smart red suit. The shop was in better condition than the apartment, but it still looked like the last occupants had left quickly—or, if they'd truly been evicted, perhaps *reluctantly* was a better word. Nothing important remained, but the place hadn't been swept or washed or readied for sale in any manner.

"I'll consider this." Delaney rubbed her chin as she strode through the shop. "It's a little small." It was actually larger than she'd expected. "Light's good, but might get a little cold in the winter." It was winter now, technically. Mid-March. Delaney loved this time of year, when winter and spring intersected, like lovers making up after a nasty fight, the weather edgy and unpredictable.

"There's a lot of interest in this space." Ronnie clutched her clipboard to her chest as she looked around. She could be looking at the inside of a spaceship and hold that same expression.

Motorcycle shops were going out of business, all over the place, including the one that had recently vacated. After suddenly finding herself on Three Rebels Street last week, in front of a shop-apartment combo for sale, Delaney had done her research. The previous tenants, who she now knew had been evicted, were brothers who ran a shop by day and lived upstairs by night. They sold mostly new bikes and motorcycle gear. Repairs and maintenance were basic. Their website was still up, despite the fact that Dude's Bikes had closed. Dude's appeared to focus mostly on male riders, leaving Delaney to wonder if Dude's was just about dudes or if one of the owners was, indeed, named Dude.

"What's the story on this place?"

Ronnie glanced at her clipboard. "The owner wants to sell. After the last renters' lease ran out, they were given the option of buying or moving. I don't think their shop was doing well, because they couldn't afford to buy. They weren't even paying their rent. And they weren't quick about moving. The rest, as they say, is history."

If the last motorcycle shop had failed, buying would be a gamble. But any business venture was a gamble.

Life was a gamble.

"There are a couple of people looking, after you." Ronnie continued, "About five."

Delaney could respect white lies in the sales biz but seriously? Five? Five or so people were waiting to check out the bike shop with an overhead apartment suitable for one small, low-maintenance tenant? She had no idea how two brothers had managed up there.

She strolled through the space, wanting a good feel. She needed to touch things, inhale the shop, draw its molecules into her lungs and taste its history before she could decide on the symbiosis of her dream space. Triple M Classics—short for Martin Monroe's Motorcycles, named after her father—would own her as much as she would it, so this relationship was going to be deep and mutual. Through the front window, she could see the parkway that ran the length of the county. At just past eighteen-hundred hours, rush hour was a jam of red taillights in the waning daylight. No amount of time would erase Delaney's memory of her last tour here, when she had to commute to work every day. Pure hell. It would be nice to go right upstairs to her cozy little apartment after closing, rather than having to sit in that mess.

Across the street was a row of shops, including a grocery story and an Italian restaurant. Food. Check.

On the south side, the shop butted up to the woods, which had a downward slope of grass and weeds that led to the trees. Privacy. Double check. Plus, Delaney figured if there was a tornado, that slope could count as a ditch, and would probably be the safest place to run. She laughed at herself. This wasn't Omaha. Virginia tornado season consisted of a few warnings that rarely panned out.

Delaney withdrew the listing, printed from the internet, from her back pocket, crammed together with a grocery receipt for extra firm tofu, Tater Tots and Ben and Jerry's Cherry Garcia. "This is the price, right?" She handed over the paper. Money would be tight, but Delaney should be able to manage for a little while until things got going.

That is, if she was going to do this.

Was she really going to do this?

All her adult life Delaney had moved around, from station to station. Forts, camps, bases. Not shops. Not *homes*. She'd never put down roots. Never had anything permanent other than her childhood home with Dad. Never owned a thing she couldn't cram into a duffel bag.

Ronnie looked at the paper. "No." She sniffed. "There's a newer listing." She flipped through her clipboard, laid it on the counter and pointed. "Here we go."

Delaney looked at the asking price, choked a little bit, almost thanked Ronnie for her time and left. That would be the smart thing to do. Sometimes childhood dreams just needed to stay dreams.

She strode around once more, mentally saying goodbye to everything that she'd never even made hers. Even though all of this had been a panster move, it felt like all the blood in her veins had been replaced with disappointment. She stopped by the far wall, where a ratty piece of paper hung by a sliver of tape. Delaney smoothed out the curled edges and read the flyer.

Fiftieth Annual Classic Motorcycle Show.

Dogwood County Fairgrounds.

The event was in July. There was a contest, including prizes. The grand prize for the winning classic cycle was five grand plus a feature article in *Ride* magazine.

The disappointment started to drain away. Five grand wouldn't pay all the bills, but exposure in a major motorcycle magazine would be a boon for business. Plus, there was something about that poster, just hanging there like that.

It seemed like a sign.

"Oh!" Ronnie's sharp exclamation came from behind. "Oh, what is that?"

Delaney turned just in time to see a large dog waltz through the open bay door. He halted at the sound of Ronnie's voice, one paw raised, ears pinned. He looked like a pit bull, his colors white and chocolate brown. The chocolate dominated his right side and ran up around his right eye. The other side of his face, including his muzzle, was white, as well as his chest and most of his left flank, though he had chocolate splotches there, too. He reminded Delaney of Chunk, the pit bull Dad had found in the neighbor's cornfield back when Delaney was about eight years old.

It had been one of those thick, windy Omaha summer nights, and Dad was sweaty, shirt stripped and stuffed in the back of his jeans, when Chunk had followed him home through the corn maze to the front porch, where he'd plopped down and refused to budge. Delaney had been watching *Goonies* on cable, and right when she saw Dad hit the porch she'd called out, "Sloth love Chunk!"—their favorite line. The dog had peeked inside, startled, and everyone had laughed. Chunk, even though he wasn't Chunk yet, had been covered in blood-gorged ticks and Dad had spent the evening showing Delaney how to squeeze them in just the right place to snap them out of the dog's skin. *Gotta make sure you don't leave the heads buried,* Dad had said. Chunk had been their dog after that, fiercely loyal and a permanent fixture at the foot of Delaney's bed at night up until the day he died in his sleep at an indeterminate ripe old age.

Only now did it occur to Delaney that she had no idea whatsoever what Dad had been doing in the neighbor's cornfield. Though it would explain the abundance of fresh corn chowder all summer long.

Ronnie took a couple of steps backward, wobbly in her heels. "Stay very still," she hissed. "This looks like a dangerous breed."

The pittie sniffed the air. His eyes were wide. "Nah." Delaney tucked her hands in the back pockets of her jeans and waited to see what the dog would do. He'd come in here with such purpose. "He looks confused. Not dangerous."

After a moment of stillness, the dog trotted over to the door behind the register. He sat down, his ears perked expectantly. He waited, but when nothing happened, he reached out with his paw and scratched the door.

"What is happening?" Ronnie whispered, hand on her chest. Nails and lips were a perfectly matched red. Rather than being pleasing, Delaney found the combo contrived. Ronnie screamed stop sign rather than alluring siren.

"Let's find out." Delaney went behind the counter, toward the door where the dog sat. She put her hand on the knob and the pittie rose, shaking out his legs, like he was readying to go inside. She turned the knob, but it was locked. "Do you have the key?"

"I'm not sure that's a good idea." Ronnie's gaze was on the dog.

"I need to see the room anyway." Delaney offered her knuckles to the pit bull. He gave her a tiny bump with a cold, wet nose, and refocused on the door.

Ronnie dug through her pockets, then winged a key at Delaney from across the room. The key flew way to Delaney's right.

She lunged and made a grab.

"Wow." Ronnie forgot herself. "Good arm."

The key slid easily into the knob and the door opened.

The dog rushed inside, a little whine escaping his throat as he pushed into the darkness. Delaney followed, fumbling against the wall. Just inside on the left, she flicked the switch and dim light flooded a large work space/storeroom. There were rows of metal shelves, empty, along with a larger open space that could be used to work on more bikes once Delaney had a staff of mechanics, or to store bikes and merchandise for sale. A second bay door—the back bay—covered half the rear wall. Off in the far corner of the concrete floor was a shaggy, worn dog bed, where the pit bull settled into a ball. His head rested between his paws, but his eyes were open. He huffed, not completely satisfied with what he'd found, even though the bed had been his destination.

Delaney's heart suddenly felt too big for her chest. They'd cleaned out everything but the dog bed—and, apparently, the dog.

"I'll call animal control." Ronnie's voice came from behind her shoulder. She was no longer whispering or on edge. Now that the dog was safely balled in the corner, Ronnie considered him with cold eyes.

He lifted his head and looked around, expectant.

Scared.

Lost.

His tail thumped against the bed, just as a child might wring his hands or fidget.

"Animal control?" Delaney wrinkled her nose. "As in, the pound? You want to send him to the pound?"

Ronnie shrugged. "Are you going to take him home?"

"I don't have a home." Delaney was staying at a hotel, ten minutes away. Now that she'd officially retired from the Marine Corps she'd jumped head first into civilian life. Up first was getting off Quantico Marine Base and into normal quarters. If you could call an apartment over a bike shop normal. "Besides." Delaney gestured to the black Honda Rebel 500 parked out in front of the shop, just visible through the doorway that Ronnie had propped open. "Even if I had a home, I couldn't put the dog on my bike."

"Well, there you go." Ronnie shrugged. She slipped her cell phone from the front pocket of her suit.

"Wait." Delaney held up a hand. She crouched down and walked toward the bed. "He's wearing a collar." Delaney extended the same hand the pit bull had bumped with his nose earlier. He crawled forward, using his paws to inch closer, like he was stretching, and sniffed around Delaney's knuckles. She brushed them back, against his muzzle and then down to his neck, where she felt around for an ID tag. Her fingers closed over smooth, flat metal. Delaney peered at the tag. "Sinbad," she read. Meh. Maybe. He did have an eye patch. "There's a phone number."

Ronnie sighed.

"I'll call." Delaney slipped her phone from the back of her jeans and tapped in the number. "Do you think I'm just going to reach the guys who rented this shop?" She mused aloud. "Do you think they really meant to leave him here?" She suddenly remembered seeing a dog that looked like this one in a picture on the Dude's Bikes website.

"I don't know them," Ronnie said. "I don't ride motor-cycles."

Delaney was busy thinking about all the ways she might be able to buy this place without Ronnie getting any commission when a bright, cheery voice popped on the other end of the line. "Pittie Place, this is Sunny."

"Hey, Sunny. My name's Delaney Monroe. I'm over here on Three Rebels Street." For about the millionth time since Dad had died she squelched the urge to text him. Last time it had been to tell him that, after roaming around on her bike, crying inside her helmet over his death, she'd suddenly found herself on Three Rebels Street. This time she wanted to tell him that she was going to *live* on Three Rebels Street. "I'm at a motorcycle shop that used to be called Dude's? There's a dog here. A brown and white pittie named Sinbad. He's got a collar with your number on it."

A long pause followed, along with some background noise that sounded like Sunny was questioning someone else about the dog's whereabouts. Finally, her voice came back on the line. "Sorry," she said. "Did you say Sinbad? We didn't even know he was missing."

"Yep. That's what his collar says. Sinbad. Like the pirate." Delaney noted that the dog gave no visible reaction when his name was mentioned.

"He got out somehow," Sunny said, and Delaney could tell by her tone she spoke mostly to herself, "and found his way back to the shop. Isn't that something."

"Is he yours?"

The pittie curled into a ball and huffed a sigh.

"He is now. I'll come get him right away."

Delaney waited outside with Sinbad on a leash that she found hanging inside the storeroom. Talk about douchebags.

The Dudes had stripped the store of every last nut and bolt but left the dog bed, the dog leash and the dog.

Ronnie had bailed, with a promise to get back to her on the shop and apartment, and Delaney was left with the pittie. Together, they watched the fireball of a setting sun on the horizon. "Don't worry." Delaney squatted down next to the dog, who sat on the pavement and stared into the woods like he, too, wondered if he could hide there from tornados. Up close he smelled clean and woodsy. He'd probably traipsed through there to get back to the shop. "Those stupid Dudes didn't deserve you."

Delaney laid a hand on his back and he flinched. She dropped her hand away just as an old Ford truck, snow-white, pulled into the lot. A long, slender blonde emerged; solid posture and a strong gait. She wore blue jeans and an old peacoat. Delaney slackened her grip on the leash, to see if the pittie would run to her. He perked up his ears, but didn't budge. He looked anxiously toward the shop, then shifted his weight from paw to paw.

This guy had been passed around. He was an orphan. Dad used to fidget, especially during times he forgot himself, like when he wasn't working on a bike or riding. He'd be all over the place, sweeping or scrubbing or organizing, like he didn't know where to settle. Maybe afraid to. He only slept when he passed out from exhaustion. Delaney would find him on the couch in the morning before school, zonked out in a sea of throw pillows and blankets, TV muttering in the background. Delaney would fix herself a bowl of Sugar Smacks—back when it was okay for a cereal to be named Sugar Smacks—then sit by his feet and watch *The Price Is Right* before running for the bus. Sometimes Dad would wake up in time for the Showcase Showdown and they'd take bets on who would win. Sometimes they'd ask each other what they'd do with the money if they ever won *The Price Is Right*. Their answers always matched: open my own motorcycle shop.

"Hey!" The blonde spotted them, even though Delaney and the dog hadn't budged. She headed their way, her strides quick and focused. She held a leash in one hand. "I'm Sunny," she said, as Delaney rose to meet her. "Hey there, Sinbad. Hey, boy." Sunny's voice changed, filling with warmth.

He pushed his muzzle forward and smacked his tail on the ground. It seemed like he knew her, but was trying to remember how she fit into his vagabond life.

Only after she'd greeted and made sure Sinbad was okay did Sunny extend her hand toward Delaney. "Sunny."

"Delaney."

They shook hands like women do, just a gentle touch hello, no clasping, owning, dueling or innuendo. Sunny glanced around. "You found him out here?"

Delaney tilted her head toward the shop. "I was with a real estate agent, checking it out. The bay was open and this guy just came trotting inside. There's a dog bed in the storeroom. He settled right in."

Sunny's mouth turned to a grim line, the opposite of her pretty and cheerful name. Delaney imagined Sunny got told to smile a lot.

"The guys who owned this shop adopted Sinbad less than a year ago. As far as I can tell, they weren't abusive. But he was apparently just an ornament. As soon as the shop failed, they bailed, gave him back to me with some story about moving somewhere they can't have a dog but will come back for him once they have more space."

Delaney looked down at the pit bull, who kept equal amounts of empty space all around his body, like he favored no direction. Or, maybe he had no direction. She found herself disliking the Dudes even more than before. They hadn't even bought their dog a new tag, with their phone number on it. Hadn't even committed to the level of a cheap piece of metal. She wondered if they knew what that kind of thing did to a person—being part of a world where you mattered only within other people's framework of existence. Delaney wondered if the Dudes knew what it was like to not have anyone be *all in* on you.

It was a deeply lonely feeling, one Delaney had never felt until she stood staring down at her father's wrecked body.

"I run a dog rescue," Sunny explained, as she switched out leashes, unclasping the one Delaney had found in the shop and attaching the one she'd brought. "It's called Pittie Place. Poor Sinbad has been passed around since he was born."

"I can tell."

"You buying this shop?" Sunny's voice brightened.

"I hope to." Delaney shrugged.

"That your bike?" She nodded at the Rebel.

Delaney followed the look, then stuffed her hands in her back pockets. "That's one of them."

"Nice. Are you new to the area?"

"No, but I've been living on Quantico. Time to get my own space."

"Marine?"

"Yeah. Just retired. Been in since I was seventeen."

"Impressive."

Delaney shrugged.

"Alright. Not really the chatty type, are you?" Now Sunny did smile. It was a deep, genuine, beautiful thing. "Well, it's cold out here. I'm sure you've got somewhere you need to be. I'm going to get Sinbad back to the rescue. Start over from scratch. Huh, boy?" Sunny petted behind his ears and he seemed to smile a little bit. "Thanks again for calling. Nice meeting you and let me know if I can help in any way. I've lived here all my life and know all the curvy back roads." She glanced at the bike and winked.

Cute. "Thanks." Sunny started to walk away but Delaney called her back. "Hey. One thing you might be able to help me with. I need a gym, now that I won't be using the one on base. Like ASAP. Nothing fluffy. Somewhere I can get some serious work done."

"A gym?" Sunny dug around in her coat pocket. "I've got just the place." She pulled out a dog-eared business card and passed it over. "The guy that owns this place is also a Marine Corps vet. If you want hard-core, this is your jam."

Semper Fit. Yeah. Delaney should fit right in. As much as she ever fit in, anyway. "Thanks, I'll check it out."

Sunny raised her hand in a wave as she walked Sinbad to her truck. She hustled him into the passenger seat, then came back around to the driver's side.

"Hey!" Delaney called out again.

Sunny halted. "What. You the type that only wants to talk when someone's trying to leave?"

Ha. Cute and clever. "I don't think Sinbad is his name."

Sunny's brows knitted.

"I just—" Delaney shrugged "—don't think that's who he is. It won't fix all his problems, but finding his real name should be the next step."

Sunny poked her tongue in her cheek, then laughed and shook her head. "Well, I'll keep that in mind, Delaney. Thank you."

Sunny backed up and drove past slowly, offering a wave. The pit bull, upright in the passenger seat, stared right at Delaney as they went past. His eyes were droopy and sad. Delaney watched him go, the empty leash from the storeroom still clasped in her hand and dangling on the cold ground.

She stood there until the sun had set and the sky went dark, didn't even realize she was shivering until the cold had seeped into her bones. Time to head back to her hotel and wait for Ronnie to reach out about the next step. This might be a little crazy, and she might be sticking her neck out, but Delaney was convinced that she had to give this a try.

Triple M Classics deserved a chance, and now that Dad was dead, Delaney was the only one who could make that happen.

two

"For someone who just closed a case, you should be in a better mood."

Sean gave his partner a weary look as he leaned back in his chair and stretched his arms over his head. His whole body was stiff. "That case was over before it started. I knew it was the ex-boyfriend from the second I took that woman's statement. And I knew she was just as shady as he is."

Sonia Castillo shrugged. "It's always the ex. Be happy. You got it done."

"Meh." Sean reached for his duffel bag under his desk. "I'm going to hit the gym tomorrow. Sweat this whole week out."

"Man, you have it bad. You just can't resist the long chase, can you?" Castillo leaned against the door frame, coffee cup in hand, ankles crossed. "But you're not supposed to actually want to take months or years to make a collar. The whole idea is to catch the bad guys."

Sean shook his head. Sonia could be such a sap sometimes.

She really believed in all this good and evil shit, when the truth was, the world was about a million shades of gray. "Didn't you think it'd be different?" Sean cleared his desk of today's mess: coffee cups, a paper plate, a clump of staples. He'd started making that a closing routine at the end of each shift. He'd read a book about starting your day with a made bed and ending it with cleaning up all the messes you'd made along the way. It was supposed to leave him with a sense of ownership and accomplishment. Instead, it just made him feel sorry for mothers everywhere.

"Thought what would be different?"

"When you were a kid and you wanted to be a cop. Didn't you think that collaring 'bad guys' meant taking down the bandit in the mask who held up the innocent bank teller, not cuffing the scumbag boyfriend stealing dope from his ex-girlfriend's apartment, after he gave her a good beating?" And when Sean had cuffed the scumbag boyfriend, the girlfriend had started crying and begged Sean not to arrest him because she *still loved him*. "Didn't you think that 'protect and serve' actually meant *protect and serve?*"

Castillo nibbled on the green plastic stopper from her coffee cup for a second before lofting it into the trash. It hit a pile of papers and disappeared. "I wanted to be Jennifer Lopez when I was a kid."

Sean flipped off the lights and edged Sonia out of the office. "You should've done that, Castillo. What the hell were you thinking?"

"Aw, Sean." Sonia wrapped an arm around his waist and gave him a buddy hug. "Don't sweat it. You'll get a hard chase soon, I'm sure."

Sean went home and got some shut-eye, then woke in time for the mid-morning class at the gym. He'd learned to live on four hours of sleep for years, but the one place he couldn't avoid showing his hand if he was tired was Semper Fit. The truth was he wanted to see Red so he could schedule a massage, and odds were she'd be there. But he couldn't just show up to see the gym owner's girlfriend without Santos giving him a rash of shit, so he'd have to work out first.

He sat in his car until the last possible second, eyes closed, dozing in the wind that blew in through the open windows before he forced himself awake. His lungs were full of clover and honeysuckle and all the spring things. Semper Fit was packed, as usual. There was no downtime at this gym, its success due to a variety of factors like location and results, but mostly the no bullshit vibe. Those that wanted to flex and curl in front of mirrors were quickly weeded out and what was left was a community, staff and programming that would pick you apart, layer by excruciating layer, until your ego was curled in the fetal position in the corner, begging for mercy.

Sean eyed the whiteboard, where the workout had been written in elegant red letters—back squats, box jumps, handstand walks, toes-to-bars. Handstand walks? Ugh. Zoe, who was clapping her hands and calling everybody in for the pre-workout prep, had obviously coached the earlier class, too.

"What the hell you doing here, Callahan?" Rhett Santos cuffed him on the shoulder as his deep voice boomed over Sean's head.

"Not trying to read your chicken scratch, thank God," Sean said. "You should let Zoe write the workout every day."

"Why would that matter to you? You only come in once a month."

"Some of us work for a living, Santos. Don't have all day to mess around on the monkey bars." Sean nodded at the rig, where some people were already doing a kipping warm-up.

"Alright!" Zoe raised her voice. Her diamond nose ring

sparkled when her nostrils flared. "Everybody quiet while I go over the workout. That includes you, Santos."

A chorus of *ooooooh*s went around the gym as everyone cast glances at the six-foot-five gym owner who took Zoe's reprimand with a huge grin. Red, who came sprinting out of the office, laughed the loudest. Fit and bursting with energy, she was a far cry from the quietly withdrawn woman hiding under oversize clothes Sean had met over a year ago. Red gave Rhett's ass a smack and he grabbed her around the neck in a fake choke hold, which turned into a hug.

"Hey, Sean," Red whispered, her eyes going big when she spied him. "You need to come see me about a massage. It's been a while."

"It's like you read my mind." Sean was still laughing when he turned his head to face Zoe and the whiteboard. His gaze trailed past her, to the right-hand corner of the gym.

Humphrey, nestled in his dog bed a few feet away, caught Sean's eye. Rhett's old beagle was the official gym dog. A rescue who had barely escaped death about ten times over, Humphrey went just about everywhere with the Marine Corps vet. The old guy trotted at Rhett's side without a leash, slept in the corner while everyone banged their weights around, even went with Santos to the grocery store, where the management allowed him in to shop despite not technically being a service dog. Usually, at the start of the workout, Humphrey was snoozing in his bed by himself. Today, a woman Sean had never seen before squatted next to him, petting his ears while she smiled softly. It was a Polaroid moment, because Humphrey usually only tolerated touch from Santos or Red. Everyone else just had to admire him with words.

The strange woman, this dog witcher, glanced up at that moment.

Her eyes caught, then held Sean's. Big and bright, Sean

could tell even from across the space that they were an unusual light brown, like butterscotch.

No. Not like butterscotch. Like *scotch* scotch. Specifically, like Highland Park Fifty Year. From Glasgow, a rich, fruity, complex scotch that Sean had been treated to by the grateful, wealthy father of a woman Sean had extracted from a bank robbery years ago. Sean didn't have any trauma about that day, even though guns had been drawn and his life had been on the line, but he'd readily admit that even ten years later, that scotch haunted him. Sometimes, at night, he could still feel it on his tongue, rolling and warming like silk, tasting like strawberries, oranges, raisins and vanilla. The bite that dragged across the end of the swallow was like the caress of a banshee. Both soft and rough. A danger you craved.

The woman's smile fell. She turned away. She stood up and ran a hand through her short, dark hair and squared her shoulders, which were bare in a plain gray tank top.

Sean had stared too long, losing himself in those whiskey eyes. And it was hard not to keep staring, at the little V of feathery hair at the nape of her neck or the smooth, cut muscles of her arms and shoulders. She was a sweet, hard, dark-haired pixie with the eyes of a desert cat, and Sean wanted to follow her back to whatever magical, secret, dark place she'd come from and curl his body around hers.

Shit. Jesus. WTF?

He forced his gaze back to Zoe, whose voice had grown strangely muted to Sean's ears. He realized his heart rate was jacked, his pulse thudding in his neck. He tried to pull himself together when they were released to do the warm-up, but he couldn't shake those eyes. It wasn't so much the color, even though it was absolutely the color, but everything swimming inside them.

"Eh, Santos." Sean tried to catch him while they all bear-crawled across the gym. Santos was so tall his bear crawl looked awkward and clunky. "Who's the new girl?" He pointed to the rear of the gym, where Highland Park had finished her bear crawl and was executing high-leg kicks that nearly touched her nose. She was all alone inside a sea of chattering people, oblivious to their conversations.

Rhett was quiet while he watched her a second. He turned to Sean with a shrug. "Don't know. But a hundred bucks says she's a marine."

"Her name's Delaney." Red's voice came on Sean's other side. She stared up at him with a knowing smile. "She's a drop-in. This is her first time here. Came in with a business card. Doesn't talk much."

Sean felt his cheeks warm. Overly curious by nature but a master at keeping that fact to himself, he hated when people guessed his thoughts. He didn't mind Rhett knowing his interest had been piqued, but Red was another story. Not that she'd say anything. To anybody. Ever. But Sean respected the little massage therapist who'd come into Santos's life and turned it around for the better. Sean didn't need her thinking he was a perv, especially when he'd briefly dated her sister, Sunny.

"Just get it done." Rhett shook his head with a smile. "It's hard enough to get you in here to work out. You don't need any distractions."

This was all true. "But she was petting Humphrey," Sean said. "You see that?"

Rhett shrugged. "Humphrey makes his own decisions."

As they moved from warm-up to workout, Sean did his best to focus on the job at hand and not on Delaney. If he doubted her toughness, he only needed to watch her with the barbell. Though impressed, Sean was a little disappointed. If he'd been able to offer her some pointers, he would've had an excuse to talk to her. But Delaney could likely give him pointers, if he was honest.

When they were all collecting wooden boxes to jump on for the rest of the workout, Sean found himself directly behind the newcomer. The boxes weren't typically heavy for someone who was fit, but they could be awkward to maneuver.

"Need help?" Sean almost regretted his words as soon as they popped out. At this gym, everybody collected and cleaned up their own equipment, no questions asked. If you couldn't lift it, you couldn't use it.

Delaney peered at him from around her box. "I'm good. Thanks." She hauled her box to the corner of the gym closest to Humphrey and didn't give Sean a second glance.

Sean grabbed his own equipment and set up his workout space, but watched, out of the corner of his eye, as Delaney warmed up her handstand walk. She flipped right up on her hands and executed a tight, smooth walk from one end of the gym to the other, then dropped down, one foot at a time, with the grace of a ballerina. Humphrey seemed to watch her, too, even though everyone knew he had cataracts. Sean was glad he wasn't the only one who struggled to keep his eyes to himself.

The music rose from the speakers, belting out a hip-hop playlist. Then Rhett shouted, "Three, two, one, go!" and Sean shook himself free of her spell and focused on his workout. When it came time to do a handstand walk, Sean groaned inwardly. He hadn't done them in ages and knew he should probably scale the movement to something he could handle better. But today, Sean's male pride was real. Delaney flipped onto her hands at one end of the thirty-meter marker and Sean did the same at the other. His walks had never been super-clean, his legs bent awkwardly and pace clunky, but as he started moving down the floor he surged with pride. Was he really going to pull this off after a spotty year at the gym and his last recorded handstand walk a distant memory?

That was when Sean felt his balance go. Worried he might flip over on his head, he tried to bail sideways. He smacked into someone and they both went tumbling to the floor. "Shit, I'm sorry." He looked down at his victim, pinned under his bulky weight, and died a little bit inside.

Delaney glared up at him, her amber eyes on fire.

Rhett dropped out of his handstand walk with grace, despite his height, and planted his hands on his hips. "Callahan. You're done with handstands today. Go get a set of dumbbells."

Sean rose to his feet. "Roger that," he agreed. He wanted to help Delaney up, maybe apologize again, but she'd already flipped back onto her hands and finished her walk. She jumped to the rig and knocked out ten toes-to-bars like a gymnast.

Sean sunk into his work and wondered how much of the burn was lactic acid and how much was embarrassment. At the end of twenty minutes, when time was called, Sean slumped to the floor against his box and listened to the grateful thump of his heart. Only when Rhett smacked him on the shoulder did he remember it was time for high fives.

Sean offered and accepted fist bumps amongst the sea of people cleaning up equipment. He didn't spy Delaney anywhere until he found himself directly behind her, as she was washing the chalk and grime off her hands at the sink. Plastered on the wall over the faucet was a poster for an upcoming summer fundraiser workout for Canine Warriors, several months away. An outdoor workout in July? Ugh. Pass. Sean could donate without actually attending, right? "Hey, sorry again about the spill," he said, determined to keep it cool this time. He offered a fist.

She turned to look at him, hands dripping wet. She lifted an elbow to tap his fist. "Don't worry about it. I've been done worse." She looked like she was stifling a grin as she swiped her hands on her shorts, then was off, headed for the cubbies where people stowed their bags and coats. She said something to Red, who was getting a drink from the water fountain. Red smiled, said something back to her. They talked a few more seconds, before Delaney smiled, too. Looked like it might be pretty, but Sean was too far away and could only see her profile.

Then she was gone, out the door. Sean resisted the urge to ask Red if the new girl was going to join the gym. He put away all his stuff, feeling mentally worse than when he got here, even though physically his body was thanking him. Just as he'd tipped his box onto the stack, outside a motorcycle roared to life and rolled past the open bay door. The rider wore a silver helmet and red jacket, blue jeans and black motorcycle boots. She had to have put all that stuff on in the parking lot, but Sean knew exactly who was driving that bike.

He watched her go, and as the bike disappeared around a curve in the road, Castillo's words echoed through his mind: *Don't sweat it, Sean. You'll get a hard chase soon.*

Sean was a mile from home when he made the split-second decision to stop at the grocery store for some Guinness. Nothing wrong with topping off a brutal, embarrassing workout with a cold one.

He'd just pulled into the parking lot when he spied a first responder vehicle, lights rolling, parked along the fire lane of the supermarket. Sean wasn't on duty but he was headed into the store, anyway. Couldn't hurt to see if he could be of help. He may not be the greatest at handstand walks, but he was good at his job. He grabbed his badge from the glove box and hustled inside to a group of county firefighters in the produce section, kneeling on the floor, making a circle around someone. Sean pushed his way through gawking shoppers to get to the scene.

A small woman in blue jeans and a white T-shirt sat on the floor, near the apple case, with her knees to her chest, arms curled around her shins, head to her knees. A few spilled apples littered the floor beside her. She rocked herself gently. One firefighter knelt beside her, hand on her back, talking softly. Another first responder had a dog on a leash, straining to get to the woman. The dog looked like a pit bull, on the smaller side, all black, with a little white patch down her chest. She wore a camo-colored vest with the words *Do Not Pet, SGM Trinity* embroidered on the side.

"That's a service dog," Sean said. "Let it go."

The firefighter—a kid, no more than early twenties—looked at Sean with wide, confused eyes before Sean pulled his badge from his shirt and let it hang from its chain. The kid let go of the dog. SGM Trinity rushed to the woman, pressed her muzzle in and licked at the woman's face until she finally peeked up. The licking continued, all over the woman's face until she stopped rocking. "Okay," she murmured. Her hand went to Trinity's head, swiping over each ear. "Good girl. Off."

Trinity stopped licking and stood next to the woman, quiet and alert. She looked like a little black ball of thunder.

"You okay, ma'am?" The firefighter by the woman's side still had his hand on her shoulder. She seemed to notice the touch for the first time and flinched.

The guy was clearly young, confused and unsure—probably one of the volunteers—so Sean stepped in and made a gesture. The firefighter drew his hand away. The woman pulled a deep, shaky breath. Her eyes were big and her skin clammy. She reached for Trinity and petted over the dog's back in long, steadying strokes. She petted so hard it looked like she leaned into the dog for support. The dog made no reaction, other than standing still and allowing the woman to pet her.

"You okay, ma'am?" the firefighter repeated.

The woman nodded rapidly. She looked around at the crowd that had gathered and shrunk into herself, like a turtle in its shell.

"Everyone back to shopping." Sean raised his voice and pointed toward the corners of the supermarket. He waved a hand at the crowd. "Go back to your business."

People reluctantly dispersed.

"Cashier called 9-1-1," the firefighter who'd been holding the dog said. "Woman freaked out in the produce section, was on the ground, with a dog in her face."

"It's clearly a service dog."

The kid shrugged. "When we got here, one of the employees shoved her leash into my hands. He'd pulled the dog off the lady."

"Understood."

The firefighter next to the woman rose and offered her his hand. She shook her head. "I'm fine." Her voice was almost a whisper. "Go. Please."

Damn. They were all just doing their jobs, but nobody here had any idea what they were dealing with. Sean walked over to the shopping carts and grabbed two of the smaller ones in each hand. He lined them up a couple yards away from the woman, her dog and her spilled apples. The firefighters stepped out of his way as he repeated that with more carts, until she was circled off by a row of carts, with the apple stand at her back. Sean stood just outside of the circle he'd created while the firefighters packed up.

After about five minutes alone inside her space, the woman finally stood. She was just a wisp of a thing, black hair in braids, big eyes, brown skin and couldn't weigh a buck-ten with rocks in her pockets. Her gaze fixed on Sean, who'd hung nearby. "Thanks," she said, her voice weak.

Sean pushed aside one of the carts and stepped into the circle, but still kept his distance. "You alright, Miss...?"

"Tabitha," she said.

"You okay, Tabitha?" The perspiration on her face was drying and her breaths were winding down.

Tabitha nodded. "Panic attack came out of nowhere. Trinity had it under control." She gestured toward the dog. "One of the employees pulled her away from me. He was—" she scanned the store, but obviously didn't see the guy "—stacking apples, and I guess he thought she was hurting me, but licking my face is one of the things she was trained to do."

Sean nodded. He knew that people often had the best intentions but sometimes misunderstood and made things worse.

"Thanks for..." Tabitha trailed off, her gaze following the line of carts. Realization slowly filled her eyes. "Oh, geez. Everyone's looking." Her eyes cast down. "Aww. Look at all the apples I dumped."

"Apples are tough." He pointed at Trinity's vest, changing the subject. "You in the service?"

Tabitha's face relaxed. "I was." The tension in her body started to dissipate, starting with her shoulders and working its way down. "Been out for a while."

Sean could tell that her brain was defogging and she was starting to feel relieved and embarrassed all at once. She wanted to flee, but also wanted to trust in her dog and accomplish her task. Only now did he spy the hand basket on the ground, a few feet from Trinity. It was full of apples, like she planned to make a dozen pies. The odds of Tabitha finishing her shopping and making those pies were probably about seventy/thirty right now, in favor of fleeing. "Why don't I stay close while you finish your shopping?"

"I…" Tabitha's eyes went to Sean's badge, then to the fire-fighter who still stood outside the circle of carts. "Really?"

"Long as we hit the beer aisle." Sean offered a grin that he hoped was comforting. The woman reminded him of his niece. They were about the same age—late twenties? Same build. Same aura of innocence. Only difference was Lizzie was pale as a ghost and went all shades of pink when she was embarrassed.

Tabitha smiled. "Thank you, Officer…?"

"Callahan. Detective Callahan."

"Detective Callahan," she repeated. Then Tabitha picked up her basket and led Trinity through the produce, methodi-cally choosing fruit and vegetables like she wanted to repre-sent all the colors of the rainbow.

"She seems okay, physically," the firefighter said, once Tabitha was back on her feet and moving around. "She re-fuses to go to the hospital. You got this?"

Sean nodded. "Thanks for coming out."

Sean stayed close but kept his distance, briefly wondering what the woman had been through. He thought of Rhett and Humphrey, which was a natural leap to Pete, who trained ser-vice dogs for military veterans. Odds were high that Trinity was one of Pete's. But Sean wouldn't be asking Tabitha about that, or even speaking to her again. His task, right now, as he'd so recently mentioned to Castillo, was to protect and serve. He hadn't enjoyed his shift yesterday and he'd made a huge mess of things this morning at the gym, but right now, right in this moment, he could be of some good.

Tabitha checked out and he watched until she was safely out the door, fruit in one hand and dog in the other, a little wave over her shoulder, head held high, like she was determined to rise above it all. Sean bought his Guinness and decided the morning hadn't been such a bust after all.

three

The bike has arrived, Delaney typed as the caption. *She got to Triple M Classics on Three Rebels Street in one piece.* Then she clicked Post and the photo of Dad's 1933 Indian Four filled out his Facebook wall.

In the picture, the motorcycle dominated the freshly painted concrete floor of Delaney's new shop, the sun glinting off the polished black fuel tank and the word *Indian* scrolled in gold. It'd cost a pretty penny to ship, but there was nothing to be done about that. Despite the many offers Dad had gotten over the years, and the handful Delaney received from all his biker buddies when Dad passed, the motorcycle would literally only be sold over Delaney's dead body. In the family for as long as he could remember, the bike was the only material object Dad had ever given a crap about. He cared for it like a child, which meant he gave the motorcycle the same diligence he had raising Delaney: a light-pressured patience, keeping her and the bike both in running shape in deliberate, necessary increments. Total neglect was a crime but too much attention or interference spoiled the authenticity of the piece.

You gotta let it be what it's supposed to be, Dad liked to say, whether he was talking about bikes or his daughter. It was the same phrase he used when people tried to get him to modernize the Indian or when nosy neighborhood mothers told him that Delaney needed more instruction in the ways of being female, and that raising her like a boy, around all those motorcycles and grease and big guys in leather, wasn't good for her.

Delaney wondered what those do-gooder soccer moms would think of her now. A thirty-seven-year-old, single Marine Corps veteran who'd just spent her life savings on a motorcycle shop and who posted regularly to her dead father's Facebook wall.

That's so sad. The exact words of Tammy Rollison's mother the day she poked her head into Delaney's bedroom and saw that the only amusements were books, motorcycle magazines, a baseball and catcher's mitt, and two battered board games—Sorry! and Monopoly, both missing lots of pieces. Tammy Rollison had all the Barbie videos, a huge dollhouse her father had made by hand and stocked with miniature people and furniture, and about a dozen different brushes, bands and implements with which to style her hair.

The joke was on them. Delaney liked helping her father repair and build motorcycles more than anything, second only to playing catch. She couldn't stand the Barbie videos and though she secretly loved the dollhouse—all that tiny stuff fascinated her—Delaney would never give up her pixie cut.

Delaney scrolled through the handful of posts she'd put on Dad's wall since he'd died, which included photos of her retirement ceremony and a happy birthday message he'd never seen, and considered deleting them, even though nobody would ever see them. Dad had never wanted a Facebook page and only joined so that he could follow Delaney's posts and some of the online motorcycle groups. When he'd died and Delaney went to delete the page, she'd discovered that Dad had only one other friend besides herself—a person named Lauren Bacall, using the old film star's photo, and zero posts—but over five hundred friend requests queued up that went back a decade. Well, wasn't that just like Dad. Everybody considered themselves Dad's best friend but Dad claimed no one but his daughter. And, apparently, Lauren Bacall.

Delaney couldn't bring herself to delete anything. She closed up her laptop and checked her phone. A text from Boom, owner of the bike shop Dad had worked at all his life, Delaney's second home, and one of Delaney's many "uncles."

How you doing, Pip?

Delaney couldn't remember a single instance of Boom using her real name. He'd called her Pipsqueak all her life, because that's exactly what she'd been around all those big guys in the bike shop. Half a dozen bikers who either worked Boom's shop or frequented it, all of whom rode together, all of whom acted like Delaney was one of their own. Even as she grew and eventually made it to five feet eight inches, the guys called her Pip. Or Squeak. Or Pippie. Or Pipsqueak.

All good, Boom-Boom.

Delaney was pretty sure his real name was Lamar but nobody ever called him that. Boom came in like a smack of thunder, both in size and sound. A friendly smack of thunder, unless you got on his bad side, but a storm in and of himself.

You get the truck home ok?

I'm here. Truck's out front. Bike got here today. All good.

She'd flown back to Omaha after she closed on the sale of the shop so that she could drive the Ford back here. Boom had offered to buy that, too, even though he knew Delaney wouldn't part with it.

Take good care of it. And my girl.

Will do. 😚

Delaney didn't have a father anymore, but Boom had certainly tried to step in. "Come back to Omaha, Squeaky," Boom had said at Dad's memorial service, which was held at Boom's bike shop, the only church any of them had ever known, "Free Bird" playing out the speakers in the corners and everyone drunk on Maker's Mark. "We'll take care of you."

"I can't," she'd said. She'd looked around the shop at Boom, Zip, Donnie and Sal, and she'd only felt lonelier because she couldn't really see the group of men that had helped raise her. She could only see that Dad was missing from that group. "I can't stay here."

Boom had looked at her a long time, his bloodshot eyes warm and the corners of his downturned mouth buried beneath his salt-'n'-pepper beard. "Okay, Pippie. But you know you got a place to be if you ever need us."

Delaney clicked off her phone and went for a shower. She was greasy from unloading the bike today, even though the delivery guys had looked over her head and all around the shop to see who was really there to receive such a prize.

"That's a sweet ride," the smaller of the two guys had said.

He was wiry and had greasy hair and eyed Delaney as much as he did the motorcycle when he spoke.

"It is." Why argue? "Leave her right there. She needs a little work."

"She?"

Delaney shrugged. "My dad and I used to argue about it. We eventually decided the bike is both genders and agreed to call them '33. But I still call her *she* a lot."

"Would you sell her?"

"Nope. Never."

The look the guy gave her was typical—almost offended, like a woman didn't deserve such a bike. Delaney ignored it, officially done with that nonsense, as much as she was officially done with this day. She hopped under the warm, wet spray and closed her eyes. Despite not having many things to her name, closing on the shop and moving in had been a months-long process that left her exhausted. She hadn't even had time to make it back to Semper Fit. As she rubbed soap over the side that had sported a large bruise after her last visit she was reminded of the guy who'd knocked her over with his clumsy handstand walk.

She laughed, despite herself. Typical male ego. Intolerable, really, and not even worth her time. Except for the way he'd looked at her when he apologized. And when he'd offered to help carry her box. *Dude*, she'd wanted to say. *I'm a motor transport mechanic. I lift all the heavy things.* But something had stopped her. She still couldn't pinpoint what, but call it instinct. Delaney trusted her intuition. It was the only thing she could rely on to help navigate her atypical life. She grew up in the boys club, which had the benefit of making her think she was just one of the guys. By that same token, thinking she was just one of the guys, when she really wasn't, could be dangerous. The boys club didn't always have a welcome sign, even if she could outrun most of them. Especially because she could outrun most of them.

She had to be careful.

The guy who knocked her over with his eager handstand walk had a lot going on behind his hard-set facade. On the taller side, with a muscular frame, clean cut, sandy hair and an aura of authority, he would've been imposing if Delaney hadn't noticed the faint scar just near the corner of his left steely gray eye. Marine, she'd immediately thought, which didn't make any sense. He could've gotten that scar anywhere, doing anything, in any branch of the military, or on the playground as a kid. But a little squeeze had run through all her muscles when she'd spotted that line of pale, barely discernable skin. His eyes had changed, almost like he'd noticed her noticing it, and in that brief moment Delaney had gotten a peek somewhere he didn't want peeking.

Marine, she thought again, as she dried herself off with a big, fluffy pink towel. Not that that made him safe, or her friend. Or anyone to keep thinking about, the way she was right now. Delaney brushed him out of her head.

She didn't have a bed yet to go in the little bedroom, because her goods on Quantico had been military issue and shopping for furniture had come second to getting the truck and the bike and to setting up the shop, but Delaney had slept on the ground countless nights of her life. A sleeping bag and pillow on the hardwood floor of her very own studio apartment, above her very own motorcycle shop, felt downright luxurious.

Delaney slid inside the bedroll and jammed the pillow into her neck, her back to the wall and her Glock 43 within reach.

She slept hard. Didn't even remember falling asleep until she suddenly woke. Delaney sat up straight inside the bedroll. She blinked in the darkness, trying to remember where she was. Camp Leatherneck came first, which was common, and then, most unusually, Camp Lejeune. But the smells were all wrong. No heat. No sand. Not even motor oil or brake fluid. The world was dark and strange, but smelled like spring; like cool wind and pollen. Like the air of a free man; smells Delaney had fought for, for years, but hadn't really experienced in a long, long time.

I'm in my new apartment.

As soon as the thought registered, the scratching that had woken her came again. A clawing sound that came from below, somewhere in the shop.

Delaney grabbed the Glock and tiptoed to the stairs. She took each step on the balls of her feet, cautious and quiet as her eyes adjusted to the dark. When she got to the bottom she whipped around the corner, weapon drawn.

There was nothing there but '33, shining in the dark.

Scratch. Scratch. Scratch.

Something clawed at the front door. Through the glass, which had been scraped clean of the Dude's title and operating hours, and was now bare and awaiting the shop's new details, Delaney saw the shadowy figure of an animal.

Oh, wow. Could it be?

Two months later?

She unlocked the door and in came Sinbad, whooshing past her until he was behind the counter. There he sat, just like he had back in March, and waited patiently to be let into the storeroom.

Delaney glanced at her watch: 0300. She wasn't going to wake Sunny at this hour. "Okay, boy." She slid the Glock to the counter, grabbed the ring of shop keys and found the one to the storeroom. "Your bed's still in there. Glad I didn't get rid of it." She'd thought about it, but at the last second, Delaney had left the scruffy thing right where it was. Getting rid of it seemed wrong. In her heart, it felt like the dog had just as much a right to this space as Delaney did.

Maybe more.

She poked the key in the knob and paused. "You can come upstairs if you want. It's cold and dreary in there." Delaney headed for the stairs and patted her thighs. "C'mon, boy. Wanna come upstairs where it's warm? You can sleep by me."

The pit bull whined and slapped his tail on the ground. He pointed his nose at the storeroom.

"Alright." Delaney frowned as she opened up the back room and watched the dog race over to the tattered bed, where he curled into a ball and closed his eyes. It was like setting something free after too long in captivity and watching it return to its jail cell, comfortable only because it was all he'd ever known. "I'll be upstairs." Delaney collected her weapon and pointed at the ceiling. "If you need me." Sinbad sighed but didn't open his eyes. He also didn't follow her as she climbed the stairs and slid back into her sleeping bag.

Even though everything was quiet after that, it took Delaney a while to drift off. She kept thinking about the pittie downstairs, in that cold storeroom, on that scruffy bed. Only when she reminded herself that he couldn't go anywhere, and would be safe until morning, did she let the tug of sleep overtake her.

By morning, when Delaney crawled out of the bedroll and shook off the dreams, she hoped to find the dog poking around the apartment, but all was silent. Knowing she didn't have any dog food, Delaney hit the kitchen, just across the room, nestled in a nook by one of the windows. There was a stove, a row of cabinets and drawers done in cherry, a sink, and a stainless steel refrigerator that had conveyed with the sale. The backsplash between the granite counter and the cabinets above was a cool blue that made Delaney think of

K-Bay, her tour at Kaneohe, Hawai'i. On the adjacent wall was a table with tall chairs, flanked by two windows, where she could sit to eat.

Delaney wouldn't be eating there today. She pulled eggs and leftover tofu from the fridge, and whipped up a quick scramble in a cast-iron frying pan she'd taken from Dad's. She'd gone through the house before putting it up for sale, taking his personal things, donating others, and leaving the appliances and furniture to convey. But there was no way she was leaving this pan, which she and Dad had used to cook almost everything they ate. Along with the tofu and eggs, she grabbed two pieces of bread from the loaf on the counter, soft, because the toaster wasn't unpacked yet, and a bottle of water, and took the food downstairs.

Delaney chuckled when she saw the pit bull peeking around the corner of the back room, nostrils flaring as he took in the scents of breakfast. She found a bowl in one of the boxes near the stairs, then put half the scramble and a slice of whole wheat bread inside. "Sorry, boy," she said, as she set the breakfast down at the pittie's feet. "I don't have any dog food. And I don't eat meat. I hope you like it."

He ate every last bite. When he was done, Delaney poured some water into the bowl and watched as the dog's pink tongue lapped it all up. She slid down the wall until her butt hit the floor and rested next to the dog. She had her own half of breakfast on a paper plate and was eating it with a plastic fork. When the dog gave her moony eyes, she gave him a bite from her fork. "What's your real name?" Delaney narrowed her eyes. "It's not Sinbad."

The dog cocked his head to the side and waited, expecting more food.

"One more bite, and the rest is mine." When the food was all gone, Delaney opened the bay door. The late May sky was bright blue and the wind smelled like Sinbad's fur. She'd better call Sunny, who was probably freaking out right about now.

By the time Delaney went up to the apartment, searched around for her cell phone, found it in the pants pocket of yesterday's jeans and returned downstairs, Sinbad was gone. She got a pit in her stomach as she went through the shop, checking the ratty old dog bed twice. She shouldn't have opened the door, but she honestly hadn't thought the dog would leave, just go do his business. Delaney peered out the bay, her hand on the cold metal and the wind rolling over her face. She stuck her pinkies in the corners of her mouth and whistled, since she didn't really think the dog would come if she called out for Sinbad.

Nothing.

"Aw, damn." Delaney found Sunny's number in her phone history and called, but only got voice mail. She left a message about the pit bull so that Sunny could at least start the search, then went upstairs and dressed for the gym—no more putting it off. By the time she was ready to head out there was a text message on her phone.

Sinbad's here. But thank you for calling! I need to find out how he keeps escaping.

So he'd gone back to Pittie Place. Delaney mulled that over while she geared up for the ride to Semper Fit. Poor guy didn't know where to be, just kept going back and forth between the two places, settling nowhere and trusting no one. She wondered how many times the dog had come by in the months since Delaney had met him, only to return to Pittie Place when nobody was here to let him inside. Sunny might not have even been aware of his comings and goings. Now that she was, Delaney figured Sunny would probably fix whatever hole was in her fence and she'd never see him again. She closed up the storeroom, shutting out the view of the empty dog bed. The urge to text Dad was the strongest yet.

Chunk's brother keeps showing up to my shop on Three Rebels Street. He's just like you, can't sit still. He was here last night but now he's gone.

Sure, she could text Boom, but she couldn't text Boom *those* words. Only Dad would understand *those* words. Delaney swiped beneath her eyes and grabbed her helmet. *Suck it up, Pippie*, Dad would say. *No use crying over a spilled motorcycle.* Dad always made morbid jokes like that, and if he could've joked about his own death he would've. Either way, he was right.

Better get going so she wasn't late.

"You're going to be late."

Tabitha glanced at her watch. "It's not even eight thirty." Auntie El didn't know what time the class was, but saying she was going to be late had been Auntie's way of motivating Tabitha since she was a kid. "I have plenty of time."

"You can never be too early." Auntie El shook a bent, arthritic finger. "Or too careful."

"I know that, Auntie El." *Couldn't you, though?* Tabitha thought. You really could be *too* early. Let's talk about those people who camped out overnight in front of retail stores so they could be the first to buy the next best thing. That was surely *too* early, but there was no point arguing with her auntie, which would be taken as sass. Auntie El didn't do sass.

"Don't go thinking you'll have that same nice detective at the gym to help you if you have another panic attack." Auntie El sat at the kitchen table, pencil poised over her morning crossword puzzle, yellow mug of coffee on the place mat next

to her. She glanced down at the paper. "Eleven-letter word
for *happy coincidence*."

"I don't think that." Tabitha thought about that cop from
back in March while she got Trinity's vest fastened. She'd
looked Detective Callahan up online immediately after the
incident at the supermarket. Everyone in that scenario had
meant well, from the store clerks who'd called 9-1-1 to the
firefighters who'd rushed to the scene. But only the cop had
truly seemed to understand what was going on, and to know
exactly what to do. He was older than Tabitha, strong, both
in physical appearance and in spirit, and seemed like the kind
of guy who needed to protect the world from all the bad stuff.
Tabitha had written him a thank-you note and planned to send
it to the county police station where he worked. She'd put a
stamp on the envelope and everything, but had lost her courage and never mailed it.

"The gym knows about Trinity?" Auntie El shifted in her
chair and regarded the dog over the rims of her glasses. She'd
been skeptical from the start about a dog being able to help
with PTSD and panic attacks, and even though Auntie El
had been around for the year of training that Tabitha had put
in with the dog, it was like she had to be convinced anew
every day.

"She's a service dog, Auntie El. She can go anywhere I can
go." Tabitha laced up her sneakers and took a deep breath.
She hadn't been to a real gym in years. She couldn't help but
wonder what would cause more harm: persistent thoughts
of a random panic attack happening again, like it had at the
supermarket, or trying to push away persistent thoughts of a
random attack. "But, yes. This is the gym Pete told me about.
They're doing a big fundraiser for Canine Warriors in July. I
called Semper Fit and talked to the owner and there is abso-

lutely no problem with bringing Trinity. In fact, he said he has a dog of his own that hangs out there."

Auntie El's eyebrows rose. "Alright, then. You be strong, Tabby."

"Yes, ma'am." Tabitha attached Trinity's leash and paused in the doorway. *"Serendipity,"* she said.

"How's that?" Auntie El peered up from her crossword.

"Eleven-letter word for *happy coincidence*," Tabitha said. *"Serendipity."*

four

Callie was curled against his left hip, a tiny spot of warmth in the large, empty bed. Sean blinked his eyes open to the alarm clock on the nightstand: 8:34. Damn. He'd slept in again. "You're a terrible cat," he chided the sleeping ball. "Aren't you guys supposed to walk on our faces and throw things on the floor when we sleep too late?"

Callie didn't budge, the insult landing on tiny, deaf ears. She'd always been a snuggler, a dream come true on cold, lonely nights and rainy days. A gift for his ex-wife when things went bad, Callie had always preferred Sean, and Kim hadn't even tried to take her when she left. *I don't like cats, Sean,* Kim had said. *I never understood why you got her in the first place. I wanted you home to keep me company. Not some stupid cat.*

Sean gave the cat one last stroke and murmured, "You're not stupid, are you?" before he slid out of the covers and hit the bathroom. After he splashed some cold water on his face he looked in the mirror and decided he'd make it to the 0930 at Semper Fit no matter what. This was his last day off before his shift started again tomorrow and he'd been really good about hitting the gym almost daily.

Callie leaped onto the bathroom sink and sat like a statue, tall and straight, with her tail curled around her feet, and watched Sean get dressed. She was a calico; dark gray with peach-colored patches, one of which cut her chin directly in half. She tilted her head up.

"Stop showing me your peach fuzz," Sean said. "I'm doing this for my health." Which was the truth. At least partly. He wasn't going to deny that he'd hoped each day for weeks that he'd see Delaney, the tough girl with the wildcat eyes. No such luck, but in the words of Rhett Santos, if it took a pretty woman to get him into the gym on a regular basis, then so be it. Things could be worse.

Not that Sean held much hope. Spring had flown by and Delaney never showed. When he pulled into the parking lot of Semper Fit ten minutes late, he almost didn't go inside. A marine through and through, Rhett could be a real hard-ass about tardiness. But then Sean spotted the motorcycle: a black Honda Rebel. He couldn't be one hundred percent sure this was the bike Delaney rode, but there were no other motorcycles that showed up regularly to Semper Fit. Odds were high.

A rush of adrenaline filled his veins. He slipped inside, willing to take any and all crap for his lateness, and was glad to see a large group warming up to melt into and not draw attention. Everyone was doing Samson lunges so Sean dropped his bag by the cubbies and fell right in. He scanned the room, trying to seem casual, when a low whisper came near his ear.

"Yeah, she's here," Rhett's voice said. "But you're so late, you probably didn't notice."

"Just for once," Sean said, turning to grin at his Marine Corps brother, "don't bust my balls, okay?"

Rhett didn't even crack a smile. "Why? Is it your birthday?"

Sean laughed, his mood surging upward as he went through the rest of the warm-up. He scanned the room until he found her. Dark, short hair. Slender body with hard muscles. Bright, pretty face. There was something inherently earthy about her. She could be one of those wood nymphs who lived in the trees. A living, breathing contrast of masculine and feminine. Strength and vulnerability. Somewhere in her thirties, but that was tricky because she was probably older than she looked. There was so much Sean could read, just by watching. She was legit tough. Probably single—no ring, not even the silicone kind so popular in gym settings—but it was more than that. There was something nomadic that suggested a long solo flight. She wasn't fussy, based on the haircut, short nails, lack of makeup. Less easy to read, but still present, was a cloud of grief—Sean couldn't say what but it was there, in her skeptical gaze, careful movements and the way she kept rolling her shoulder back, trying to shift away weight too heavy to carry.

Delaney looked up and caught him staring, just like their last encounter. Sean quickly moved outside to get ready for the metabolic conditioning, or "cardio" portion of the workout. He'd lunged past the whiteboard to get a peek, since he'd missed the intro, and saw that today's workout was running a 5K. He'd groaned inwardly at that, even though he was a good runner. It'd been a while since he'd done more than a collection of 400- or 800-meter sprints. Runs like today were atypical for gym programming, but this was the time of year Rhett always ramped up the mileage. Sean hadn't done any steady mileage for years, and when Sean did run he preferred middle distance. Marathons were punishing and 5Ks were puke fests.

"Scale this run to keep it half hour or less," Rhett was

speaking to the group that gathered outside. "Across the street, into the woods, you'll find markers to turn around for one mile, two miles and for five kilometers. Faster runners up front. Check your ego at the door. I don't need faster runners trying to get around a throng of people only doing a mile or two."

Sean realized he was up front because he'd gone outside before everyone else. Zoe and Duke—a super fit secret service agent who'd been coming for as long as Sean could remember—were there. Both would definitely beat everyone inside. He almost excused himself to the middle of the pack, just to be safe, until he glanced over and saw Delaney right next to him. "Confident, huh?" The words slipped out before he could stop himself.

She squinted a death glare. Looked just like Clint Eastwood in a spaghetti Western, right before he blew somebody's brains out.

"I just meant, you don't know anybody here," Sean explained. "I didn't mean you aren't fast."

Delaney tilted her head back. *The Good, the Bad and the Ugly* stare remained. "Let's make a deal," she finally said. "If you beat me in this run, you get to be all full of yourself and tell me I told you so. But if I win..." she paused to blow a few stray strands of hair from her eyes "...you stop staring at me. Deal?"

This was the first time Sean had heard her speak more than a couple of words. She had a little rasp in her voice. What some people might call a whiskey voice. Well, of course she did.

"What do you say, hotshot?" she pressed.

What else could he say? He couldn't deny staring at her. And he wouldn't back down. He'd made this bed, now he had to lie in it. Sean could only hope his rusty legs would come back fast.

"Deal."

★ ★ ★

Sean lay on his back, just inside the gym, eyes closed while his heart pounded so hard it might burst right out of his throat. He ran the finish through his mind over and over again, how the sight of the bay door only a few feet away had seemed like that metaphorical oasis after a long desert trek. The 5K had been a cat and mouse game of staying right with each other, never dropping too far back and keeping just behind redlining. Sean hadn't run that fast since he was in his twenties, and he'd wanted to quit, or at least slow down, many times after the first mile. The only thing that kept him going was watching Delaney's long, toned legs work the trail, her feet expertly striking and pushing the ground away from her in fluid, even strokes. She never slowed.

Despite the shock to his system, Sean was taller and had longer legs, which gave him an advantage from the get-go. The rest he made up with pure grit, and he really thought he had a chance at the end. When it came down to the last four hundred meters, Sean opened up the tank, ticking up the speed with the tiniest bit of reserve he'd held on to for just this moment.

Turned out Delaney had done the same. She stayed right with him, and it wasn't until they burst through the bay door in tandem that a verdict was delivered:

Only two people had beaten them inside. Zoe and Duke. Zoe gave Delaney a quicker time by one second. Duke gave the extra second to Sean. The tiebreaker came down to Rhett, the coach, who declared it…

A tie.

Sean had sunk to the floor, too spent to argue. Delaney walked around the gym, hands on her hips as she gulped in air. Her dark hair was slicked back with sweat and her skin glistened. She didn't speak, but her eyes said it all. She either thought she took the race or she was irritated by the tie, but she wasn't going to argue with the coach.

By the time everyone else finished and fist bumps were being exchanged, Sean clambered to his feet and sucked down huge gulps of water. "Good job." Delaney put her fist out.

No matter what else she might be, Delaney was not a bad sport. Sean tapped her knuckles. "You, too. Not sure where this leaves us on the bet, though."

Her eyes glittered. Her lips were bright pink from the exertion. A faint rose color tinged her cheeks. "Well, I think that's obvious."

Sean used the hem of his T-shirt to mop sweat from his face, still dripping from his pores, even twenty minutes later. Delaney's gaze followed the motion. He was pretty sure of what she was going to say. *I don't care about this run or this tie. Quit gawking at me like a teenager.* She wasn't wrong. "You're going to let me have the win?" Sean nodded in Duke's direction, shirt stripped, skin dripping with sweat. "Duke's a secret service agent. He doesn't miss a thing."

Delaney grabbed her water bottle from the floor and squirted some in her mouth. She swallowed hard. "Duke took an extra second to turn around and check the clock. Zoe was looking right at it. You and I both know I won that race." She shrugged. "But that's okay. I don't need charity."

"Charity?"

"That's right." She crossed her arms over her chest.

Sean had just parted his lips to ask her what was obvious about the bet, when Hobbs popped between them with a big grin. "Callahan, you superstar. I haven't seen you run that fast in…well, ever." Hobbs, the most boisterous coach at Semper Fit, stripped his shirt and rubbed the sweat from his face. He'd joined the run today and finished in the top third. On a normal day, Hobbs would've beat Sean. But today was not a normal day. "Hi." He turned to Delaney. "I don't think we've met. I'm Hobbs. I'm one of the coaches here."

If Hobbs's tone had been any slicker he would've sounded like Joey, from *Friends*: *How you doin'?* He flexed his chest, making his pecs bounce.

Delaney's gaze went from his bare chest to his eyes. Her lips had the tiniest smirk at the corners.

"You new?" Hobbs sank into his stance, feeling confident. The ladies always went for his casual charm. Sean figured it had something to do with the way his completely harmless nature came through at the exact same time as his shameless flirting.

"New to what?"

"Um." Hobbs was momentarily stopped by her reply. "The gym."

"I've come twice."

"You going to join?"

"Probably."

"Nice." Hobbs slipped his shirt back over his head. "New to the area?"

"Not really."

"Alright, then." Hobbs seemed to be picking up on her clipped replies. "Well, you ran great today, but if you need anyone to help you work on your running a little more, I know just the guy." And there it was. Despite all her warning signs, he went for it. Typical Hobbs.

"Generous of you." Delaney took another swig from her water bottle. "If I need lessons on how to run slower, I'll look you up. Have a nice day, gentlemen." With that, she turned and walked away, stopping at the cubbies to collect her helmet, boots and bag. She took everything outside, disappearing into the sunshine.

"Dang." Hobbs choked out a laugh. "Guess she doesn't mess around."

"I wanted to warn you. But that was so much more fun."

"I like it." Hobbs looked back toward the bay door, where Delaney had vanished. "I've definitely got my eye on her."

"Hobbs." Rhett's voice came from behind Sean's back. "Don't start. We want her to join, not slit her wrists."

Hobbs made a pffft sound and waved his hand. "She ain't afraid of me."

"Get a bucket and mop up the sweat." Rhett pointed to the corner, where the mop lived. "Everybody's dripping all over my damn floor."

Hobbs gave a sigh, then a salute. "Yessir."

Once he was gone, Rhett fixed Sean with a knowing look. He grinned a little bit. Sean was expecting a dig or a joke, but all he eventually got was, "Good work today, Callahan. I'm glad to see your motivation is back."

Then he was off, in the direction of Red, who'd finished in the middle of the pack. Her copper hair spilled out of her ponytail and her face was all smiles as Rhett approached. They couldn't have looked more different if they'd tried—Rhett tall as a basketball player, black hair and brown skin, and Red just past five feet and the spring sun barely kissing her pale skin. Over a year into their relationship and they still acted like lovesick fools regardless if anyone looked on.

Sean turned away. His lungs were better now, but his throat was still tight. He'd probably have metcon cough all day. Worth it, though.

"Hey, man, you took her in that race," Duke said as Sean headed past him, toward the door. Duke stretched his arms over his head, chest and arms like boulders, and quads to match.

"He totally didn't," Zoe countered. She was busy jotting down people's running times on the whiteboard.

"Did you mean to race her?" Duke arched an eyebrow. "I just saw you two barreling toward the gym. Wasn't sure if it was intentional or like a last-minute thing, chasing each other."

"He's chasing her for sure," Zoe said with a cackle. She laughed again, happy with her joke.

"It was a bet," Sean admitted. Despite the silence that followed, he wouldn't be giving them any more information.

"Uh-huh." Zoe grinned. "Well, what now?"

The light feeling that Sean had gotten when he saw Delaney's bike out front dulled. Even his win, near win or tie for today's 5K wasn't going to bring the feeling back. Delaney had made it very clear she didn't want him staring at her, beating her in a race or even chatting with her about it after. Sean had gotten the message, loud and clear: *leave me alone.*

The chase was over, before it'd even begun.

Sean had just stepped out the bay when he noticed that Delaney was still in the parking lot. She wasn't at her motorcycle, and was instead leaning in the driver's side window of an old, beat-up four-door, her helmet at her feet. She made slight gestures, her facial expression going from knit, concerned brows to a small, encouraging smile.

It took Sean a moment to recognize the person behind the wheel. Small. Dark hair. Thin. *Tabitha.* The woman from the grocery store. And right there, in the passenger seat, wearing a seat belt and her camo vest, was Trinity.

Sean dipped back around the corner, not because he was spying but because he didn't want the women to think he was spying. Even though, at this point, he was totally spying. He could only catch pieces of their conversation on the wind, just enough to figure out that they'd been stationed together somewhere. Delaney's voice sounded encouraging, Tabitha's frustrated. Sean got the idea that maybe Tabitha had come to the gym for the 0930 and hadn't had the courage to actually go inside. Without saying it, Sean knew that the reason behind that lay with the incident in the grocery store. After another minute or so, Delaney said something like "catch you later" and then, maybe thirty seconds after that, the revving of her motorcycle filled the air.

"What the hell are you doing, Callahan?" Rhett was suddenly by his side.

"Back off, Santos," Sean joked. "I've been whipped once already today."

Santos clapped him on the back. It stung a little bit. "I think you'll survive."

Sean laughed and headed for his car. He'd just made it to the door and was fumbling in his bag for his keys when a soft voice came over his shoulder.

"Officer Callahan?"

He turned to see Tabitha standing there, Trinity by her side. Tabitha looked small and helpless, all knees and elbows in her gym shorts and tank top, but her eyes had a spark of hope.

"Hey, Tabitha." Sean didn't even pretend he didn't remember her name. "Long time, no see. How you feeling?"

"Good." Her voice wavered. She sniffed deeply, then let out a long exhale. Trinity inched closer to her body. "I just wanted to thank you again. I wrote you a thank-you letter, you know." Tabitha had a strong Southern accent that suggested she'd lived farther south most of her life. All the vowels were dragged out and the *r* on *letter* disappeared. "But I was too chicken to mail it."

"That's okay." Sean swallowed the urge to hug the girl. She seemed so sad and lonely, but an embrace might be misunderstood and so was out of the question. They didn't know each other well and Sean needed to be one hundred percent certain he didn't violate her boundaries. "You come to work out today?" He pointed at the building.

"We did." Without pause, Tabitha referred to herself and Trinity as one unit. "But I was too chicken to go in. Guess I'm a chicken a lot." She pursed her lips together and eyed the gym wistfully. "I didn't used to be a chicken. I used to be strong. Confident."

"You're not chicken." Sean's words came out harder than he meant, but he didn't dial it back. Tabitha's brown eyes widened in surprise, so Sean pressed on. "You're learning to live again. Nothing's like it was before, is it?" Sean spoke on pure instinct, but didn't wait for Tabitha's answer. "So you have to relearn. That's okay. Takes time. Be patient with yourself." He glanced at Trinity. "And trust her to do her job."

Tabitha swallowed deeply and stood a little bit taller. "Yes, sir," she said. "You're right. You're absolutely right." She glanced down the road, in the direction Delaney had disappeared on her motorcycle. Sean hoped that Tabitha would say something about her, give him details as to how the two knew each other. "Do you think I should go inside and tell the owner why I didn't show up today? He was expecting me."

Sean glanced over his shoulder. He couldn't see Santos but he knew he was in there. Santos was salty as fuck and didn't tolerate laziness, tardiness or excuses. But Tabitha was none of those things, and Rhett would treat her with rare kindness. Sean knew this without question. "You should," Sean said. "Go talk to him. Then maybe you'll be more comfortable next time you come."

Tabitha nodded, and eventually smiled. Then, without warning, she dropped the leash and slipped her arms around Sean's back. Sean froze, arms stuck out at his sides like a robot. She held him tight, head to his chest for a few seconds, before she pulled back and collected Trinity's lead. "Thank you, Detective."

"Yes, ma'am." That was all Sean could summon. His throat had gone tight.

Tabitha had turned to go, but stopped and smiled. "I just ran into a lady I knew at Camp Leatherneck." She pointed down the road. "Isn't that funny? I come here. I can't go inside. Then I run into her. Then I run into you. It's like..." Tabitha trailed off, staring at the sunny sky for a second. "Serendipity."

"Sure." Sean's brain scrambled to remember the exact meaning of that word. Something about good luck. Mostly, his brain had gotten stuck on the fact that Tabitha had known Delaney at Camp Leatherneck. And now, Sean knew just a little bit more about the wildcat than he had before. Maybe this wasn't such a bad day after all.

"Thank you, Detective." Tabitha disappeared inside.

"No," Sean said, even though she was gone. He could still feel her hug. "Thank you."

five

It took Delaney another few weeks to get the shop up and running to the point where she was ready for the grand opening. Her biggest worry had been about business being slow. A lot of motorcycle shops struggled and the guys who'd rented this space before her, and failed, were a case in point. But part of her motivation for sticking with this area—aside from not being able to live in Omaha without Dad—was that plenty of people around here had money, which meant that they could afford to indulge in vintage cycles. The closest vintage shop was hours away, so she was confident in a captive customer base. In the time since she'd gotten the space, Delaney had amped up her marketing by introducing herself to motorcycle groups and the people who conducted riding courses, and meeting the owners of the shops across the street. It didn't hurt that it was June, which was prime biking season. Everybody was pulling their motorcycles out of storage and novices were looking into buying them.

Things are off to a great start!

That would be the caption for the photo she'd post later to the Triple M Classics Instagram account, and to Dad's Facebook page. She snapped a few pictures of the crowd, many of them clustered around '33, which had been shined up and put on display for the grand opening. On the other side of the store was a table with refreshments—appetizers and wine from the Italian restaurant across the street. Around the perimeter of the shop were glossy photos of vintage motorcycles—a 1950 Vincent Black Shadow, a 1972 R75/5 BMW, Dad sitting on '33—along with a couple deployment pics and various prints of celebrity riders and their bikes whom Delaney liked: Peter Fonda on the famous chopper from *Easy Rider*; Keanu Reeves and his Norton Commando; Pink, midriff bared, with her custom Indian Scout; Charlie Hunnam and his Harley Dyna Super Glide; and of course, Norman Reedus, both on his blacked-out Tiger and just Norman, no bike, surrounded by zombies, all of them throwing the camera the bird. Other than that little bit of flash, the rest of the shop was just nuts and bolts bikes and gear, an honest reflection of the serious riders she wanted to draw.

It seemed to be working. Her grand opening was only three hours old and already she had work lined up. An older guy with a British accent had bought a '77 Triumph Bonneville Silver Jubilee last fall and wanted Delaney to take out the shitty Lucas electrical and custom build a new system.

"Is that your specialty?" A tall woman in a Harley jacket who'd been eavesdropping stepped into the conversation. "British bikes?"

"No, ma'am. I can do them all." Another thing that would set Delaney apart. She'd been working on bikes since she was knee-high. Dad did not discriminate or specialize. He liked all bikes, vintage jobs being his favorite. "British, American,

Japanese," Delaney said. "I have experience with each. I have a soft spot for American bikes, obviously." She nodded in the direction of the Indian Four.

The woman smiled. "Well, in that case, I got a Shovelhead I need you to look at."

"Sure," Delaney said. "Is it on the road?"

"Yeah, I've been riding it." The woman pulled her blond hair into a ponytail and affixed it with a tie. She looked to be in her forties by the fine lines around her eyes that she didn't try to mask with makeup. Her eyebrows were sculpted, though, plucked and primed, like a kiss of feminine vibes amidst the sea of leather and denim. "But it's acting funny."

Delaney wondered if the supposed Shovelhead was a mislabeled Ironhead. She wouldn't know unless she looked at it. "Bring it in," she said.

"Don't gotta ask me twice."

Most of the people who crammed the grand opening were riders of some kind, whether hard-core or weekenders, but some were thinking of getting into it, and a few had no interest at all, they had just spotted her colorful banners from the road or just liked to look at old motorcycles. A lot of people who stopped by were into riding but had never gone vintage and had a lot of questions.

"It's not for everybody," Delaney told one young woman who didn't even have her motorcycle license yet. "Vintage bikes are fun but they're a different breed from modern bikes. They're slower. They're going to need ongoing work. And unlike today's bikes, it was assumed they were going to be worked on by the owner. The assumption was anyone buying a bike had some working knowledge on how to keep it running."

The young lady's eyes began to glaze over, her lips parted in thought. "I think I'll hold off," she said, her gaze darting to the '33 that was surrounded consistently by at least three or four people.

"Do your research and know what you're getting into," Delaney advised. "If you don't enjoy doing your homework, you won't enjoy the bike, either."

"That's solid advice," an older guy chimed in. He wore denim and leather from head to toe, had a set of gray Willie Nelson braids and had come in an hour ago with a big smile, talking about Dude's Bikes. "Wasn't a great shop," he'd said. "Those brothers might know bikes but they had no business dealing with the public. They were shady at best and, between you and me—" he lowered his voice "—I think they were dealing in more than motorcycles."

Delaney had wanted to ask more about that but there'd been too many people around, so she made a note to bring the topic up later, if she got a chance.

"This your Indian?" someone called out, a young man in blue jeans and an old Metallica shirt.

"Hey, are you selling the print with Daryl and the zombies?" someone else asked.

"Did you make this food yourself?"

"Yes, it's her bike," the older guy with the braids yelled back. "She's not selling that print, is my guess, and the food is from Nonni's, across the way." He turned back. "I recognize the garlic bread."

Delaney offered a grateful smile. Normally she'd have been annoyed at someone taking over, but this guy reminded her a little of Dad. Not in appearance—Dad had looked more like Clint Black than Willie Nelson—but in his easygoing but confident bearing and an almost quiet protectiveness that came out in the way he'd handled the crowd. "Thanks," she said. "I might have to hire you."

"Hey, don't offer unless you mean it." The guy struck a big

grin and stuck out his hand. "Walt. Harley to the core. But I like what you're doing."

"Delaney." She shook his large, bony hand. "You know how to work on bikes?"

"Harleys. Could feel my way around the others. This is great, what you've done so far. How thick is this concrete?" He tapped his boot toe.

"Four inches."

"Nice. Great job on the paint color."

"I know, right? Now I can drop all the carburetor float springs I want."

Walt laughed big.

Delaney was just about to ask him if he'd been serious about a job when a young girl gave a little shriek. The room quieted and turned in her direction.

"Aww, he's cute," the girl's mother said, peering down at something Delaney couldn't see in the crowd. "Don't feed him, though."

Delaney navigated her way to the food and sighed. Leave it to Sinbad to show up, uninvited, to the grand opening of Triple M Classics. And go right to the buffet table. He sat and whapped his tail against the floor.

"He must be the motorcycle shop dog," the girl said. She had curly red hair in a ponytail, pale skin and copper freckles. She reached to pet him but her mother caught her hand and pulled it away.

"Ask first." The mom nodded toward Delaney.

"He's actually not mine," Delaney said. "He keeps showing up, though. C'mere, boy." Delaney grabbed a paper plate from the table and loaded it with a few meatballs. She took it to the back room and Sinbad followed. He pushed ahead of her, motivated by both the food and his dog bed, which was now a permanent fixture. "Here. This is one of the few times you'll find meat in my shop, so enjoy." She gave him the plate and left him in peace, bumping into Walt on her way back to the showroom.

"I remember the dog." Walt nodded in Sinbad's direction. He was licking and nibbling at the meatballs rather than wolfing them down like any normal dog would. "The Dude's Bikes guys had him here. Used him in their advertising. They didn't really seem to care about him. They weren't mean to him but they just—" Walt shrugged "—didn't care. I think they only got him to help sell their bikes. Part of an image they wanted to project. I overheard one of the brothers saying the dog wasn't mean enough. They should have gotten a meaner dog."

"I'm glad they don't have him anymore." Delaney watched the dog play with his food. Sinbad's delicate treatment with the meatballs seemed less about being cautious and more like he was simply savoring good food. "This is the third time he's shown up out of nowhere, wanting to get into the back room." Delaney nodded at the bed. "But he doesn't stick around. He hoofs it between here and Sunny's dog rescue. Do you know Pittie Place?"

Walt shrugged. "The girlfriend likes cats."

Delaney smiled as they made their way back out to the crowd, leaving Sinbad with his meal and his prized bed. "Smart. Cats are cool." She drew her cell phone from her pocket. "I need to text Sunny and let her know Sinbad got out again."

She'd just sent the message when she spotted two new men inside the shop. She had no idea how long they'd been buried in the thick crowd, but one of them was poking around the newly stocked shelves and the other was very close to '33, sitting pretty and shiny in her prime spot. One of the guys was tall, bulky and bald while the other was a good four inches shorter, looked almost breakable and had a brown beard, thick as a carpet.

Delaney got an itchy feeling in her stomach as she watched these men touch everything. It wasn't unlike the feeling she'd get in Afghanistan when a vehicle became inoperable during a convoy. She and her team would leave camp to identify the problem and tow the vehicle back. Basically, everyone had to depend on her and the crew of mechanics, which lit a fire of adrenaline and kept her on edge.

There, it served a purpose. If Delaney was on edge, she'd be alert, and her adrenaline might help keep everyone alive. Nobody was going to die today. The logical part of her brain told her that. But the primitive part was having a different reaction to these two men, who were now talking to Walt. Walt nodded in her direction, and the two men faced her with expressions that could only be described as threatened.

Delaney figured out who they were even before the larger of the two walked over and extended his hand in her direction. "Hi, I'm Dude."

Delaney held up her hand in a wave. "Delaney."

Dude rested his meaty fingers on his hip, pretending he hadn't gone for the handshake. "You sure moved in quick." He filled up the space, leaning an elbow on the counter and stretching his legs out, ankles crossed.

"I guess. Opportunity came and I grabbed it."

An irritated glint rippled through Dude's eyes. He straightened up a little, making himself taller. "This is my brother, Dick," he said as the smaller guy joined the group, positioning himself in front of Dude, as if he'd calculated just how close he could get to Delaney to be intimidating without actually crossing into her personal space. His carpet glittered with what must've been some kind of beard conditioner.

"Hi, Dick." Delaney still didn't offer her hand. "Welcome to Triple M Classics. You guys into riding?"

Dick's eyes glinted like coals, matching the sparkle in his beard. "We used to lease this space," he said. "We're Dude's Bikes."

"Oh." Delaney nodded. "I think I remember reading about your shop. What happened? You guys just decide to pack it in, or what?"

Dude's eyes narrowed. He held her gaze long enough to let her get a peek inside, and what Delaney saw there gave her unexpected pause. Dude didn't particularly like her being here. This was not a welcoming visit. "Well, you'll probably find out soon enough," he said. "Bike shops are hard going around here. Not trying to bring you down on your opening day, but it's probably best you don't go into this thinking it will be easy."

"I don't think anything of the sort," Delaney said. "Most things worth doing aren't easy."

Dick smiled, but it held no kindness. "You'll have to excuse my brother," he said. "He's a little bitter about losing the shop. No, I take that back. He's a *lot* bitter. But I told him we needed to be nice. It's not your fault we lost the place. So we decided to come out here and—" Dick paused, looked Delaney up and down, with no attempt at hiding it "—give you our best wishes for success."

For a second, Delaney's body went cold. Then she quickly shook her head and looked around at the crowd of happy, chatting people. "Well, I appreciate you guys coming out."

"How long you had that '33?" Dude pointed over his shoulder in the direction of Dad's bike.

"Been in the family for generations."

"It's sweet. You planning on selling it?"

"Never. I'm going to enter her in the Classic Motorcycle Show, though. I think she's got a shot."

"Our dad has judged that show," Dude said, his tone conversational but still not quite friendly. "It's a tough win. Big prize."

"I'm counting on it."

Dick chuckled under his breath.

"Well I'll be a sonofabitch." Dude's eyes were trained over Delaney's shoulder.

She followed his gaze and saw Sinbad, circling the buffet table. He'd obviously finished his meatballs and was sniffing for more.

"Sinbad!" Dude squatted down and opened his big arms, like he was welcoming an old friend.

The dog didn't budge. He looked over at the brothers but there wasn't a hint of affection or even recognition. The pit bull's attachment to this shop was just that—to the shop. To the building, the dog bed, to any sustenance that might be available, whether from the buffet table or from breakfast that Delaney cooked up.

But not to those men.

She thought of Dad. How he'd never wanted to leave Omaha, no matter where Delaney was stationed. She'd practically had to drag him to Hawai'i when she was stationed at K-Bay. "Who does that, Dad?" she'd demanded. "Who refuses to visit his daughter in Hawai'i? Especially when he lives in friggin' Omaha?"

"If I could ride my bike, I'd be there in a heartbeat. You know that, Lanie. But getting on a plane and all that. I just…" Then he'd trail off, recognizing his own lameness.

"There's pork lumpia," she'd teased. "And poke. And malasadas. And sticky rice. Sticky rice for days, Dad. You can even get a Spam burger at McDonald's. I shit you not."

It was the food that finally got him. With a paid, round-trip ticket, Dad had run out of excuses and just couldn't resist the lure of the cuisine. He'd left behind the bike shop where he spent his days and the sunken sofa where he spent his nights and came out to Hawai'i for two weeks of lying on the beach and eating everything in sight, and for once in her life Delaney had seen her father settle down and relax, even if it was just for a little while.

"Why do you have our dog?" Dude said as he rose to his feet. "We gave him back to the rescue." His big cheeks were flushed pink.

"He keeps coming back here." Delaney's voice was tight. "He comes and goes between this place and Sunny's."

Dude's beady eyes flitted between the dog, his brother and Delaney. "I told you we shouldn't leave him. We should take him home," he said. "Give it another try."

"He wasn't the right fit," Dick said. "He couldn't guard crap. All he wanted to do was play with people. We agreed it was best he go back to the rescue. We'll get a better dog once we open up the new shop."

"I don't want a better dog. We already paid for Sinbad. We can train him to guard stuff, Dick."

They went on like that for half a minute, like they were a couple instead of brothers, back and forth about the dog, their excuses sounding lame, their argument petty. Delaney didn't wonder in the slightest why their business had failed, focused as these two grown men were on themselves and whatever other drama they were involved in.

"Hey, I'm going to save you two some time." It was getting late, people were heading out and Delaney was getting tired. She stepped over to Sinbad and stroked his head with just the tips of her fingers. He didn't flinch this time, his attention rapt on the remaining meatballs. His nostrils flared as he tilted his head back, catching the scent of the food. "You're not taking him anywhere."

Dude narrowed his eyes. He stood to his full height and crossed his arms over his chest. He went to speak, but nothing came out. Delaney suspected he wasn't used to being challenged by anyone, let alone a woman.

"Well it ain't up to you," Dick said. He slid his hands into the front pockets of his jeans. Though Dick was much smaller, Delaney knew that he was the meaner of the two.

"Well, I say it is up to me," Delaney countered. She stepped close enough to Sinbad that her knee brushed his shoulder. Again, the pittie didn't flinch. "He's in my shop. Around here, my word is law. You gave him up and I've already texted Sunny."

"We just needed some time." Dude's bald head beaded with sweat. "We'll be in a new place soon. More room for him." He reached for Sinbad, but the pit bull leaned back, resting some of his weight on Delaney's legs.

Delaney didn't raise her voice when she looked Dude dead in the eye. "I said no. You can't have him."

Silence fell over their small group. Walt, who had been most certainly listening in, chuckled under his breath. The brothers exchanged glances. Delaney could tell that Dude was waiting for Dick to tell him what to do.

Dick leaned in closer, and when he spoke his breath came in beer-scented puffs. "What you gonna do if I just grab him? Huh? You think you can stop me?"

Delaney's adrenaline fizzed up as her body tensed. But she'd been trained to stay calm. She knew how to breathe through it, to keep a clear head. "I think maybe I can," she said, her voice level. "With what I have behind that counter." She tilted her head at the register, a few feet away. Her Glock wasn't back there. It was upstairs, locked away. But Dick didn't know that.

He slowly pulled back and offered a thin smile. His gaze flitted to Sinbad, but held no affection. "You best watch your step, little lady. You might be feeling pretty big about yourself right now with your brand-new shop, your fancy bike and all these people here." He gestured to the crowd. "But we have what you would call a bit of—" Dick leaned closer and lowered his voice "—*influence* in the bike business around here. You might want to rethink making me your enemy."

Delaney silently studied Dick's eyes. She slipped her first two fingers beneath Sinbad's collar and gently held him still. In that moment, she felt the slight tremble of his body against her legs. The shiver would rumble, then die off, then rumble, and die off, like the pittie was allowing Delaney to absorb some of his anxiety.

"I think you and your brother were just leaving," she finally said. "Isn't that right?"

Dick straightened up and tilted his head at his brother, in the direction of the exit. "This isn't over," he said. "See you around, Delaney." He dragged over her name. The brothers left without another word, but both looked back over their shoulders as they departed out the bay door, the sun setting in a red line at their backs. Dick's mean eyes narrowed, his gaze lingering until Dude snapped his fingers in front of his brother's face and they both disappeared.

Tabitha tried the door, but it was locked. She sighed and looked down at Trinity, whose black fur looked blue in the setting sun. "I did it again," she told the pittie. "Sat in the car too long, chickened out and missed the party."

Trinity whined.

Stomach tight, Tabitha had just turned to go when a clicking sound came from the door, followed by the jangle of a little bell. "Hey." A familiar voice rode over her shoulder. "So you made it after all."

"Sergeant Monroe." Tabitha turned to find the lean, mean woman with short, dark hair standing just inside the shop, door held open with her back.

"Relax, Corporal. I'm just Delaney now." She tipped her head toward the inside and smiled. "C'mon in."

Tabitha followed Delaney inside, noticing how strong she looked. Even at Camp Leatherneck, hidden under her BDUs, Gunnery Sergeant Monroe cut an imposing figure. Just by the lines of her jaw, her erect posture, and the complete and total command she held over herself and everyone around her, Tabitha had known that Sergeant Monroe was not to be messed with. What she hadn't expected was the depth of her, the power of her spirit, which rose up and shone like a beacon on the most tragic day in Tabitha's life.

She brushed all that aside and focused on the motorcycle shop. "Wow, Sarg...uh...Delaney. This is amazing." Not that Tabitha knew anything about motorcycles. But the shop was supercool with an old bike shined up and on display, a bunch of memorabilia on the walls, and sitting happily near a buffet table, a large, brown and white pit bull. Trinity paid him no attention whatsoever. The pit bull, who was male, sniffed the air when she came inside. "We both have pit bulls," Tabitha said. "Though mine is a lot smaller."

"This guy's not actually mine." Delaney patted his head and tossed him a meatball from the plate of leftover food on the table. The buffet was wrecked, like it got hit by a mob of teens, with just a few meatballs left, some sad, wilted lettuce in the bottom of a clear, plastic bowl, a plate with brownie crumbs, and the heels of some garlic bread. "His collar says Sinbad. Apparently he used to live here. He keeps sneaking away from Sunny's place and comes here."

"Sunny?" The name perked Tabitha's ears. She watched Sinbad settle on the floor with his meatball and start to lick off the sauce. She'd never seen a dog eat that way, so careful and deliberate. "He's from Pittie Place, then. So is Trinity, originally." She nodded at her polite girl, who watched Sinbad eat his meatball with her head cocked to the side. "Sunny gave Trinity to Pete, who runs Canine Warriors. He helped me train her to be a service dog. We chose her because she's on the smaller side, and so am I."

"She looks perfect for you." Delaney smiled at Trinity but didn't try to pet her. Her gaze shifted to Tabitha and her eyes softened. "Sorry you missed the food. But at least you came inside, eh?"

"I'm not hungry anyway." Which was a lie, but Tabitha had seen Auntie El before she left the house, deveining shrimp and cooking down okra to get all the slime out of it. That meant gumbo for dinner.

"How long did you sit in the car before you saw everyone leave?" Delaney had never been one to mince words. She handed Sinbad the last meatball, which he took gently and settled between his paws. "I mean, I don't blame you. I had a big crowd today. Too much for me, even. I'm whipped."

"Not long, actually. I took Trinity to the park today. We were forest bathing. That's this thing where you soak up the trees and sky and get close to nature. There's a Japanese word for it, but I don't remember what it is." When Tabitha had left the house she'd been intent on coming to Delaney's grand opening. Instead, she'd found herself on the trails, in the county park. She'd kept in the shade, to avoid the heat, the hard ground keeping her rooted, the rush of the water making her feel loose and fluid, and the scent of the blue sky a balm on every secret wound beneath the surface that tried to fester in her soul.

"Still spiritual as ever, huh?" Delaney gave a soft grin. "I always admired that about you."

Tabitha felt her cheeks go hot. "Maybe not as much these days. But I try."

Her voice must've given her away because Delaney quickly changed the subject.

"I'm just about to go upstairs and cook some dinner. That is, after I get this guy back home." She waggled her fingers at Sinbad. "You want to join me?"

A heavy brew of emotions filled Tabitha. She'd been invited to dinner by a woman she'd admired for a long time, even though she hadn't seen her in years. She felt excitement. Pride. But also anxiety. There was no way in hell she could ever measure up to a woman like Delaney, who put in so many years in the corps and now owned her own shop. All Tabitha had done was get out as quick as she could and run back home to her great-aunt. Trinity must've sensed the shift because she stood up and pressed close to Tabitha's legs. "I can't. But thank you. So much. My, uh—" she pointed toward the door "—my auntie El is making gumbo." She glanced at her watch. "I have to get back. I just wanted to pop in after the hike and see your shop. Thank you again for talking to me at the gym. I still haven't worked out there, but I will. And also thanks again for...for..."

Delaney stepped in and clapped her hands on Tabitha's shoulders. She gave a squeeze. "It's cool, Tabitha. All good. I wouldn't miss out on gumbo, either. As for the gym, no big thing. You'll go inside and work out. I'll make sure of it. And as for the other thing." Delaney's eyes narrowed. "Don't even mention it. We all did what we needed to do that day."

Tabitha felt her throat grow tight, so she slipped her fingers beneath the elastic band she wore on her wrist and gave it a couple of snaps. Trinity pawed at her leg, without using her nails. Tabitha drew a deep breath and felt the tension pass. She took a treat from her pocket and gave it to Trinity, who nibbled it gently. "Good girl."

Delaney's eyes took in all of it. She grabbed something from the counter and pressed it into Tabitha's palm. A business card. "Text me before your next gym visit. I'll make sure I go the same time, if I can."

Tabitha slipped the card in her shorts pocket. "Thanks. That would be great. I did go in, by the way. That day. After you left."

"Oh, yeah?" Delaney's eyes brightened. It was pretty obvious when she was happy because Delaney's eyes were this unusual gold color that lit up like champagne.

"Yeah. I went in and met the owner and his wife. Rhett was cool and his wife was really nice. She's a massage therapist and told me I could come by anytime for a free intro session. I didn't even know massage therapists did intro sessions. Their old beagle was the cutest. The beagle wouldn't let me touch him, but that's okay. I'm used to nobody touching my dog, either." Tabitha clamped her mouth shut. Why was she babbling so much?

"I don't think they're married, but yeah, they're a great pair." Delaney grinned big. "So next time you go, you're all set to actually work out."

"I think so." Tabitha wanted to be positive but also didn't want to lie to Delaney.

"You will."

Delaney was obviously more confident than Tabitha was. Which, somehow, made Tabitha feel more confident. Apparently Delaney's courage was contagious. It certainly had been that day in Afghanistan. "Good night. Thanks for having me and enjoy your dinner." Tabitha squashed the urge to go upstairs and see how Delaney had decorated her apartment. She envisioned simple, but warm. Functional, but colorful.

"'Night, Tabitha." Delaney pointed at the business card. "Don't forget to text."

"'Night, Sarge." Tabitha left with a good feeling.

six

Castillo always did this little thing, just before they served a warrant. She tested her badass persona on her camera phone, turning the corners of her mouth down just slightly and letting her dark eyes narrow until they looked like a creature peering at you from a dark cave entrance. Sean had seen the face a million times and it still made the hairs rise on his arms. Nobody would guess the woman behind that face was a mother of three who baked cookies on her days off for her daughters' various sports teams. What made her a good detective also made her a good mother: her ride-or-die vigilance in both endeavors.

Once Castillo had her face right, she smoothed her chest, maybe checking her vest.

"Ready?" Sean rested his hand on the door of their minivan—the perfect undercover police vehicle—waiting for his partner's approval.

Castillo patted her red lipstick into place with a forefinger. "Ready."

They pushed open the gate on the tall, junkyard chain-link fence, ignoring the rusty Beware of Dog sign, and wove their way through piles of tires, metal parts, broken bicycles, wood and trash. They approached the residence—a small, single level structure with rotting siding—in the cool early hours of the morning. The house was in about as good a shape as the junk that surrounded it, but it sat on a couple dozen acres of land that Sean was certain held stolen cars and parts. He and Castillo had put in enough work to know there was a chop shop, or various installments of such, buried on this property. "Let's see if Mr. Richardson is up yet." Sean brushed aside a set of brass wind chimes shaped like birds that hung over a gimpy rocking chair.

"Rest of the crew's pulling up." Castillo looked over her shoulder.

"Damn." A warrant for this much property was going to take a lot of help to get the search done, but Sean had wanted the stealth approach on this job. Cole Richardson had a long rap sheet of minor infractions that went back to his teenage years. He lived alone, having inherited the holdings from his grandfather, who had raised him, and, according to court records, regularly beat him. There had been many different women in and out of the residence over time, several who had called in domestic disturbances and then refused to press charges. Sean had been working on him for nearly a year, starting with a string of stolen vehicles and vehicle parts in the county and surrounding areas. The first lead on Richardson had been a single photo of a catalytic converter on social media, posted and quickly taken down. From there, it had been a steady game of cat and mouse that Sean played with patience and persistence until finally, with enough undercover digging and stakeouts, it had garnered him his warrant. Based on everything he'd learned, Sean had a gut feeling Richardson wasn't going to take this warrant lying down.

Right before Castillo went to knock, Sean stopped her. "Remember, this guy is really bad news. That last domestic call? The woman's face looked like hamburger."

Castillo's expression didn't change. "Yep. Why do you think I was so happy to get this warrant?" She rapped sharply on the door and waited. After some time passed, the faded lace curtains that covered the window shifted. Some rustling sounds came from inside but nobody came to the door.

Castillo rapped again. "Mr. Richardson," she called. "Dogwood County Police. We have a warrant to search your premises."

A little more rustling, then nothing.

Sean turned to Castillo, her cold-blooded stare in place, and said, as calmly as he might discuss the weather, "He's going to run."

A bang from a slammed door came from out back.

Sean and Castillo regarded each other. She popped her gum, something she called mint berry, even though Sean wanted to know how it could be mint *and* berry, and lifted one shoulder slightly. *What you gonna do?*

Sean took off, leaving Castillo with a slightly stunned expression. He wove his way through piles of junk, hopping over some and threading around others. Out back he caught sight of Richardson fleeing through the overgrown grasses toward a barn nestled just inside clumps of ancient pin oaks, harboring maples and hollies and all the creepy crawlies. Richardson wasn't under arrest yet, but based on what they found after executing the warrant, he most likely would be.

Sean wasn't going to lose him. Not after all the work he'd put in. He dug deep, and despite the lack of athletic clothing and Richardson's head start, Sean picked up speed. Richardson—who turned out to be surprisingly spry—also cranked up the heat.

Tall, overgrown grass turned into dirt, with sticks and low-lying shrubs that clawed at and caught Sean's shins. Thorns snagged his pant legs and tore at his skin. He was wearing knockoff oxfords, but Richardson had sneakers, a fact Sean knew because he could see the waffle treads on the bottom of Richardson's shoes.

Sean drove hard, but it wasn't enough. Richardson didn't slow and Sean's lungs were burning. Sean was starting to drag. He recalled the race against Delaney, where he'd felt exactly the same way.

Sean's breath came in heavy gasps, his undershirt soaked beneath his body armor. "Cole!" He called out Richardson's first name, a tactic he'd learned long ago.

Sure enough, Richardson's pace faltered. He looked over his shoulder.

Classic mistake.

Richardson stumbled. His body jerked, then went face-first to the ground.

Sean gave a final push and raced up alongside him, just as the man was scrambling to his knees. "Freeze, Cole!"

Richardson fell back to the ground, maybe knowing he wouldn't make it this time. Sweat dripped from Sean's nose and landed on Richardson's dirty white undershirt as he knelt on the ground and pinned one arm, then the next, behind Richardson's back. "You're under arrest," Sean panted, his heart slamming into his chest as his words rushed out. "For...interfering...with a police...investigation. You also..." Sean paused, still gasping for air "...have the right...to remain...silent."

Which Sean would now do, his voice officially gone.

★ ★ ★

"What is going on with you?" Castillo narrowed her eyes as she poured a shot of whiskey into Sean's glass. The day had been long and hard, and by the time they'd finished with the search warrant and were back at the station, Sean noted the end of their shift and pulled out a selection of airplane bottles from last year's Secret Santa gift exchange, which he kept stashed in his bottom drawer.

"What're you talking about?" Sean took his first sip. Cheaper stuff than what he kept at home, so it didn't have the same depth of flavors, but the warmth of the scotch filled his head and soothed his nerves. Like getting a high five for a long, successful day.

"What do you mean, what am I talking about?" Castillo had the opposite of her cave creature face on now. This was her unrestrained, lots of white teeth, eyes twinkling, "I'm going to tease you mercilessly" face. "I haven't seen you run that fast..." Castillo tilted her head to the side "...ever."

"Not fast enough, though."

"Right. But still, you tried. Tell me about that." Castillo tossed back her drink and wrinkled her nose. She was a bourbon girl, through and through. *No to the barley*, she would say. *I'm American. I want corn in my fermented mash. Better yet, give me tequila.*

"I don't know." Sean tried to shrug it off. He pounded his chest with his fist, clearing his throat from letting the whiskey go down the wrong pipe. "I've been inspired, I guess you could say." No point in lying to his partner. She could see right through him. And for good reason. There was no difference, in Sean's opinion, between brothers in arms in the corps and brothers in arms on the force. If you couldn't trust your brothers and sisters, you were going to have a problem.

"Inspired by who?" Forgetting herself, Castillo grabbed a second airplane bottle of scotch and poured it into her glass.

"It's really nothing." It really wasn't. Except it kind of was. Even though Sean had put Delaney behind him, there was no arguing that she'd brought out the best in his running today. Would he have chased down Richardson a month ago, before that race? "Just somebody at the gym who's inspired me to get my butt back in shape."

Sean didn't leave his messes for other people to clean up and he always got his man. He would've busted Richardson one way or another, would've discovered the chop shop and recovered the parts and pieces to over a dozen vehicles, including the pivotal catalytic converter that started the chase.

But would he have run as hard as he had today? Probably not. Not that Delaney had created something inside of him that hadn't been there before. She'd just *reminded* Sean that he had that fifth gear. One he hadn't used in ages. And since then Sean had been motivated to keep going, to get even faster, if he could. He'd even gone on a couple of jogs on his own, despite not having seen Delaney again.

"Holy shit." Castillo slugged her second glass. She made the *ohmagawd* face. "There's a girl. You've met a girl."

"Not a girl," Sean countered. He pointed a finger and sipped at his drink, which was the proper way to drink scotch. Not throw it back like a defeated hero in an old Western. "A woman. A really strong, fast, wild...woman."

"Gee-suz!" Castillo punched him in the shoulder. Sean didn't even flinch, though his scotch sloshed in the glass. "I've never seen you act like this." She narrowed her gaze. "Not about Kim anyway. And not with the rebound chick you dated last year, who was secretly in love with someone else."

"Sunny," Sean corrected. "Her name is Sunny. We're still friends."

"That's nice." Castillo smoothed out her lipstick. Somehow, that deep red color she wore never came off, no matter how long the day or how many arrests they made. It didn't even leave an annoying ring on her favorite coffee cup, which was printed with Mr. Monk's list of phobias, starting with *Fear of Germs* and ending with *Fear of Elevators*. "But tell me more about this other girl. I'm sorry, I mean—" Castillo fanned out her fingers "—woman."

Sean shrugged and polished off his drink. "No more to tell. She's been to my gym a couple times. I've made a fool of myself both times. Once, I knocked her over and the next she almost beat me in a 5K."

"Almost?" Castillo plopped in her desk chair and woke up her computer, like she might actually be contemplating doing the paperwork for today's mess right now.

"Jury's out. In the end, our race was declared a tie."

Castillo tapped on her keyboard, her fingers going light and fast. "Ties are bullshit."

"You're telling me."

After a long moment of silent typing, Castillo looked up with a sly smile. "I'm going to trust my instincts and let it lie for now. But you keep me posted on this situation."

"She's not interested. Plus, I haven't seen her in a few weeks. Case closed." Sean pushed Castillo out of her chair. He grabbed her jacket from the desk and pressed it into her hands. "Go home to your man and kids. I'll finish the report."

"Nah, I can't let you do that," Castillo said, even as she pulled on her coat. "Just do it tomorrow. You've had enough today, chasing down that car thief like you're some movie star or a badass on *Grand Theft Auto*."

Sean laughed, leveled out on scotch, his anxiety from the day gone but his weary body not ready for sleep. "It's no big deal. Go home, Castillo. I got nobody waiting for me right now, other than my cat."

"Hey, don't discount that pussy," Castillo snorted as she rounded the corner. "She's got needs, too."

Sean smiled as he took over the report Castillo had started. He could do it on autopilot and still get home at a decent hour. "Go home."

"Yes, sir."

"That's better."

seven

The grand opening seemed like a success, despite her unpleasant interaction with the guys from Dude's Bikes. But a week later, Delaney had only made a few sales and lined up a couple small jobs. No major work sat on her floor yet and despite her advertising, things were pretty quiet.

Rather than mope, Delaney decided that this was the perfect time to put the Qua-sinterbronze clutch in '33. She'd inspected every inch of the bike after shipment, and nothing had gotten dinged up, but the clutch had been slipping when the throttle rolled open for some time now. Dad had never gotten around to fixing it, and now, he'd never have the chance.

As she set up her workspace, the thought briefly crossed Delaney's mind that if Dad had fixed the clutch, he might've been riding '33, instead of his Harley Softail, when that asshole changed lanes without looking. Man, that would've pissed Dad off. That would've pissed him off so much he probably would've come back to haunt Jerry Meyers—the man who'd murdered Dad with his obscene, gas-guzzling SUV. If Dad had survived the crash and not hemorrhaged out on the side of the road, he would've been pissed enough at Jerry Meyers to make his life a living hell. But if Jerry Meyers had ruined the Indian Four? Even from beyond, Dad wouldn't have been able to let that go. Jerry's wife would've found him dead in his bed one day, the only clues a ghostly scent of motor oil and some rye bread crumbs. Dad loved a good tuna on rye.

Delaney wasn't sure how long she waited, frozen, as the oil drained from '33 into a pan, while she pictured what Dad might've looked like at his death. She didn't want these images in her head, but because she'd never actually seen Dad at the site of the accident, her brain made things up as replacement. He probably looked something like he had at the morgue, when she'd gone to identify him. The closed eyes and shredded flesh hadn't bothered her as much as the fact that he'd seemed so much smaller than he was in real life. Delaney remembered thinking, *How big the soul must be. How much must it fill you up? Now that it's gone, Dad looks like a shell.*

Delaney closed her eyes to quiet the burning behind them. Once it passed, her lashes fluttered open and she faced the clutch cover. There were two of them because her eyes were blurry, but once that passed, and the clutch cover was back down to one, Delaney removed it. The gasket beneath tore when she pulled it out, which she expected. She grabbed a razor blade from her setup and scraped off all the stuck-on bits. She heard Dad's voice in her head: *The gasket needs a perfect seal.* Delaney was seven the first time she helped with a clutch. She remembered that her hair was in braids—Boom showed her how because he did his daughter's cornrows—and that she wore jeans and work boots that matched Dad's. It was an exciting time because in the past he'd let her mop up oil or polish bikes or fetch him tools, but he'd never let her actually get into the guts of the motorcycle before.

Don't cut yourself, Dad had said as he handed her the razor blade. *Even a tiny touch will make you bleed. Scrape slow and careful.*

Delaney hadn't been afraid of blood. She'd been afraid to disappoint Dad, because that might mean he'd never let her help with the guts again, and she'd be forever stuck wiping up oil and fetching wrenches. She'd trade all the blood in her body for Dad's approval.

She hadn't cut herself, and she got all the sticky bits off so that the new gasket had a fine seal. Dad had been pleased, and by the time Delaney was twelve, she was fixing clutches all by herself.

Fixing the clutch on '33 today was bittersweet. Delaney took out the spring bolts and then laid out her clutch pack one plate at a time, on the workbench next to her, along with the jutter springs. Just as she suspected, the '33's friction plates were discolored and the steel plates blue from overheating. Delaney grabbed the tray holding the new Qua-sinterbronze, where the plates had been soaking in oil since this morning. She didn't have much worry they'd do well in the bike, as Delaney had worked with sintered bronze her entire career in motor transport. She slid the plates on, seven in all, in the same order she'd taken out the old ones, then replaced the springs and pressure plate, added a brand-new gasket, and finally the cover. She tightened the bolts and had just finished putting in new oil, enjoying the bite of the breeze to cut the humidity as it floated through the open bay, when her favorite furry friend poked his head inside.

"Sinbad." Delaney stood and wiped her oily hands on her jeans. The name still sounded wrong, but she didn't know what else to call him. "What you up to, my man?" She lifted her phone and texted Sunny the dog emoji. Last time Sunny had picked up the pit bull, on the day of the grand opening, they'd agreed that until this problem was solved, texting short-hand was in order.

"Just text the dog emoji and I'll be over ASAP," Sunny had said.

After she hit Send, Delaney faced Sinbad. "You look hot." The pittie was panting against the humid air, his pink tongue lolling to the side, making it look like he was smiling. "I thought you might show up again. Even though Sunny said she fixed the hole in her fence." Delaney had a feeling that fixing a hole wasn't going to stand between this dog and his need to wander. His front paws were coated in dirt, like he'd just dug himself a new tunnel out of prison. Delaney nodded toward one of her shallow kitchen bowls, which she'd filled with water and left just inside the bay.

The dog lifted his muzzle into the air, as though sniffing it out, then turned and dove into the bowl, nose first. Loud, thirsty slurps followed. Water splashed outside the bowl with his aggressive lapping. When he was done, he sauntered over to Delaney and sat.

"Door's open." Delaney nodded toward the storeroom. That was part of her opening routine for the shop now. Open the bay, unlock the main door, flip the sign from Closed to Open, wake up the register, change the water in the dog bowl and open the storeroom, just in case Sinbad arrived while she wasn't looking and needed his bed.

Today, Sinbad didn't budge. In fact, he circled the motorcy-cle, sniffing the wheels, the seat, the kickstand, even the clutch cover. When he faced Delaney again, he had a little bit of oil on his face, a smear next to the eye that didn't have the patch.

"Look at you." Delaney clucked her tongue. "Sunny's not going to like you getting all dirty over here. I'll be labeled the bad aunt who lets the kids eat junk food and stay up all night. She won't let you keep coming. Not that she's letting you come now."

Sinbad woofed, which marked the first time Delaney had heard him speak. It wasn't just any old bark, either. This was a bark with attitude. The pit bull tilted his head back, danced on his front paws and gave a determined woof that truly sounded like he was trying to talk to her.

"The hell you say." Delaney squatted down and opened her arms, hoping the dog would come to her.

He stuck close to the bike instead, circling it a second time, his tail wagging a mile a minute.

"Are you kidding me?" Delaney watched the dog dance and spin and get all excited. "You like the bike?" She wracked her brain, but could think of no good reason why Sinbad would like the motorcycle. Maybe that was the only reason he'd stayed with the Dudes at all? Maybe he would've been running back to Sunny's shelter every day if the Dudes hadn't owned a bike shop. And maybe he hadn't noticed the bike the last time he was here, because there was a buffet of meatballs to distract him. Delaney smiled to herself, kind of liking the idea that this poor, homeless dog who had never had anyone to trust had a thing for motorcycles.

Why not? The motorcycle was the ultimate symbol of freedom.

You don't have to follow anybody's rules, Dad would say. *It's just you, your bike and the road. You can go around everyone else. You can fit places the cars can't. You don't need walls. You can park anywhere. You can fix any problems yourself, unlike all these fancy, computerized, gas-guzzling monsters. And when you're riding, it's just you, the road and the wind.*

Delaney lifted a shop rag off her countertop and wiped the rest of the grease from her fingertips. "Well, go ahead. Check her out. She's not just any motorcycle, my friend," she said to the dog. "This bike here is an American classic. Back in the day, only the wealthy could afford it."

The pit bull woofed again, this time leaning back, rump in the air, into what yogis called "down dog."

"It's true," Delaney insisted. "A four cylinder in 1933 was a luxury item. Clearly not something my backlist of poor, low-life thieves would've been able to afford. Which raises the question of where my great-granddaddy would've got it in the first place."

Sinbad settled next to the bike, head between his paws, and huffed.

Delaney laughed and strode around the shop, tidying up the goods and thinking things were kind of perfect right now. Twenty years in the Marine Corps in the books. Her own bike shop. A wild dog.

The picture of Peter Fonda on the *Easy Rider* chopper caught her eye. "Wyatt," she said, without really thinking. She looked over at the dog, perfectly content lazing next to the motorcycle. "How do you feel about the name Wyatt?"

The pit bull thumped his tail.

"It's better than Sinbad. And it certainly fits your personality."

"I talk to the dogs like they're people, too."

The voice coming from the open bay startled her, but Delaney's reaction turned to a smile when she spied Sunny's blond head peeking around the entrance. She stepped inside, fully decked out in workout attire that was various shades of perfectly coordinating pink. Delaney figured Sunny must work hard to look so fashionable when she spent most of her day with dogs.

"I'm a lot ruder to people," Delaney admitted.

Sunny snorted. "You and me both."

"I've renamed him," Delaney said as Sunny came inside

and faced the pittie with a grin. "His name's Wyatt. Because he's clearly born to be wild."

Sunny narrowed her eyes in thought, then laughed. "I get it. My sister usually names the dogs, really nails their personalities, but she was out of town when I got this one." She squatted down and held out the leash. Wyatt turned his head away. "What're you doing, boy? You can't keep coming out here. Getting all dirty. Taking up Delaney's time."

"He likes the bike." Delaney nodded at '33. "Hasn't even visited his dog bed yet."

"He likes the bike? That's weird, isn't it?"

"No weirder than me, I guess."

Sunny laughed and shook her head at the pit bull, who showed no signs of budging. "My boyfriend runs Canine Warriors. Pete takes some of the dogs I rescue and rehabilitates them into service dogs for military veterans. I wish this guy was a good candidate." She nodded at Wyatt, who rolled over to his side and sighed, content as pie. "But he's clearly a free spirit of the most extreme variety." Sunny's gaze raked over Delaney, a little smirk on the corner of her mouth. "I'd ask you to foster him, but you're kind of already doing that, against your will. Thanks for that, by the way. I know a lot of people wouldn't be as patient as you about a stray coming into their shop all the time."

"No skin off my nose. I kinda like him. I guess we can split custody," Delaney joked.

"I think that would suit him fine." Sunny coiled up the leash and circled the motorcycle. "That's a cool ride." A pair of sneakers covered in a floral print topped off her outfit. Delaney wondered if she'd just worked out or was getting ready to. "It's not like most of the motorcycles I see."

"Nah, it's vintage from 1933. It was my dad's favorite thing in the world."

"I can see why Sinba…er, Wyatt…is attached. You been working on it?" Sunny motioned to the mess on the floor. "Both you and the dog are pretty dirty."

"Yeah, getting her running a little smoother. Wyatt's clearly a digger." Delaney nodded toward his muddy paws. "We're the opposite of you. All pretty in pink."

Sunny beamed a smile that matched her name. "Getting ready to get pretty gross. I teach spin classes in between running the rescue. Hey." She snapped her fingers. "How'd you like the gym? Did you go? I've been meaning to ask. What'd you think of Rhett? He's kind of a grump but he dates my sister, so…" She trailed off with a shrug.

Delaney mentally organized the fleet of questions. "I did go. Twice. I liked it well enough to join, but haven't been in a while because opening the shop has been taking up all my time. I met Rhett Santos, the owner. He's cool. He's no bullshit, I'm no bullshit…we get along. That must mean that Red is your sister."

"Right." Sunny pointed a finger. "I forgot they call her that. To me, she'll always be Cici, even though her name is Constance."

Now that it was out, Delaney could see the resemblance. Sunny was clearly a blonde and had about three inches in height on Red. Sunny was willowy in build, like a runway model, whereas Red was more athletic. But they shared a pair of striking blue eyes and something in the gentle slopes of their foreheads. "Red's who got me set up. Free class. Membership. All that. She's in the office a lot, doing admin stuff. Really cool chick. Pretty good athlete, too."

"She's also the resident massage therapist. She's really good with her hands. She works on my dogs."

"Ha." Delaney grinned. "She needs to work on Wyatt. Settle his butt down a little."

"He's never around long enough."

"Well—" Delaney bent down and started gathering up her things, starting with the oil pan "—he's welcome to hang out here with the bike. The bay will be open all day, so he can come and go as he pleases. I worry about him getting hit by a car but it seems like he sticks to the woods. I think your rescue is a straight shot through there." Delaney pointed over her shoulder, toward the back of the shop where the forest was untouched by developers.

"Isn't that dangerous?" Sunny nibbled on her lower lip. "Although," she continued, "he's getting out anyway. He keeps digging huge holes under my fence and even though it hasn't happened yet, other dogs might get out through his escape tunnels." In the end, Sunny shrugged. "Alright, Wyatt. We get it. Nobody can keep you penned in." She squatted down and stroked along his ears. "But we have to take care of you. You're making it hard."

"Didn't you say your boyfriend trains dogs? And did he… Hey." Things clicked into place. "Did he train a dog named Trinity? For a lady named Tabitha?" Mentioning the shy, former chaplain's assistant reminded Delaney of her earlier thoughts about the size of Dad's soul. Which weren't the typical kind of thoughts Delaney had any given day.

Sunny's eyes got big as the ocean. "Trinity? Yes! She was mine at first. A couple years back. One of eight from the *Matrix* litter. We name our litters after movies and TV shows and that sort of thing," Sunny explained. "Makes it easier to remember names and it's fun. Trinity's mom, Oracle, had been bred so many times." Sunny paused and shook her head. "Then she was dumped at the shelter, pregnant. They called me. Trinity ended up having the perfect personality to be a psychiatric dog. She was laid-back, yet confident. Plus she was tiny for her breed. And if I remember right, Tabitha is a wisp of a thing."

"That's her."

"So you know her?"

"We served together at Camp Leatherneck. Years ago. I don't know her well. Our paths crossed once." Delaney stopped short of saying that the day their paths had crossed had been one of the most challenging days of her life, and certainly one of the most challenging for Tabitha. "I bumped into her at the gym, actually."

"Oh, great." Sunny smiled. "She's getting out and about. Tabitha worked with Pete and Trinity so hard. I could tell that she had never wanted something so much in her life than to work with that dog. That's so cool that you know her. What a small world, huh?"

"Yeah. Real small. So has Pete ever tried to train this one?" Delaney nodded at Wyatt, who was still happily settled near the '33.

"Yeah. Pete tried to train him. Said he's never met a more stubborn dog. He got some of the commands but never quite mastered *stay*."

"Ha. Me neither."

Sunny paused to smirk at her. "Maybe he should give it another go." Sunny sighed and attached the leash to Wyatt's collar. "Speaking of. We should get going. C'mon, boy. Back to my place. We'll see what Pete can do with you this weekend."

Wyatt whined, but clambered to his muddy feet.

"See you later, buddy." Delaney waggled her fingers at him as he trotted after Sunny, a spot of clean, bright pink against the blue sky, a muddy dog and a bike shop.

"Thanks, Delaney. Hopefully I can keep him contained this time." Sunny gave a wave as they disappeared.

Once they were gone, the shop seemed too quiet. Whereas

Delaney had been enjoying the solitary time with her bike, knowing Dad would be proud she was keeping it in prime shape, now all she could think about was how Dad would never ride it again. That, and Tabitha, the poor kid with demons that continued to haunt her. Delaney finished cleaning up her mess and smiled at the muddy paw prints and the short white hairs stuck in the motor oil, even as her throat tightened.

Only one way to beat these kind of blues.

Delaney grabbed her helmet off the counter and pulled it on, then straddled '33 and rolled it out the bay. She kicked twice to prime, then fired it up. The bike rocked gently, back and forth. Once Delaney got going, it'd be a smooth ride, though. Delaney needed a smooth ride right now.

As clear as the day had been, the night was lit up with thunderstorms. June had been fickle so far, caught between warm and cool temps, but it had definitely been more wet than dry. Tonight's storm wasn't an Omaha thunderstorm by any means—those suckers sounded like the gods were waging full-out war in the sky. But this Virginia storm was wild enough to wake Delaney from a dead sleep. The world lit up for a half a second, then ceded to darkness as the thunder gurgled around and seemed to swallow the apartment. Delaney's phone lit up, on silent for the night. She rubbed the sleep from her eyes and grabbed it off the nightstand, even though it was probably just a shipping notification or spam. Instead, there was a text from Sunny.

Do you have Wyatt?

Delaney's pulse rose. She checked the time—just after midnight. For a split second, Delaney wondered why Sunny would know the pittie was missing so late at night, but then, she didn't know Sunny's schedule. Delaney had been early to bed, early to rise for so long there was no use in trying to do anything else. Sounded like Sunny was a night owl.

She threw back the covers and headed downstairs. Wyatt hadn't shown up since this morning, when Sunny took him home, but that didn't mean he wasn't outside the shop door right now, standing in the rain, waiting to curl into his dog bed. Delaney opened the door and was met with fat drops of cold rain that reminded her she was only wearing her "Mauna Kea: Ski a Volcano!" tank top. There was no dog waiting to get inside. She flicked on the outdoor lights and stepped out into the wet, in her bare feet, just as the sky burst into light. The heavens rumbled while she peeked around, but saw no dog.

"Wyatt!" she called. Nothing. She whistled. Still nothing. The pit bull was nowhere to be seen.

Delaney stood in the rain for several seconds, peering into the darkness and calling Wyatt's various names, including "hey, doggo!" When he didn't appear, she went back inside and headed for the rear workshop. There was no way he could be inside the locked room, but she checked anyway. As expected, the dog bed was empty. Damn. She hated to think the poor guy was out in this mess. If he'd left Sunny's place, why hadn't he come here? Was there somewhere else he went that nobody knew about? Or was he lost?

Delaney shuddered and combed her hands through her wet hair, then wiped the rain from her face and arms with a clean shop rag. She didn't know what to do. Should she wait up for him? Go look for him? What if he'd been hit by a car? Delaney realized that, in her haste to check for Wyatt, she hadn't texted Sunny back. Her phone was upstairs, in the apartment. She turned to go, but at the last second, Delaney grabbed the chain to the back bay and raised the door just enough for a dog to get through. If Wyatt showed up while she was gone, she wanted him to be able to get in, out of the storm, as quickly as possible.

The sky rumbled and burst and it felt like the shop actually shook with the force of the storm. Delaney rushed upstairs and sat on the edge of her bed while she texted Sunny.

He's not here. Are you sure he's not there?

Ten minutes went by. Fifteen. Twenty. Maybe Sunny had gone out to look for Wyatt in the storm. Well, of course she had. Delaney tapped her foot nervously. No way she would fall back to sleep until she heard back. She grabbed her jeans from the foot of the bed and jumped into them, crossed the room to the kitchen, snagged her flashlight from the top of the fridge and headed back downstairs. An umbrella seemed like a bad idea in a thunderstorm, so she left it behind in favor of a windbreaker with a hood that she had hanging off the shelves in the workshop. She jammed her feet into her motorcycle boots, which were right next to '33, not far from the dog bed—strategic planning—and left the door raised in case she and Wyatt missed each other.

Using her flashlight to create a trail, Delaney followed the beam across the parking spaces out back, toward the woods. She knew that the worst place to be during an electrical storm was under a tree—or, in her case, smack-dab in the middle of a forest of trees—but while she'd been waiting to hear back from Sunny she'd been counting the seconds between flashes and rumbles. Her last check had been at forty, putting the storm far enough out to not be a danger.

The sky grew darker the nearer she got to the trees and the more she left the world of electrical lighting behind. Now it was just Delaney and her flashlight. The concentric circles of her beam only caught about a yard at a time, but the whole world was muddy and soaked. Her motorcycle boots grabbed at the muck and kept her steady as she took her first tentative steps onto a discernable trail. This wasn't a path that some park service had made, merely a worn groove through the surrounding oaks, maples and hollies that had been created by the feet of short-cutters, teenagers and dogs who couldn't make up their minds where to call home.

Delaney kept to the makeshift trail so she could find her way back out, but occasionally whistled or called out her array of names for the pit bull. Though the storm had moved off, rain continued to drum against her windbreaker and roll down the slope of her nose. The day had been warm, but the night had cooled and she started to feel the chill on her skin from the soaked tank top beneath her jacket.

She paused to pull out her phone and check for a message from Sunny. A text was there, but Delaney's heart sank as she read it.

I can't find him anywhere. He's really not with you?

"Dammit." Delaney sighed and shoved her phone back in her coat pocket. This was pointless. The dog could be anywhere. She stuck her pinkies in the corner of her mouth and gave another loud, long, sharp whistle. She pushed back her hood and closed her eyes, straining for any sound above the raindrops pattering on the leaves and gurgling into the ditches. Nothing. She'd just turned around, ready to head back home, when suddenly, the rain stopped. Like she was back in Hawai'i, where the rain would start and stop on a dime, the drumming just quit. In that moment of sudden silence, she heard it, low but unmistakable: the whining, yelping, desperate sound of a scared or trapped animal.

"Wyatt?" Delaney's voice rose, even though she tried to

control the wave of excitement that gripped her core. She stuck her pinkies in her mouth and whistled again.

The yelping grew more frantic, rising in pitch.

West. The noise was coming from the west.

Delaney trained her beam into the forest and tore inside, going as quickly as she could without running into tree trunks. Branches and sticks tore at her jeans, her boots sticking in the mud as she clomped her way toward the whining sound, which was growing louder and closer.

What happened next was a complete departure from everything she'd been trained to do, her entire military career. She got excited and lost her cool, rushing toward the sound of what she knew to be Wyatt, trapped somewhere, hurt or scared or both, and she tripped in the darkness, on either a tree root or a rock, face-planting in the mud, flashlight flying from her hand on impact.

When she lifted her head from the ground, her gaze connected with the circular beam of light that shone to the bottom of a muddy ravine. She crawled on her belly, collected the flashlight and peered down. There, at the bottom, yelping in the pale glow, was Wyatt. The sides of the pit were steep.

Delaney let out a great sigh. This explained everything. Wyatt had obviously spent the day digging a new escape tunnel out of Sunny's place, only to be caught in a storm and trapped in a ditch too slick to climb out of. The good news was he didn't appear to be hurt. The bad news was, Delaney had to get him out. She trained her flashlight all around the outer rim of the ditch and determined it to be a calculated risk. The ravine looked shallow enough to scale, boost Wyatt out, then climb out herself. If she got stuck, she could probably grab on to one of the roots or secure footing on a jutting rock.

Wyatt was barking frantically now that he'd seen Delaney. She tried to calm him with a soothing tone as she took her steps into the ravine with the edges of her boots, to keep steady and upright. Once she made it to the bottom, the pittie waggled up to her and pushed against her legs. "Okay, boy. I'm going to boost you up first. I'll come after."

The dog made a growling-whining sound from the back of his throat that sounded a lot like agreement.

"Okay. C'mon." Delaney laced her fingers together, just like she would to boost a fellow marine. Rather than wait for Wyatt to step into her palms, Delaney braced her hands under his bottom and shoved him upward. The flashlight lay on the ground, lighting up the opposite side, so she couldn't really see what was happening, but she felt the pittie scramble, as if he clawed at the side of the ravine with his paws to get to the top.

After a moment, the weight left Delaney's hands and Wyatt woofed from over her head. She grabbed the flashlight from the ground and shone it upward, revealing that the dog had, indeed, found his way out of the pit. "Okay, buddy," she said. "My turn." Delaney tucked the flashlight in her coat pocket and felt around for a good hold. Eventually her fingers lit on an exposed root, which she grabbed greedily. Delaney felt the root separate from the side of the ground, like a rope, but hold fast to wherever it was attached. She planted her feet and rappelled up the side of the ravine, using the upper body strength she had cultivated for the past twenty years to keep her steady when her boots slid against the muddy wall. Back when Delaney had enlisted in the marines, women didn't have to do pull-ups, a seventy-second flexed arm hang instead being the goal to earn max points toward a first class PFT. Delaney had done pull-ups anyway, working her way up to fifteen by the time she was done with basic training.

Despite being variously teased, hated and admired, Delaney knew without a doubt that she was having the last laugh. She grappled toward the top of the ravine, Wyatt's face in the bouncing beam of her flashlight, when her feet slipped and she slid back to the bottom, landing on her ass in the mud. Wyatt woofed and made a scrambling sound. Delaney groaned and shone the light upward, saw that he was trying to scramble back down in her direction.

"No, boy! Wyatt! Stay!" Delaney held up her free hand, like she could ward him off. Wyatt's paws were sliding and he was tossing his head. Knowing the pittie would come rushing back down to square one if she didn't haul ass, Delaney quickly regrouped, grabbed the root for a second time and rappelled up the side of the pit as fast as her legs would go. Her arms were on fire but she held steady, calling out, "Stay, Wyatt! I'm almost there!" until she finally reached the edge. A determined nudge from Wyatt's muzzle was her reward.

Delaney pulled herself over the rim, then squatted there a second, catching her breath, before she patted Wyatt's muddy fur. "I'm here, boy," she said. "C'mon. Let's go home and get dry."

The pit bull followed along, no leash needed, as Delaney hoofed it back along the makeshift trail. The light from the shop, which Delaney could see from the partially raised bay door, was like a beacon in the night.

Once they reached the shop, Delaney ducked under the door as Wyatt raced inside. The pittie dove into his bed, circling three times before he sank down with a huff. Delaney grabbed two shop rags from the shelves and rubbed them both, one in each hand, over his fur, drying him, brushing off mud and calming his nerves. "You're going to need a bath tomorrow. You're seriously filthy."

Wyatt huffed, but allowed Delaney to use six shop rags on his wet body before he laid his grateful head down and, curled into a tight ball, sighed with satisfaction.

"Well, good for you," Delaney murmured, not a trace of

sarcasm in her voice. "You made it. Now sleep off the night, safe in your dreams, whatever they may be." She grabbed a blanket from the shelves and draped it over the dog's slumbering body.

Once he was breathing hard and steady, Delaney texted Sunny.

He's here. He's safe. Go to bed.

Delaney grabbed the chain and lowered the bay door, clicking it in place to lock. She went to snap off the light, ready to hit the shower, then climb back into her warm bed, when she suddenly became aware of the oddly vacant feeling to the workshop. She blinked, thinking she must be exhausted or dreaming. But no. She was here and now, with a safe but shivering dog snoozing at her feet and her body covered in rain and mud.

But Dad's Indian Four was gone.

eight

The day started with a small white envelope on his tidy desk. In the old days, before Sean was doing the tidy-your-area thing every night, he might not have noticed the envelope amongst his messy piles. But today, there it was, a neat rectangle against the backdrop of his green blotter. The return address started with *T. Steele*. The name didn't ring a bell. Sean ripped it open and pulled out a greeting card with a cartoon dog on the cover. The dog sat on a green patch of grass and wore a red collar. *Just Wanted to Say Thanks* was printed in the sky above. Inside was a short note.

Detective Callahan,

Thank you for being so kind. Don't say you were just doing your job because you and I both know that not everyone would've done what you did at the grocery store. Trinity and I will forever appreciate your help that day.

Blessings,
Tabitha.

"What's that?" Castillo was suddenly there, reading over his shoulder.

Sean closed up the card. "Nunya."

Castillo rolled her eyes. "All your business is my business. Get used to it."

"Just a thank-you card. No big deal." Even though it was. Not because he'd been thanked, as he never expected thanks, but because Tabitha had screwed up the courage to mail it. Sean had kind of been dragging this morning and now he felt his mood lifting.

"Oh, yeah? Well, in that case—" Castillo dropped some papers on his desk "—we've got a case."

Sean lifted the report and scanned it, noting it was about a stolen motorcycle. His pulse rose as he slowed down and read through the details. This wasn't just any bike someone had nabbed on a side street. This was a pricey, antique bike, stolen from a motorcycle shop.

Then he saw the name attached to the report.

Delaney Monroe, owner of Triple M Classics, located only ten miles from the police station and even closer to Semper Fit.

Sean's heart sank as quickly as his pulse had risen. Delaney wasn't a common name. A Delaney who rode motorcycles narrowed the field even more. So when he and Sonia headed out to the shop to talk to the owner, Sean didn't have the typical edge of adrenaline that fired up his belly and told him this day was going to be a good one.

"What's wrong with you?" Castillo glared at him over her coffee cup. She ran the lid along her bottom lip. "You're off, somehow. Gloomy, when you should be oddly thrilled about a stolen vehicle."

Sean shot her a glare. "It's nothing," he said. "Just…drop it for now."

Castillo's lips parted, like she might have a sassy comment, but then she closed her mouth and shrugged.

Triple M Classics was a brand-new, stand-alone shop located across the street from Nonnie's, Sean's favorite Italian restaurant. He'd never actually been to the shop, though he recalled it being named Dude's Bikes not long ago. Before that, it was just a battery and oil change gig that was as old as the road it lived on, all the way back to when that road wasn't even paved. Living quarters were above the shop, and from the info Sean had gleaned on his background search, Delaney Monroe lived alone and was the sole owner. He parked the minivan next to an old, white Ford truck, which he hadn't seen her drive, but he supposed she'd need a vehicle other than a motorcycle to get around in. The shop was open for business, as indicated by the sign on the front door. A little bell jangled when Sean and Castillo stepped inside.

The shop was full of sunshine, due to a wide-open bay door on the far side of the store. Small pools of water from last night's storms sparkled in the divots of the worn asphalt outside. Twigs and leaves shaken from the trees floated there. One small section of the store had shelves lined with inventory— an array of stock parts, helmets, jackets, magazines and memorabilia. A counter with a register was stationed near a back door, which was closed. A staircase led to the apartment above. The center space was wide-open, with two large workspaces in either corner, away from the merchandise. On the far side a motorcycle was up on a lift, something off-road, maybe a Pioneer.

On the other side of the Pioneer—which Sean could see was an OSSA as he got closer—was Delaney, clad in rugged blue jeans, motorcycle boots and a plain white T-shirt smeared with oil. The sides of her short, dark hair had been hastily pinned back in several places, which gave her an unexpected flash of softness. She had a wrench in her hand and was intent on her work. Well after the bell over the door sounded, Delaney turned to face them, tucking the wrench in her back pocket. Sean smiled, despite himself. She looked like one of the greasers, if Danny Zuko had had an adorable sister who decided the Pink Ladies weren't her style.

"You gotta be shitting me," she said, once recognition lit her eyes.

"Cat quick and tiger tough." The words slipped out of Sean's mouth.

Delaney's eyebrows rose at the same time that Castillo shot him a *what the hell* look.

"The OSSA," Sean said quickly, pointing at the Pioneer. "That's their slogan. Cat quick and tiger tough."

"Oh." Delaney's face relaxed. If she smiled, she glanced at the bike to hide it. "Yeah. You're right." She almost sounded disappointed, like she'd wanted to be irritated at his appearance, but couldn't muster it now.

"She yours?"

"Um, no." Delaney glanced at the bike again. "I'm fixing her up for a client. He took her on the trails over the weekend. Brought her in this morning."

Sean could see the air filter had been removed and the chain was in a pan of oil. "Got business already. That's great."

"Yeah, this guy has money. He doesn't like to get dirty unless he's riding, so he's paying me to do the maintenance." She shrugged.

"Sorry," Sean said, after a pause. "I'm Detective Callahan." Sean's police persona kicked in. "This is my partner, Detective Castillo."

Castillo nodded and drew her little notepad from the breast pocket of her suit jacket. She had on her All Business Face, which was different from her Creature Face and her Mom Face. It was kind of a mix of the two, all hard chin and cautious eyes, with a promise of not getting pissed if everyone played nice.

"Thanks for coming." Delaney glanced at Castillo but kept her eyes trained on Sean. It was clear she wanted to know what the game was. Were they supposed to know each other or not? She didn't care what the rules were, no matter how hinky. She just wanted to get down to business. Her emotions were raw, just under the surface of her smooth skin and tired eyes, the dark circles beneath them telling Sean she hadn't slept much. He also noted caked mud on her motorcycle boots and a set of muddy paw prints that trailed from the door behind the counter and over to the bay. There didn't seem to be a dog anywhere, though. Sean wondered if he was upstairs, in the apartment.

"So your motorcycle was stolen." Castillo jumped right in. "Why don't you show us where it was?"

"Sure." Delaney glanced once more at Sean before she turned and headed for the door behind the counter. She pushed it open and secured the doorstop with a drag of her boot. Behind it was a large space that could work as a second workspace as well as storage. "It was right there." She pointed to a spot behind a row of shelves, not far from a bay door that matched the one out front.

Sean walked over to the spot and stopped near a worn dog bed that was muddy and wet. Paw prints led from the door to the bed. Next to the paw prints were muddy boot prints that matched the size of Delaney's feet. Small. Maybe a size six, women's. There were no tire tracks, suggesting the motorcycle had not been out in the rain.

"You noticed the bike missing last night?"

"Yeah." Delaney rubbed her hands over her face, leaving

behind a couple streaks of motor oil. "I went out in the storm to look for my dog. Well…" she paused, her eyes closing and a rueful grin shadowing her lips "…he's not really my dog. There's a pit bull that used to live here, and he keeps showing up at random times. He's supposed to be at this dog rescue. But he keeps digging out and coming back here. I text the lady who runs the place, she comes to get him. But last night she texted me instead. Said he was missing and wanted to know if he was here. He wasn't, so I went out to find him." Delaney took a breath. "I was worried. The dog was lost in a thunderstorm. He uses the woods," she explained, pointing over her shoulder, "to get between my place and Sunny's."

"Sunny's." The caffeine from this morning's coffee suddenly kicked up a notch in Sean's veins. So Sunny and Delaney knew each other. He briefly wondered if they'd talked about him. Then he reminded himself not to be a typical male. They probably had much better things to talk about. "Write that down," he told Castillo, to distract both women from noticing his sudden awkwardness.

Castillo shot him a glare. "Aye, aye, Captain." She made a long, slow mark on her notepad with her pencil, some kind of bull's eye, just to be a smart-ass.

"I went out in the woods to find the dog," Delaney continued. "The bike was here when I left. It was about half past midnight. I found Wyatt, brought him back here. By the time we made it to the storeroom, the bike was gone. That was at 1:24 a.m."

"Exactly 1:24?" Castillo actually wrote that on her pad.

"I looked at my watch."

"Twelve thirty to 1:24. That's a very narrow window," Castillo said.

Sean approached the bay and saw that it locked on the floor and opened with a chain. He played with the lock, saw that it worked. Sean grabbed the chain and raised the door, which was old and rusty and made a loud grinding noise. When he looked back at Delaney he saw that she watched closely, her eyes extra bright.

"It was open," she admitted. "I, um…left it open a ways." Her voice dropped at the end of her sentence. "I thought that the dog might come to the shop. That we might miss each other. I didn't want him out here in the rain so I left the door raised while I went to look for him." She sounded guilty but also defensive. "I know it was stupid, but I'm not sure I'd do anything different."

Silence passed. Everyone in the room knew what nobody said. With a door wide-open, under the cover of night, stealing a motorcycle was easy. Drive it away or just wheel it right out, into the bed of a truck and take off. There wasn't a lot to it. And, as with most stolen motorcycles, there wasn't much hope, either.

"Did you leave the key in it, too?" Castillo raised an eyebrow.

"The bike was in my storeroom. I thought it was safe."

"What about security cameras?" Sean looked around the door and near the eaves for the usual location.

"I have them out front." Delaney sounded defeated. "I haven't put one back here yet. I planned to, but I just opened and I didn't see an immediate need."

"Okay." Castillo huffed a little sigh. "Ma'am, my partner here is going to check out the shop and surrounding area. Why don't you and I go sit down and get all the details, okay?"

"Actually…" Sean took the chain and lowered the door, shutting out the sunlight. "Why don't you do the sleuthing today. I'll get the details from Miss Monroe."

Castillo's eyes narrowed. Sean hated taking down the details. Sean was always the guy inspecting the area, picking up on the little crumbs and following the tracks, with almost no input from anyone. He let the facts drive the case, and enjoyed putting the pieces of the puzzle together from environmental clues and his own instincts. Sean was almost never the guy who sat at the kitchen table or on the living room sofa with the crying mom, the angry dad, the confused girlfriend, the lying boyfriend. Castillo weathered that task well with her various personas, like a method actor who could become exactly what the crying mother or lying boyfriend needed in order to get the most accurate information.

Today, though, Sean wanted to be the one to get the details. Yeah, he was probably being a little selfish, as any excuse to get to know Delaney better was one he would take. But mostly, it was her eyes. In the couple of times Sean had been around Delaney he'd seen anger, surprise, determination and doubt. Today, the glint was gone. There was nothing there but a hollow sadness, like the loss of the bike was so much more than the loss of the bike. Her eyes were like those of an animal in captivity. Like her very freedom had been stolen.

And to Sean, that just wasn't acceptable.

Delaney was too distraught over the missing motorcycle to dwell on her shock that the guy from the gym was now the head detective on her case. She invited him upstairs where they could sit and be comfortable while he collected her information. He paused inside the shop, turning in a slow circle while he studied the bike on the lift, the merchandise and finally the pictures hanging around the perimeter of her shop. The detective's gaze lingered on the north wall, and Delaney tried to figure out which photo had grabbed his attention.

"That the bike?" He pointed at the picture of Dad sitting on '33.

"Yep." Delaney stared at the photo as long as the detective had.

"I'll get a picture of that before I go," Detective Callahan said.

"Sure." They went upstairs to the apartment and Delaney pulled two beers from the fridge. She offered one to the detective, but he shook his head. Delaney motioned for him to sit and while he settled in the recliner she sipped and tried to decide if she was surprised or not that Callahan was a cop. The answer was both yes and no. No, in that he had that rough edge to him that would be required for his job and was common at the types of gyms Delaney frequented. He took his physical health at least semiseriously and he was built like a brick house, to use a cliché she liked particularly well, because brick houses were old-fashioned, sturdy, tough and attractive. Right now the detective wore a white dress shirt with slacks and a jacket, his badge around his neck on a chain and presumably his weapon holstered at the waist, but Delaney had seen him at the gym, in shorts and T-shirts. She knew his clothes covered an impressive set of muscles, even if he was clumsy at body-weight movements and a little rusty overall. Those were all the reasons Delaney was not surprised that Detective Callahan was a cop.

What did surprise her was this immediate situation. Detective Callahan, sitting in her living room, regarding her with a hint of softness in his gray eyes as they talked about the missing motorcycle. Delaney knew Callahan was the guy who should be downstairs, checking out the site where the bike got nabbed, looking for tire tracks out front, combing around for clues or whatever it was detectives did in these situations. She knew it by his partner's reaction when Callahan suggested they switch roles and she knew it by what little she had learned about this guy at the gym. Detective Callahan liked to be the guy on the trail with the magnifying glass, not the guy on the couch talking to the upset victim, refusing to have a beer, even if he wanted one, because he was on duty.

"What's the history of this bike?" Callahan pulled out a notepad and pencil. "Just, nuts and bolts. How long you've had it. Where you got it. That kind of thing."

"It was my great-grandfather's, originally. I never met him, but the story was he won the bike in a poker game. I have no idea if that's true, but I do know that he wouldn't have been able to just go out and buy the bike. We're a long line of mechanics. The '33 is a four cylinder, made at the height of the Great Depression, so it was a luxury item. No way my people had four hundred dollars to drop on a motorcycle, so my great-grandfather definitely got it otherwise. After he died, the bike became my grandfather's, who I also never met, then my father's. When my dad died, the bike became mine. I just had it shipped here from Omaha."

"Who knew about the motorcycle?" Callahan knocked out a couple of tiny mints from a plastic container hidden in his breast pocket and popped them in his mouth. "Mint?"

"No, thanks."

Callahan put the mints away and waited.

"All my father's biker friends knew the '33 well. That's a long list, and they're all over the country." Delaney honestly couldn't think of anyone who would steal Dad's bike, off the top of her head, even though plenty of his friends had wanted to buy it. Some of Dad's crew had been shady, but they were blue collar kind of shady, not the type to steal from one of their own.

"Anyone show any particular interest in the bike, out of that group?"

"Everyone in his core riding group. The guy that owns the shop he worked at and three other guys. They all asked, each in their own way, if I was going to hang on to the bike after Dad died. They were willing to buy it if I wasn't. They're like family, though. Like my uncles. They helped raise me."

Detective Callahan was quiet, writing in his pad. "Those the guys downstairs? In the photo of you as a little girl, surrounded by five men?"

"Yeah, that's them." Delaney tried to keep her surprise to herself.

"I'll need those names."

"Sure." Delaney didn't repeat, *they're like family.* The detective was only doing his job. She was, however, dreading the fact that Boom, Zip, Donnie and Sal were going to find out she'd lost '33. She needed to give Detective Callahan alternatives. "The guy who delivered the motorcycle was really into it. And I just had a grand opening two weeks ago," Delaney added. "At least a hundred people came to that, throughout the day. The bike was parked right downstairs and everybody liked checking it out. People even took pictures of it." Delaney swigged her beer and wallowed in the bitter aftertaste. She normally didn't day drink, but she needed something to keep her hands busy if she was going to sit here and be judged by a cop who was probably thinking she was asking to get her bike stolen by leaving a door wide-open. Not to mention this was the same guy she'd raced in a 5K last time she'd seen him, and their parting hadn't exactly been friendly.

Callahan kept writing. He had the perfect poker face, with his hard, square jaw, lips that didn't turn either up or down at the corners, and eyes that went between her, the pad and the apartment, like he was recording information, scoping out the place and watching her reaction all at the same time. "Did you keep a list of people who came to the grand opening?"

Delaney's lips paused at the edge of the beer bottle. "I did. I had a registry book. Like when you go to a funeral. People were supposed to sign it. I thought it would be a cool keep-sake, plus I'd have names and phone numbers of potential clients. It's downstairs."

"I'll need that book."

"Definitely." Delaney rose, but Callahan motioned with his hand for her to sit back down.

"Later. We've got more to talk about."

Delaney hesitated, then sank back down. This was a side of Callahan she hadn't seen. This whole cop thing. At the gym, he kept to himself, even though he seemed to know everyone. He wasn't loud or flashy, rude or bossy. Just quietly confident and possibly a little bit jaded with life. Now, as a detective, he was still quietly confident, but with a huge edge. Callahan was laser focused and completely in charge. None of his baggage came with him to the job.

He leaned forward. "Anybody close to you have a reason to take the bike? Other than your...uncles?"

She didn't even hesitate. "I'm not close to anybody but my uncles."

"No disgruntled ex? Somebody who had a score to settle or a debt to pay? Knows your routines closely?"

Delaney shook her head. "My last serious relationship was in Hawai'i, years ago. Quantico was my last tour before retirement. I had my head down, all business, just to make my twenty, get out and open my shop. I'm not on Tinder and I'm not in any knitting circles. The only person I was close to in any meaningful way is dead."

Callahan looked up from his notepad, and for a flash of a second, his emotions peeked out from behind his cop persona. A change that ran through his eyes, like a single sparkle in a far-off ocean. He cleared his throat and changed topics. "What's the bike worth, Miss Monroe?"

Delaney let out a great gush of air. She'd been waiting for

this part. She felt stupid enough already for leaving the door open, inviting anyone and everyone to steal Dad's prized bike. Which is all Delaney cared about—the bike she and her father had worked on together and shared since she was knee-high. Detective Callahan was about to learn just what an idiot she was. "Depends. But...anywhere between twenty and sixty grand." With the amount of work Dad had put into it, the care he and Delaney had taken with it, they were probably talking near the higher end. Delaney kept that to herself because frankly, she didn't care. '33 was priceless.

Detective Callahan leaned back in the recliner. He squared his shoulders and eyed Delaney like he'd read every word that ran through her mind. "Who do you think did this? Any idea at all?"

Delaney polished off her beer and set the bottle on the edge of the coffee table. She'd gone through that very question multiple times ever since the shock of seeing that empty spot of concrete next to Wyatt's dog bed.

"It's such a small window of opportunity," Callahan repeated what his partner had said. "Less than an hour between when you last saw it downstairs and when it went missing. What it boils down to is this—who steals a bike, in the rain, while the owner is gone for less than an hour?"

The silence ticked by, seconds weighted by concrete.

"I thought the same thing," Delaney finally spoke. "How could anyone possibly know I was going to leave my storeroom open and be there to steal the bike?" That was one of the reasons Delaney had stood there, dripping wet and muddy, stunned, for probably a full minute before she went and searched the entire shop for the motorcycle. Maybe she was going crazy and had actually parked it on the main floor. Maybe someone had moved it as a joke. Maybe if she blinked enough times, the bike would reappear. When none of those things turned out to be true, Delaney had gone upstairs for her Glock and toured every inch of her shop, apartment and perimeter, and came up with nothing. The bike was just gone. One minute it was there, less than sixty minutes later, it wasn't. Then she'd locked everything up, squatted down on her heels next to Wyatt's slumbering body and buried her face in her palms for a long, long time.

"There was this one moment—" Delaney's voice dropped while she relived the memory "—when the rain just stopped. That's the only reason I found the dog. I could hear him whining, once the rain stopped. That's the *exact* moment the bike could've been stolen. If they drove it away, that is. Because who rides a bike in a downpour?" That thought, more than anything, had haunted her all night. The moment '33 had been taken was likely the same one she'd rescued Wyatt.

"Everything suggests this crime was planned, but it certainly looks like a crime of opportunity."

"I just don't get it." Delaney opened her palms in her lap and stared at them, determined to keep the burning behind her eyes from leaking out. "Somebody might've been planning to steal the bike. But nobody could've known I'd go out looking for the dog."

Silence passed before Callahan pressed on. "How'd the dog get out? You said the dog's been visiting awhile? Leaves Sunny's place and comes here?"

"Yeah, for months. Even before I bought the shop." Delaney rose up and started pacing the apartment. If Wyatt had been a pawn in a plan to steal her bike, then Sunny was the most likely suspect. But that was ridiculous. When Sunny had shown up this morning to get Wyatt she'd been genuinely stunned about the missing cycle. She'd even apologized.

"Look how much trouble you're causing," Sunny had scolded Wyatt. "You're filthy. You made Delaney go out into a storm to find you and now her best bike is gone. Aw, Delaney." Sunny's blue eyes had filled with gloom. "I'm so sorry. I swear he's going straight to Pete's and he's not coming out until he's trained."

"Don't be mad at him." Delaney had bent down to pet his ears, and rather than flinching, Wyatt had allowed her touch this time. "It's not his fault. Or yours."

"I'll need to talk to everyone who works for Sunny," Callahan said, as though he'd already been through the idea of Sunny having something to do with the stolen motorcycle and had rejected it. "This might all go back to the dog."

"The Dudes," Delaney said, pausing her walk around the apartment. "The brothers who owned Dude's Bikes came to the grand opening. Wyatt—that's what I named the dog—was here and they saw him. The dog was theirs when they lived here, which is why he keeps coming back. They gave him back to Sunny when they were forced to move out. The dog likes the shop, especially his dog bed in the back room, but he wanted nothing to do with those guys. The Dudes wanted to take Wyatt when they saw him, but I said no. They were not pleased." Delaney's heart was thudding in her ears now. "They saw the '33. They went so far as to basically threaten me. Said they controlled the bike scene around here and I shouldn't make them my enemy."

"Is that right?"

"Yeah. I kind of blew it off at the time, but now I'm starting to wonder. Plus, someone suggested that Dude's Bikes dealt in more than motorcycles."

Callahan's writing slowed a little bit. "Okay." He finally looked up from his pad. "I've got some leads. In the meantime, you let me know immediately if those brothers come around here again."

The hard edge to Callahan's voice took Delaney off guard,

but it also made her feel safe, which wasn't a feeling she was used to. "I will."

She waited for him to get up, but the detective stayed seated, regarding her thoughtfully from his seat in the recliner. He had one foot on top of the opposite knee, creating a shelf for his notepad. She hugged herself, her bare arms suddenly cold, like she was back in last night's rain.

"When did your dad die?"

The words fell around Delaney like soft feathers. If anyone else had asked, she might've clammed up or asked them to leave. But again, this guy was just trying to do his job. "Five months ago. Right before I retired. He didn't make the ceremony." Delaney was proud her words came out so steady.

"That sucks." Callahan's steady gaze suggested he was not just paying her lip service. "What happened?"

Delaney looked him dead in the eye. "Motorcycle accident." She kept contact and waited for the detective to ask if Dad had been wearing a helmet or if he'd been speeding. The answer to the first question was yes and the second no.

"He was on his motorcycle in December…in Omaha?"

"All he needed was a warm day. It was a warm day."

Callahan nodded. "Somebody change lanes without looking?"

Her first reaction was that Callahan had looked it all up before he got here. Maybe he read the accident report. But her second reaction was that Callahan, as a police officer, had probably seen his fair share of road accidents and knew how common it was for drivers to simply not look out for motorcyclists. On a bike, you definitely had to be a defensive driver. "Yes," she said. "My father was murdered with a goddamn SUV."

Callahan nodded, giving no visible reaction. "I'm sorry."

It's not your fault, Delaney almost said. But she knew that wasn't what Callahan meant. "Thank you."

He waited one more heartbeat before he rose and tucked the notebook in his pocket. "I'll be in touch, Miss Monroe. Hopefully we can figure out what happened and track down your bike."

"Delaney," she said, as she offered her hand. "It's Delaney."

Detective Callahan clasped her fingers gently. "I'll be in touch, Delaney."

Delaney wanted to return the handshake with a firm clasp, to show the detective that she was both in charge of this situation and of her emotions. But she felt powerless right now, and, up until the moment the detective had taken over, a little hopeless. Her hand stayed soft inside his rough one. She tilted her head up. The glint in Callahan's eye had gone from hard-nosed detective to something softer, almost intimate.

A flush ran through Delaney's body. She cleared her throat and slowly withdrew her hand. "Thank you, Detective. I really appreciate your help."

"That's what I'm here for."

Delaney smiled, despite her sadness, and found herself wishing she'd held on just a little longer.

nine

"Did you tell her the recovery rate on motorcycles?" Castillo said as she edged the minivan onto the road. "Intact or in pieces?"

"No." Sean skimmed his notes. "She's depressed enough already."

"You're acting weird." Castillo took a sharp turn that made Sean slide roughly into the door. "Usually right about now we'd be sighing over the lady who left her shop wide-open with a fifty-thousand-dollar bike inside. You would've been the one to start the joking. You also would've been the one to check out the shop and perimeter."

Sean ignored her probing. "What'd you find, by the way?"

"No tracks. Too much rain." Castillo changed lanes in front of a rig that was going at least ten miles over the speed limit. Sean knew she was tempting the trucker to honk or flip her off, but the rig merely slowed down. "I did find a cozy spot under the eaves. Neat little corner where one could hide in the dark, stay dry, watch the back door and smoke cigarettes."

"So maybe someone was watching the shop. How many?"

"Three butts. Newports."

"Three. So he waited awhile."

"Or he's a chain-smoker. Our girl smoke?"

"No." Sean sputtered a laugh. "Not with those lungs."

Silence passed before Castillo whipped her head around to face Sean. "Oh, my God. That's her, isn't it? That's the girl. The *woman*, I mean." Her fingers fluttered open and her grumpy face broke into a sneaky grin. "I thought it seemed like you two knew each other."

"No."

"Yes." Castillo glanced back at the road. "Absolutely yes. You two had this vibe going. Then you want to do the interview. This explains everything." Castillo punched him in the arm. "This is the woman from the gym. Who 'inspired' you. Who beat you at the 5K run."

"It was a tie."

"Liar." Castillo punched him again.

Sean swatted her away with his notebook. "Face the damn road. You trying to kill us?"

Castillo turned forward, the grin not fading even a little. "Dang, Callahan. You always go for the chase, don't you?" She shook her head. "Don't get me wrong. I can see the appeal. She's adorable, but…" Castillo shook her head again.

"But what?"

"What you've been into since the divorce." Castillo pulled up to the station and put the van in Park. She faced Sean, hands flying all over the place while she spoke. "After what you went through with Kim, I can see the appeal of a strong, independent woman. Kim was always that damsel in distress."

"Lazy," Sean corrected. "Kim was lazy. Liked to be pampered. I thought it was cute when I met her. Not so cute after five years."

"Right. So first chick you date after your divorce is the lady with the dogs."

"Sunny."

"Right. And she's strong and independent. But she's also got the clothes and the hair and the cute little spin outfits. So she's definitely not Kim, but she's not *not* Kim."

"She's not Kim at all."

"But that chick," Castillo said, hitching a thumb over her shoulder in the direction of Delaney's shop, "is a badass. Like, a flat-out, serious badass. She will eat you for dinner, Callahan. She's not just playing at the biker chick persona. She actually fixes the damn things. And I think she can fix a lot more than motorcycles. I saw a picture of her in the shop? Up on the wall? Next to Daryl from *The Walking Dead*? My girl's wearing BDUs, holding an assault rifle and leaning against an MRAP...with five dudes in the background. You see it? That chick is for real."

Sean didn't answer. He'd seen the picture, but he and Castillo didn't actually have to answer most of each other's questions. Fifty percent were rhetorical and the other fifty percent were answered with cop telepathy.

"Wait, wait, wait." Castillo was getting ready to open the minivan door but paused. "Sunny. The dogs." She snapped her fingers. "These two ladies know each other."

Again, Sean didn't answer. None of this mattered, right? What mattered was the job. Working the case. Finding the motorcycle.

Castillo bent over, laughing, her back shaking. When she finally lifted her head she had tears in her eyes. "You're in trouble, Callahan. I can't wait to see how this plays out." She got out of the minivan, but Sean didn't follow. He slid into the driver's seat and fastened his seat belt. "Where you going? It's lunchtime." Castillo glanced at her watch.

"Going to talk to the Dudes," Sean said. "That's our best lead."

Richard and Dale Worley lived in an apartment about half an hour's drive from Delaney's shop. They were like Abbott and Costello, with reverse heights, neither one funny.

"I didn't take that chick's bike, though I'm not surprised somebody did," the big guy said. His name was Dale but everyone called him Dude.

"Why's that?" Sean looked around the apartment. From where he stood in the galley kitchen, he could see a messy living room, coffee table covered in pizza boxes and beer cans, and a television running on Fox News.

The smaller one, Richard—aka Dick—snorted. "She won't know how to take care of that bike. Won't treat it right. I'm sure one of the many other people who saw it the other day felt the same."

A sizzle of irritation ran up Sean's spine. "She owns a vintage motorcycle shop. Why wouldn't she know how to take care of it?"

Dick made a derisive sound and bit into his sandwich, which looked like ham and cheese on Wonder Bread. "Well, it's missing, isn't it?"

"Exactly," Dude piped in. "I give that shop six months, tops. Yeah, some people might take pity on her or be interested at first—oh, look at the cute little lady running her own bike shop, how sweet—but once she starts breaking their shit, they'll sing a different tune."

The zip of irritation turned to a slow burn through Sean's veins. For the first time in a long time, he felt a wave of dizziness wash through him. Over the last decade and a half, the vertigo had dissipated, but had never quite gone away. It'd been months, though. The last time he'd felt it had been at a Nationals game when two drunks in the row in front of him got in a shoving match and dumped their beer on him. He rubbed the scar near his eye with the heel of his hand, drew a deep breath and blew it out slowly. The feeling passed. "You give the shop six months, huh? So you give it about six months less than your shop lasted?"

Sean had done some digging online before he came up to the apartment, learning everything he could about Dude's Bikes and its owners. When he'd pulled up their website—which was still live—the home page had sported a picture of a white-and-brown pit bull with a brown eye patch, which he presumed to be Wyatt. The dog stood near an orange Harley Street Rod. *Our bikes are a dangerous breed!* the caption read, though the dog didn't look dangerous at all. He looked sweet, and a little sad, like he didn't really want to be in the Dude's stupid picture.

Dude's chewing slowed, which was a relief because the guy had really big horse teeth that chomped and fat lips that smacked. Worse than nails on a chalkboard. Dude exchanged a look with Dick. They knew they'd been insulted but also seemed to know better than to say anything.

"We got prospects on a better location," Dick said. "Our lease running out was a good thing. She won't last there, either."

"Shop's by a major thoroughfare. I see bikes on the road all the time this time of year."

"Yeah. Well." Dude stuck his hand in a bag of chips and drew out a fistful. "We'll see."

"The bike aside," Sean moved on. "Miss Monroe said you showed a lot of interest in her dog. A pit bull that was at the shop. Used to be yours?" Sean didn't see any sign of a dog, not a white-and-brown pit bull or any other kind of animal. There were no leashes, bowls, dog smells, nothing. Nothing but Dude and Dick's pigsty of a bachelor pad.

Dude and Dick held their shared look for a heartbeat too long. "Sinbad's ours. But she wouldn't let us have him." Dude picked up his sandwich and resumed eating. "He was really excited to see us, too. It was clear he wanted to come with us but the bi—Miss Monroe held on to his collar and wouldn't let him follow."

Sean let a long silence pass, his eyes narrowed at the men. "I was told you returned the dog to Pittie Place."

"We did," Dick chimed in. "On a temporary basis. We're tight with the owner. Sunny would've been okay with us taking him back. She wants what's best for the dog."

"That last sentence, at least," Sean said, closing up his notebook, "is the truth. One last question. Did either of you threaten Miss Monroe?"

"Is that what she said?" Dick didn't wait for a reply. "Because that's a lie."

"Yeah," Dude agreed. "Nobody threatened anybody. Why would we? It's not like we're afraid of her."

"Maybe you're mad she bought the shop you couldn't afford." Sean noted the moment of silence. "You wouldn't have to be afraid of her. You're just pissed that she's there. And on top of all that, she won't give you the dog back. Am I on to something?"

"No." Dick's response was too quick, too forceful. "Listen, Detective. We didn't threaten her. And we didn't take her bike. Now if you'll excuse us, we have important things to do."

"Uh-huh. Thank you for your time, gentlemen." Sean handed over his business card. "If you think of anything, give me a call."

Dick took the card and tossed it on the kitchen counter, on top of a bag of smashed hamburger buns.

"What do you guys do now?" Sean paused in the doorway, taking the opportunity to peek into the mudroom. Two sets of muddy boots lay on a filthy rug. "Ever since your shop failed?"

Dude's chewing paused again. The sandwich was gone and he was on the last cheekful of ham and cheese, which now sounded crunchy because he'd shoved in a few chips. "We're doing some online sales and stuff." He dusted the grease from his fingers and gestured toward a computer that rested on a dining room table just behind the kitchen.

"Mmm-hmm." Sean took one more sweep of the apartment, everything he could see, from dirty kitchen to messy living room to dinged up laptop. No ashtrays or odor of stale tar or any other signs that the men smoked, at least not inside. "Have a nice day."

Sean toured the parking area before heading back to his minivan. The spaces were marked by apartment number, with one space for every apartment. At the end of each row there were several spots marked Visitor. In the brothers' space was a pickup truck. Sean peeked inside the open bed. Trash. Old wood. Leaves. Dirt.

There were no motorcycles that he could see, and every single spot had been taken. Not that Sean had expected to find the stolen bike sitting out in front of the apartment. Still, he made notes and took pictures.

Back at the station he found Castillo just finishing up her lunch. She always ate at her desk, had some kind of salad and a vanilla yogurt. "How'd it go?"

Sean shrugged. "They could've done it. They own a pickup and don't have much money or good job prospects. They're sexist, don't like Delaney and they're liars."

Castillo dragged her spoon out of her mouth slowly and tossed the empty yogurt cup in the trash. "But?"

"Delaney said something about maybe they ran more through that shop than bikes. I'll look into it. If they are dealing, they've probably slipped at some point. They don't seem too bright."

"If I had a dollar for every stupid criminal."

"You'd be a wealthy woman." Sean slumped in his chair and resumed his online sleuthing of Dude and Dick. Time to poke around their social media, because stupid people were always stupidest on social media.

"Do you like them for it, though?" Castillo fixed her lipstick with a compact from her purse.

Sean shrugged. "It's too early to say. I need to pay Sunny a visit next."

Castillo got a knowing grin on her face. "That should be fun."

"Shut up." Sean clicked around and brought up the Facebook business page for Dude's Bikes, which was also still active. The header photo was a picture of Wyatt, in front of the shop, sitting between Dude and Dick. "This is all business."

"Sure it is."

Sean didn't answer, though he could feel Castillo, only a few feet away, reading his mind. This might be a little messy, but in the end, Sean never had a problem keeping things professional. If failing at marriage had taught him one thing, it was that no matter what, at the end of the day, you still had to follow your gut.

Sean would be following his. Time to pay a call on Detective Rawls, in Narcotics. Sean had known him a long time and they crossed paths frequently. If anyone knew whether or not the Worley brothers were dealing, it was Rawls.

ten

Delaney leaned against the building, next to the front door, ankles crossed, displaying a set of long, muscled legs that made Tabitha feel scrawny. Her upper body was even more impressive in a crop top with no sleeves—biceps that were cut in all the right ways and abs for days. She was scrolling on her cell phone, oblivious to the world around her. Or so it appeared.

"Hey, Steele," she said, without looking up, as Tabitha and Trinity approached. Then she put her phone away and met Tabitha's eyes. "You made it."

Tabitha had a sudden memory of Delaney, strong and in charge, her leveling gaze going deep into Tabitha's soul, her steady hand on Tabitha's shoulder while Tabitha stared down at her own blood-covered hands. "What's your name?" Delaney's voice had been close to her ear. "Your name?"

"*Steele,*" she'd whispered.

"Okay, Steele. Keep the pressure." Delaney had taken her

hands and pressed them back on Captain Dorsey's leg, which had felt slick, like oil. "Don't let go."

Tabitha shook the memory away and forced a smile. "I made it," she agreed.

"Cool." Delaney glanced down at Trinity and gave a soft smile. "Ready?" She tilted her head toward the gym.

"Yes." No. But she had to.

"You can do this." Delaney held the door open for them.

The gym was as full as it had been the last time Tabitha visited, with about a dozen people near the whiteboard, waiting for the class to start, and another dozen in a separate attached room, being schooled in something involving barbells. Rhett, the owner, held a PVC pipe and was calling out instructions.

"You're back!" Rhett's redheaded wife—or had Delaney said girlfriend—appeared in front of them, smiling. "Tabitha, right?"

"That's right."

"Constance." She reminded her. "Or, everyone around here calls me Red. Just in case you forgot."

"I like Constance."

"You'd be the first. Or maybe the second. I'm assuming my mom liked it." Constance smiled. Her gaze shifted. "Hey, Delaney. Good to see you."

"Good to see you, too, Red." Delaney waved as she walked over to stow her motorcycle helmet and bag in the cubbies.

"Since you filled out the waiver last time you visited, you're all set to go," Constance said. "First session is free, to see if you like it here. Then we'll go from there."

Tabitha smiled. There was something about Constance that made the air easier to breathe, not so thick and difficult to draw in. Tabitha's heart loosened up in her chest and her jaw unclenched. She got Trinity settled in the agreed upon spot that kept her close but also safe from the barbells and other gym equipment that got slung around. Trinity was right next to Humphrey, who raised his head and regarded her with blue-tinted eyes. He sniffed the air a little bit, then settled back down on his dog bed with a puff of his jowls.

"He likes her," Constance said with a grin.

Tabitha smiled, feeling more relaxed the longer she spent in this gym. The energy was high, which would typically put her on edge, but here it was different. Here, the energy allowed you to get lost, not suffocated. Constance led her over to a large whiteboard, where a young, muscular woman with a nose piercing called out to get everyone's attention. Her hair was done in space puffs and she wore a shirt with Black Girl Magic printed across the front. Tabitha had done high intensity group fitness many times but hadn't seriously worked out in at least a year and a half. Even today's simple chipper of jumping rope, push-ups, pull-ups, sit-ups and wall balls looked intimidating.

Delaney fell in just as the coach, who introduced herself as Zoe, started explaining the workout for the day. Delaney gave Tabitha a reassuring shoulder pat but Tabitha could tell she was distracted by something. She kept checking her phone and a shadow of worry tinged her every move. Tabitha wanted to say something but wasn't sure Delaney would appreciate the interest. In all honesty, Tabitha just hoped she kept her shit together without another grocery store episode. One minute she was picking out apples for Auntie El's famous pie and the next she was on the floor, heart pounding, covered in flop sweat, everyone staring.

But her first experience at Semper Fit reminded her why she loved the high intensity and closeness of a group. For the next hour she was so busy trying to survive physically, so busy trying to just breathe, she had no time to break down mentally. Yeah, it was tough, and her heart and lungs begged her to quit, but when Tabitha finished her last rep and lay in a puddle on the floor, near the open bay in hopes of catching a breeze over her sweaty body, a feeling of calm washed over her that she hadn't felt in a long time.

Delaney stood over her, fist extended. Tabitha bumped it. "How was that, kiddo?"

Tabitha closed her eyes, mostly to block out the fact that Delaney wasn't even sweating, and smiled. "I forgot how much I like to have my ass handed to me."

"That's my girl."

Tabitha lay there awhile longer, eyes closed, enjoying the breeze as it dried the sweat on her clammy skin. Her mind was a clean slate—at least for now. She was going to bask in that for as long as she could. After some time had passed, Tabitha sensed a presence over her. Assuming Delaney had come back to check on her, she extended her hand.

The firm grasp that hauled her to her feet in one quick motion shocked Tabitha's eyes open. She stood facing a well-built man with beachy blond hair and the kind of classic good looks that either got taken for granted, or got dismissed as being *too* good-looking. His grin was wide as the blue sky, the high energy that lit him up floating all around, inviting everyone in for a party. "New girl," he said, his voice laced with unexpected affection. "You crushed the hell outta that workout."

Tabitha stammered something, hating herself as the words came out as nonsense. This kind of energy always took her off guard, crashing into her like a Mack truck. Guys as good-looking as him never wasted their time on a quiet, introverted, quirky thing like Tabitha.

"Hey, don't be modest," he said, the admiration thick, his gaze drinking her in like she was the postworkout recovery beverage.

Delaney was suddenly at her side. "Hobbs, right?" She squared off with the guy, who appeared to shrink a little.

"Delaney," he said, his smile fading. "Right?"

"Right." Delaney's eyes narrowed. "Maybe now's not the time for your usual thing. All the—" she flexed and posed and brushed across her chin with her thumb "—if you know what I mean."

Hobbs's grin vanished completely. Something silent passed between them, and despite the guy being pretty muscular Tabitha honestly wasn't sure which way things would go if a fight went down.

"Hobbs." Constance was suddenly there, like a guardian angel, lurking in the shadows. "This is Tabitha. She's trying us out today. That's her service dog, over there with Humphrey."

Hobbs tore his gaze from Delaney, went briefly to Constance and finally rested on Trinity, who was lying right on the dog bed next to Humphrey. "Oh," he said. His party-time energy died like a balloon that had leaked out all the air. "Look at that. I've never seen old Humphrey share his bed."

"Me, either." Constance sounded genuinely shocked. "Aren't they cute." She turned to Tabitha. "Humphrey really only likes Rhett. He tolerates me. And he does seem to have a thing for Delaney."

"Trinity usually keeps her distance," Tabitha admitted. "But it looks like she knows how to relax here."

"She knows you're doing good," Constance said with a shrug.

"Sorry." Hobbs turned back to Tabitha. His whole face had softened, the chummy persona gone. "Nice to meet you, Tabitha. I'm one of the coaches here. Hope you come on board."

"Thank you." Tabitha was relaxed enough now to study him. His personality hadn't retreated so much as it had matured, shushing whatever it was inside that made him dance around like a clown. Tabitha was reminded of her time as a youth counselor in school and in church. There was always that kid who acted the clown because he didn't want anyone to see the sadness inside.

Hobbs cleared his throat. "Till next time." He gave a nod and melted into the dispersing crowd, his jubilant voice returning as he said goodbye to someone he was obviously familiar with.

"Well, how about that." Constance lowered her voice and gave a small grin. "First time I've ever seen Hobbs back down."

"Guess he's not as dumb as he looks," Delaney said.

Tabitha suppressed a laugh. "Oh, I don't know," she said. "I don't think he's dumb at all. I think it's an act."

Delaney's eyebrows raised, then she shrugged. "I need to go, Steele." She had her phone in her hand. "But you did great today. Now you just need to come back tomorrow. Right?"

"Yes, ma'am," Tabitha said as they headed over to the dogs. Only a few inches of space existed between Trinity and Humphrey. Trinity sat up as Tabitha approached. Tabitha was almost sad to split them up. "All set, girl? You like it here, huh?"

Trinity flapped her tail so hard it smacked Humphrey's side. Humphrey didn't even flinch.

"I guess that's a yes," Tabitha said with a laugh. "And look. There are signs all over about the fundraiser at Pete's place." Tabitha pointed at a poster on the wall behind Trinity's head. "Isn't that cool?"

Trinity didn't look at the poster, obviously, but she did appear to smile. Tabitha smiled back. "C'mon, girl, let's get home."

Normally, Tabitha pressed the speed limit just a little in her rush to get back to the house. Today, she rolled the windows down and enjoyed the breeze. She was physically tired from the workout and mentally tired from meeting new people, but there was something else there, too. A positive sort of anxiousness to get back into the gym and do it all over again, with all those same people. Constance was soothing, Zoe was motivating, Delaney was a confidence builder and that guy Hobbs—Tabitha wasn't sure what he was. But something about him made her smile. The whole morning made her smile.

"Fist bump." Tabitha held out her hand. Trinity, sitting up in the passenger seat inside her harness, raised her left paw. It was one of the last commands Pete had taught her, but—Tabitha decided, as her skin met Trinity's furry foot—one of the best.

eleven

Delaney's world was quiet for days. She didn't hear from the police, '33 didn't miraculously reappear and, most notably, Wyatt didn't come back. Delaney wasn't sure why that gave her a gouged feeling in the pit of her stomach. She should be happy that the dog was safe at Sunny's boyfriend's place, getting trained. But Delaney had to admit she missed turning around and finding that goofy pit bull pawing at her storeroom door, begging for food or mooning at her motorcycles. She had bikes to work on, which was good, but even that was a solitary activity unless people came in the shop to buy stuff.

With the motorcycle stolen and Wyatt safely contained, Delaney hadn't felt this alone since she found out Dad had died. Her mood was interrupted by a ding from her phone. A text message.

Que pasa, chingona.

Sal. Of the group, he was the second most likely, after Boom, to check on her daily. And to their credit, they had. One or the other of them, including Donnie and Zip, had checked up on her every single day since Dad's death.

Hanging in there. Thanks.

Delaney had sent them all a group text right after Sean had left the apartment the other day. She didn't want them finding out about '33 from the police. She hated that she couldn't see any of their faces, because in person she would've known right away if they were disappointed in her, but over text the responses had been limited to sympathy, outrage at the thief and requests for her to be extra careful. Delaney could picture all of their expressions, though. Boom would have a tight mouth hidden beneath his beard. Sal wore his heart on his sleeve, so he probably would've hugged her first. Donnie would do that thing with his eyebrows that made you think he was mad at you when he was really trying to figure something out and Zip would be unreadable.

Any news?

Not yet.

Just text if you need anything.

Done working for the day, Delaney settled with her laptop behind the front counter and posted a picture of Dad's '56 Ford pickup, parked out front of Triple M Classics, on his Facebook page. *Still got this*, was her caption. At least nobody

outside his riding circle would know that Delaney had allowed
Dad's prized bike to be stolen, or to see that his crazy daughter
talked to him on a social media site that he'd never used when
he was alive, and clearly wasn't going to access from heaven.

Well. Nobody but Lauren Bacall, anyway. Delaney had at
first thought she was one of the many rotating girlfriends that
Dad kept company with—all in the shadows when she was a
little girl but sometimes at the shop or the house once Delaney
was grown. They were down-to-earth, no-strings-attached
types who pulled beers at night for a living and wanted a serious relationship about as much as Dad did. But an early visit
to Bacall's page showed nothing but the black-and-white picture of the film star, blond hair sculpted around her dreamy
eyes and high cheekbones. There was no personal information
or photos, and if she had other friends, they weren't visible.
Delaney was convinced Dad had accidentally added a bot account one day and had probably received tons of instant mes-
sages begging for money to save some foreign prince—all of
which he probably never even saw.

Delaney watched the clouds gather in the sky outside the
bay door. More rain was coming, so there probably wouldn't
be many more customers this evening. She would close up in
an hour and hit the gym. Not only had she promised to be
there for Tabitha, she was hoping Detective Callahan might
show up. Though he would be off duty, she could sneak in a
question or two about leads on the motorcycle.

And that's it. There was no other reason Delaney wanted
Callahan to show up at the gym. She certainly didn't need to
be knocked over again and she wasn't in the mood for a foot
race as she hadn't been sleeping well since the bike got stolen
and Wyatt got drafted to training camp.

Still. It couldn't hurt to know a little bit more about the detective who was searching for Dad's prized motorcycle. Del-

aney turned back to her computer and googled the county police department, hoping to find photos or biographies or anything that he might be in. The first link to come up was the department's home page. She almost clicked on it, but just below that was a link to a YouTube video, something about a lip sync challenge. Delaney thought a second, then remembered that a couple of years ago this challenge was going around the internet: police departments lip-syncing to popular songs. Looked like Callahan's department had taken part. Curious, Delaney clicked on it.

The opening beats, snapping fingers and call to "open up the champagne!" let Delaney know instantly that Callahan's department had chosen to do "My House" by Flo Rida. A large man in uniform popped out of an office and strutted down a hallway, lip-syncing and gesturing with a huge smile plastered on his face. Other people joined him, including someone in a McGruff the Crime Dog costume, an assortment of men and women having fun singing, tossing papers, riding atop rolling carts, disappearing into rooms. This went on for about thirty seconds of the song before the officer sank into an elevator and the silver doors slid shut. Delaney almost closed out the video but then, nobody closes out a video when doors slide shut because doors sliding shut means a surprise was going to pop out next.

The elevator doors opened again and Delaney choked on her water. Out popped Detective Callahan, dressed in a white collared shirt, navy vest and slacks, handcuffs attached at his side and badge on a chain around his neck. He strutted down the hall, singing his heart out, his face looking mean and his arms going in broad, bold gestures.

Delaney sputtered a laugh, her palms covering her nose and mouth just as Callahan's partner, Castillo, fell in beside him. She was dressed just as smartly in navy and white, but she was much more in her element than Callahan, her curvy body popping and working the beat effortlessly. Castillo had obviously been waiting for this moment all her life, and when the time came, she shined. They joined a few more people in uniforms and danced and sang their way outside to the front of the police station, cars and trucks parked on the lawn, people in various forms of gear all around as the camera panned away, up into the sky, high above the building as the song faded out.

"Oh. My. God." Delaney had a hard time wiping the smile off her face, the first smile she'd had in days. "What did I just see?" she said aloud, to the empty shop. Clearly, she'd just witnessed hard-ass Detective Callahan lip-syncing and dancing for all the world to see. She wasn't sure what to do with that. Who would agree to such a thing? Other than Castillo, who clearly needed her own music video. But all those other guys? They were on the internet forever, making fools of themselves.

For some reason, Callahan's words from the other day popped in her head. *Cat quick and tiger tough.* That's what he'd said upon seeing the OSSA in the shop downstairs, demonstrating that Callahan both knew a thing or two about motorcycles and that he had a quick wit. Delaney laughed softly and wiped up the mess she'd made with her water, the smile never leaving her face as she went upstairs to change into her gym clothes.

She'd wanted to run into Detective Callahan before she saw the video. Now it was almost compulsive. Obviously the detective couldn't have known, when he took part in this video years ago, that a heartbroken woman who needed a cheap, quick laugh would click on the link and get just the dose of humor she needed. But it sure felt like it. For some dumb reason, Detective Callahan's goofy "My House" rendition felt personal.

Like he'd sang that song just for her.

★ ★ ★

Humphrey the Beagle, Master of the Gym, was curled up on his bed in the corner when Delaney arrived. She squatted down and spent some time letting him sniff her knuckles before she stroked his ears. He had scars all over his face, but they were old and well healed. "Been through a battle or two, eh, boy?"

"The stories he could tell."

Delaney looked over her shoulder and saw Red approaching, her hair up in a ponytail and a big smile on her face. Now that Delaney knew that she and Sunny were sisters she found herself doing a mental comparison of similarities. Their eyes were a definite, both sharing a striking blue. The difference in their hair was like if someone added ten drops of red to Sunny's blond, mixed it up in one of those paint spinners at the hardware store and gave the result to Red. Personality wise, both women were friendly and approachable but Red seemed like she kept more to herself, Sunny the more extroverted of the two. "Doesn't seem like they'd be happy stories," Delaney said. "Except maybe the one where he met you and Rhett."

"My sister, Sunny, rescued him initially. Snagged him from a puppy mill. But his heart belongs to Rhett. I still can't get over how he lets you pet his ears like that."

"No kidding?" Delaney gave them a few more strokes for good measure before she stood up. "Not much for the human touch, Humphrey?"

"Humans haven't been Humphrey's best friend." Red frowned. "But he took to Rhett instantly. Everybody in here can coo at him or let him sniff them but they've all learned if they reach for him, he's probably going to flinch."

"Reminds me of someone." There went that feeling again, sadness that Wyatt hadn't been by, when Delaney should be happy he was safe, either at Sunny's or her boyfriend's, and not stuck in the middle of the woods during a thunderstorm.

"Oh, really? And here I was going to ask you if I could check out your ASISs." Red folded her arms over her chest and grinned.

"My wha…?"

Red nodded toward Delaney's waist. "Your anterior superior iliac spines. When you stood up just now, it looked like you might have a lateral pelvic tilt. Your hips are off just a little bit. I could check to see if one side of your pelvis is higher than the other. But if you're like Humphrey, I wouldn't want to make you uncomfortable."

"Oh." It took Delaney a moment to process everything Red had just said. Delaney recalled Sunny saying that her sister was a massage therapist. "No, I wasn't talking about me." Delaney laughed and ran her hands through her hair. "When I said 'reminds me of someone' I meant Wyatt. This other dog. He escapes from Sunny's place and comes over to my motorcycle shop. The one that used to be named Sinbad."

Red tilted her chin up. "Oh, wow. You're the shop girl? Yeah. Of course you are. That makes sense."

"Yep. That's me."

Red tsked her tongue. "I've heard all about Sinbad. Small world." Then her expression got serious. "Do you want me to check, then? The ASISs?"

"Go for it." Delaney opened her arms wide, then let them fall back to her sides. Why was she being awkward? Going overboard to prove that she was not like Humphrey wasn't going to prove that she was not like Humphrey. "What do I have to do?"

"Just stand there." Red kneeled down and felt around the front of Delaney's hips, both thumbs landing on either of the bony ridges of her pelvis. So that's what an ASIS was. Red leaned back and drew an invisible line, thumbs meeting just under Delaney's navel. Red squinted. Then she ran her hands around to the back and sunk her fingertips into Delaney's shorts, right around the bones at the top of her butt and looked up at the ceiling. "Yeah," Red said, after feeling around for a while. "Left is higher than the right. More than half an inch, I think, though I'm just doing a very quick scan right here."

"What causes that?"

"Could be dysfunction of the SI joint," Red said as she rose up. "I'd have to do a thorough intake, but if you've been in the Marine Corps for twenty years, I'm not surprised. Carrying heavy packs, etcetera. You should come in for a massage." Red smiled. "I prefer dogs, but I do humans, too."

"Ha. That's cute. Sunny told me you massage the dogs."

"Sunny's and Pete's."

"Well, that's one of the coolest things I've ever heard, Red." Delaney grinned at her and Red's cheeks got a little pink to match her hair. Cute. "Thanks for the assessment. I'll get back to you on the massage. Speaking of Sunny, do you think she'll be in? I'm wondering how Wyatt-Formerly-Sinbad is doing."

Red started laughing so hard her eyes teared up. "Sunny doesn't have a membership here," she said between chuckles. "She thinks we're all crazy." Red waved a hand around at the group gathering in front of the whiteboard, ready for the warm-up. "Sunny teaches spin classes."

Delaney smiled. On one level, Sunny wasn't wrong. They were all a little crazy here. "That's alright. I'll just text her." Delaney almost went to the cubbies to get her phone and text while she was thinking about it, but both Detective Callahan and Tabitha walked in at that moment. Tabitha waved hello but Callahan didn't notice her at first, his strides steady and straight as he headed toward one of the restrooms. He had a bag on his shoulder and was wearing slacks and a dress shirt, his badge on a chain around his neck. A glance at the clock showed he only had a couple of minutes to change and be on time for class. Nobody liked to be late if Rhett was coaching the class; he was worse than Delaney's seventh grade history teacher who gave you an extra page of homework for every minute you were tardy.

Tabitha got Trinity settled next to Humphrey and fell in beside Delaney and Red.

"Hey, Tabitha. Glad you came back. Working out?" Red nodded toward the group as she headed in that direction.

"Definitely." Tabitha seemed in high spirits.

"Yep." Delaney shook herself and followed along, training her eyes at the whiteboard to see what was on the menu for today. Hopefully not handstand walks. Last thing she needed was clumsy Callahan smashing into her. Delaney felt the corners of her mouth turning up.

Looked like front squats, dead lifts, 400s and lateral burpees over the barbell. Delaney felt her heart jack up with excitement, even as Tabitha groaned beside her. "I'm going to die," she whispered.

Delaney elbowed her in the ribs. "You'll be fine."

"Detective Callahan told me the same thing."

"You guys know each other?" Delaney snapped her head in Tabitha's direction.

"A little. He helped me out recently." Tabitha pretended like she was zipping her lips as she nodded in Rhett's direction.

Rhett had just finished his intro to the workout when Callahan sidled up behind Delaney, off to her left. She caught him in her periphery, not seeing him so much as she smelled his mintiness.

"Alright, let's get warm." Rhett clapped his hands together, sending everyone scattering to do a 400m run. Delaney hoped the detective would run next to her so she could casually bring up the stolen bike but Rhett called him back. "You were late, Callahan. I want ten burpees before you start your run."

Delaney finally looked Callahan's way and caught his eye, just as he dropped without protest to the ground and executed a push-up. As he stood and finished the burpee with a jump, arms stretched overhead, the "My House" video popped into Delaney's memory. She pictured Callahan's Mean Cop Face as he lip-synced, *Morning comes and you know that you wanna stay*...and she burst into laughter. She immediately covered her mouth with her fingertips, even as Callahan offered her a slight, confused grin.

Rhett's gaze shot in her direction. "I agree that this is hysterical, but why aren't you running, Marine?"

Delaney bit down on her lower lip and swallowed her laughter. She almost said, *I'm retired*, but knew what Rhett's response would be. *Once a marine, always a marine.* She gave Callahan one final chuckle and took off outside, through the open bay door, into the gray sky that was just starting to pop with the opening strains of a new thunderstorm.

Tabitha was a much slower runner and fell in with one of the other ladies, but somehow, Callahan caught up with Delaney. He came sprinting up beside her, his feet heavy and breathing labored.

"Still swallowing those burpees, huh?" Delaney teased. "You need to learn to be on time, Detective."

"Well," Callahan gasped, "I was busy trying to find your motorcycle, Miss Monroe. So the least you can do is not laugh at me while I'm doing my penance."

Delaney immediately wondered if he'd found anything, but kept that question to herself. It would clearly be rude to grill him considering he could barely talk and they hadn't even said hello. "If you step up your running game, you won't be so out of breath on a measly four hundred meter." Delaney put the pedal to the metal and took off, leaving Callahan in her dust.

He caught up to her again and streaked inside the bay just as she did, almost tripping over Duke, the secret service agent, who raised up his giant arms in protest. He reminded her of Boom, both of them sharing an intimidating physical presence with a teddy bear's heart tucked deep inside.

Delaney and Callahan gave the workout their full attention after that, Rhett eyeing them with hopeful suspicion, like he was just waiting for a reason to assign them penalty burpees.

At the end of the hour, Callahan settled on the bench where Delaney was packing her gym bag. "I have nothing to share yet," he said, even though she hadn't asked. "I've talked to Dude's Bikes and looked into the drug angle. Nothing definitive yet. Next up is a visit to Pittie Place. I'll keep you updated."

"Alright." Delaney didn't press. She was disappointed but not surprised. "By the way." She glanced at Tabitha, who seemed to have struck up a new friendship with the woman she'd run with earlier. The woman was a petite blonde and appeared to be giving Tabitha running tips. "How do you know Tabitha?"

"Met her at the grocery store," Callahan said. "Not long ago. She was having some trouble. I just happened to be there."

Delaney looked over toward Trinity, who patiently waited next to Humphrey on his bed. "I think she's going to fit in here. She can lose herself a little bit. Get outside of her own head. Make some friends she can trust, too."

Callahan followed her gaze. "Yeah," he agreed. He silently packed his bag after that, his demeanor changed from the playful side to the cop side as soon as he'd brought up the case. Delaney respected that, but he clearly wasn't as fun. "I wasn't laughing at you having to do burpees, by the way."

Callahan looked up from his bag. "Sure you weren't."

"I was..." Delaney bit back her words. She'd been about to tell him what had really made her giggle, but then she watched the detective's gray eyes soften with curiosity and decided to restrain her comments about the video. Suddenly, it became a private joke that she didn't want to share. "I was laughing because you really think you won that 5K race, don't you?" That was the best Delaney could think up.

Callahan snorted. "You know I did."

"You know *I* did."

"There's only one way to settle this." Callahan pointed his water bottle at her, then took a sip.

"How's that?"

"Rematch." Callahan shrugged. No-brainer.

Delaney laughed. "I see."

"Unless you're scared."

Delaney laughed again, louder this time. She grabbed her bag and slung it over her shoulder. "I'll do a rematch. Anytime, anywhere. But this time..." she started to walk away, then peeked over her shoulder "...it's a 10K. Deal?"

Was that a sneaky flash of joy that crossed Callahan's face? "Deal," he said, all too quickly.

Delaney smiled to herself, unexpectedly reliving that feeling she'd gotten when Callahan had touched her hand the other day. For the first time, she was looking forward to the detective giving her a hard chase.

Constance had been right. Humphrey had a thing for Delaney. Tabitha watched her interact with the beagle once the detective had chatted her up and headed out with a smile. The little dog rolled onto his side and let Delaney pet light strokes with her fingertips over his fur. Tabitha stood and headed her way. The detective waved to her from the doorway. Based on their interaction, Tabitha was guessing that Sean Callahan felt the same way about Delaney as the beagle did.

"How well do you know Sean?" Tabitha asked as Delaney said goodbye to Humphrey, rose and grabbed her bag.

Delaney's face blanked. "Who?"

Tabitha pointed at the door. "Detective Callahan. You were just talking and laughing with him."

Recognition lit Delaney's expression. Her eyes blinked rapidly. "I didn't even know Callahan's first name."

"Well, everyone seems to call him Callahan."

"True."

"Massages." Constance suddenly appeared, holding business cards. "Both of you. Just text me."

"Thanks, Red." Delaney took the card and examined it.

"I'm not sure," Tabitha said, even though she took the card. "But I'll think about it." She wasn't working right now and no way in heck was Auntie El going to spring for a massage. She'd had many jobs since she'd gotten out of the navy—just local shops where she thought she could hide herself restocking groceries or folding sweaters or dressing the mannequins—but she'd been late too many times, ignored customers too many times, freaked out and hid in the bathroom too many times. It was always something. All of this was pre-Trinity, and Tabitha was hoping, with a little more time, she could try again soon. Until then, money was tight. The only way she could afford Semper Fit was the veteran's discount.

"Remember what I said. First one's free." Constance headed into the office, where she slid her arms around Rhett's unsuspecting waist from behind.

"Gosh, those two are sweet." Tabitha got butterflies in her stomach.

Delaney chuckled under her breath. "They do give a girl sugar shock."

Tabitha offered a guilty smile. "You're probably not a romantic. But I can't help it."

"I can be romantic," Delaney said, but her voice got all squeaky and weird, like she knew it was a lie.

"Are you dating Sean?" Tabitha was surprised at herself, as soon as the question popped out.

"Callahan?" Delaney looked down at the floor. "No." She waved a hand. "We actually get on each other's nerves. Well, he gets on mine, anyway. And he's working my case. Somebody stole my motorcycle. The one that was my dad's." Her voice went soft and her humor faded.

Tabitha thought back to the grand opening. "The old one? From the shop?"

"Yeah, that's the one." Delaney pressed her lips together in a grim line.

"I'm sorry. Who would do that?" Tabitha regretted her naive question. People did all sorts of things for all sorts of bad or confusing reasons all the time. Figuring out why used to be one of her specialties.

"That's what Callahan is trying to find out."

"I hope he does."

"Me, too. Hey." Delaney pointed at the business card in Tabitha's hand. "Schedule that."

"I don't know—"

"Trust me when I say, people don't do massages for free. It's too much work." Delaney pointed in Constance's direction. "She's being nice because she knows you need it. She's Sunny's sister, you know. She massages the dogs."

"Oh, wow. I thought she looked familiar," Tabitha mused, thinking back. "I never met her, but now that I think about it, I saw Constance at Pete's once or twice. Always in the background. What a small world."

"No kidding."

Tabitha looked down at Trinity. "That means she's massaged you, I bet."

Trinity wagged her tail.

"See?" Delaney arched an eyebrow. "The dog knows."

twelve

"Good to see you, Detective." Sunny winked at her own formality as they exchanged a brief hug in the doorway of her home. She wore blue jeans and an old Underdog cartoon T-shirt and smelled like dog shampoo. Bright and cheerful as she'd always been, there was a steady calm to Sunny's personality that had been lacking before she and Pete became a thing. Whatever Sunny had been looking for, she'd found in the quiet, confident army veteran who took many of her rescue dogs and transformed them into service dogs for military vets. "C'mon in," Sunny said, "and I'll fix you a scotch. I know what you like."

"This is true." Sean followed Sunny inside the main house, the rebuilt dog rescue in perfect view from the dining room. With its fresh wood and log cabin–style design, the building was nicer than the original, with no sign of the fire that had almost taken the whole place out. "I'm on duty," Sean said. "I'll just have water."

"Sure." Sunny disappeared into the kitchen.

Sean peered out the bay window and saw that Roger had all the rescue dogs out for playtime in the fenced-in acreage. The youthful twenty-year-old had been working at Pittie Place since he was a troubled teenager and had proved his dedication for so long that he lived in the log cabin house out back, right next to the dogs. Roger was a permanent fixture, and was most definitely not a suspect in the motorcycle theft.

"Water," Sunny said with a smile, raising two glasses as she appeared in the dining room. "But the expensive scotch you like is still behind the bar, if you want it. I haven't touched it since the last time you had some."

"Don't tempt me." Sean took the water and slugged it back. The air was thick with humidity today, which never agreed with him. Alcohol would be a bad idea, even if he wasn't on the job. "Let's go out and look around. I just want to see the grounds. Get a roster of your employees."

"Trust me, you're not going to find that beautiful motorcycle on my property." Sunny gestured for Sean to follow as they headed through the kitchen and out into the sunshine. "I would've just asked Delaney to teach me how to ride. Or, let's be honest, I'd just ask her if I could ride on the back."

Sean smiled, picturing the two ladies riding a motorcycle together. Bruiser Delaney in her greaser outfit up front, and Sunny on the back, all long legs and probably designer motorcycle boots, if there was such a thing. Sean smiled to himself, but then wiped it off his face as Sunny glanced over her shoulder at him. "I know you don't have the bike, Sunny." As soon as they were in the fenced-in yard, the dogs came rushing over, Roger keeping careful watch from afar as he walked around with a pooper-scooper.

"I can't think of any of my kids who would take it, either."

"You still have volunteers from the juvenile detention center?" A few of the dogs milled around Sean's legs, wagging their tails and eyeing him expectantly. He waited until they'd calmed down before he reached out to offer pets. Most of them were bully breeds but there were a few off-brands, too, mixes of shepherd and hound and terrier. They had all been abused or neglected or dumped in some way.

"Yes." Sunny's voice grew tight. "I still participate in the Jobs for Disadvantaged Youth program. Which means they often come with a juvie history. But they're all vetted. Nobody with a violent history can work here."

"Sunny." Sean held up a calming hand. "I'm glad you participate in the program. And I'm not suggesting you hired a motorcycle thief. I'm just checking all angles. The kids in detention are not lost causes. But they are all troubled." Sean had been in law enforcement long enough to know the truth of the world: people weren't just good and bad. Everybody had the good and the bad, and the way they behaved depended on a lot of different buttons being pushed. You put anybody under the right kind of stress and they'd do things nobody ever expected. "Who's this guy?" A black-and-tan pittie stayed back from the bunch, his skinny body a glaring contrast to his large head. Sean could count every rib, and the sight made it hurt to breathe.

"That's Harry." Sunny's voice went soft. "He was found in Greenview Park last month, tied to a tree. He'd been left to starve. He was there for weeks. Drank rainwater and ate mud. We weren't sure he was going to make it. But you did, didn't you? Yes, you did, my good boy." Sunny squatted down and opened her arms. Harry trotted over and rested his head right on her shoulder, like he was giving her a hug.

Sean's heart broke a little bit, like it always did when he was here. Of all the things he saw on a daily basis, it was the starved, abused dog hugging his rescuer that made Sean want to cry. He cleared his throat. "Where's the one who escapes? The one who goes to Delaney's shop?"

Sunny glanced up from behind Harry's head, her arms around the dog's skinny shoulders. "Wyatt's with Pete, getting trained. Delaney renamed him. After the *Easy Rider* character? I guess he liked her motorcycle. The one that got stolen."

"Well, that fits."

"Yep."

"Can you show me how he'd get out?" Sean surveyed the wide expanse of land. There was the main house, where Sunny lived, with Roger's separate quarters in the back, where the quarters for the dogs was attached—all rebuilt after the fire last year—and then about a half dozen cabins all along Sunny's acreage that she rented out seasonally for semi-rustic vacationers.

"Sure." Sunny waved a hand. They walked along the wooden fence, out of view from Roger's quarters. Sunny pointed out a couple of places where the dog had dug under, which were refilled with dirt and logs. "The ground has been soft from so much rain. He's the only one of the bunch who digs or who wants to escape. All the others are happy as pigs in mud to be here. The fence runs pretty far, but all the cabins are outside it. I don't need renters having instant access to my rescues." Sunny stared into the woods, where a path that led to the cabins disappeared. "Roger keeps a pretty good eye, but sometimes he'd lose track of Wyatt and then he'd be gone. The couple times he got out at night, he was slipping out a back door Roger hadn't locked. Wyatt could pull down the door handle like Fezzi." Sunny twisted her lips in a smile when mentioning Red's three-legged pit bull who'd been trained to help their late father with various tasks.

"And you don't think anyone might've been letting him out?" Sean suggested. "On purpose?"

"Wyatt always had the muddy paws to prove his crime," Sunny said with a chuckle. "He's just a wanderer. That was one of the reasons the original owner gave for bringing him to me. They couldn't keep up with his physical demands." Sunny shrugged. "Or some such bullshit."

"You mean the Dudes?"

Sunny rolled her eyes. "Yes. The Dudes."

"You don't care for them."

"I do not."

Neither did Sean. After talking with Rawls the other day Sean had learned even more about the Worley brothers. Though they'd managed to avoid arrest, they'd been associated on multiple occasions with a biker group infamous for violence and possession charges. Dude's Bikes was even named in an arrest report for a dozen different men picked up at an after-hours party that had turned into a drunken brawl. Sean didn't imagine the shop was as clean as it appeared in the report, just because nothing illicit was found that night. He also didn't imagine Dude's Bikes to have been a fun living space for Wyatt.

"Alright, Sunny. I know you're a busy lady. I'm not going to take up any more of your time. If it's okay, I'll just poke around the grounds while you get me that list of volunteers. And the renters."

"Sure thing." Sunny grinned. "You're sure working your ass off on this case, Sean."

Sean shrugged. "It's my job."

"Yeah," Sunny agreed. "Still."

"It was her father's bike. He died several months ago in an accident. The bike means a lot to her." Sean knew that Sunny and Red had lost their father a couple of years ago, so this piece of information would hit home, and hopefully end Sunny's probing.

Sunny's smile fell. "I didn't know that. It kind of makes sense, though. She's got kind of a sad aura about her, doesn't she? Underneath that coat of steel, anyway."

"Yeah."

Sunny lingered a moment, then pressed on, despite Sean's diversionary tactic. "Cici tells me you knew Delaney before this happened. From the gym. What a coincidence, huh?"

"It's a small world." A small, tight world that everyone thought was so big. If Sean had learned one thing in his career it was that the world was just a bunch of overlapping circles. Sean couldn't afford to look at the straight lines in his job. He had to study the whole picture, which was more like a messy scribble than neat compartments.

"Cici also told me that you and Delaney are kind of a pair at the gym." The twinkle in Sunny's eyes accompanied a sly grin. "A competitive pair, that is," she quickly amended. "Like, on each other's nerves…but kind of in a cute way."

Sean almost said, *I'll take that scotch now, thanks*, but instead just grunted dismissively. "Delaney and I have had a couple of run-ins," he said. "Literally. But I've got nothing else to say about that." And for some reason, he really didn't. In the past, he might've talked to Sunny about the new girl in town. Despite their past, he and Sunny were friends. But he didn't want to talk to her about Delaney. He didn't want to talk to anyone about Delaney. Which was an odd, unprecedented protectiveness Sean couldn't explain. Sean's job was to protect and serve after all, but the motorcycle girl had dug inside him somehow, and like Wyatt, would have the muddy paws to prove it.

"Alright." Sunny gave another wink. "Anything else I can do for you, Detective?"

"I think I'm good for now," Sean said, relieved Sunny let it drop, when that wasn't usually her style. He watched her walk off to the house to get the list, then turned his attention back to the grounds. Typically, the case was solved in the details. And Sean didn't want to miss any of the details.

"Whoever took this motorcycle isn't riding it all over town," Castillo pointed out. "It's too distinctive. Eventually, somebody would spot it and give us a call. Which means, that gorgeous bike is probably in pieces by now. Damn shame."

Sean usually appreciated Castillo's practicality. But today, it was getting on his nerves.

Her facial expression said it all. *How long are we going to spend on this?*

"No security camera at the shop, but Sunny had them installed all over her property after the fire last year. If the case gets thin, or if we establish a clear link to the dog, I can look at that footage. For now, I've got a list of names to cross-check with the list of people who went to the grand opening of Triple M Classics."

"You don't think the thief was stupid enough to sign his name in Miss Monroe's book, do you?" Castillo scooped up a bite of yogurt and stuck it in her mouth. "Never mind," she mumbled through her mouthful. "Don't answer that."

Sean slumped to his desk. "It's not exactly a bike you steal to chop into parts, either. How many people are in the market for motorcycle parts from 1933? And how easy would it be to sell those parts if they're stolen?"

"Black market." Castillo shrugged. "Either parts or the whole bike."

"Maybe." Sean scanned the book Delaney had given him from her grand opening. He'd looked at it a few times now, but with Sunny's employees and cabin renters fresh in his mind, a match would jump out. "My eyes are still on those

Dick brothers. Especially now that I know they're into shady shit. I kind of like them for this."

"Dude brothers," Castillo corrected. "It was Dude's Bikes. Not Dick's Bikes."

"Yeah, I know."

Castillo's snort-laugh was real. A few heads within the vicinity of their desks turned. She waved a hand at them. "Nothing to see here."

"Then again." Sean's eyes narrowed as he spied a name in Delaney's book, printed in bold, fat letters, that matched one of Sunny's volunteers. *Janie Ramirez.* Say what? A girl? Sean dug out the sheet from Sunny. According to that data, Janie was sixteen and was not marked as being from the Jobs for Disadvantaged Youth program. She was just a regular teenage volunteer, someone who either loved dogs or was trying to flesh out her college transcripts.

"You got something?" Castillo rolled over in her chair and peeked over his shoulder.

"I don't know." Sean checked the names again. "I got a match on both lists but it just doesn't seem likely. Sixteen-year-old girl? Stealing an antique bike? Sitting in the rain at midnight, smoking cigarettes, then pinching the bike? I'm just not feeling that. She had school the next morning. Plus, how many teenage girls know how to ride a motorcycle, let alone have the balls to steal one?"

Castillo eyed the match. "You never know who she's working with, Sean. She could just be the intel. Maybe this is gang related. Drug related. She's being used by brothers or cousins or the wrong crowd. Hang on. Let me look up her address." Castillo rolled away and clicked on her keyboard, her slender fingers working so fast they made Sean's eyes cross. "She lives in a nice neighborhood," Castillo reported. A few more clicks. "Looks like she's an honor roll student. Head of the Diversity

Club. Excuse me, *founder* of the Diversity Club." Castillo faced Sean with raised eyebrows. "I tend to agree with you. This girl's not out stealing motorcycles. But it can't hurt to ask."

Sean stood up and slid on his jacket. "I'll check it out. You can take the lead on something else if you want. I know you think this is a lost cause."

Castillo gave him a wry smile. "Good luck. I get why you're after it, Sean. Just text if you need me."

Sean grinned. "If I feel threatened at Meadow Rose Estates, I'll text 9-1-1."

"You do that, Callahan."

Janie Ramirez was everything Sean thought she'd be, and more. She was an athletic, studious, well-mannered young lady who wore her dark hair in a side braid and her owl-shaped glasses perched on her tiny nose. She was bilingual, which Sean figured out when she spoke to her grandmother in Spanish—who insisted on staying during the casual inter-view—and to Sean in English. Apparently the grandmother's English wasn't great because Janie said, with no attempt to dis-guise her words, "I love motorcycles, but I'm not allowed to ride until I'm eighteen. My older brothers all ride and I'm not even allowed to ride with them. I got the flyer for the grand opening of Delaney's shop from Sunny. She handed some out for Delaney. Delaney's *the* coolest, am I right?"

And Grandma didn't even bat an eye.

"Yeah," Sean agreed, without hesitation. "She's pretty cool."

"I would've gotten in so much trouble for going to that grand opening." Janie pushed her glasses up the bridge of her nose. "My parents think I need to focus only on school and the track team. I'm only allowed to volunteer at Pittie Place one day a week."

The grandmother's full attention was on her knitting. Her

bent, arthritic fingers worked the needles through a mass of green yarn, the start of a sweater or a blanket piled in the old woman's lap. She wore a dress with a faded flower print and had her gray hair in a bun. Sean wished he'd had a grandmother who knitted and wore old lady dresses. And parents who told him he should focus on his academics and the track team. Janie Ramirez was a lucky kid. "So you saw the Indian motorcycle?"

"Everybody saw it. Delaney had it on display. She told me she'd be starting a ladies' riding club in the future and that I should check it out once I'm old enough. She wasn't pushy or trying to sell anything, she just wanted to share her knowledge and foster my interest in motorcycles. That's why I like her. She's cool and experienced and knows bikes in and out, and since she's a girl, I can trust her."

Sean nodded in agreement. This was all great news, of course. The kind of stuff that warmed a jaded cop's heart. But it didn't help his case. Clearly the only thing that linked Janie to both Pittie Place and Triple M Classics was the flyer for the grand opening. Janie worked at Pittie Place. Sunny had flyers for Triple M Classics. Janie, already a motor head, went to the grand opening. That's why her name was on both lists. Still, as long as he was here. "How many brothers you have?"

"Five."

"And they all ride motorcycles?"

"Yeah, but two are married and don't live here and one is in the army and doesn't live here. Carlos and Manny live here but share one Harley they bought together last year." Janie glanced at her grandmother, who hadn't dropped a stitch, despite the frequent glances in Sean's direction. Sean didn't buy her frail-old-lady-knitting-at-the-kitchen-table persona for a second. If she thought her granddaughter was being coerced or was in harm's way, those knitting needles would be doing a lot more than working some yarn. "I told Carlos and Manny about the old motorcycle and the shop and they thought it was cool and planned to go see it for themselves. But I don't think they'd steal it."

"You don't *think* they'd steal it?" Janie's matter-of-factness had a special place in Sean's heart.

Janie shrugged. "They're boys. They both had their share of stupidity when they were teens. All my brothers did. Typical stuff, I guess, but they never stole anything. Not like those two guys who came to Delaney's opening."

Sean glanced up from his notepad. "Which guys?" Even though he was pretty sure he already knew.

"I think they used to own the shop. One's fat, one's skinny? They were seriously scoping out Delaney's shop. I even saw the skinny one go upstairs, which I know isn't part of the shop because Delaney had it blocked off. At first I thought maybe he knew her really well or was dating her. But once he knew I saw him, he came back down. Acted really funny. Then I realized later that Delaney didn't know him and it was obvious to everyone they didn't like each other."

"Really." Sean wrote that down, his brain racing. "You say anything?"

"I know I should have. It seemed too late. I didn't know how to bring it up. Will you tell her for me?"

"Oh, I'll tell her. You see those guys do anything else?"

"Just act like big jerks, in general. They were fighting over the dog. But the dog wanted nothing to do with them."

Sean smiled and handed Janie his card. "Thanks for all your help, Janie. If you see or hear anything, give me a call." He rose up and slid his jacket from the back of the chair. The grandmother dropped her knitting to the table and ushered him to the door.

"Bye." Janie waved at him as he left. "Good luck. Say hi to Delaney for me."

Sean raised his hand as the grandmother shut the door in his face. He got behind the wheel of the minivan and decided that it couldn't hurt to pay Delaney a visit, regroup and fill her in on his progress.

thirteen

"Walt!" Delaney smiled as she recognized the older guy with Willie Nelson braids who entered her shop late in the evening. He had his full-size helmet tucked under his arm, which Delaney was surprised to see. She would've pegged Walt as the half helmet type, worn grudgingly to satisfy the law.

"Hey, Delaney." Walt grinned, exposing crooked teeth. "Thought I'd come see how things are going." His gaze swept over the Pioneer that was finished and waiting for its owner and the Shovelhead that Mary Sue, from the grand opening, had brought in this morning. "Looks like it's going well."

"It's going okay," Delaney said, even though it had been pretty slow. "I can't complain."

"Where's '33?" Walt toured the shop.

"You're not going to believe this." Delaney didn't like to talk about it. Just speaking out loud about the missing bike made her stomach cramp. "The bike got stolen last week. Went missing out the back." She nodded toward the storeroom. "In the middle of that bad storm we had."

Walt smiled. "You're kidding." Then his smile faded. "You're not kidding."

Delaney shook her head.

"That's a damn shame, kid." He shook his head. "Any idea who took it?"

"Not really." Delaney still didn't think it was real. At least once a day she would go into the back room to check that the motorcycle was really gone. Once she was back there she'd spy Wyatt's empty dog bed, and that only made her feel worse.

"You report it to the police?" Walt's question might've seemed silly, but Delaney could picture him doing sit-ins in the sixties, chanting *Hell no, we won't go!*, so the thread of distrust that ran through his question fit as well as the gray braids.

"They've been here. They're working the case. But..." Delaney trailed off, not wanting to say aloud what everybody knew about motorcycles that went missing. "The Classic Motorcycle Show at the fairgrounds is coming up fast. The grand prize will get lots of exposure, including advertising in *Ride* magazine. That would be so great for the business, especially since the shop is new. Plus, the bikers around here will get to see how much I know. They'll see firsthand that I'm legit, despite anything those guys from Dude's Bikes might have to say about me. I know '33 would have a good shot at a ribbon."

"I know the show. And heck, yes. Your bike would do well. And you'd meet a lot of great people who can spread the word."

"But not if I don't have it."

Walt's smile fell. "Well, damn, honey. I hope the police have some luck." His face looked pained, like he truly felt as bad as Delaney did about the stolen bike.

"I'm glad you came in. At the grand opening, you said

something about those brothers dealing more than bikes. Were you talking about drugs?"

"Well, I haven't lived up this way in a while. Just came back to the area, but—" Walt cast a look around, even though they were alone "—word in some biker groups was Dude's was the place to hit for all kinds of junk. Coke. Smack. You name it. They're not good people. Have they been hassling you at all?"

Delaney shook her head. "I haven't seen them again."

"Good. Stay away from them."

"They better stay away from *me*." Delaney could tell by the look on Walt's face that he didn't quite buy her bravado. He seemed like a concerned father, with a tinge of regret. Delaney cleared her throat and plastered a smile on her face. "I heard you roar up. What're you riding?" She poked her head out the bay and saw a newer model black Fat Boy parked near her Ford pickup. Walt wasn't kidding when he'd said he was a Harley guy, through and through. She stepped outside to get a closer look at the bike that glittered in the fading sunset. "What year is this?"

"Twenty-nineteen," Walt said as he followed her outside.

"Nice." Delaney nodded her appreciation as she toured a circle around the bike. "You got the Milwaukee-Eight. A 107 or 114?"

"It's a 114," Walt said proudly. He drew a pack of cigarettes from his pocket and tapped one out.

"Hell, yeah. You like it?"

"Hell, yeah." Walt echoed with a grin. "She slings some torque."

"I bet."

Walt stuck a smoke between his lips and flicked open a silver lighter. "You care?" he asked, just before he put the flame to the tip.

Delaney shook her head. She'd inhaled worse over the course of her life.

"I know it's a bad habit—" Walt sucked the cherry to life "—but I've been at it so long I couldn't quit if I tried."

Just as Delaney was about to tell Walt he was fooling himself, a familiar minivan pulled into the parking lot.

Walt drew deeply on his cigarette and eyed the vehicle. "You get a lot of soccer moms?"

Before she could answer, Detective Callahan stepped out, his white button-down looking wrinkled, the badge he usually wore around his neck absent, and his eyes tired, even from a distance. There was no indication whatsoever to an onlooker that Sean was a cop, and Delaney decided not to mention it.

"Evening." Sean approached with a mixed air of formality and fatigue. "I know you're closing up soon, but if you've got a minute…"

"Sure." Delaney turned to Walt, who was busy grinding his cigarette out under his boot. "Sorry, Walt. I never got a chance to ask what you're looking for. We can go back inside and take care of whatever you need, first."

"Nah, it's okay." Walt shrugged his shoulders, wide but thin, and slightly rounded with age. He had the sort of build that probably could never keep weight on during his youth, only gaining some girth when he hit middle age and everything started to slow. "I was only checking on you. You remind me of my daughter, but she lives in Seattle, so I don't get to see her much. This guy needs help way more than I do." Walt eyed the minivan with a smirk. "Brother, you need to get you some new wheels."

Sean laughed. It looked genuine, the crinkles at the corners of his eyes highlighting the bright gray of his irises, like undecided storm clouds. "I actually have an old Harley," he said. "But I'd need to dig it out of storage."

"You should do that," Walt said.

Sean stuck out his hand. "Sean Callahan."

Walt slowly extended his. "Walt." They shook, then Walt turned to Delaney. "I can come back sometime next week and catch up." He smiled. "See if you need my help with that Shovelhead in there. Meantime, I hope your bike turns up."

"Thanks, Walt. Nice seeing you." Once he'd settled on his bike and had his helmet strapped, Delaney turned to Sean. "Thanks for coming out." She was too afraid of bitter disappointment to ask if he had any news of '33.

At that moment, Walt revved up the Fat Boy, so they both stopped talking until he'd zoomed away with a wave. As soon as he was gone, Sean slipped a notebook and pencil from his inside pocket and jotted something down. He stuffed that away and drew a baggie out of another pocket, then bent down.

"What're you doing?" Even as she asked, Delaney could see Sean lifting the cigarette butt and dropping it into the tiny baggie. "Seriously?" she said. "Just like on TV."

Sean closed up the bag but didn't put it in his pocket. Delaney didn't blame him. "Not just like TV," Sean said. "There won't be a DNA hit within an hour. It doesn't work that fast and this isn't a murder case, so it's not priority. But it looks like the same brand of butts we found behind your shop. I'm just going to take it along and see what I see."

"I met Walt at the grand opening," Delaney offered. "I barely know him. He seemed really upset for me when I told him the bike had been stolen. He also said I remind him of his daughter." The sky was starting to get dark. "Let's go inside. I'm about to close. We can talk upstairs."

While Delaney closed out her register, Sean toured the shop, movements slow, brow furrowed, hands doing curious things. He went into the storeroom and was gone awhile.

Once Delaney was finished and the store locked, she poked

her head back there and found Sean standing outside the door, which he'd rolled open partway. "It was like this?" he said, without meeting her gaze. "The door?"

"Yeah." Delaney closed the distance between them and watched Sean furrow his brow. "I left it open before I went to find Wyatt. In case he came back while I was gone. Maybe two feet."

Sean grabbed the chain and adjusted the door until the gap was a couple feet. "Like that?"

"Yeah. Pretty much."

"And when you got back, the door was just like you left it?"

"Yeah," Delaney repeated. "I think so."

Sean's brows knitted and he shook his head.

"What?" Delaney rolled her shoulders back, trying to shove off the feeling that she was just an idiot who should never have been left with the care of Dad's prized bike. She should've let Boom have '33. He'd have taken good care of her and she wouldn't be missing right now.

"I don't know," Sean admitted. He rolled down the bay, which squeaked like mad, and locked up. "There's just something bothering me. Can't put my finger on it."

Delaney watched him examine the door awhile longer before she tugged on his shirtsleeve. "C'mon, Detective." She tilted her head toward the shop. "Let's go upstairs to talk."

Sean broke himself free and followed her out of the storeroom and to the stairs, his steps a respectful distance behind as Delaney climbed up to her living space.

The upstairs always felt like a new world when she rounded the corner, even though her apartment was literally only a few yards from her shop. Downstairs was cool and crisp, smelled of motor oil and leather and whatever flowers were carrying on the summer wind, and upstairs was warm and homey, smelled of tea with honey mixed with the pine candle Delaney liked to light because Christmas tree was her favorite scent. The floor was hardwood, but the couch and recliner were soft and inviting, where an old quilt she'd found at a thrift shop and pretended was her grandmother's was draped just so, and the ceiling fan, newly installed with blades shaped like giant leaves, offering a cool circulation of air.

Delaney gestured toward the couch. "Make yourself comfortable."

"Thanks." Sean took her at her word. He stripped the jacket, followed by the tie, laying both on the arm of the couch before he loosened the top button of his wrinkled white shirt. He sank to the sofa and did a sort of man-spreading that wasn't territorial, just stretched out, like he was relieved to be off his feet.

"Can I get you anything?" Delaney walked to the window over the high-legged table that was supposed to serve as the spot she took her meals—even though she regularly ate on the couch, in front of ESPN, most often a bowl of granola cereal or a peanut butter sandwich—and jammed it closed. She hooked the rusty latch, which always stopped about a quarter inch shy, then turned back to Sean. "I still have beer in the fridge. Or water. If you need something stronger, I've got some Heaven's Door I bought for my dad. He loved a good bourbon." Delaney heard her voice drop at the end of her sentence and drew a deep breath to steady her voice. "Unless you're still on duty."

"I'm off duty now. A beer would be great."

Delaney grabbed two IPAs from the fridge, popped off both bottle caps and handed one over. "You sure? Your ears perked up when I mentioned the bourbon."

Sean gave an easy laugh, different from the one outside.

This laugh was lower, had a little regret attached to it. "I get in trouble with whiskey. The beer's good."

"Ha." Delaney sank to the opposite end of the couch. "Trouble's not all bad."

Sean regarded her comment with a smirk as he drank the steam off his beer. He set the bottle on the table before he spoke. "I visited a young lady today named Janie Ramirez. She works at Sunny's place. She signed your grand opening register."

Delaney sipped her IPA. Any excitement Sean's words might've brewed faded fast. "If I'm remembering right," Delaney said, thinking back and filtering the people through her mind like she was watching a movie, "she was a little firecracker. Teenager. Side braid?"

"That's her."

"I remember thinking that the name Janie both fit perfectly and didn't fit at all. She's definitely no plain Jane." Delaney laughed. "That girl knows way more about bikes than a lot of the weekend warriors I meet. She's going to be something else on the road once she's allowed to ride."

"Agreed. I don't think she or her brothers had anything to do with your motorcycle. But she did tell me she saw the Dudes here that evening. In fact, she said she saw Dick Worley sneak upstairs that night."

Delaney froze. She had to be still a moment to let Sean's words sink in. "Up here?"

"That's what Janie said. This is why I wanted to come over right away. Have you noticed anything missing or out of place?"

She hadn't, but now Delaney had to think about it. "No," she said, after closing her eyes briefly. "Not that I can think of. Seriously, though. One of those men came up here?"

"Janie saw him go up, but when he caught her looking, he

came back down. So I don't think he actually made it into the apartment. I'm just being cautious."

"Well, that's not good." Delaney rubbed her hands over her arms, creeped out that one of those dudes had tried to get up here.

"No, it's not," Sean agreed. "This is even more reason for you to contact me immediately if they come by."

"Don't worry." Delaney didn't even pretend to have it all under control this time. "I will." She slid her hands up to her face and rubbed her eyes. "My father would've made quick work of those brothers," she said, trying to keep herself from tearing up. "If there was one thing that got him mad it was anyone messing with me. God help those dudes if they stole my dad's bike. Because Dad's ghost will tear them a new one."

Sean laughed and leaned back into the couch cushions. "You were really close to your father. It doesn't take a detective to see that. He probably taught you everything you know about bikes, bike repair, everything you already knew going into your motor transport MOS in the Marine Corps. Am I right?"

Delaney held her beer up near her face to hide whatever it was she felt about Detective Callahan knowing her background. It was no surprise he'd dug into her bio. If he hadn't, he wouldn't be good at his job. But in his favor was that Sean was making no secret of the fact that he'd learned what he could about her. He might be nosy but he wasn't sneaky. "My dad taught me everything I know about everything."

"What about your mom?"

"What about her?" The words slipped out too quickly. Delaney clamped her mouth shut. A man like Callahan would learn more about Delaney by what she didn't say than what she did. The bumbling guy at the gym was someone else entirely when he had the detective hat on.

"Was she in the picture?"

Delaney set her beer on the coffee table and sighed. "If we're going to talk about my mother, I'm going to have to open the whiskey."

Delaney disappeared into the bedroom, one of only two other rooms in this cozy studio apartment—the other presumably the bathroom—and came out a few minutes later wearing gray sweatpants with Go Big Red! printed down the side and a long-sleeved, oversize pajama top that fell off of one shoulder. She looked simultaneously small and vulnerable, and sleek and strong.

"Sorry," she said, with a rueful smile. "I had to get out of those clothes." She stopped at the dining table by the window and opened up a bottle, which Sean presumed was the Heaven's Door bourbon. The pleasant sound of liquor glugging into two glasses followed. "My parents were just teenagers when they had me," Delaney said as she passed a glass over to Sean. "They were the wild, unsupervised types. Dad took care of himself most of his life. His parents came and went but weren't around much, so Dad spent his life dodging child protective services. My mother's parents were older. Poor. Didn't pay much attention to her. Sometime after I was born, my mother freaked out and bailed. Struggled with addiction, on and off. Dad was the only steady force in my life I ever knew. When I was little she'd pop in every now and again, but she never stayed. By the time I was a teenager I refused to see her. She still sends me birthday cards and tries to make contact—her cards have followed me all over the world—but I never respond. Sometimes she catches me off guard and gets me on the phone. I always keep it brief. But I haven't talked to her in probably…" she looked up at the ceiling, her lips moving, like she was counting "…five years?"

Sean raised his glass of Heaven's Door. This was Bob Dylan's creation. He'd read about it somewhere. He took a sip. Modest at first, without the aggressive punch of a cheaper whiskey. The flavor profile flowed in slowly: vanilla, layered over oak, with some kind of toasty note, like bread from a campfire. The intensity came at the finish, where it burst and lingered on his tongue. Overall, it was like an old-fashioned romance, with a proper introduction and courtship before the fire. Sean had always been a scotch man, but that didn't mean he couldn't be seduced by Tennessee bourbon from one of the greatest songwriters of all time. Especially since he could see Delaney's tough exterior slowly crumbling before him. "You're originally from Omaha. Is that where your mom is?"

"She's moved all over the place. Goes with one guy to the next. Last I heard she was in Newport News. Just a couple hours south."

"She's close by and you've never seen her?"

"I know. You think I'm harsh." Delaney shook her head dismissively. "I've got nothing to say to her. The time for all the mother-daughter stuff has come and gone. You don't get to dirt your kid and then expect a magic redo when they're all grown-up and somebody else has put in all the work."

"How do you really feel?"

Delaney offered a soft smile.

"I was raised by my older sister, Mary," Sean admitted. He noted that he hadn't even finished his beer as he abandoned it in favor of the bourbon. "She's twenty years older than I am. I wasn't planned, either. I have vague memories of my parents when I was little. Just like—" Sean put his hand up near his ear and rolled it around "—flashes of their voices and fuzzy images. Old people with white hair and glasses. Though in reality they were only in their fifties. Sometimes I wonder if what I remember is real or made-up. They were very hands-off. Died within a year of each other. Heart attack for Dad and untreated diabetes for Mom. She didn't 'believe in it,' from what my sister said."

Delaney pulled her legs beneath her and tucked herself into a ball in the corner of the sofa. She sipped her bourbon and her voice got quiet, almost dreamy. "You were alone a lot, weren't you?"

Sean paused, his glass halfway to his lips. "Takes one to know one, huh?"

She rolled back her bare shoulder in a slinky shrug that made her look wise. "Somebody's got to raise the kids. Somebody's got to pay the bills. When there's only one person to do all that, the kid has to fend for herself a lot. I can tell you've been fending for yourself for a long time."

Used to being the detective in the room, Sean was taken aback. "I got no complaints."

Delaney offered a knowing smile. "You sound like my dad. Despite his rough upbringing, he never complained. Because he never complained, I felt like I never could, either. Certainly makes you work harder and take more responsibility for your life. I basically wanted to be everything he was and I guess I kind of am." She pointed downward, toward the shop.

Sean took another sip of the bourbon, felt it going to his head. He needed to put it down now if he was going to drive home. "This Dylan's whiskey?"

"Yeah." She smiled at his guess.

"Bet you've got Dylan over there, too." Sean nodded toward the stack of vinyl he'd spotted next to what looked like a stereo system. He got up, not waiting for her answer, and went to the records. He leafed through them as Delaney came up beside him. "So who taught your dad everything he knew?" Sean picked up the dangling thread of their earlier conversation.

Delaney watched Sean's hands as he flipped through the

vinyl. Sean made sure he handled *Duke Ellington and John Coltrane, Damn the Torpedoes, Howlin' Wolf, The Wall, Morrison Hotel*, and *(Pronounced 'Leh-'nérd 'Skin-'nérd)* with care. He wondered if the LPs were also her father's or if she'd bought them herself. Sean was usually good at games like that, but in this case, it could go either way, so he mentally decided on a mix of the two.

"Dad taught himself. He had to, if he wanted to go anywhere. The Indian Four had been out back, in a shed, for as long as he could remember, but it didn't run well, and nobody used it. His father told him if he could fix it, he could have it." Delaney shrugged. "So he did. He learned everything he could about it, saved up money, hitchhiked to bike shops. He fixed up the bike and got it running, and it's been running ever since. It was his freedom, I guess. He'd finally found a way to escape. He could take off and it'd be just him and the road, and if he broke down, he wouldn't have to rely on anyone because he could fix things himself."

"Hmm," Sean said, considering her words. "I agree with the last part."

"What do you mean?" Delaney's eyes narrowed, just as Sean's fingers lit on what he'd been searching for: a black cover, an arena in darkness except for a sea of glowing flames from people's lighters.

"Aha." Sean pulled out the record. *"Before the Flood."* He flipped it over. "Bob Dylan and The Band. Including—" he scanned the tracks "—'Knockin' on Heaven's Door.'" He smiled and slipped the vinyl halfway out. "May I?"

Delaney glanced at the record player, which, like most of her stuff, looked vintage. "Sure. But what did you mean," she said, "that you agree with 'the last part'?"

Sean raised the lid of the record player. Delaney slipped

the LP from his hands. He didn't argue. She blew away any dust that might be on the vinyl and placed it on the turntable.

"You said that your father liked that he could take off on the bike and go places, and that it was important to him that he know how to fix it himself, because no one else was going to fix it for him. Just like no one had ever fixed anything for him."

Delaney carefully laid the needle on the fourth track. Just as the opening strains of Dylan's guitar melted out the speakers, she turned and fixed him with her whiskey eyes. "What didn't you agree with?"

Sean hesitated. He'd taken a risk when he said that, but there was no undoing it. "The part about your dad working so hard to learn how to fix the motorcycle. You said he worked so hard to fix it because it was his freedom. And yeah, I agree there's an obvious element of truth about his need for escape."

Delaney crossed her arms over her chest. "But?"

"But." Sean watched her bite down on her lower lip and felt the struggle of the whiskey and his common sense warring in his head. The bourbon made him wonder what her lips tasted like—Heaven's Door?—and his common sense reminded him that this was how his last failed relationship had started. He'd been drinking, they were close, things got steamy. Maybe— just maybe—Sean needed to rein himself in this time. Not screw things up before they even got started. Even though Delaney, vulnerable and tipsy, was almost irresistible. "Have you ever considered that, rather than looking for freedom, maybe he was looking for connection? Maybe your dad learned everything he could about that motorcycle because it's the only family legacy he had. The only connection he had to his father before him. Everyone else had died or left. Everyone else had given up on him. Maybe he fixed up the bike because it was there, waiting for him to find, waiting for him to rescue it from the shed. Waiting for him to reconnect the missing pieces and bring it back to life."

Delaney stared at him, her eyes bright, her lips parted slightly. The room was silent but for the strains of Dylan and The Band:

Knock, knock, knockin'...

She closed her mouth and swallowed deeply. Her eyes sparkled brighter. Then she looked around the room, avoiding his gaze.

"I'm sorry," Sean said because that was all he had to offer when what he really wanted to do was fold her into his arms and let someone else absorb some of the sad for a while. But that would be a mistake. Sean knew that if he took her in his arms, he wouldn't want to let her go. "I overstepped."

Delaney cleared her throat, and as the song faded to black and the next track started—"It Ain't Me, Babe"—she smiled a little bit. "You really got an old Harley in storage? Or you make that shit up to close Walt's mouth?"

Sean turned his sigh of relief into a gentle laugh. He couldn't tell if her reaction was forced recovery or genuine humor, but either way, he'd take it. "Nah, I really do. It's an '83 Disc Glide. My sister's husband gave it to me when I turned sixteen. He hadn't ridden it in years because of his bad back. He said I could have it if I didn't tell my sister and if I was careful. I used to race it down the back roads, before everything around here was built up. I hung on to it, even after I'd deployed. Left it at my sister's, where no one took care of it. I hung on to it, even after I got married. My ex kept trying to make me get rid of it, said it was a useless piece of junk. But I just couldn't."

Delaney sniffed away the remnants of whatever had gotten hold of her. "Did you say an '83 Disc Glide?"

"Yeah."

"Do you mean a Willie Glide?" Her eyes narrowed skeptically.

"Yeah," Sean said. "That's what Tom called it. A Willie G." He shrugged.

"You're lying."

Sean laughed. "I'm really not." It was clear at this point that Delaney knew far more about motorcycles than he did. "Why?"

"Harley only made about eight hundred of those," she said. "If you really have one, you have a gem."

"No shit?" And all this time Kim had called that bike junk.

"Does it run?"

"About as well as I do."

"Ha." She ran her hands through her hair, pushing back the dark waves that curled around her ears. It was a habit she had that Sean had noticed and grown fond of. "Which means the Willie needs work."

"Ouch." Sean walked over to the coffee table, retrieved his whiskey and threw it back. What the hell. Couldn't let it go to waste. "We won't know how much work until we run the 10K. I'm off tomorrow. You game?" He couldn't believe he was actually bringing up the rematch; either Delaney had forgotten or had decided to let it go, and there went Sean, opening his big mouth. Even though he preferred middistance and had felt pretty sure of himself when they'd made the bet, his resolve was now faltering.

She stretched her arms over her head, looking sleepy. "I'm game, if we go early. And I'll even sweeten the pot. You win, I'll fix up your Willie, free of charge."

"Um." Sean couldn't resist, his tongue loose on whiskey. "My willy is just fine, but if you're offering…"

Delaney laughed so hard the gravel in her voice came out

like an undercurrent. "The bike, Callahan. I'll fix up your bike. The labor, that is. You have to buy the parts."

"Seriously? Then let's postpone the race. Give me time to train."

"Nope." Delaney cocked her head to the side. "One-time offer. Take it or leave it."

"I'll definitely take it."

"What do I get when I win?" She pushed her chin out.

"*When* you win?"

Delaney grinned. This might've been the first time Sean was treated to a full-on, unrestrained smile that lit up her whole face.

Leave it to facing an impossible footrace to realize you have so very little to give. The best Sean had to offer was his job. He'd hunt that motorcycle thief to the ends of the earth, both because Sean always got his man and because he wanted Delaney to have her dad's bike back. His talents ended there, and because he was likely to lose this race, he had to be careful about what he offered. "I'll make you dinner," he heard himself say. As soon as the words left his mouth, the heat of the bourbon crept up the back of his neck. Not only were his culinary skills limited to sandwiches and boxed mac 'n' cheese, he'd just reminded himself not to get too close, too fast. He wasn't worried, though. There was no way in hell Delaney was going to agree.

Then she stuck out her hand. "Alright, Detective. Deal."

fourteen

Delaney had a little more Heaven's Door, then crawled under the thrift shop quilt made from pinks and greens, her secret favorite color combo, and fell asleep on the couch. She woke the next morning to the sound of the needle scratching at the end of the Bob Dylan album. Faint beams of sunlight pushed through the half inch along the bottom of the window where the shade hadn't quite met the sill. She sat up and stretched, feeling remarkably levelheaded considering she didn't usually drink. But whiskey, in small amounts, had been a part of her life since she could remember. Dad wasn't a heavy drinker, and he didn't buy pricey stuff, but there was always a bottle of Maker's Mark behind the counter and he and the guys usually ended the day with two fingers. When Delaney was little he'd let her stick her pinky in the glass and taste it. It was only a drop and it made her nose wrinkle but she didn't care. If her guys were doing it, she was going to do it, too.

Delaney checked her phone, half expecting a cancellation text. Nothing from Sean, but there was a text from Boom.

Happy Independence Day!

She checked her watch. Well hell. It was the Fourth of July. Now that she thought about it, she'd seen pop-up stands selling fireworks all over the place but hadn't really paid them much thought, other than getting a creepy-crawly feeling down her spine. Delaney wasn't going to lie, setting off fireworks had been fun as a kid. She and Dad would drive into Missouri and load up on all the fireworks that were illegal in Nebraska and once it got dark they'd spend hours setting off bottle rockets, spinners, smoke bombs and firecrackers. The multicolored spray under the dark sky, the smoke rising high as the moon, the smell of sulfur and the dying edge of that year's crop of June bugs buzzing in the streetlamps had made everything seem magical.

But explosions were different when you'd spent a good chunk of your life hoping your convoy didn't hit an IED.

Thanks, Boom. You too.

You doing ok, Pip?

Yeah, I'm good. Going for a run.

[vomit emoji] Any news on the bike?

Not yet.

Hang in there, Pip.

Delaney decided not to tell Boom, or any of the other guys, that one of the Dudes had tried to come up here, into her apartment. She hadn't told the guys anything about the Dudes because that would open up a long line of aggressive questions Delaney wasn't prepared to handle over text. She toured her apartment, giving everything a once-over with new eyes. What could he possibly have been after?

No point in driving herself crazy about it. Delaney shook it off, dressed for the 10K in shorts and an airy tank top, then bypassed the kitchen, deciding to run fasted. Many people loaded up on big breakfasts, but fitness had been a part of Delaney's life so long she knew what worked for her and what didn't. The big breakfast would come after the run, not before, unless she felt like hurling a few miles in.

As she laced up her shoes she tried to tell herself that she'd agreed to do this today because of the bourbon and that she should probably lay off making deals unless completely sober, but that would all be a lie. She wanted to run and she wanted to win this race, and she would make that bet again, in the light of day, with no liquor running through her veins. Delaney hated to admit it, but she'd made this bet because she'd come to like how she felt around the big, gruff detective and by running this race she had an excuse to be around him some more. Plain and simple.

She headed downstairs and grabbed her truck keys. She'd have to wear completely different clothes to ride the Rebel, so she would meet Sean at the bike trail that ran along the highway in the old Ford. Delaney arrived early and parked in the supermarket lot. She waited only five minutes before Sean arrived, also early.

"You can still back out," he teased as they met by her truck and walked up the slope of hill that led to the bike path.

"That's no way to give yourself a pep talk, Detective."

Delaney messed with the buttons on her GPS watch, trying to decide if she was going to use it, as they'd already mapped out their route.

"Turnaround spot's by the entrance to the park," Sean reminded her.

"I know." Delaney stared at the watch, waiting for it to acquire a signal. "Trying to decide if I want to try to go for a personal best today or just take it easy."

"Oh, really." Sean gave her a fake glare.

He looked different today, for some reason. Maybe he hadn't shaved or his hair wasn't combed as neat, when typically everything about Sean was as neat and crisp as the mints he ate. Maybe Delaney had never seen him in the reddish wash of morning sunshine, or with a backdrop of traffic whizzing by. He seemed less like a detective, less like a fitness geek. Before now, Delaney could picture Sean in one of two scenarios: Detective Sean and Gym Sean. She could envision Detective Sean chasing down a perp, talking on his radio, cuffing a suspect or, strangely, doing paperwork at his desk. She could envision Gym Sean knocking her over during handstands or gasping in a puddle on the floor after their 5K race. Then there was the Sean from the "My House" video, which was an entity unto itself, but today was completely different from all that. Today, Sean just looked like a rugged, handsome guy going out for a weekend run. Just a runner named Sean.

And she didn't hate it.

"When's the last time you ran a 10K?" he said.

"Um." Delaney shook herself out of her own head. "Two weeks ago. You?"

"Eh." Sean looked up at the sky, like he was mentally sorting days or months. "Two years ago?"

Delaney laughed and looked back to her watch. Still no signal. "Good luck today, then." She'd decided on her strategy: start out below race pace, allowing Sean to think she was giving the first half of the run around 80 percent. Pick up the pace for the next two miles and then, for the last one, open up the gas tank.

"Oh, I don't know." Sean started bouncing on his toes, like he was getting ready to run the Rocky Steps up the Philadelphia Museum of Art. "I think I have a…three, two, one, go!"

And he took off.

Delaney looked up from her watch in time to see Sean tear a blue streak down the bike path. He didn't stop and say he was kidding. He didn't turn around and come back for a proper start. He really kept running. He really had just cheated, and was not ashamed of it. Delaney burst into laughter. "Okay, Detective," she said, just as her watch beeped with acquired GPS. "Game on."

Sean had no idea in hell what he was going to cook. That was the first thought he had as he crested the final ridge of the bike path and spied Delaney down the other side of the slope. She was sprawled across the hood of her truck, forearm shading her eyes, either sunbathing or asleep while she waited for him to finish. Her legs looked long and lean, feet planted on the hood, her tank top riding up a little and exposing an impressive set of abs. Sean could almost forgive her easy win, given the view.

Still, she had won, and not just by a little bit. It was clear Sean's endurance had taken a hit with his neglect, which might've been the most disappointing thing about this. For the last painful mile, he was way more angry at himself for letting life get in the way of what used to be his favorite running distance than he was thinking about what sort of dinner he might make for the road warrior snoozing in the sunshine. This was an opportunity, both to get back into a solid running routine and to amp up his cooking skills. He couldn't very well fix Delaney a grilled cheese sandwich with canned tomato soup to celebrate her crushing victory.

When Sean arrived at the truck and Delaney still didn't budge, he couldn't resist. He grabbed his water bottle from where he'd left it by her truck tire and poured a little on her exposed abs. The water pooled in her belly button and slid down over her glistening skin.

"That feels good," was all she said. No shrieking or jumping up to retaliate. She withdrew her arm and blinked in the bright light. "All done?" She peeked at her watch. "Hoo, boy. Took you a while."

Sean wasn't sure what reaction she'd been hoping for but he smiled at her. "I'm definitely all done," he agreed.

"Good, because I've got to be home soon to get some work done." Delaney smiled and slid off the hood of her truck. She planted her hands on her hips. "What'll you be cooking? And when can I expect it?"

"You don't mess around."

Delaney stretched her arms out to her sides, probably to catch the inviting breeze that was rolling up Sean's back. "I won, fair and square. And eating is like, one of my favorite things to do, so don't give me any of that 'we'll set up a time at some point' crap. I want hard, concrete details."

Sean really wanted to be depressed about the fact he wasn't going to get his motorcycle fixed for free, but then, he probably would have paid her for her time anyway. "I'm back on shift in a couple days. How about tomorrow night? After your shop closes?"

"Alright. But let's make it an hour after my shop closes." Delaney pulled her truck key out of a hidden zippered pocket in her running shorts. "I'm getting a massage from Red. She offered me a free intro massage, which is like, unheard of."

"Damn. I never got a free intro massage."

"Guess she prefers girls."

"Well, she's not stupid," Sean agreed. "After all, she prefers the dogs over all of us."

"True. So…eight o'clock? Should I dress up? Will it be a black tie affair?"

"Don't push your luck. I'll text you my address." Now he had to clean up his apartment and learn how to cook. In twenty-four hours. "Any dietary restrictions?"

And then she said it. Three little words that were sure to take Sean's culinary expansion into a whole new world of fuckery: "I'm a vegetarian."

Trinity gave no outward reaction to the random explosions that had been going off all day, but every single one made Tabitha's body jerk reflexively. Trinity came to her and settled by her side. "I'm okay, Trinity," she said, for about the fifth time that day. Trinity gave her that look that seemed like she was smiling, mouth closed but lips turned up at the corners. "You're probably the only dog in the history of the world who can smile."

Trinity did some kind of tiny dance that involved spinning and tossing her head, highlighting how small she was for her breed. Tabitha laughed and all the tension in her body melted away.

"Just why." Auntie El pulled a tray of brownies from the oven and shook her head. She set the pan on the top of the stove and fisted her generous hip as she glared out the kitchen window. "When did it start being okay to set off fireworks anytime except after the sun goes down? These fools been cracking things off all day."

And then some, Tabitha thought. She'd heard random firecrackers all week long and every single one made her body freeze and her heart race. But the smell of chocolate and Trinity's presence were helping keep the edge off.

"You sure you want to go to the gym?" Auntie El closed up the café curtains over the window, as though this could keep out the sound of the fireworks. "It'll be dark soon."

"Working out will help." Tabitha laid her hand over her chest. "Besides, the music is so loud it will drown out any explosions."

"Alright." Auntie El came over to press the back of her hand to Tabitha's forehead and peer into her eyes. The action was more clinical than motherly, her nursing instincts taking over, even though she'd been retired for years. Auntie El must've been satisfied with whatever she felt and saw because she settled at the table with a grunt and lifted the pencil that lay atop this morning's unfinished crossword. "Those brownies will be cool by the time you're home."

Tabitha stuck her face over the pan and inhaled the hot, chocolatey steam. Few things in life could compete with this sort of therapy. Tabitha would eat three, back to back, and Auntie El would take the rest to her Bible study.

"Reverend Stokes asked again today when you'll be coming back. He wants you to run the Sunday school, like you did before."

The hot chocolate lost its sweet edge, leaving only a harsh alkaline scent in Tabitha's nose. It bathed the back of her throat, making it hard to swallow. "I don't know, Auntie El. Trinity doesn't like church."

"Trinity doesn't like church," Auntie El echoed with scorn. "How do you know? You haven't taken her." She wrote something into her crossword, frowned, then erased it. "I don't like this baseball-themed puzzle. Ten-letter word for *out of left field*."

Tabitha stroked Trinity's head. She was close by, like she

enjoyed the smell of the brownies, too. She counted on her fingers, then said, "Unexpected."

"Ah." Auntie El filled the blocks in with a smile. "That's it."

"I'll see you later." Tabitha secured Trinity's vest and headed out to the gym before Auntie El could bring up church again.

Only once she'd pulled into the parking lot and didn't spy a motorcycle did Tabitha realize she hadn't texted Delaney to see if she'd be working out tonight. Her mind had been so frazzled it'd slipped by. She almost put the car in reverse and hightailed it back home but then Clementine appeared, a woman she'd met during her last workout. Clementine was new to the gym as well, though she was a really good runner and had been giving Tabitha tips on her form during the warm-up and again after the workout. Tabitha had always thought that running was just putting one foot in front of the other, really fast, but she'd been surprised how much Clementine could share on the subject.

"I own a running shop," she'd said. "You should stop by."

"Maybe I will." Tabitha had always hated running but maybe she would've fared better in the navy if she'd had Clementine for pointers.

"Hey, Tabitha." Clementine peeked in the car window. "Hey, Trinity." She waved at the dog, who was buckled in the back seat with her pet harness. "Did you see today's workout?" Clementine held up her phone, which she could use to access the app that both showed the daily workouts and tracked their weights and scores. "It looks brutal. Lots of weights." Clementine flexed a tiny bicep. "But that's what I'm here for. Buff up a little bit to improve my running."

"I don't look," Tabitha admitted. She got out of the car and opened the door for Trinity. "I don't want to give myself excuses to bail."

"That's a good idea." Clementine had bright green eyes like

freshly mowed grass. The color made her seem both earthy and exotic. "But it would kill me not to look."

They headed inside to a much smaller group of people than Tabitha's last workout, which, after some thought, made sense. Everyone would be out doing what normal people do on the evening of the Fourth of July: cookouts, pool parties, airplane shows and fireworks in DC or at the county stadium. Now that she thought about it, Tabitha was kind of surprised that the gym was even open for the 7:30 p.m. class.

"Welcome, my diehards." Hobbs was at the whiteboard, waving everyone closer. Today he wore a blue Semper Fit T-shirt that completely covered the pecs he liked to display and a pair of American flag shorts. He was of medium height, but his personality and huge, charming grin made him seem like a much larger man. His voice was welcoming and playful, and Tabitha wondered what kind of coach he would be. She hoped he wasn't the sort that let everyone break all the gym rules or do rude things like take up all the space or clean up early. Hobbs seemed, so far, like that kind of guy. Then again, Tabitha had a hard time picturing Rhett hiring someone like that for his gym.

"This workout is called 1776, and I'm sure I don't have to explain why." Hobbs pointed at the board, where a long workout with a lot of reps was written in red and blue dryerase marker. "In case you're wondering, yes, all the reps do add up to 1776."

A woman wearing a hijab and a long-sleeved athletic shirt groaned good-naturedly. Besides her, only Tabitha, Clementine and Zoe were present. Zoe wore a pair of bike shorts that highlighted every muscle and a blue sports bra with a lot of pretty straps, no shirt, so every abdominal muscle was bared, along with a navel ring. Tabitha noted the navel and nose piercings and wondered how many more Zoe had.

"Looks like it's Ladies' Night," Hobbs said with an appreciative grin. "Including our favorite female furry friend." He glanced over his shoulder at Trinity, who was doing circles around Humphrey's empty dog bed, probably wishing the old beagle were there to keep her company. "Let's hit this thing, ladies. Grab some rowers and give me 250 meters." Hobbs clapped his hands together, then pointed at the rowing machines lined up along the far wall. Then he pumped up the music.

As the hour progressed, Tabitha discovered Hobbs had a talent for being the smoothest coach on record. Whereas Rhett was unabashedly in your face like a drill sergeant, Hobbs managed to get you to do what he wanted while making you think it was your idea all along. "Look at that heavy barbell." Hobbs crossed his arms and smiled down at Clementine's weights as he made his preworkout rounds. "Feeling aggressive, huh?"

Based on what Tabitha had seen last time, Clementine was aggressive, maybe wanted to be able to lift more than she could safely just yet and would need someone to keep her in check.

"Well." Clementine puffed out a sigh and deadlifted the bar. "Yeah, that does feel a little heavy. I'll strip some weight."

"Good choice." Hobbs smiled and moved on to Tabitha. "How we doing, New Kid on the Block?"

Tabitha smiled, her opinion of Hobbs slowly changing. She did three cleans without him asking, just to prove she hadn't gone too heavy. To her surprise he said, "How are we feeling about going ten pounds heavier today? You're slinging that bar like it's the wild wild West, Annie Oakley."

Tabitha smiled, despite herself, and left to get a couple of five-pound plates.

After Hobbs shouted, "Three, two, one, go!" the next half an hour was a huge blur of booming hip-hop, sweat, pain and a heart that was racing for all the right reasons. When Tabitha was done, she crawled to the open bay door and collapsed in front of it, hoping for a summer breeze to cut through the thick humidity of the July twilight. She lay there, gasping, feeling good, feeling proud, as she'd used a barbell weight that was heavier than she'd ever used in a workout, even though it was way lighter than Clementine's and way, way lighter than Zoe's. Tabitha felt strong, felt a sense of control, like the foundation of her being was settling in, gaining footing, solidifying. She'd forgotten the power that lifting steel had on her soul.

Then something exploded.

The sound was loud, sudden and sustained.

A rational person would've known that it was fireworks. Tabitha had been hearing them all day. But that wasn't how her brain worked anymore.

One minute Tabitha was lying in the doorway, gasping and coming down off her workout high, and the next minute she was staring up at Hobbs, his eyes narrowed in concern, his body so close she could smell the sweetness of his laundry soap. The world came back to her in small increments, like a paint by number that slowly filled with color.

She was on her back, a comforting weight atop her chest. Something strong, and just as comforting, gripped her hand. As her brain unfogged, Tabitha's pulse slowed, and her lungs stopped squeezing shut like Ziploc bags sucked of all air. Trinity was lying across her chest, front paws draped over her shoulders, like she'd been trained to do. Hobbs was the one holding her hand. His palm and fingers were both rough and soft, offering gentle pressure that kept her grounded without overwhelming her.

Some time passed where nobody said anything and Tabitha just tried to find her voice. "I am the sky," she whispered, her eyes closing again. "I am the sky." She imagined herself a vast, endless blue, her anxiety nothing but a series of storm clouds that could be blown away.

"Damn straight you're the sky." All the teasing humor was gone from Hobbs's voice, but the inner warmth remained. His hand gave a gentle squeeze.

Tabitha felt her lungs opening as her heart wound down, the heavy thumps filling her ears. The scent of Trinity's fur bathed the inside of Tabitha's sinuses, making her pulse slow even more. After another minute or so, Tabitha said, "Off," and Trinity crawled away from her chest. Tabitha sat up, her head a little dizzy.

"Easy." Hobbs's free hand touched lightly on her back, steadying her.

Tabitha blinked rapidly. All the sweat had dried on her skin, which was cool and clammy. Zoe and Clementine were a couple of feet away, watching. Concern creased Clementine's face but Zoe had an encouraging smile on hers. "There you go," she said. "Feeling better? The fireworks stopped."

"Stopped?" Hobbs shot her a grin. "You mean you went across the street and threatened those kids with their life."

Zoe's lips twisted. "I made a gentle suggestion they go home to set off their fireworks. The park is not the place for things that light other things on fire."

"Uh-huh." Hobbs turned back to Tabitha. "You want some water?"

"Please."

Clementine was holding Tabitha's water bottle, collected from the spot on the floor where she'd worked out. All her equipment had been cleaned and put away. The floor, once littered with barbells, boxes and chalk was now spotless. The other woman who'd done the workout was in the far corner, stowing away the mop and bucket. She must've cleaned up all of Tabitha's stuff. Tabitha wondered how long she'd been on the ground, with Trinity on her chest. She felt guilty for not cleaning up her own equipment, but also grateful to everyone here, helping in some way. Clementine handed her the bottle and Tabitha took a long draw from the straw. The water opened up her throat and washed away the faint, prickly traces of panic that remained.

"Good girl," Hobbs said to Trinity, who sat nearby. "That was the damnedest thing." His eyes sparkled with appreciation. "Soon as your attack started, she was on top of your chest. Ran over and settled right in."

Tabitha reached out and petted Trinity's ear. The feel of her fur wiped away the last specks of panic. "It's called Deep Pressure Therapy. Pete helped me train Trinity to drape over my chest in the right situations."

"Pete?" Clementine stepped closer, her face relaxing. She settled on one knee and offered a smile. "Trinity is one of Pete's? Funny. My daughter works at the animal shelter. Pete goes there a lot."

"Really?" Tabitha looked Clementine over. "You don't seem old enough to have a daughter who works."

Clementine shrugged. "She's sixteen."

"If I ever have kids, I hope I look like you when my daughter is sixteen," Zoe piped in.

"No kidding," Tabitha agreed, glad for the distraction.

Clementine laughed and batted their comments away. "Hey," she said, steering the conversation back to Tabitha. "I'm sorry about those fireworks. Those had to be illegal. They scared me, and I don't mind loud noises."

"The world is always going to have explosions." Tabitha repeated something her therapist had said. "The way I deal with them will define me." Her words came out breathless, so she stopped talking. She stayed seated for a little while longer.

Eventually Clementine rose and Zoe collected her gear. The woman who'd cleaned up Tabitha's stuff appeared by her side.

"Thanks so much for doing that," Tabitha said. "I really appreciate it."

"It was nothing." She shrugged. "My name's Fariba, by the way."

"Tabitha. Nice to meet you."

"Same. You going to be okay?" Fariba had pretty eyes and a tentative smile.

Tabitha nodded. "Thanks again."

"You guys can take off," Hobbs said. "I'll stay put."

"G'night, everyone." Fariba collected her things and waved a hand as she headed for the door.

"Take it easy, Tabitha." Zoe offered her fist and Tabitha bumped it. "See you soon."

"Coming tomorrow?" Clementine gave a tentative smile.

"Probably. Thanks." Once they were gone, Tabitha turned to Hobbs, who'd released her hand but guarded the side that Trinity wasn't covering. "You probably have somewhere to be. I'm sorry. Give me just one more minute."

"I've got all night, Tabby," Hobbs said, the humor returning full force to his voice. "Take your time."

Tabby. Nobody called her that but Auntie El. Tabitha usually discouraged the nickname because it made her sound like an alley cat. "Don't you have a fireworks show to get to?" Tabitha felt herself gaining strength, all the atoms that made up her body normalizing between the steadying forces of Trinity on one side and Hobbs on the other.

"Nope." Hobbs shook his head. "There's a reason I'm coaching tonight. Rhett wanted to cancel. I offered to cover."

Tabitha wanted to know why he'd be one of the few Americans who didn't want to run around blowing things up on Independence Day, especially given his party personality, but she didn't want to pry. Then again, Hobbs had just seen her at her worst. "Why not? You seem like the kind of guy who'd be into noisy celebrations."

Hobbs laughed. "I know, right?" His easy grin fell away. "I just don't like this day. It's dumb."

Tabitha felt like there was more, but let it rest. She decided to test her legs. As she rose, Hobbs jumped up and offered his hand. She didn't need him for support, but she let him grasp her gently by the fingers anyway. She liked the feel of his sandpaper palms, gritty from so much barbell and gymnastics. He peered into her eyes. "Can you drive? You're welcome to hang out here for a while. I'm going to do paperwork." He nodded toward the office.

"I'll be okay."

"Alright." Hobbs released her. "Good job today on your workout. You're moving weight really easily. I expect big things."

Don't get your hopes up. The words rose but stopped at her lips. "Thanks," Tabitha said instead. "For everything." She nodded toward the bay, where she'd opened her eyes and found Hobbs staring down at her.

"Anytime, Tabby." Then he gave a wave and disappeared into the office, not one joke or flexing or clowning to be had.

Tabitha headed to her car with Trinity, feeling hollowed out but suddenly starving for Auntie El's chocolate brownies. This night had been unexpected, but the funny part was, she wasn't exactly sorry for it, either.

fifteen

Sean had never bought tofu in his life. The only vegetarian he had ever known had been a girl in high school named Karen who ate fish but claimed it didn't count because it "wasn't meat." When pressed with how she could be a vegetarian if she ate living creatures, albeit from the sea, she gave a lengthy explanation about grazing cows and methane emissions, plus chickens with shaved beaks crammed into small spaces, versus the freedom of the open ocean.

Even at that age, Sean had a good bullshit detector, which meant he knew that Delaney was probably the first real vegetarian he had known. Despite thinking he knew what a vegetarian was, he still texted her about a dozen times that day, making sure he was on the right track.

Are you vegetarian or vegan?

Vegetarian.

So you don't eat meat but you'll eat cheese and eggs?

Correct. Though I do get my cheese and eggs from a local farm, rather than the big chains.

So it's about the animals for you. You want them to be treated with respect.

I try to treat everyone with respect. We're all animals. I don't differentiate.

Sean realized he'd gone down a twisty, turny rabbit hole, one he would not mind spending more time in if Delaney was going to be there, but for now he just needed to know what to fix for dinner. He backpedaled out of the murky ethical swamp.

Ok. So no meat. But eggs, cheese, dairy, honey are all ok?

Honey? Are you using honey in your dish? #impressed

Shit. Not only did Delaney think he was using honey, she'd called tonight's dinner a *dish*. A dish implied a whole lot more than the current situation going on in Sean's kitchen, which involved a block of extra firm tofu, a couple bunches of broccolini—which he guessed was a fancy word for skinny broccoli—and white rice, which any idiot could pull off. He also had some fresh ginger and a couple cans of stir-fry vegetables, which had those baby corns you saw in Chinese takeout. Sean wasn't sure why he'd bought them, other than the baby corns seemed like the hallmark of stir-fry, which was what he was trying to pull off.

What's your favorite food?

Sean realized it was probably too late for that question, which should've come before the tofu, snobby broccoli and baby corns but it was probably too late for a lot of things, such as cultivating the ability to knock Delaney's socks off with his cooking skills.

Peanut butter.

"Seriously?" Sean tossed his phone down and glowered at his recipes. Not only could he have made Delaney a peanut butter sandwich without going grocery shopping, he knew exactly how to do it without poring over online videos.

Callie, who'd been prancing around the countertops, hoping Sean would stop what he was doing and feed her, glared at his sudden mood swing.

Sean had no idea how he was going to work peanut butter into his dish. He'd already spent more than an hour today watching the videos. He'd even bought a wok, thinking maybe this would prompt him to cook stir-fry more than just once. If he was wrong, the worst thing that happened was he was out sixty bucks trying to impress a beautiful woman.

He got out his mini blender, which he'd only used for protein shakes, and threw in some of the fresh ginger, chopped, along with a couple of garlic cloves and an assortment of things from jars, like soy sauce and rice vinegar. He squinted at the recipe on his iPad, trying to remember if the olive oil went in now or later, saw it was now, added it, then hit Blend. After a minute he opened up the blender, stuck in his pinky and gave it a taste. Not bad. He poured the marinade over the tofu, which he'd cubed into a bowl, and figured he just might pull this off. He'd eaten a crumble of the tofu earlier, and when it tasted like absolutely nothing, Sean had turned to the internet and found out that this was the whole point of tofu. It was supposed to taste like nothing. That was the magic, one article declared. With a little bit of preparation and a lot of playfulness, you could make tofu taste like anything you wanted!

"I don't know what's playful about it," Sean grumbled, "but the sauce is good." He stuffed the tofu into the fridge to marinate.

Last step was to clean. Callie watched, stiff in her cat statue pose, while Sean hustled around the apartment, dusting, vacuuming, swishing the toilet. He set the table with the nice dishes, which meant they weren't paper plates, but the actual dishes his sister, Mary, had given him after his divorce. They were blue with yellow and orange stripes. Mary said, "These are the most masculine dishes I have. I never use them," and set them on the counter of Sean's new bachelor pad, along with some groceries, a chocolate Bundt cake and two pieces of wall art, both religious in nature.

She'd regarded her little brother over her black-rimmed glasses and Sean had waited for a comment full of veiled disappointment that Sean hadn't stuck out his marriage with Kim. "Kim didn't have enough drive for you," Mary had said, surprising him. "It wasn't particularly noticeable until she refused to have your children and start a respectable family. I could tolerate her lounging and laziness before that, but after a certain age, that behavior becomes unseemly and unacceptable. I hope she finds her path, the good Lord willing, but I'm pleased you are no longer being led into Satan's Valley."

Sean hadn't known what to say to all that. In all his youth of being forced to go to church he'd not once figured out what Satan's Valley was, though it had always sounded a little pervy. One thing he did know was that of all the negative places you could be where Mary was concerned—the corner, the doghouse—Satan's Valley was the worst. She had too many years on him to be like a sister and was too busy being a mother to her own children to have much space to offer Sean. She approached raising him as a responsibility assigned by God, not to be questioned, only enacted with a firm hand. Sean had long ago stopped trying to connect with her and had just taken his relationship with his sister for what it was worth: lucky he hadn't been in the foster care system. "Okay," he'd said about the plates, the cake, the advice on Kim and the Jesus wall hanging. "Thanks."

Sean hadn't cared much at the time, but he was glad to have the dishes now. He couldn't serve Delaney tofu stir-fry on paper plates. He set out forks and napkins and then finished off the table with a vase full of pink and green flowers, hoping they would provide a distraction from the apartment, which was uncluttered but not superclean.

Callie broke her statue pose and leaned forward into a stretch, her eyes closing as she pushed her peach chin into the air. "You like it?" Sean stroked along her back as she purred. "Don't come around at dinner, expecting treats. There won't be any meat tonight."

She flopped on the counter and offered her tummy for pets.

"Very accommodating of you. Wish me luck."

Delaney rode the Rebel to Sean's apartment. The complex was in an older section of town, probably been there twenty years, with a crowded array of parking spots that weren't numbered. Delaney might've spent some time trying to find a spot, but that was another benefit of riding a motorcycle—you could park in places even the most compact of cars couldn't dare to go. She found a slot in the back of the complex, next to a streetlamp, and wedged herself near an old four-door with a sheet of plastic serving as the driver's side window. She removed her helmet and stripped her gloves, relieved to be free of them in this humidity, and used her mirror to fix her hair as best she could. She'd pinned it back before leaving home so mostly she just needed to revive the smashed helmet look. Once she was satisfied, Delaney turned to the building and wondered where number sixteen might be.

A group of teenagers milled around an old sedan across the lot, their cigarette smoke heavy on the summer wind and their laughter punctuated with curse words. The sounds of their voices slowed as she neared them, approaching a stairwell that had numbers and arrows, like halls in a hotel room. The teens gave Delaney a once-over while she found number sixteen. They looked like they might call out, whistle or make a comment, but then, as was often the case, they thought better of it, based on whatever they saw. They resumed their conversation as she climbed the stairs to the second level. In a dark hallway that reeked of tobacco and spicy food she found Sean's place—a red door with black numbers—and rapped with her knuckles.

Scuffing came from inside. When the door opened, the spicy smell that had rimmed the stale odors of the hallway bloomed. Ginger. Soy. Peppers. Music from somewhere inside rode out on the aromas, like the tail on a kite.

"Stir-fry?"

Sean, dressed in jeans and a Nationals T-shirt, held the door open with his back and ushered her inside. "Good guess," he said, looking a little disappointed that she'd ruined the surprise.

"Smells great." Delaney looked him up and down, deciding she could add another persona to her list. Along with Gym Sean, Detective Sean and Runner Sean there was now Just Sean, the one who might lie closest to his core. Just a guy in denim and cotton, barefoot, puttering around his kitchen, making stir-fry. "Where can I put these?" Delaney held up the helmet and gloves.

Sean took them from her and set them on a table next to a lamp with a cheap plastic shade. Delaney peeled off her riding jacket, then bent down and stripped her boots, leaving them by the front door before she followed Sean deeper inside. The music grew louder, sounded like jazz. The apartment wasn't unlike her own, with one large space, the kitchen bleeding into the living room, which held an old tan sofa, a matching love seat, a coffee table and a bookshelf. A giant flat-screen television was mounted on the wall facing the couch. A couple of other doors at the far end probably led to a bedroom and a bath.

"You didn't have to do that." Sean eyed her feet, then his own. "I'm not worried about my floors. I just hate shoes."

"Me, too." Delaney looked down at the worn hardwood, which had a randomly thrown rug here and there. "Ever since I lived in Hawai'i, the shoes come off at the door. Unless I'm working in the shop."

"Fine by me." Sean spread his arms out. "Make yourself comfortable."

Delaney tried to orient herself to the decor and the way that things were arranged, but she couldn't get a solid foothold. Half of the apartment screamed bachelor pad—the giant TV, the keys and wallet tossed carelessly on an end table, the old furniture. But then there was a random sprinkling of homey touches that didn't quite fit, like pretty blue pot holders hung over the stove, in pristine condition; a shelf of knickknacks on the wall opposite the television, which looked like glass clowns in different poses; and a cross-stitched wall hanging of a Bible verse, peeking from the short amount of wall space between the living room and bedroom door. After a quick thought back to her conversation with Sean over whiskey,

Delaney came to a conclusion: Sean's sister, Mary, had helped him decorate when he first moved in. He'd put up the clowns and the cross-stitch out of respect, in case she visited, or, not really caring, he simply hadn't bothered to take them down.

There was a sink full of dishes and the remnants of whatever Sean had cooked up for dinner was all over the countertops like a vegetable murder scene: garlic skins and broccoli stems on a wooden cutting board, empty cans overturned in haste, a small blender coated in a dark sauce. On the stove, where Sean had his back to her while he put on his finishing touches, was a covered saucepan which had bubbled white starch down the sides and onto the burners, and a wok that looked brand-new, despite the food inside. Sean gave it all a big stir. "Go ahead and pour whatever you'd like to drink," he said over the sizzling of the food. "I put a pitcher of water and a bottle of wine on the table." He pointed in the direction of wherever they were going to dine.

Delaney found the table, tucked in a nook just behind the kitchen and across from the living room. No matter what the rest of the apartment looked like, the sight before her made her exhale softly. Atop a small wooden table Sean had set out dishes that were bright blue, yellow and orange. Polished flatware had been carefully set to the right of one plate and the left of another, atop linen napkins that had been folded in half. There was a wineglass and a water glass for each setting. In the middle of the table, near their plates, was a clear, sweaty pitcher of ice water with lemon slices floating on top and a bottle of rosé with a corkscrew next to it. Right smack in the middle of the table was a frosted mint vase holding a couple dozen pink and green roses. At first, Delaney thought they might be separate flowers, but upon closer inspection she could see that the roses were a soft dogwood green in the center that slowly got pinker until the final outer rim of petals was the color of cotton candy. She stared at the flowers for a moment, suddenly able to catch their sweet aroma, and wondered if there was any way Sean could've possibly known that pink and green was her favorite color combination or if this had been a random coincidence.

"Feel free to open the wine." Sean came around the corner, bearing a bowl of white rice and a much larger bowl of stir-fry. He set both on the table, right in two blank spots that had obviously been reserved for the food.

Delaney grabbed the blush and the corkscrew and filled each glass a third of the way, then filled each water glass to the top. Sean had disappeared back into the kitchen when something furry brushed Delaney's thighs. She looked down to see an orange-and-black calico cat standing in the chair next to one of the place settings.

"I hope you aren't allergic." Sean was back, holding two small spoons. "That's Callie."

"Not at all." Delaney reached out to see if the cat was interested in getting petted. She stretched her neck out and rubbed the side of her mouth across Delaney's knuckles. Delaney turned her hand over and let it run over Callie's ears, then her neck. One hand, then two. The petting was gradual. Delaney's experience with cats had been that "different strokes for different folks" was literal with them. Some liked the rump petted, others their ears, some wanted belly pets if they flopped over and offered it, and others most certainly did not and were only showing you their belly, not inviting touching.

Callie seemed to like it all. She flopped slowly, like a fish, from side to side, showing the light peach fur on her belly as she stretched out her legs.

Sean went to the opposite side of the table, where the place setting had the utensils to the right of the plate, and rested his hand on the back of the chair. "Callie." Sean spoke sternly to the cat. "Let the lady have a seat."

In true cat fashion, Callie completely ignored him.

Delaney laughed. She admired a man who was openly into cats, and it was no surprise to her that Sean was one of them. Cats appealed to people who liked a challenge, a mystery to solve, the quiet beneath the storm. Men who used animals as ornaments to proclaim their toughness, such as owning a pit bull just because of the fighting reputation attached, made her skin crawl. Delaney lifted Callie gently from the chair and set her on the floor. The cat arched her back and flicked her tail as she stalked away. "She's miffed," Delaney said with a chuckle as she slid into the vacant chair.

"She'll get over it." Sean took his own seat and pointed at the food. "It's tofu, fancy broccoli and some other veggies. I'm not going to lie, it's my first stir-fry. I hope you like it."

"It looks great." Delaney caught the sweet and sour smells of the food and felt her stomach growl. She took a large helping of rice and passed it to Sean. Then she loaded up on stir-fry and went to lift her fork. That's when she noticed the tiny spoon. Right next to her fork was a dessert spoon with a scoop of peanut butter, done in a fancy swirl. That must've been what Sean had carried in after he brought in the meal.

"You said your favorite food was peanut butter," Sean said sheepishly, when he noticed Delaney had been looking at the spoon for a really long time. "I didn't know how to incorporate it into the, uh—" he gestured at the stir-fry "—the 'dish'—" he made air quotes "—so I did that." He pointed at the spoon. "I saw it on a cooking show. The chef put the dessert into these little spoons. It was some kind of cake, like a single bite of cake with one berry on top, sitting in the spoon. I remember thinking, how stupid. Who eats one bite of cake? But the idea came in handy today."

Delaney couldn't take her eyes off the spoon. When she finally looked up, Sean had a nervous smile plastered on his face. "That was really dumb, wasn't it?" he said. "I thought back and forth on it and, judging by your face, I think I made the wrong choice."

Delaney wanted to laugh, but she didn't want Sean to think she was laughing *at* him. Who would laugh at a guy who went to the trouble to find out what your favorite food was, and, faced with peanut butter, decided to swirl it on fancy dessert spoons? Not to mention that Delaney's fancy dessert spoon was to the left of her plate, along with her fork and napkin, while Sean's utensils were in the traditional spot, to the right. Which meant that Sean had noticed, at some point, that Delaney was left-handed, and he'd placed her spoon and fork accordingly. No, she most definitely wasn't going to laugh at him.

She picked up the spoon and stuck it in her mouth, sucking off all the peanut butter. "Top-notch peanut butter." Delaney rolled the spoon around in her fingers. "I detect Jif creamy, full-fat peanut butter, from a twenty-eight-ounce jar. No graininess or excessive oiliness, with a bright peanut finish."

Sean smiled, looking both amused and relieved. "You are correct. Except it's a forty-ounce jar. I love peanut butter, too."

"Smart man."

Sean's face relaxed, the worry draining away. "You're not supposed to eat dessert first."

"Haven't you figured it out yet?" Delaney gave her spoon one more lick for good measure. "I'm a rebel."

Sean snorted. "I've had a hint or two." He pointed at her plate. "Try the tofu. I'm dying to know if I did it right." He scooped some up and tentatively put it in his mouth. Sean's nose wrinkled as he chewed and swallowed.

"You're not giving me confidence," Delaney joked as the steam from her plate rolled over her face. She scooped a bite onto her fork and slipped the tines in her mouth. The ginger and garlic came immediately, spicy and hot. Nice crunch to the broccoli, which was bright green in color so had delivered on its promise. The tofu squished on her tongue, imparting less of the ginger flavor than the veggies, but still had a creamy feel that wasn't unpleasant. "The sauce is great," she said. "And who can resist baby corns?" She stabbed one with her fork and stuck it in her mouth. "Remember that scene from *Big*?"

The lines around Sean's eyes crinkled. "When Tom Hanks is at the cocktail party?"

"And he nibbles on the little corn?" Delaney finished.

Sean leaned back in his chair. "Tell me the secret, Delaney." The way he used her first name so casually, all formality stripped away, sent a tingle up her spine. "Tell me the secret of this tofu. Because I'm eating this stir-fry and all I'm thinking is how good it would taste with some chicken."

Delaney choked on her food, giggling. "Okay," she said, setting her fork down. "First, let me just say that I think you went above and beyond on your end of the deal. You agreed to cook me dinner if you lost the race and you did that. In spades. You made a sauce and chopped up veggies and…and… *bought a wok*."

Sean forked in some more of his food and chewed through it, a half smile on his face. "Guilty," he said. "But. Tell me your secret with this stuff." He played with the cubes of tofu with his fork. "Be honest. I can take it."

"I'm being honest." Delaney took another bite and legitimately enjoyed it. "This is all amazing. But we vegetarians aren't as complicated as we seem. I'm actually really easy to please. If you had served me a grilled cheese sandwich, I'd still be a happy girl."

"Damn." Sean slammed his fist playfully on the tabletop.

"I knew it! Soon as you texted 'peanut butter' I knew I had overcomplicated things."

Delaney sipped her wine and smiled into her glass. "Let me simplify this," she said, leaning back and swirling the rose-colored liquid around. "You can give me bread and cheese. Pasta. Peanut butter. A simple salad with a splash of lemon juice and vinegar. Popcorn. Cheese and crackers." She shrugged. "People act like vegetarians are hard to please, but I'm quite the opposite. It's a lot easier to smear peanut butter on whole wheat bread than it is to grill a steak. But, if you're going to get fancy and make tofu, I can offer you some tips."

Sean lifted his glass and drained his wine. "I'm all ears." He poured some more blush into both their glasses, then leaned back in his chair and stretched his arms behind his head, making his heavily muscled torso strain against the Nationals T-shirt. "I sincerely want to know the mystery of this substance."

Delaney cleaned the last bite off her plate, enjoying the ginger and garlic and the crisp broccoli, before she laid her fork down and leaned forward on her elbows and whispered, "Paper towels."

Sean narrowed his eyes, a smile tickling the corners of his mouth while he sipped his wine. "Wait. What?"

Delaney wished she had more peanut butter, but resisted telling Sean how he could have worked it into the dish by making it Thai stir-fry. "I know you marinated your tofu," she said. "I can taste the delicious sauce. But, in order for tofu to take in the flavors you have to get all the moisture out first. You can do that by wrapping the tofu in layers of paper towels and plopping something heavy on top. I usually use a cast-iron pan. Let it sit half an hour. You'll be surprised how much moisture comes out. Some brands are drier than others."

Sean was quiet a moment, sipping his wine, his face straight and thoughtful. "That makes a lot of sense," he finally said. "My recipe didn't mention that."

Delaney shrugged. "Your dish was delicious anyway. This is just an insider tip from a woman who's been around the tofu block a few times."

Sean smiled at her joke. "A tip I will not need unless you want to have dinner with me again. Because I stick to my guns." He gestured at his empty plate. "This would have been amazing with chicken."

Delaney loaded her plate with more rice and more stir-fry and lifted her fork. "I think it's amazing just like it is."

"The flowers are beautiful," Delaney said, after she'd cleaned her plate for the second time. "I've never seen roses this color before." She studied the bouquet in the center of the table and looked like she wanted to say more, but didn't. Had she noticed that Sean had chosen flowers that matched that quilt on her sofa? All soft pinks and mint greens. He'd seen that quilt and had known that there was no way the blanket was resting on the sofa in her studio apartment unless she loved the colors. She didn't have enough evident female family to have made the blanket and handed it down, which meant she'd bought it somewhere because she found it comforting, a feeling she'd had to cultivate on her own most of her life. Sean both did and didn't want her to notice that he'd noticed.

"Thanks," Sean said. "They caught my eye when I was food shopping. There's a flower shop near the grocery store." He offered Delaney his untouched spoon of peanut butter and she didn't even pretend that she didn't want it. Once she'd polished that off, Sean faced her with a little more seriousness. "I checked a few things out after our run yesterday, and this morning before I started my tofu adventure." He paused to smile. "The cigarette butt from Walt is the same brand—Newports—as the butts we found out back of your shop. I wanted to find out more about him, but Walt notably left off his last name when he introduced himself the other evening and he didn't sign your registry. None of that necessarily means anything. A lot of people smoke Newports, and Walt doesn't seem like the kind of guy that would sign your registry anyway."

"You don't think old Walt had anything to do with this?"

Sean shrugged. "I suspect everyone. It's my job. Just give me time. I also made a phone call to each of the guys who worked with your father at the shop in Omaha. Not only do I know they had nothing to do with the theft, I take pity on the fool who ever messes with you. Those guys were more interested in making sure I was doing right by you than in that missing bike."

Delaney flashed a knowing smile. "Yeah. My uncles are something else. But hey, I didn't expect to talk about the bike tonight. You've been working your butt off, even when you're not on shift. I really appreciate it, especially since I know the odds…" She trailed off, not finishing a sentence that Sean knew wasn't hopeful.

"Hey." Sean wanted to reach out and cover her hand with his, where it rested on the table, just long enough to get her to look at him and stop staring sadly into space. But he held back. "I'm going to find that bike. Mark my words."

Delaney nodded. "I trust you. And not to sound ungrateful, but it would be amazing if we could find it before the Classic Motorcycle Show. I was really counting on entering '33 to get that exposure for my shop. Like, *banking* on it, if you catch my drift."

"I've been to that." Sean remembered going with Kim many years ago. She'd complained about the heat and the bad food from the vendors and the day spent staring at "stupid machines." Her attitude had killed any joy Sean might've other-wise found in the event and he'd never gone back.

"It looks like a fun time. I'm going either way, but my plans to enter Dad's bike are obviously shot to hell unless it magically reappears. And the local show was the clincher that made me buy the shop. I thought with the cash prize and the exposure in the magazine, I could pull it off." She sort of laughed at herself, but there was no humor in it. "Anyway. Moving off the bike." Delaney stuck her fork into the stir-fry bowl and snagged another piece of tofu, chewing it slowly.

"I'm glad you're enjoying your victory. You earned it."

"I've been enjoying my victory for two days now," she admitted. "I went to Red's house and got a massage today."

"Red's the best," Sean said. "A massage is a massage, I guess. I haven't had enough to know. But there's something different about her. She really seems to know exactly what your muscles need."

"Not just the muscles." Delaney sipped at her second glass of wine. "I felt like I was in this unusual kind of altered state. Not exactly sleep but definitely not awake. I remembered things I'd forgotten about but I was able to view them with a different lens. Kind of like an onlooker rather than being immersed in the moment. It was really..." she tilted her head from side to side "...cathartic."

"Yeah." Sean was glad to have someone else articulate what he'd also experienced during some of Red's massages. "That."

"Sunny was there, too. She got a massage before me. We talked a little bit and she's going to let me see Wyatt. I know it's weird, but I kind of miss him. Pete's had him awhile and he says Wyatt's sad. I guess once in a while Pete gets a dog with an indomitable will and they're hard to train. He says Wyatt has a deep-rooted anxiety due to abandonment."

"I don't think it's weird. You were out saving the dog when

the bike got stolen. The dog and the motorcycle are forever wired together in your brain." Sean tapped his temple with a forefinger.

"Look at you, getting all shrinkie on me." Delaney switched out her wine for her water. "I guess that's what makes you a good detective. You get into people's heads."

"I never thought about it like that." Sean wasn't sure if anyone had ever told him to his face that he was a good detective. "But thanks." The word *hard-ass* was used often. *Relentless* had been tossed around a lot, not just in his years on the police force, but his whole life, dating back to the day in middle school when someone had stolen his lunch money during PE and he'd launched an intensive manhunt, including clue collecting and interviews of his peers, and his sister had told him that if he was going to be relentless about something, it might as well be for the greater good. "Hey, did you really get your massage for free?"

"I did. I offered Red a huge tip but she refused that, too."

"Red doesn't do it for the money."

"Yeah, I picked up on that. I really hope Tabitha goes in for hers."

"How's she doing? Were you guys close at Camp Leatherneck?"

"No. I only met her once. One single, horrible day. That's one of the memories I was able to examine during the massage, in fact."

Sean waited. If Delaney wanted to tell him more, she would. If not, so be it.

"Tabitha was the chaplain's assistant." Delaney switched back to her wine. "Navy." Delaney searched his face, maybe trying to decide how closely Sean might know what she was talking about. "It was a long time ago. But I guess sometimes time doesn't heal all things." She stared into space, over Sean's shoulder. There was a window there, but he doubted she was gazing off into the parking lot littered with stray teens who suffered from lack of parental supervision. "The day I met Tabitha, her convoy had hit an IED. The chaplain had been out doing a special service in the field." Delaney shrugged. "Me and my guys went out to transport them back. See about repairing the vehicle." She looked Sean dead in the eye. "The chaplain got shrapnel in the leg. Got banged around pretty good. Was knocked out, when I got there."

The pieces of the puzzle slowly fell into place for Sean. Chaplains, or religious program specialists, as they were called now, weren't allowed to carry or use weapons. Chaplains had assistants, like Tabitha, who had many duties—one of which was to be the chaplain's bodyguard.

"There was nothing she could've done about it," Delaney said, as though she read Sean's mind. "But I can see her taking that very hard. I know I would."

"Did the chaplain die?"

"No." Delaney's brow wrinkled. "That's what's odd. I mean, I get how Tabitha might feel she failed in her job to protect the chaplain, even if there was nothing she could've done to stop it. But as far as I know, he lived. He was going to have some serious problems the rest of his life, but he was alive when he was sent home."

Sean rolled the pieces of the puzzle around in his mind. "I wonder if he passed away recently." The words slipped out. For a second, Sean forgot he wasn't alone, sitting in his office or his cop van, slowly putting the clues together. "Tabitha's anxiety is really, really fresh. There has to be a recent trigger. I bet you money the chaplain died recently."

Delaney's expression flickered and changed, her eyes widening. "He did take a pretty good hit to the head. The kind of thing that didn't kill him right away but certainly could take its toll over the years."

"Bet you money," Sean repeated. "And now Tabitha is reliving that day all over again. With fresh guilt."

"You like to make bets don't you?" Delaney switched once again to her water and smiled over the rim of the glass.

"Bad habit. I avoid casinos." Sean smiled back, glad to have the levity back in the room, then rose and collected the empty dishes and utensils. He was trying to decide how much that day might've shook up Delaney, but other than concern for Tabitha, she seemed unfazed.

Delaney followed him into the kitchen. "I can't wait to see what you fix for dinner when I win the half-marathon."

"The what?" Sean froze, plates in hand.

"That's the next level, right?" Delaney leaned against the counter and got a devilish little smile on her face. "I beat you at a 5K, a 10K, and the next level up is a half."

"You did not beat me at the 5K." Sean shoved the plates onto the only empty spot left near his sink. "And I am not running a half-marathon anytime soon."

Delaney laughed, opened his dishwasher and stuck her hand out for a plate. Looked like she was unwittingly on board with Sean's new habit of keeping his living and workspaces tidy. Thank God the dishwasher was empty. He would have been embarrassed if it had a week's worth of dirty plates, but luckily Sean rarely even bothered with the dishwasher. He just didn't make enough of a mess eating oatmeal, ham and cheese sandwiches, and loaded salads from the salad bar in the grocery store.

"Now that I think about it, the only half-marathons I've run have been in training. I did run the Marine Corps Marathon a couple times," Sean said. "Back when I was still an active duty marine. But that was ages ago."

Delaney's head popped up from her task of layering the dishes in the dishwasher. "I knew you were a marine." She wore a look of triumph on her face. "Even though you never said so."

"Before I became a cop," Sean said. "I was in Fallujah with Santos. We were just kids back then. We thought we were so tough. Which is probably a good thing, because when I look back on it now, I'm amazed we didn't lose our minds. Or at least shit our pants."

"Oh." Delaney's voice got softer, like she'd had an *aha* moment. "That's what this is." Delaney ran her fingertip near her left eye, right where Sean had his scar.

Sean contained his surprise by facing the sink. Nobody ever noticed that scar. If they did, they didn't bring it up. "Nah," he said. "I got that falling off my bike when I was a kid."

After he'd finished with the plates and utensils, Sean began handing over the dishes in the sink, and they methodically loaded the dishwasher like an old married couple. "I see," she said. "Did falling off your bike come with anything lasting? Like, I have a bad habit of driving down the middle of lonely roads, instead of the edges, because of IEDs. It's reflexive at this point and I've been pulled over a few times because of it. From, you know—" she took a long time accepting a bowl he'd offered, forcing him to look at her "—falling off my bike."

They were quiet for a minute, nothing but the clinking of dishes and soft rush of water from the faucet as Sean rinsed everything he passed over. "I saw the guy who tried to kill me. That's the clearest memory I have of that moment. Someone yelled 'sniper.' I scanned. Saw the insurgent through the window of a building. He was wearing blue. Then there was just this blinding white light. My helmet is the only reason I'm not dead."

Delaney's movements slowed. Her gaze went to the vicinity of Sean's scar.

"I get dizzy sometimes and I'm not a very deep sleeper, but it used to be a lot worse. It's a part of who I am, but it doesn't run my life."

Delaney slid bowls and glasses inside the dishwasher, arranging them much neater than Sean ever would.

"Red's massages help a lot," he admitted. "Though I've never told her about it. Santos might have, though. After I've had a massage I sleep so good that night. The effect lasts for about a week."

"I'll sleep like a baby tonight," Delaney said. "I can feel that massage, settling in my bones. I'll sleep and I won't think about the bike or the dog. I won't smell sand and motor oil in my dreams, either."

Sean grunted, followed by the hiss of water.

After a long round of quiet Delaney steered the conversation back to running. "I ran the Marine Corps Marathon, too. At Camp Leatherneck. The route is Leatherneck, Bastion and the flight line."

Sean stuck his fingers in the faucet and flicked water in her face, making her blink, both from the water and in surprise. "Why do you always have to one-up me?"

She grinned and swiped her face with her palm. Sean handed her the wok and she gave him the *Are you serious?* face so he put it back on the counter.

"I bet training for that was fun."

Delaney groaned. "It's insane. Not just because of the heat. You're at three thousand feet above sea level, the roads are either gravel or moon dust, and you're sucking in sand and smoke and fumes for miles. Add to that a high op tempo and it gets tough. But." She shrugged. "At least we got to run. It's a much less crowded race than the one in DC, that's for sure.

You're never elbowing a guy in a superhero costume or gag-ging on the perfume of the chick across from you."

"Silver linings." Sean went to hand her the chef's knife he'd used to chop the broccoli and again Delaney shook her head.

"You don't put good knives in the dishwasher." She caught his wrist and peeked at the knife. "This is a Wüsthof. Which you probably just bought. And you're trying to put it in the dishwasher. Were you raised in a barn?"

"No." He stared down at her. "But *you* probably were. Omaha."

She smiled and squeezed his wrist tight. Sean smiled back. He didn't even try to pull away. A quiet moment passed as they both realized the space that had closed between them had happened too quickly to notice. He glanced down and saw the light glinting off the Wüsthof, her slender fingers looking delicate against his forearm. It was no surprise to Sean that when he finally got close to the wildcat with whiskey-colored eyes there was an eight-inch knife in the mix.

Delaney slid her hand from his wrist to the knife, which she slipped from his fingers. She set it on the counter, then edged a little closer, officially eliminating any space between them. Sean's body had an immediate physical reaction to her thighs brushing against his and her fingertips softly tracing the inside of his palm where the knife once was. Not only had it been a long time since he'd been this close to a woman, he'd been thinking about being this close to this woman ever since he'd laid eyes on her, so the intensity was a double blow. Blood rushed everywhere.

"Tell me something, Detective." Delaney's voice was low and soft, matching the simmering heat Sean could feel com-ing from the parts of her body that touched his. "The flow-ers. Why did you buy them?"

"I thought you'd think they were pretty," he mumbled. At

least, that's what he thought he said. Ask him tomorrow, he might remember something else. Right now he was too busy trying to keep his hands to himself. When it came to women, Sean was always the one to make the first move. But like the other night in Delaney's apartment, the last thing he wanted to do was repeat his past mistakes, come on too strong and mess everything up.

"They are pretty," she agreed, even as she ran both of her hands up his arms, to his shoulders, where her palms flattened out and fingers spread. She pressed in tighter until Sean's back was flush against the counter. "But why did you buy *those* flowers?"

"They were pink and green," Sean said, unaware he was going to admit that until the words left his mouth. "Those are your favorite colors, right?" There was a chance that he was wrong. That he'd interpreted the quilt on her couch all wrong. Watch. It was probably some old thing she'd used as cushion to pack boxes during all her years of moving and had just never gotten rid of.

Her grip on his shoulders tightened. "They are my favorite colors. Not by themselves, so much. The combination of them. There's just something about them when they're together." She cocked her head to the side. "How did you know that?"

Sean shrugged. "I guessed. The quilt on your couch is pink and green."

She smiled, then leaned in close, her breasts now against his chest. If he hadn't been stupid before, Sean was about to get really stupid now. Not a sane thought entered his head as Delaney leaned in and trailed her lips over his, not really touching so much as grazing, like a teasing invitation. She smelled like the wind, her motorcycle shop, freshly washed hair. He wasn't exactly sure from which direction she was coming—if she'd just given him a really sexy hug or a sweet little kiss. The edges were all blurred and soft, like her body and her personality.

Sean went with his instincts. He could only hold back so long. He slid one hand to the back of her neck, the other resting against her rib cage. He ran his thumb along her jaw, pulled her tighter. Whether she'd wanted this to be a real kiss or not, whether he was working on her case or not, Sean was not about to lose the opportunity to finally get a taste of the woman he'd fantasized about for many lonely nights.

Delaney made a little noise of surprise, had just pressed closer, as though egging him on, when a sudden, loud noise from the countertop made her jolt in his embrace. Delaney squeezed her arms tight around him and froze. After a couple of seconds she pulled back as Sean looked over her shoulder.

The brand-new wok, still unwashed, was on the floor, along with a few stray vegetables that had been knocked free, and a smattering of oil over the linoleum. Above, perched proudly on the counter, her tail flicking as she looked down on her handiwork, was Callie.

Delaney's body slackened. She broke away, leaving Sean feeling cold and frustrated as her blurred edges parted from his. "Your cat is mad," she said, her voice raspy. "She just threw your new wok on the floor."

Sean let out a long exhale as he bent over and retrieved the wok. His pounding heart knocked in his ears and his blood slowly slithered back into place. He rested the wok on the counter, next to the cat, and gave her a stern look. "Oh, now you want to throw things on the floor?" he scolded. "Not at 0500 when I need it."

Delaney laughed and reached out to her. Callie immediately pressed into Delaney's hand and accepted pets. "You little devil," she said. Callie flopped on the counter and stretched.

After a few more pets Delaney turned to him and offered a rueful smile. "I better get going. Early day at the shop."

Sean kept his crushing disappointment to himself, even though the cat had probably done him a favor. His divorce was only a year old and his attempt to squelch his habit of rushing into things headlong was failing. As Delaney turned her back and headed for her helmet and gloves, he glared at the cat. "We'll talk later," he hissed as he followed behind Delaney.

"Dinner was great," Delaney said as she stuffed her feet into her boots. "Thanks for having me."

"You earned it." Sean lifted her jacket and held it open. His body was normalizing, more and more sentience returning to his brain. It was the same sort of aftershock he experienced after chasing down a suspect, except now he wasn't relieved and didn't welcome the sensations. "Anytime you want peanut butter on a dessert spoon," he joked, hoping to cover his disappointment at having her jerked from his arms so quickly, "you know where to come."

Delaney slid her arms into her jacket and grabbed her helmet. "Highlight of the dinner," she said with a grin.

"Liar."

She grew quiet for a moment, her eyes traveling over his torso, then back up to his lips, then his eyes. "Bring the Harley in," she said. "I'll look at it even though you lost the race."

"Really? You're serious?"

"Sure." She tilted her chin up, a twinkle in her eye. "I'll check out your Willie, Detective. Get her purring again."

Heat crept up the back of Sean's neck, his body doing a sudden reversal. "Alright, then. I'll bring her in soon."

"Good." Delaney's hand rested on the doorknob. "I'll make room for her in my shop. Give her a diagnostic and then see what needs fixing."

"That's really nice of you. I haven't ridden the Willie in a long time."

She bit down on her lower lip, near the corner of her mouth, and sort of snorted a laugh. "Understood."

Sean laughed softly and glanced out at the setting sun. July had arrived with a lazy report, rolling in on the fading flowers, sometimes hot, seldom cool, with longer days and thicker air. "Ride home safe."

"Always."

Delaney hit the road, determined to let the evening wind and cooler temps blow away the residual desire running through her veins. She hadn't planned on kissing Sean tonight, or any night. Relationships were not Delaney's forte. She'd never stuck around long enough to establish roots, either for herself or anybody else. On top of that, she didn't exactly have the female role model necessary to show her how a woman might behave in a healthy, long-term relationship. But after tonight's dinner, Delaney had to admit that she might've met her match. No, Sean hadn't won the race. But he'd damn well won something with how well he'd reacted to being on the losing end of a bet. Tasked with making dinner, he'd gone above and beyond, finding out what she liked to eat and then doing his best to provide it. He'd bought a wok, for God's sake. He'd handled tofu, with no prior experience. That had to earn him some kind of gold star.

In the end, Delaney admitted that either the flowers or the peanut butter spoon had been the tipping point for her. Who else would have the balls to act on either one of those impulses? Good detective or no, that was quite the deduction he'd pulled off based on an old quilt tossed on the back of her sofa. And the peanut butter spoon? Delaney sputtered a laugh into her helmet. Who would really do that?

Sean was a risk-taker. That much was obvious. She counted herself lucky that the cat had interrupted their intimate moment before things went too far. Not that she hadn't wanted to go far. She really, really had. But...then what? Relationships came and went, and by the time you started getting on each other's nerves and looking for a way out, it was usually time for the next deployment. Problem solved.

This time, there would be no deployment. This time, Delaney might be here to stay. If there was one thing Delaney hadn't learned how to do over the course of her nomadic life, it was *stay*.

She idled at a stoplight, almost home. Only now that the wind had cooled her off did her desire sink like the setting sun before her. She shook off all thoughts of being in Sean's arms before she got herself all worked up again. The light changed, and just as she started to edge her bike through the stoplight, she saw it.

At first, she thought her eyes were playing tricks. But even later, she would close her eyes and relive the moment when she sat in the deep orange glow of sunset, her gaze on the flow of traffic coming from the opposite direction, and she would come to the same conclusion. Even if her eyes had deceived her, her ears had not. There was no mistaking that sound.

The sound of that motorcycle, flying through the intersection, heading south while she was headed north, with no way to turn around and give chase.

The Indian Four.

sixteen

Constance said she worked out of her basement, and had given Tabitha the address. Tabitha drove out deep into the recesses of Dogwood County, mostly untouched by development, taking a long, winding country road to Constance's house. She parked in the gravel driveway of the wooden two-story home, which was getting on in years but kept freshly painted and in good order. The entrance to Healing Touch Massage was marked with a sign on the back gate, which opened to a flagstone path lined by dogwood trees whose white flowers with green centers had probably bloomed and died off a couple months ago. Stretching their necks in between the trees were orange tiger lilies and patches of impatiens. A sign on the glass door indicated that Healing Touch was open.

Tabitha stepped inside the cool air-conditioning and was met by the aromas of eucalyptus and lavender. Soft music played over hidden speakers, punctuated by the squeak of

Tabitha's sneakers over the wood floor. The entire space had
been decked out professionally, including a sofa and chairs that
surrounded a round table with a spread of magazines. Tabitha
sank to the cushions and lifted one about fitness. She tried to
read an article about the "Five Best Stretches for a Woman's
Hips," but she couldn't focus.

The problem with massages, or things like getting your
hair done, or your teeth cleaned, was you had to let people lay
their hands on you, touch your body, get inside your head. On
top of that, Auntie El had raised Tabitha to "do for herself"
as soon as she could walk. It wasn't an easy thing to allow a
stranger to floss her teeth, massage her scalp or rub oil into
her skin. She didn't even like eating out, because telling the
waiter what she wanted to eat for dinner seemed too intimate.

Yet, here she was, sitting in Constance's waiting room,
on a nice plush sofa, bathed in the sounds of spa music. Delaney had talked her into it, had texted Tabitha yesterday after
her own massage and told Tabitha she'd be crazy not to take
Red up on her offer for a free session. Tabitha agreed, only
because she thought it would take a while for Constance to
fit her in, but as soon as Tabitha texted, Constance found an
opening for the next day. Now here she sat, regretting that
impulse. Twice, Tabitha almost got up and left, but she kept
herself rooted when Trinity gave her a huff each time. How
the dog could possibly know such things, Tabitha had no
idea, but she'd come to trust Trinity implicitly. "Okay," she
agreed. "I'll stay."

Trinity settled down, head between her paws, just as Constance appeared around the corner. She looked smart and professional, which was pretty much how she looked at the gym.
The only difference was she wore navy blue scrubs, like a
nurse, instead of fitness gear. She had her hair back in her usual
ponytail and carried the same calm, open aura that seemed to

start deep inside of her and radiated outward. "Tabitha!" She smiled wide. "You're here. I'm so glad."

Tabitha wondered if Constance greeted all of her clients that way. When people made appointments, they were expected to show up, yet Constance's tone hinted at a whole lot of pleasant surprise. Tabitha tried to imagine her dentist getting that excited over her showing up on time, and she had to stifle a laugh.

"And Trinity." Constance stepped closer to the dog without attempting to pet her. "Good to see you again. I remember when you were just a pup, fighting Neo and Morpheus for nipples."

Now Tabitha did laugh. All the building tension left her body in an eruption of chuckles as she pictured the characters from *The Matrix* fighting for nursing rights.

Constance laughed with her, then nodded at her computer. "I looked over your intake form." Constance took a seat across from her. "And everything seems to be in order. Not pregnant. Not sick. No allergies."

Tabitha shook her head to all as her laughter wound down.

"Anything you'd like to focus on today?"

"Ummm." As the rest of her humor died off, Tabitha started to sweat. Her palms got clammy and her armpits damp, which then made her anxious that she'd have sweaty armpits for her massage, which then made her sweat more.

Constance walked over to a sink in the corner and proceeded to wash her hands. "Any preference for how we start the massage? Face up or down?"

"Does it make a difference?"

"Depends," she said, over the rush of the water. "Some people prefer to start face up so that any anxiety they may have will be massaged away by the time they have to flip over and put their face in the cradle."

Tabitha sorted through that comment and realized that Constance had just masterfully told Tabitha that if she had any PTSD—about her military experience or anything else in her life—then it would be just fine with her if Tabitha had trust issues and didn't want her back exposed in a dark room while someone she didn't know very well touched her bare skin. Except she hadn't put it like that, because putting it like that might've made Tabitha uncomfortable. Looked like Constance was as meticulous with her client intake as she was with her handwashing, scrubbing backward and forward and up to her elbows, like she was getting ready for surgery.

"I was thinking we'd start faceup." Constance spoke in a strong, low tone, not giving Tabitha time to answer, like she'd sensed the instant tension, and maybe even the sweat. "We can start with light pressure, see how things go, and just go by feel."

Tabitha's heart slowed immediately. She took a deep breath and let it out in a sigh. "Great," she said. "That works."

Constance dried her hands and walked over. "Come on." She gestured toward the door at the far end of the room. Tabitha and Trinity followed. They entered a dimly lit room with a massage table, white linens turned back and pretty pink lamps glowing in the corners, and the eucalyptus smell intensified. "Get undressed to your comfort," Constance said. "Then get under the covers faceup. This is your hour. You are not required to talk to me, but can if you wish to. I recommend you just relax and pretend I'm not here, unless you need to give me feedback. I can read your reactions pretty well, but if I miss something, feel free to speak up. Otherwise, your job is just to lie there and do nothing." Constance gave a little shrug. "Just be."

Tabitha nodded. Just be. She could do that. Right?

Question was, could she do that without all the thoughts

and images and feelings invading her mind like blood dripping slowly over a white canvas?

As soon as Constance left, Tabitha settled Trinity in the corner and stripped off her shirt and shorts. She folded them neatly and laid them in a pile on the chair next to Trinity. Then she removed her jewelry and laid it on the table next to the chair. She debated on her bra. The underwear was staying put, but what about the bra? The straps would be in the way. But how naked would she feel without it? Finally, Tabitha unhooked the bra and added it to the clothing pile, then slid on the table and pulled the covers to her chin. The room was cool, but the table was heated. She'd expected to be uncomfortable but it felt like heaven. Plus, Trinity was there, the warmth of her furry body almost palpable in the cozy space. Tabitha closed her eyes and braced for Constance's arrival. *I'm so stupid*, she thought. *Most people would dream of a free massage. And here you are, tensing up like an idiot.*

A soft knock came. A second later the door opened and Constance said, "All good?" her voice low, like a mom peeking in on her slumbering child.

"All good," Tabitha whispered back. She waited for the sudden pressure, followed by the elbows and the pain and the tensing and the wincing, wondering why the hell she'd come here. Instead, a soft, warm cloth, smelling of lavender, draped over her closed eyelids. Tabitha drew the scent into her lungs and her pulse slowed. An indeterminate amount of time passed. Could've been seconds or minutes, but whatever it was, it gave Tabitha time to equalize. She got used to lying there. To nothing bad happening. To feeling okay in this space. Eventually, there was light pressure on her shoulders, like someone resting their hands. It was a comforting feeling. The mother she'd never had, letting her know that she was there, in the dark room, chasing away all the demons so that

Tabitha could sleep. Tabitha settled deeper into the covers and the heated table. Her breath and her pulse chased and slowed until they caught and matched. The air got heavy, but not in a suffocating way. More like an old quilt, resting, sinking to her bones, protective.

At some point Tabitha became aware of hands on her neck, her arms, sliding between her and the table to reach her back. But that was background noise to the hazy disassociation that had happened somewhere along the line. A long, fuzzy line that Tabitha slipped into without a fight.

She was no longer waiting for the blood on the canvas. The explosive sound, that wasn't really there. The sudden, jacked heartbeats with no explanation. Her lungs sucked of air for no reason. Tabitha was vaguely aware of her body, like she was floating in the big, white fluffy clouds of a sunny, summer day. Or maybe the waves of the ocean, licking over her body under a bleached blue sky. The world buzzed around her, like she lived inside a beehive and was sustained by the murmur of the workers, keeping her alive with the beat of their wings.

Tabitha didn't remember anything after that. At some point, she woke. The room was cool and quiet. She was still on her back, had never flipped over, but could tell that her entire body had been massaged because all her muscles felt like they'd been gently rolled. She sat up, holding the covers over her chest, but nobody else was in the room except for Trinity, asleep on the floor next to the chair and Tabitha's clothes. At the sound of Tabitha rustling the sheets, Trinity's ears perked, then her eyes opened. Tabitha let her head get used to the feeling of sitting up before she swung her legs around, over the edge of the table. She sat there a moment, enjoying the wrung out feeling of her muscles. Her skin tingled pleasantly, her breath and pulse surprisingly even and slow.

Eventually Tabitha settled one foot to the cool floor, then another. She finally let the sheets go, knowing nobody was going to come in while she was dressing. She took her time getting to the chair, collecting her clothes, putting them on with deliberation. Trinity sat up and waited. Tabitha stroked her head. The last thing to go on was Tabitha's watch. Even though she'd wondered what time it was, there was no clock in the room. A quick glance revealed that well more than an hour had gone by.

Tabitha drew one final deep breath before she cracked open the door and was met by the brightness of the afternoon sun. Constance sat at her desk, in front of a computer. She glanced over her shoulder as Tabitha emerged.

"Hey, there." Constance smiled. "How you feeling?"

Tabitha thought about it for a second. She was supposed to say *fine* or *good*. That's what a normal person would say. "Unstuck," was what came out of her mouth. Once the word left her lips, Tabitha wondered if she meant physically or mentally, but it was probably both. Her insides no longer felt like plastic wrap, clinging to itself.

"Excellent." Constance didn't seem to think Tabitha's word choice was weird or required explanation.

"Um." Tabitha dug around in her short's pocket. "My aunt gave me a tip." She drew out the ten-dollar bill, knowing it was probably not a decent percentage of what the massage would've cost, but it was all Auntie El could part with.

Constance shook her head. "I don't take tips."

"Um." Tabitha fumbled with the bill, unsure of what to do now.

"I appreciate the gesture," Constance continued. "But it's a policy I have. I like to think of my services as part of the health care profession. Nobody tips their nurse, right?"

"They probably should," Tabitha said, thinking of all Auntie El's long days and nights as she slipped the bill back into her shorts. "But thank you. This was really lovely."

"It was my pleasure. Let's book you for next week. I'm trying out a few new techniques I learned at a workshop. If you're willing to be my guinea pig, the massage will be free again."

"Oh, I couldn't." Tabitha really wanted to, though. She couldn't remember the last time she'd felt that relaxed. Even when she slept, she didn't come unstuck like that.

"But you'd be helping me."

"I…" Tabitha looked down at Trinity, who seemed to be smiling. "Are you sure?"

Constance nodded. "Positive."

"Um. Okay, then."

"Great." Constance turned back to her computer. "Same day and time?"

"Yes, please."

"Great." Constance clicked on her keyboard. "You're all set, then. I'll probably see you at the gym before your appointment. You can let me know how you're feeling between massages."

"Awesome. Thank you again."

"Anytime. Bye, Trinity!" Constance waved at the dog. Trinity wagged her tail.

As Tabitha led Trinity outside, along the garden path, through the gate and to her car, the sky seemed bluer than it had when she got here. Her body felt like a towel that had been wrung out of all its heaviness and her brain as clear as the sky. The incident at the gym on the Fourth of July didn't seem as big a deal now and her memories of Afghanistan felt like they lived less deeply inside her bones. She didn't know how long these feelings would last, but she'd take whatever she could get. Days. Hours. Minutes. Any little bit helped.

★ ★ ★

Sean swung by the Dudes' apartment complex on his way to the storage shed where he kept his old Harley. He wasn't sure that they had Delaney's bike, but he also wasn't sure they weren't guilty as fuck. Off duty, all he was going to do was look around.

As he wove through the lot, looking for a bike that he knew he wasn't going to find, he replayed his and Delaney's frantic text conversation from last night.

I saw '33.

What? Where?

On the way home. On Prince Blvd. Going South. I was going north. I made a U-turn as soon as I could but it was no use. By the time I got headed in that direction, it was gone.

You sure it was your bike?

I'm sure. My motorcycle is too rare to be confused.

She had a point, even though Sean was initially in disbelief that not only was the motorcycle still in one piece and still in the area, but apparently the thief had also decided it would be a good idea to ride it around.

Don't lose sleep over it, Sean had texted, though had privately wondered if he was talking to himself. I'll look into it tomorrow.

There was no Indian Four motorcycle in or around the Dudes' apartment complex. After an intensive scouring of the area, Sean looked at his watch and cursed. He was late getting to Castillo's house and hoped Miguel hadn't been waiting for him long. When Sean had called that morning to ask to borrow his partner's husband's truck, he was surprised by Miguel's offer to help, even though he hadn't been surprised by Sonia's suspicion.

"You're suddenly back into your motorcycle hobby?" Sonia's tone had been dry and knowing.

"It's summer," Sean had said weakly. "I need something to do on off days."

"You're so full of shit."

"It's a rare bike, apparently," Sean insisted. "I'm told only eight hundred of these motorcycles were made."

"Mmm-hmm."

"Can I borrow the truck or not?"

"Of course you can borrow it." Miguel's voice had ridden over his wife's, letting Sean know that he was on speakerphone. "In fact, I'll help you load up the bike so you don't bust your face. Or worse. The bike."

Sean had laughed. "Thanks, man."

When he arrived at the Castillos' house, Miguel was leaning against his Dodge Ram, ankles crossed while he texted on his phone. "Morning, Miguel. Sorry I'm late."

"Morning." Miguel finished his text, unfazed. "No problem."

"I'm going to leave my car here. Ride with you to the storage unit. Load the bike. Bring you home. Go unload the bike at the shop, then swap out cars after."

Miguel nodded, slipping his phone into his pocket. "Or, you forget all that and I just go to the shop with you. I wouldn't mind seeing it. Even though Sonia says I'm never getting a motorcycle."

"She's not the boss of you," Sean joked.

"Yes, she is." Miguel rolled his eyes. "She told me I had to go with you so I can find out what's really going on with you and the motorcycle girl."

Sean laughed. "She thinks she's so sneaky."

"I don't know about sneaky." Miguel shook his head. "But she's bullheaded."

Once they made it to the storage unit, Sean lowered the tailgate and put a step stool he'd brought along with him on the ground nearby. He unlocked the unit and found the Harley nestled in with some boxes of Kim's stuff that she'd never come to collect. Off living in New York somewhere with her ex-boss, she obviously didn't need all this stuff that she'd demanded in the divorce. Sean didn't want their old wall art or her ugly Hummel collection anyway, so it could rot in here for all he cared. In fact, it was probably time to throw all that crap out. But, first things first. He grabbed the aluminum ramp next to the Harley and secured it to the back of the truck. He went back for the bike, then rolled the Willie G out to the truck. "You push, I'll steer," he told Miguel.

"Sounds good."

The job went quickly and smoothly, without any problems. A sheen of sweat popped over Miguel's forehead in the gathering humidity of what was destined to be a hot, sunny day.

By the time they were done and the bike was secure, they had sweated through their T-shirts. Miguel, lean and wiry, wasn't much of an outdoors guy, but he had a naturally athletic body he didn't work very hard to attain. This had always pissed Sean off because he was forever working to maintain muscle mass and beat back the body fat.

"You must really like this chick," Miguel said as they climbed inside the truck and he cranked up the AC. "It's already like an oven out there and that bike has seen better days."

Sean laughed. "Tell Sonia, nice try. Thanks for playing."

Miguel grinned and cranked the radio for the drive over

to Triple M Classics. Country music rolled out the speakers and he sang along, his voice much larger than his body. Castillo was forever complaining about Miguel's music choices, which was a mistake because now Sean could torture her whenever he wanted. If Castillo got on his nerves, Sean just cranked Florida Georgia Line or Chris Stapleton, drowned her out and got rewarded with the Creature Face. Castillo had no idea that when she used her Creature Face with him it only spelled victory.

When they pulled up to the shop, Delaney had her bay door wide-open. Sean could see her inside, talking with a group of women all decked out in riding gear. A row of Harleys lined the parking lot.

By the time Sean and Miguel got the Willie G unstrapped, rolled out of the truck and into the shop, Delaney was wrapping things up with her customers.

"You could be the vintage rep for our group," one lady said. She gripped a half helmet in her gloved hand. *Girls Gone Hog Wild* was embroidered on the back of her jacket. "Which would be cool. We don't have anybody into classics right now. Not since Val moved to Florida."

"Our first big ride of the year will be next weekend," another lady said. She wore the same jacket and had a strong, authoritative voice. "We're going to head out to Amish country up in Pennsylvania."

"I'll definitely keep it in mind." Delaney rang up a pair of gloves for one of the women and slid them into a plastic bag. "If not this weekend, then maybe the next ride."

Miguel pointed a sly finger at Delaney and mouthed, *Is that her?* Without waiting for an answer he whispered, "Daaaaaaamn."

"I know, right?" Sean muttered under his breath, glad that Miguel got him, instantly, no explanation necessary. Delaney had on blue jeans and a white tank top smeared with grease. Her short hair was ruffled, like she'd only combed her fingers through it after a fitful night's sleep. No makeup, and eyes a little bleary. But there was just something about her. She was quietly aloof, but also open and warm. Her eyes were kind, her smile rare and honest. She exuded the aura of a woman who had spent a lot of years figuring out who she was and who she still wanted to be, like she'd walked the walk for a long time.

Miguel waved a hand at him, like, *Go for it*.

"Cool." The third woman, who'd been silent thus far, glanced around the shop. "This is so great. You being here. The guys who owned this shop before you were total douchebags. They treated any woman who came in here like a child who didn't know what she was doing. Don't you worry for a second about the crap they're spreading about you. We don't believe a word of it."

Delaney's movements slowed. She caught Sean's eye as he put down the kickstand, setting the bike in the center of the floor. She raised a hand in a brief wave, then turned back to the woman. "What don't you believe a word of?"

The ladies turned their heads, following her gesture. They didn't wave, only eyed Sean and Miguel with suspicion. Sean didn't blame them. He'd been on the job long enough to decide that if he were a woman, he'd eye every single male he came across with that same look. "The Dude's Bikes guys." The tallest lady of the bunch chimed in. "They're in tight with the Old Glory Riders and the Commonwealth Cruisers. Those are the biggest biker groups around here. They pull a lot of weight. Run most of the shows and are tight with some of the motorcycle cops. The Dudes have been telling them you're all talk and no walk. That you don't really know how to fix bikes."

"That you'll be out of business within a few months," the woman with the authoritative voice added.

Delaney's face paled, her mouth turning down at the corners. "They don't even know me," she said, her voice soft, like she spoke more to herself than to anyone else.

"Doesn't matter. If they don't like you, the dudes from Dude's will trash you five ways from Sunday."

"And people just believe them?" Delaney caught Sean's eye again, but quickly looked away.

"Like I said, they pull a lot of weight," the tall lady said. "It's a boy's club, hon. We all know how that goes."

The woman who'd bought the gloves placed her hand over top of Delaney's, which was fisted on the counter. "We don't believe a word of it. And now that we've been here we're going to share our experience with everyone we know. Counteract their douchebag lies."

Delaney was quiet after that, her gaze flitting around the shop, like she didn't know where to settle. Finally, she drew a deep breath. "Thanks, ladies. I appreciate the heads-up. And the business. You all come back, okay?"

"Definitely."

"Don't you worry, hon. We got your back."

"And don't forget about the classic bike show coming up soon. At the fairgrounds. You could enter one of your bikes or maybe get a vendor stall. Get your foot in the door."

Right. The Classic Motorcycle Show. Delaney had not forgotten.

The women collected their gear and merchandise. Their goodbyes were all staggered as they headed out, brushing past Sean with a mumbled greeting. They paused, briefly, to admire the bike.

"This your Shovelhead?" the lady with the flyers said.

"Yep." Sean wanted to be polite, but his attention was on Delaney, his mind running through everything he'd just heard.

"Nice."

"Thanks."

"Morning, Detective." Delaney came from behind the counter and walked over. "I don't suppose you heard any of that." Her face was still pale, her eyes narrowed with anger, confusion, maybe some fear.

"I heard everything," Sean said. "But don't worry about it. I guarantee you I know more motorcycle cops than they do. You want me to find out if they're full of shit or not?" Sean made a mental note to dig back into the Dudes to see how many ways he could make their lives miserable.

Delaney drew a deep breath, closed her eyes briefly, then reopened them like she'd shoved everything down. She tried a smile. "Nope. I can handle this. I've got to stand on my own two feet if I'm going to make this happen, right?"

"I know you can handle it. I'd just put my ear to the ground in the department is all."

"Don't waste your time. They're full of crap." Her last words wavered a little, but she spoke quickly, changing the subject. "Is this the Disc Glide?" She turned to the bike, excitement lighting her face, despite the conversation.

"This is it. And that—" Sean pointed at Miguel, who wandered the perimeter of the shop, checking out the merchandise and the pictures on the walls "—is Miguel. He helped me get the bike here."

Miguel turned and waved. "Hey."

"Hey." Delaney waved back as she walked around the bike in a circle. She ran a hand over the seat, then squatted down, eyes narrowed, as she gave the motorcycle the same appraisal Sean would a crime scene. "Holy shit," she breathed. "You really do own an '83 Willie Glide."

"Told you so." Even though Sean hadn't known it was a big deal at the time, he'd looked the bike up since she first mentioned it being rare, and had found out she was right. This motorcycle was one of a handful.

"Holy shit," Delaney said again. "The oxblood color is amazing in the sunlight, just like they say." With the bay door open, the bike basked in a pool of morning rays.

"It's got the stock carburetor," Sean offered. "I know it needs to be either rebuilt or replaced, but I've never known which direction to go."

Delaney shook herself, like someone who'd bumped into a celebrity and didn't want to act like an idiot. She walked around the bike, checking the tires first. "These are surely expired and need replacing." She slid on the Harley and settled in, like she was getting the feel for it. "We can't fire it up until we drain it. The oil will be like gel at this point, full of particulate, so we have to get fresh oil and gas in here."

"Yeah," Sean agreed. "It's been in storage for ages."

"And that's just to start," Delaney said. "I'd bet money the throttle shaft bushings are worn and are sucking air. Basically, I need to take a closer look at everything."

Sean wished his mind was actually on the bike, but with Delaney talking shop and straddling the Harley—the only thing in his youth that had given him freedom and made him feel like he could escape the dreary path of his future—all he could think about was last night. His kitchen. That sort-of kiss. There was no question in his mind that if his cat hadn't been an asshole, things would've gone further. It was clear that Delaney was fascinated by the bike, but Sean was fascinated by her *on* the bike.

"What he means to say—" Miguel was suddenly right there, standing next to the Harley, filling Sean's awkward silence

ELYSIA WHISLER

240

"—is you should do whatever it takes to get this bike up and running. He trusts you completely."

"Right." Sean pointed at Miguel. "That."

Delaney's gaze slipped between the two men as a smile curled her lips. "Okay, gentlemen." She rubbed her palms together. "I don't think the detective knows what a gem he's got on his hands. But I do. I promise to do everything I can to get this Harley in tip-top shape."

"Sounds great. Now. About your motorcycle." Sean cleared his throat, hoping to regain his senses, despite the fact that all he wanted to do was pull her against him and taste the morning on her lips. What would that be like? Toothpaste? Coffee? Tea with sugar and cream? "I know you only saw it for a split second, but did you get a look at who was riding it?"

Delaney's smile fell. "He was completely covered. Dark clothes. Full helmet. Not on the small side or on the big side." Her eyes closed and she went quiet a moment. "Nothing stands out," she said, once her eyes opened again. She cursed under her breath. "I can't believe I was that close and couldn't ride him down. By the time I made the U-turn—"

"Good news is," Sean cut her off before she could go down the road of blaming herself, "we know the bike is still in one piece. And apparently still in the area."

"Weird, right?" Delaney's eyes narrowed.

"This case has bothered me from the start," Sean admitted. "There's just nothing typical about it. And it feels…wrong, somehow."

Delaney didn't grill him like he expected. She didn't ask him to clarify what he meant or make judgment on how so much of his work was based on gut feeling. She just made a clucking sound with her tongue, a sound that indicated she agreed with him. Her gaze went to the photo on the wall of her father sitting on the '33, her expression helpless, sad. That look reinforced something Sean had known all along: this wasn't so much about the missing bike.

"Hey." Sean wanted to reach out, but like so many other times, he quelled the impulse. "I'm on it. This case just got a lot more hopeful. I'm going to try to get footage from the stoplight camera on Prince Boulevard where you saw the bike. Maybe that will show us something you didn't see in that one split second."

She stuffed her hands in her back pockets and glowered. "Do you think it'll show Dick riding around on my dad's bike? He's about the right size."

"Well, if it does, we can arrest him."

Delaney offered a tentative smile. "I like the sound of that."

"What else you got going on today?" Sean glanced over his shoulder, to make sure Miguel was far enough away to not eavesdrop.

"Working on bikes all day. Then tomorrow I'm going over to Sunny's. She promised to let me see Wyatt."

Sean was a little disappointed that Delaney's schedule was so full, but so was his. He had a late shift tonight and now that she'd spied the '33 that's all he was going to think about. Sean was happy to hear she'd be going to visit the dog who used to randomly show up at her shop, though. He could tell she liked that wandering pittie way more than she let on. "Sounds good," he said, and watched her eyebrows rise a little, like maybe she was expecting more.

"Alright, then," was all she said.

"Alright, then."

By the time Sean rode back to Castillo's house, got the van and returned home, he found a text waiting for him from Gus, at the station.

Got the hit on the plate you asked for. Bike's registered to Walter Hanson. See attached deets.

Thanks, Gus.

Old Walt might've refrained from giving Sean his last name, but the tag on his Fat Boy had been easy enough to run down. "Now let's find out exactly who you are, Walter Hanson."

Delaney watched Sean go. He had a nice walk, because he held himself with confidence but lacked arrogance, which Delaney found unusual for a cop. He looked different to her after last night, making her focus more on his physical attributes than she had before. She found the way his clothing draped over his body pleasing—the way his T-shirt hugged his muscled torso and his jeans hid a good set of legs. His friend Miguel chatted and laughed with Sean all the way to the truck they'd arrived in, like they'd known each other a long time.

When they'd first arrived, Delaney had been busy with the Girls Gone Hog Wild group and then preoccupied with the motorcycle. Now that the shop was quiet, she could still smell Sean faintly in the air, either his shampoo or aftershave. The memory of being pressed up against his body last night, and of the brush of her lips over his, came rushing back in. When she'd given him that small kiss, Delaney hadn't really had a clear idea of where she was going with it. She'd just gone on impulse. What she hadn't expected was how quickly she'd lit him up, the way he'd immediately drawn her in.

Delaney was used to being in charge. She'd spent twenty years in the Marine Corps. She'd worked her way up in her field, all the way to motor transport maintenance chief. She'd been on her own since she was seventeen years old and now owned her dream shop. If she wanted something, she went for it. She hadn't realized until Sean had immediately upped the ante just how nice it felt to be on the receiving end of someone else's unrestrained desire.

After they drove away, Delaney walked around Sean's Harley and snapped some pictures. She made sure to get one of the spun aluminum sixteen-inch disc wheel in the back, which gave the *Disc Glide* its name. She sent them to Sal, the resident Harley expert of their group, sans caption.

Only a minute went by before Sal texted his reply.

You got an '83 Willie G in your shop??

Guy that's looking for '33 just brought it in.

That's a sweet ride. Especially the color. Oxblood!

I know. Come get it running for me.

You don't need me for that, querida.

Couldn't hurt. Might need a carburetor. Replace or rebuild?

50/50 on a rebuild. I'd replace.

Ooh. You serious. You always want to rebuild.

Jaja. This is true. You doing ok, Pippie?

Delaney didn't want to lie to Sal, so she told him all about seeing '33 on the road last night. She could feel his excitement through the phone. They texted briefly about how a sighting was better than nothing, even if Delaney had been unable to chase the thief down. She promised to keep him updated and told him to give her love to the rest of the guys. Of course, Boom texted right after that, pissed that she'd told Sal about seeing '33 before telling him. Delaney explained that she'd only texted Sal first because of the Willie G, and, of course, all was forgiven.

As much as Delaney wanted to get right to work on it, she had a couple of paying customers to take care of first. For now, she'd put '33, the Willie Glide and the Dudes out of her mind and get down to business in the motorcycle shop of her dreams. She'd put on some music, let B.B. King fill the air as she finished up work on the Triumph, from the guy who'd brought it in after the grand opening. She'd let the sunshine roll in on the wind and mingle with the scents Sean had left behind, and maybe think about him for a little while, the way he held her, traced her jaw with his thick fingers and didn't hate on his cat, even though she'd ruined his chances of getting laid. That took a special sort of guy. One that Delaney wouldn't mind thinking about for a while, instead of the alternative.

Which was that a couple of nasty men with a long reach were out to get her, had possibly stolen '33 and might have other things planned.

No, for now she'd push those thoughts aside.

For now.

seventeen

For the first time since Captain Dorsey had died, Tabitha slept all night. She didn't wake in cold sweats, her head echoing with the sound of the explosion. She didn't feel paralyzed, watching a blank canvas fill with blood. She didn't get the sensation of her skin crawling, then jolt awake, heart in her throat, lungs on fire. She didn't wake up with Trinity on her chest, forearms draped over her shoulder. This morning, when Tabitha woke, the sun splashed a circular pattern of beams over her blue comforter and Trinity was in her dog bed, fast asleep.

Tabitha stretched, her muscles loose and hungry. A glance at her phone revealed she'd have little time to get ready if she wanted to make the morning workout, which her body was begging to do. She jumped out of bed and pulled on some shorts and a tank top, took Trinity on a walk to do her business, ignored Auntie El's snarky comments on her unexpected energy level, and was off to the gym before Auntie could even throw out a clue to this morning's crossword.

The gym was busy that morning, with multiple programs running. Rhett was doing a class in Spanish and Hobbs was by the whiteboard when Tabitha streaked in, with a minute to spare. Clementine, who was smaller than everyone, peeked through the crowd and waved. Tabitha waved back and got Trinity settled next to Humphrey, who sniffed the air and then started thumping his tail. He shrank from Tabitha's attempt to pet him, but when Trinity started licking his face he leaned into it and wagged his tail even harder.

"Let's go, Tabby!" Hobbs called, his good-natured grin pointed in her direction. "We're ready to roll!"

"Want me to punch him?" Delaney's voice came from over her shoulder.

Tabitha turned to see that she hadn't been the last one in, as Delaney followed her to the group in front of the whiteboard. "No, it's okay," Tabitha whispered. As soon as she'd seen Hobbs was coaching that day her insides had grown oddly warm, giving even more energy to her already eager muscles. "He's not so bad after all. I sort of had an episode on the Fourth of July and he was really nice about it."

Delaney's eyebrows knitted, but she said no more. Tabitha settled in next to Clementine, who gave her a smile as Hobbs started the class intro. Looked like the workout was going to have a lot of running, and Tabitha was even happier now that she'd come early. The temperature outside was already in the high eighties with 80 percent humidity and would be brutal by this afternoon.

"Running," Clementine hissed. "Yesssss."

"But also overhead squats," Tabitha pointed out. "Ughhh."

"I know, right?" Clementine gave an exaggerated shiver.

"You're in a good mood," Delaney said, once they started warming up.

"I got that massage you made me schedule," Tabitha admitted. "Thanks for that. Constance was amazing. I mean, I don't really remember much of the massage, but it was like—" Tabitha thought back to yesterday's time on the table "—she knew exactly how much pressure to give the sore muscles versus the not so sore ones and also how to get me to relax and…" Tabitha trailed off. She shrugged. It was a mystery to her, but who was she to question mysteries?

"Say no more," Delaney agreed, nodding.

The rest of the class was a blur of trying to run without dying—"Breathe, Tabitha, breathe!" Clementine kept shouting—and attempting overhead squats with no more than a PVC pipe and Hobbs constantly at her side, jovially telling her to keep her chest up and her heels down. Delaney kicked the crap out of everyone but Rhett, who had her on the running but couldn't keep up with her overhead squats. They finished about dead even. Clementine, despite her short stride, could almost outrun Rhett, but her overhead squats were only a little better than Tabitha's. Tabitha was pretty sure she only beat the seventy-year-old grandma, who scaled all of her runs and did regular squats, but she wasn't complaining. When she was done, Tabitha felt even better than she had when she woke this morning. She sat inside the open bay with her water bottle and basked in the sun. Her body was worn-out in a good way, her mind was open and full of the blue sky, and she had some new friends who accepted her for who she was—what they knew of her, anyway.

"Great job, Tab." Clementine appeared in the doorway and gave her a fist bump.

"Thanks. You, too." Even as Tabitha spoke, her gaze drifted to Hobbs, a few feet away, inside a circle of really fit women who were neglecting cleaning up their equipment to listen to whatever story he was telling, gestures broad as his smile. The morning light showed off his tanned skin and made his blond hair look like he spent every day at the beach, getting loved on by the sun and the sea. He was only missing a whistle and a tank top with Lifeguard printed across the front.

"What about you, Clementine?" Hobbs caught sight of them nearby. "What do you do for a living?"

"I own a running shop," Clementine said. "Run Like Hell, over on Madison."

Hobbs pointed at her and grinned. "No surprise there. You're clearly all about the miles."

"Yeah. I'm here to get a few days of strength training in every week to supplement."

"Awesome." Hobbs nodded. "You're doing great so far. I can see where you're struggling with some hip and hamstring mobility, from all the running and no lifting. But you'll slowly fix that as you build muscle and get comfortable in positions you're not used to. Like overhead squats." He winked, which was definitely flirty without being creepy.

"Ain't that the truth." Clementine laughed at herself and pantomimed falling flat on her face.

"What about you, Tabby?" Hobbs turned to her. His easy charm changed, though it was hard for Tabitha to pinpoint how. He wasn't less warm, just retracted somehow. Kind of like how the older brother's best friend acts toward the little sister. "What do you do in your other life?" Hobbs held up a hand. "Wait. Don't tell me." He leaned back and appraised her. "Librarian." Then he changed his mind. "Teacher." He changed it again, his choices rapid-fire and leaving Tabitha no time to argue. "Accountant."

"I'm actually not anything right now." Tabitha wished she had something to say in this moment, but she wasn't ready to tell anyone that she couldn't even stock shelves in the grocery store without losing her shit. "When I was in the navy, I was a chaplain's assistant."

"Oh, how interesting." Clementine's voice was bright. "That sounds really important. Good for you, Tab."

Hobbs grew thoughtful, less talkative. His smile changed, as did his eyes, like he withdrew even further. Tabitha was left feeling a little hollowed out, even after her amazing sleep. This was how guys like him always acted around women like her. Party Animal Hot Guy didn't know how to be around Religious Librarian Accountant. No surprise there.

"Are you planning on doing something in that field? As a civilian?" Clementine pressed the bottom of her foot against the side of the wall and leaned into it, stretching her calf.

"Umm." Tabitha suddenly didn't feel so light and airy. Her stomach grew tight. "I don't think so."

A crease formed between Hobbs's eyebrows.

From across the room, Tabitha caught Delaney's eye. She had packed up her things but stopped to pet Humphrey before she left. As usual, the beagle didn't flinch from her touch, soon rolled over and offered his belly. Tabitha felt the knots inside of her loosening as Delaney held her gaze. Delaney offered a soft, knowing smile.

"I'll see you guys later." Tabitha plucked her phone from her pocket. "I've got to get home. I live with my great-aunt and she's getting up there in years."

"Alrighty, Tabby." Hobbs's voice got its boom back. "See you soon."

Tabitha just waved, no longer in the mood to talk.

"See you later." Clementine checked her watch. "I've got to get to the shop, too."

As soon as Tabitha walked away, Hobbs fell back into his boisterous story, the women around him laughing and still neglecting their equipment. She gathered Trinity and her bag and headed out. Delaney fell in beside her and hooked an arm around her shoulders as they walked into the sunshine. "Hang in there, girl."

After Tabitha drove away, Delaney tossed her bag in the truck and headed back into the gym. The gaggle of smitten women had dispersed, finally cleaning up their shit under Rhett's piercing gaze. Hobbs was busy mopping the floor of remnant DNA. Delaney marched right up to him, planted her hands on her hips and said, "Stop it."

Hobbs fixed her with a set of sky-blue eyes that matched his beach bum personality. "Mopping?"

"Don't play dumb with me." Delaney wasn't sure he was actually playing dumb, or was just dumb, but she didn't care. "I'm talking about Tabitha."

Hobbs, who'd dunked his mop in the bucket, lifted it from the piney smelling water and wrung it out by pressing the bucket handle forward. "I don't know what you mean."

"You know exactly what I mean. You walk around here acting like you're God's gift and then, after you somehow reel Tabitha in, you do a one-eighty and blow her off. Typical for your kind. But Tabitha doesn't deserve that."

"My kind?" Hobbs released the handle of the mop wringer and turned to face her.

"Yeah. Your kind. Use 'em and lose 'em. Don't even pretend I'm wrong."

Hobbs fixed Delaney with the most serious look she'd ever seen on his grinning face. "Let me get this straight." He set the mop head on the floor and leaned into the handle. "Last time you were here, you got mad at me for being too flirty. Now I'm being too cold. Make up your mind. Which way do you want me to be?"

Delaney stepped a little closer and lowered her voice. "It's not going to be any way. Not with her. I don't know what happened on the Fourth of July, but something made her trust you. And now you're acting like Prince Charming to every girl in the gym but her. Not cool."

Hobbs surprised her by meeting her gaze with solid resolve. Any hint of the party boy was gone, wrung out as hard as he'd twisted the mop head. "Calm down, Devil Dog. Please stop treating me like I'm stupid." He held up a hand as Delaney parted her lips to speak. "Trust me, I get where you're coming from. And I understand you wanting to protect her. But I'm not the asshole you think I am. I definitely don't want to do anything to hurt Tabitha. Okay? You're just going to have to trust me on that."

Delaney stared into his eyes for a long time, and to his credit, he didn't look away, like he offered himself up for inspection. Delaney didn't hate what she saw. There was something there that she'd missed before. Something in his eyes, behind all the bullshit. Then his gaze shifted downward and Delaney felt her anger rush back in. Was he really checking out her tits? After all this?

"Why are you wearing a Go Big Red shirt?" Hobbs pointed, and only then did Delaney remember what tank top she'd worn today. The shirt was so old you could barely read the words across her chest, cracked and eaten away by the laundry, unless you were up close.

Delaney's ire started to cautiously fizzle away. "Because I was born and raised a Huskers fan. Why do you care?"

"Because so was I." He leaned into his mop again. He looked a little bit like a janitor with an attitude now. "Where you from?"

"Omaha." Delaney thrust the word out, like a challenge. "You?"

"Same. My whole life. Until Camp Lejeune, where I met Rhett."

"Wait." Delaney paused to process. "*You* were a marine?"

Hobbs stuck his mop back in the water and turned to wheel the bucket away. "Don't act so surprised," he called over his shoulder.

Delaney parted her lips but then shut her mouth and let him go.

Well. I'll be damned.

Pittie Place and Canine Warriors—which Delaney was told had become a joint venture over the last month—was like Disneyland for orphan dogs. At least, that was the pitch Delaney would write if she were putting together an ad campaign for Sunny's rescue and Pete's training center. There was a big sign, shaped like a dog bone, on a wooden post in the ground, with the words *Pittie Place* emblazoned in the center and surrounded by black paw prints. Next to it was a twin, with the post on the opposite side, so that the two signs met in the middle and looked like puzzle pieces that fit together. This one read Canine Warriors, beneath which was a dog silhouette adorned with dog tags. A flagstone path led to a fence, surrounding a building that looked like an elegant log cabin with a backdrop of endless woods. Once behind the fence, Delaney could see the wide expanse of open grounds to run and play that surrounded the building. Despite the other dogs running free, chasing each other, lying under trees or playing in a series of kiddie pools with shallow water, Wyatt didn't rush to join them when Pete unhooked the leash from his collar.

"Stay," Pete said gently. That one word revealed his soft Virginia accent, just a little twist to the vowel sound that danced over Delaney's ears.

Wyatt eyed the dogs in the kiddie pool with longing and

shifted his paws, but didn't move. Delaney watched, fascinated by Pete's dog magic. Wyatt's jitters had ebbed considerably, even though Delaney could still sense a slightly anxious vibe from the pittie. Pete, who had a down-home country look in his Virginia Tech T-shirt, blue jeans and work boots, tipped the brim of his baseball cap with the back of his wrist and said, "Come." He tapped his thigh and strode toward the large building. Wyatt followed, keeping right by Pete's heel as Pete strode confidently through the pack of playful dogs.

Sunny and Delaney fell in behind as Pete led them to that elegant log cabin—what Sunny called the "doggy abode." The building was large enough to house rescues awaiting fosters and forever homes, she'd explained, as well as the main caretaker, Roger, who was polite, but focused, busy keeping the dogs in line with the natural smoothness of someone who'd been doing this a long time and loved his job.

Pete stopped next to an enclosed space near the rear of the building. A small fence surrounded a litter of puppies, five total, in varying shades of black and brown and white, what might be bully breeds or mixes. Inside the fence was an assortment of entertainments, like a playground for kids, but for dog babies instead. There was a tunnel to crawl through, a little platform to climb, and a handcrafted trellis with chew toys dangling from it. The puppies were clustered under the trellis, reaching for the toys with paws and mouths, trying to catch them as they swung around.

As soon as they reached the enclosure Pete stopped and said to Wyatt, "Down."

Wyatt sank onto his stomach and watched the puppies while his tail flapped on the ground. Pete slipped him a treat so small Delaney never saw it leave Pete's fingers as Wyatt took it into his mouth and chewed it.

Delaney's eyebrows rose at Sunny.

"I told you he was good." Sunny eyed Pete with a look Delaney recognized as a smitten woman. She couldn't blame her. Pete was quietly commanding, made a woman feel safe in such a way that you knew he would protect you if necessary but would never use that power to harm you.

"That's ingenious," Delaney said, laughing as she watched the puppies try to snag the chew toys that dangled from the trellis.

"Roger made that," Sunny said with a grin. "Those are the *Breakfast Club* pups."

"Ha. Cute. Like Trinity was from the *Matrix* litter."

"Right." Pointing at each one, Sunny said, "The one trying not to get dirty is Claire. The goofy one is Allison. The one who's wrestling all the others for their toys is Andrew. The one who overthinks before he leaps is Brian. And that one—" Sunny pointed to the only puppy who was running through the tunnel, ignoring all the others "—is Bender."

"Oh, wow." Delaney shook her head. "They're amazing. Bender has my heart already."

"Did you say Trinity?" Pete's eyes lit up.

"Yeah. Tabitha and I were in Afghanistan together."

"How are they doing?" The hope that flickered over Pete's features told Delaney everything she needed to know about this guy, if she hadn't known before.

"She's getting by, from what I can tell. Has already made herself a home at Semper Fit."

"That's great." Pete stripped off his ball cap and tapped it against his palm. "Tabitha and Trinity were such a good fit, they were like pieces of a jigsaw. Trinity was the perfect size. Perfect temperament. Took about a year to train them."

"Train *them*?"

"Yes," Sunny piped in. "The veterans have to work very

hard with their dogs before they can graduate and take them home."

"I bet." Delaney turned her attention back to the pups, who squeaked and rolled, bumping into each other, running over to the fence to see who the humans were, then rushing back to the trellis to have another go at getting those chew toys down. Dad would've loved this place, where all the dogs were wild and free and allowed to be themselves.

"We got a call from the local animal shelter last night. There's a girl over there named Lily who is absolutely rabid about animal welfare and has my number programmed into her cell. The whole litter was dropped off at their back door, inside a refrigerator box. The shelter is full, so Lily called me." Sunny shook her head. "But hey. At least whoever abandoned them didn't dump them in the woods. Or drown them in the Potomac."

Delaney glanced over at Wyatt, who was still lying on the ground, patiently watching the puppies. He didn't behave exactly like the dog who'd stolen into her shop so many times to find his dog bed or beg for food, constantly digging escape tunnels to run away from the only people who had ever treated him right. But he didn't look one hundred percent comfortable in his own skin, either. Not that that was a bad thing. Like a human kid, Wyatt was young and wild and still figuring himself out.

Sunny elbowed her in the ribs. "You say Bender has your heart—" she nodded at the puppy tearing through the tunnel "—but something tells me the dog who's really got a hold on you is outside the fence."

Delaney tore her gaze away from Wyatt. Sunny had a glint in her pretty blue eyes. "I'm worried about his safety. I'm busy in the shop and I leave the bay open when it's not so humid. So far all he's done is take off to go between your place and mine. I don't want him to get stuck in a ditch again. Or get hit by a car."

Sunny pointed at her boyfriend. "That's why this big lug trained him. He can teach you the commands. And Wyatt already likes you and your shop." After some silence Sunny cocked her head to the side. "You came all the way out here just to visit him. For God's sake, you *named* him."

Delaney eyed the lonely pit bull with the brown eye patch and sad face, nose twitching in the air as he watched the puppies run and play. Something about him made Delaney think of a young man who'd never had a chance to be a kid, envious of the playful abandon of the youth before him. He reminded her so much of Dad. Maybe too much of Dad.

"I don't know."

"Foster him," Pete piped in. "You don't have to be his forever home. Just give him a safe space to figure out if you're a good fit for each other."

Delaney's eyes locked with Wyatt's. He'd been lying still, admiring the puppies, but when he saw Delaney his tail started thumping. Why did it feel like Wyatt was desperately trying to tell her something important all the time? Something only he knew. Something Delaney needed to hear. She just needed to figure out what he was saying. "Okay." Delaney smiled, despite herself.

"You got to be anywhere?" Pete said.

"Shop's closed for the night. Worked out this morning. I'm done for the day."

"Good. Let's spend some time working with him. If you feel comfortable keeping him safe, you can take him home tonight."

Delaney felt a little twinge of excitement that she hadn't been expecting and didn't really understand. This had to be about more than missing her childhood buddy, Chunk. This had to be about more than Dad dying. It might be about those things, but it wasn't *only* about those things.

"Break." Pete tapped his thigh and led Wyatt away from the puppy play station, into a wider space, away from the other dogs, out near the woods. Delaney could spy a path into the trees outside the fence, along with a log cabin, nestled into the foliage.

"I rent out cabins," Sunny explained, following Delaney's gaze. "People with money get to hang out on my grounds and see all the dogs. Generates a lot of donations."

"Smart." Delaney could appreciate a fellow businesswoman. "So what happens to the Breakfast Club?"

"Some might go to Pete." Sunny nodded in his direction. "He lives a mile that way, through the woods, but we've connected operations so now the two of us have over twenty acres to work with. Others will be adopted. Puppies aren't as difficult to home as the older dogs." Her gaze rested with Wyatt.

"That's amazing. I know a few people who would benefit from a rescue dog." Delaney thought of Vanguard, from her first tour on Leatherneck. He'd kept in touch, after an IED took out his convoy and sent him home with one less leg.

"I'll set you up with a few of Pete's business cards before you go."

"Thanks."

"You guys up for a walk?" Pete called out.

"Yeah." Delaney shrugged. "Sure."

They spent the next fifteen minutes walking the grounds, until they ended up at another large building, nestled in the woods. There was a sign here, same as the one out front of Sunny's, but just the Canine Warriors portion. "This is my side of the operation," Pete said. "So Sunny works closely with the local animal shelter, other kill shelters in the surrounding counties and states, and foster homes. Pups are vetted by me to see which, if any, are viable for service dog training. If so, we match them with veterans who have submitted applications for a dog. Personality is important, as well as size, as well as disability."

"So what kind of personality? I'm guessing Wyatt wouldn't be suitable." Delaney smiled at him so that Wyatt would know her comment wasn't meant as an insult.

"No, he's too restless. I usually look for an amiable, confident personality in the dog. One that will be obedient and calm, even if the handler is terrified."

"Makes complete sense." Delaney eyed Wyatt. "You might just run away, huh, boy?"

"Size matters, too," Pete continued. "Smaller dogs are better at certain tasks and larger ones for others. Take Tabitha, for example. Trinity was perfect for her because she's the smallest pit bull that I've ever seen. Too big a dog wouldn't have worked for Tabitha, because we definitely wanted to train Trinity for deep pressure therapy and we couldn't have a huge dog lying on top of Tabitha's chest."

Delaney nodded in agreement. A lot more went into this than she'd thought.

"And then we look at what kind of service the dog will be providing. In Tabitha's example, she applied for a service dog from me because she needed a psychiatric service dog and the VA doesn't cover dogs for psychiatric issues like PTSD or MST."

"Really? I didn't realize that."

"They say there's not enough research to show that service dogs help people with PTSD or other psychological trauma and that there's risk of dependency—a reliance by the human on the animal to function without learning to do so themselves." Pete removed his hat and ran a hand through his hair.

"That doesn't make any sense to me," Delaney said. "I can

see how much Trinity helps Tabitha do things she wouldn't otherwise be doing."

"I tend to agree with you," Pete said, glancing down at Wyatt, who tilted his nose in the air and danced around, like he was eager to show Delaney everything he'd learned in the weeks since she'd last seen him. "Which is why I do provide service dogs for that sort of trauma."

"This is an amazing thing that you do."

"It's not a one-man operation." Pete waved away her compliment, hat in hand, before he plopped it back on his head. "There are a lot of moving parts, starting with Sunny and her crew and then on to me and mine. I have a slew of volunteers who come in, learn how to train the dogs, then work with them and the veterans who apply. It can take months to years to train a dog and costs thousands of dollars, so donations are essential. That's why your gym is having a fundraiser here next weekend. You've probably seen the signs."

"I have," Delaney said. "I wouldn't miss it."

"Cool. Come on and I'll show you what we've been learning."

Delaney spent the next two hours learning all the commands she'd heard Pete use with Wyatt, as well as a few others. He showed her how to use tiny treats as a reward system to reinforce the commands. Wyatt would now do most of the commands without treats, but Pete still gave him some at times.

"It's good for him," Pete emphasized. "He doesn't get enough treats to get fat. It's just a reward that snaps his brain out of the rut he's gotten stuck in of going back and forth and all around, searching for a place to be. The real thing he needs to control is inside—" Pete rubbed his chest "—not his outside." He raised his arms and gestured around the grounds. "The training just reminds him that he doesn't need to worry so much. That someone is here to help him. To care about him, guide him and protect him. Just as rules for our children help keep them safe, so does the training for Wyatt." Pete handed her a few treats. "Here. Try for yourself."

Delaney tried out the commands and treats, then tried out the commands without treats. Wyatt complied with equal eagerness. By the time she felt confident in taking Wyatt back to the shop the setting sun's rays shone down over the grounds in hazy, multicolored beams that looked like they came directly from heaven,

"If you can, maybe keep him inside, with the bay door closed, for a few days." Pete was frank as he slipped a leash on Wyatt and led him toward the front of the house, where Delaney had parked. "Just long enough to get him accustomed to his new surroundings. To sort of let him know that's where you're going to be. That he's safe there. Without giving him the chance to run back to Sunny's place."

"I can do that. It's getting too hot to leave the shop open, anyway."

When they neared the front of the house, Delaney spied her Rebel and slapped a palm to her forehead. "I rode my bike here," she said. "I'm going to have to go home and swap it out for my truck to take Wyatt home."

"I'll bring him," Pete said, unlatching the gate. "I've got my truck."

They walked out front, to the long driveway that led up to Sunny's pretty house. Delaney recognized it as a restored Queen Anne, with fish scale siding and turrets. The home only reinforced her opinion that this place was Disneyland for orphan dogs. "My dad did all the restoration before he passed away of cancer a couple of years ago," Sunny said, when she noticed Delaney studying the house.

"It's beautiful." Delaney had always liked the Queen Anne style, something about the architecture's reminiscence of old castles. She suddenly felt a new kinship with the dog rescuer who'd also lost her father. For a moment, their gazes connected and held, and though neither one of them said anything, Sunny's sad smile told Delaney everything that went unspoken.

Wyatt whined and strained against his leash, breaking the spell. Pete's brow creased. For the first time since Delaney had met the trainer, he looked confused. Pete undid the leash, apparently to see what the dog would do, and watched as Wyatt rushed forward and came within inches of Delaney's motorcycle. He sniffed around the Rebel, his nostrils flaring.

"Well, this is new," Pete said, half-amused. "I've never seen a dog react like this to a motorcycle. Do you have other dogs around this bike or something?"

"No. But I've seen him act this way before," Delaney admitted, remembering her grand opening and Wyatt's reaction to '33. "He got all excited around my dad's bike. The one that was stolen. Though at the time I thought it was just my imagination."

"He's a secret biker dog," Sunny quipped, giggling.

"Well, if this is true," Pete said, grinning at the pittie as he circled the bike, "then he's going to the right place."

"Alright," Delaney said, before she slipped on her helmet. "You know the way, Pete?"

"I know the shop. Meet you there."

By the time Delaney made it home, the sky was dark and her body was feeling the tug of fatigue. The muscle aches from the day were settling deep in her bones and making her dream of crawling under the covers. But she had to take care of Wyatt first—make sure he was comfortable. She unlocked the shop and stripped off her gear. Just as she was unlocking the back room, Pete pulled up in his truck. He parked next to Delaney's old Ford and took his time admiring it. When he came into the shop with Wyatt in tow he pointed over his shoulder, toward the parking lot. "You don't just do vintage bikes, huh? That old step-side is sweet."

"Thanks. That was my dad's, too."

"He kept it in good shape."

"He kept everything in good shape. People who had antiques but kept them covered up to rot drove him crazy. He used to say, 'If you're just going to sit and stare at it, what's the point? Life ain't about being pretty.'"

Pete chuckled. "I like your dad already."

"Yeah." Delaney kept the sudden sadness out of her voice. "He was something else." Weird how grief came in waves like that. Like the tides of the ocean. One second you're doing fine, then you turn your back and get clobbered by a monster.

Wyatt wasn't having it, all this talk about the truck. He made a beeline for the back room and disappeared inside.

"His old dog bed is in there," Delaney explained. "That's where his previous owners had him sleep, I guess."

Pete's lips twitched in disapproval. He followed Wyatt into the back room and surveyed the cold, concrete space. The shelves were no longer bare, as Delaney had stocked them with gear, parts, oil and such, but it was still a cold, hard workshop. Wyatt was already on his bed, digging at it with his front paws, like he was trying to create a comfy spot in the fraying material. Delaney had washed the bed after her and Wyatt's adventure in the rainstorm, just in case Wyatt ever came back here and needed it.

"I tried inviting him upstairs one night." Delaney watched as Wyatt settled into a tight ball and rested his head on his paws. He huffed a contented sigh. "He wouldn't come."

"Tomorrow, take his dog bed and put it just outside this door." Pete pointed at the entrance to the shop. "See what he does. He might be a little put out at first, but he'll get over it. Then after a few days, move the bed to the foot of your stairs. I assume the stairs at the back of the shop lead up to your apartment?"

"Right."

"Then eventually you put the bed upstairs, in the apartment. It's like a gradual shift to a new space. Like when you acclimate fish to a new tank."

"Makes sense. I'll try that. Thanks." Delaney's understanding of why Sunny was so into Pete deepened. On the surface, he came off as just a regular, down-home—albeit handsome—guy. But once you got to know him it became readily apparent that his knowledge and dedication to caring for others was his entire reason for being.

Pete set down the two metal bowls he'd been carrying, presumably Wyatt's food and water dishes. He strode over to the shelves and poked around the room, casing the perimeter. "Good," he said, once his appraisal was complete. "Nothing on the low shelves he can get into. No poisons back here, like any coolants, or anything he can chew on that could hurt him. Nothing I'm missing, right?"

"Nope." Delaney hadn't even thought of that. "But thanks for checking."

"Yes, ma'am." Pete reached the bay door, grasped the chain and raised it a few feet. He bent down and stuck his head out.

"Back there is the wooded area that stretches between Sunny and me. Wyatt would use it to travel between us."

Pete nodded. "I see it." He opened the door a little wider and stepped one foot out, peering around the building. Wyatt didn't move a muscle. His breathing had deepened and his rib cage expanded slow and steady. Pete squinted in the darkness. He drew something from his coat and clicked. When the concrete strip that surrounded the shop lit up Delaney realized Pete held a flashlight. He gave a low, appreciative whistle.

"That's a sweet bike," he said. "I'm not sure on your reasoning behind parking that out back. I don't think I would."

Delaney's blood grew icy. All the good feelings over seeing Wyatt again and even the fatigue that had been building suddenly vanished. "What are you talking about?" She rushed over to Pete, the jangled nerves leaking into her voice and making Wyatt's eyes pop open. "I don't have any motorcycles outside..." Her voice trailed off as she got a look at what Pete was seeing.

There, right outside the shop, illuminated in the darkness by the small beam of Pete's flashlight, shining in all its classic glory, was '33.

eighteen

"You're sure it's your dad's bike?" Sean said it, even though he knew it was a stupid thing to ask.

"Of course I'm sure." Delaney sounded dazed, both adamant and uncertain, if that was possible.

"Are you inside? Are you safe?" Sean's first thought hadn't been how great it was that her stolen motorcycle had been returned, even though that was great. His first thought had been that someone was going out of their way to fuck with Delaney, and that person might still be around her shop, waiting to see her reaction. In his career Sean had met many scumbags who got off on that kind of thing—their end game wouldn't have been to steal a motorcycle, but to torture their victims psychologically.

"I'm inside," Delaney said. "All the doors are locked. Pete checked out the whole perimeter of the shop while I rode the bike around for a few minutes, just to see if it still runs. It's perfectly fine. It's inside now."

Sean felt a stab of regret. He was working her case. He was supposed to protect her, even though he knew she could protect herself. At least Pete had done exactly what he should have. "I'm coming over," Sean said, without even thinking to ask her if it was okay. He was about to amend his statement and get permission when Delaney spoke, surprising him.

"Okay. I'll wait up for you."

By the time Sean got there, Delaney had showered and changed into pink pajama pants covered in tiny green flowers and a white tank top. Her hair was wet and brushed back, but a few strands of hair had dried and framed her face. Her eyes looked tired and she kept worrying her bottom lip with her teeth as she took Sean into the back room to show him where the bike was now and where it had been found.

"I understand the need you felt to ride the bike around and bring it inside," Sean said. "But that's going to make dusting it for prints that much harder now that you've touched it."

Delaney rolled her eyes at herself. "Shit."

Sean shrugged, not wanting to make her feel worse. "A decent criminal would've worn gloves anyway. But we'll see what we get."

"Okay. Do you still think it was the Dudes?"

"I'm not sure," Sean said honestly. "I still suspect them. But I also looked up your buddy Walt."

"Old Walt?"

Sean nodded. "Walter Hanson is sixty-one years old and listed a Williamsburg address. Divorced. Retired teacher. Taught auto shop to high schoolers for thirty years. He's heavy into riding and goes to a lot of rallies throughout the year, per his social media accounts."

"Wow." Delaney eyed Sean with a look he hadn't seen before. If he didn't know any better, he'd say she was impressed. "You really did your homework."

"I didn't see any sign of '33 on any of his accounts," Sean continued. "And I don't see evidence of him being tied to shady groups who would deal in stolen bikes or parts. But he'd definitely have the know-how to take it apart."

Delaney was quiet awhile. Sean could tell her wheels were turning by the different expressions that rolled over her face. "By the way, that's Wyatt," she said, when she finally spoke. She pointed to a white pit bull with tan splotches, one of which surrounded his entire right eye, like a patch. He looked exactly like the dog on the Dude's website and Facebook pages. The pittie lay on a ragged dog bed, his body in a tight circle. The stolen motorcycle was parked nearby. "The dog I've told you about. I'm fostering him. He likes motorcycles," Delaney explained. "So I put Dad's bike next to him."

"That's weird, isn't it?" Sean said, momentarily forgetting his real purpose, which was to investigate. "Do dogs normally like motorcycles?"

"Some do." Delaney nodded. "But he gets really excited when he sees them."

Sean paused to squat down and check out the dog a little closer. He wagged his tail, so Sean offered a hand. Wyatt licked his knuckles. He smelled woodsy. "He's cute." Sean rose, leaving Wyatt to his sleep. Delaney opened the bay door and showed him where the bike had been parked. "So, under the eaves. In the dark. You get a camera back here yet?"

"I'm going to." Delaney's voice became gruff, like she knew Sean would be disappointed. "First thing tomorrow." After a round of silence she added, "Come on. Who on earth would think the thief would bring the motorcycle back?"

"You know that's not the point."

"I know. I'm getting a camera. No need to lecture."

Sean withdrew his penlight from his pocket and clicked it

on, trailing it over the ground. There weren't any tracks. "You didn't see anything? Or anyone?"

"I came home and found the bike out here. That's it."

"Delaney." Sean drew a deep breath and chose his words carefully. "Is there anyone in your life, or your past, who was obsessive? Or abusive? An ex? A stalker?"

She shook her head. "Well," she amended, "there have been a few incidents on deployment. But then, there always are. Nothing outside the ordinary."

"Explain."

Delaney shrugged and spread her hands open. "Normal stuff. Groping. Comments. A guy who drinks too much and comes into your quarters at night and has to have his ass handed to him because you know more hand-to-hand combat than he does. That kind of thing. Par for the course."

"Par for the course? None of that is normal, Delaney."

Delaney's face tightened. She looked angry, but not necessarily at him. "They are for women, Sean. We put up with that stuff on a daily basis, in the military or not. Unfortunately, they are normal. Should they be? No. But they are. This shouldn't be news to you."

Sean sighed. "These things are on record?"

Delaney shrugged again. "Some of them. You learn early on not to rock the boat. Because then you're not a team player. Or, you were asking for it somehow. Again, this shouldn't be news to you. I learned to handle all that shit myself. Luckily I'm good at handling things myself."

"Anyone from any of those incidents living around here?" She was right, of course. None of this should be news to him, after being a cop for so many years. But the thought of Delaney having to fend off unwanted advances, possibly assault, sent his blood pressure up. It was hard enough being on deployment, just trying to do your job, get through the day, without having to worry about friendly fire. "Anyone in your life who would think stealing your motorcycle and then giving it back was a fun way to mess with you?"

Delaney was quiet awhile. She shook her head. "No."

"Let's get you inside," Sean said. "You look exhausted. Did Pete check out the apartment before he left?"

"No, but I've been up there."

"I'd still like to check it out before I go, if that's okay."

"There really aren't a whole lot of places to hide up there, Detective. But I'm not going to argue."

They passed by Wyatt, who was fast asleep. "Does he stay in here?" Sean asked as Delaney propped open the back room door.

"For now. His choice. I'm going to try to get him upstairs with Pete's acclimation plan. I'm supposed to move the bed gradually toward the apartment steps."

"Pete's a smart guy."

"I know, right? He and Sunny are perfect for each other," Delaney said as they entered the shop. "Talk about a match made in heaven."

"Yeah. They've known each other a long time. Childhood best friends, I'm told. The three of them. Pete, Sunny and Red. I never stood a chance." The words slipped out before Sean remembered who he was talking to. He hoped the flush that ran up the back of his neck didn't creep around to the front.

Delaney looked over her shoulder, brows knitted, as they headed up the steps to her apartment. "Stood a chance with what?"

"Um." Sean blew out a sigh. Damn. She looked so adorable in those pajamas. Sexy and muscular bare arms in the tank top, then soft flowery pajama bottoms in pink and green, her favorite colors, showing off the perfect contrast that was Delaney Monroe. There was some kind of tattoo peeking out from under the strap of the tank, right where it covered her shoulder blade. Something small and black.

They took the last steps into her apartment and she turned, hands on her hips, waiting. There was only one lamp on, near the couch. Her figure looked wispy in the dim light.

"Sunny and I dated, briefly." He should have found a way to bring this up sooner. "It was a year ago. I had separated from my ex but we weren't technically divorced yet. Sunny and I met while I was investigating the lady who used to live next door to her. She ran a puppy mill, mistreated her dogs. Sunny was always battling to save them. A lot went on between those two and the neighbor eventually set Sunny's dog rescue on fire. She's in jail now." Sean watched Delaney's face closely for a reaction.

Delaney's lips parted and her eyes got big. "Wow," she said. "Unreal."

"It was just for a few months. Never got serious. Never got beyond..." Sean trailed off. Now he was making it worse. "Like you said, she and Pete are perfect for each other. They figured that out while Sunny and I were...were...together... But that's...that's not important."

"Wait." Delaney's horror suddenly turned to humor.

"What?"

"When I said *unreal* I was talking about the fire. I can't believe someone was cruel enough to set Sunny's rescue on fire. I'm glad that woman is in jail and I hope nobody got hurt."

"Oh, right." Sean rubbed the back of his neck. "No, nobody got hurt. Well, not permanently. Your boy Humphrey at the gym almost died, but Pete saved his life."

"Wow," Delaney repeated. "That poor little dog really has been through the wringer. Red said as much."

"Yeah."

Delaney's eyes narrowed, lips twitching into a smile. "Did you think I was going to be upset that you dated Sunny?"

"No," Sean said quickly. "Well. I thought maybe you'd find it awkward. Since we all know each other. And since we…" He made a motion in the air between him and Delaney. "Stop laughing at me like that." Even as he said it, Sean laughed, too. "C'mon. Give me a break. Some women would be uncomfortable."

"Well, there are a lot of things to consider about that, Detective." Delaney cocked her head to the side. "One, I didn't know you then. Two, it's none of my business. Three, I'd totally date Sunny. So at least I know you have good taste."

The feeling of dread that had been building in Sean dissipated like a cold sweat. He should've known Delaney wouldn't care about that kind of thing. "Thanks," he said, hoping that Delaney didn't think he'd been presumptuous about what was going on between them. He didn't want to act like he was anything special, even though he also secretly hoped he meant *something*. Sean cleared his throat. "I hope that didn't come off wrong."

"I don't see how."

"I wasn't presuming you'd care about my past just because…" Sean shrugged. "I didn't want you to think that I was…" *Shut up, Sean.*

Delaney grinned. "This is kind of cute. What you're doing right now."

Sean's neck got hot again. He decided to change the subject. "I should let you get to bed. Everything is locked downstairs. You'll be okay?"

"I'll be okay. I'm used to taking care of myself."

"I know. But it's literally my job to protect you, and I always do my job to the best of my ability."

Instead of being offended that Sean might be hinting at her

weakness or need for a male presence, Delaney's smile and posture softened, as if his words had created the opposite effect. "I know you do."

Sean really, really wanted to kiss her good-night. She was all smooth bare shoulders and tough girl vibes, wrapped up in a bouquet of shampoo coming from her damp, dark hair.

"Was there something else?" Her posture softened even more, her skin sun-kissed against the white top. "You look uncertain."

"No," Sean said, unable to move for some reason. This was the part where he should check out the apartment, like he'd said he was going to.

"You sure?" She stepped closer, erasing the space between them, and turned her face up. Her whiskey eyes sparkled in the dim light. "You seem...unsure. Kind of like—" one of her hands lit on his hip, the barest of touches "—you're trying to decide whether or not to kiss me now. Since we didn't really finish the other night."

A wave of desire rolled through Sean's body. It would be so easy to wrap an arm around her waist and crush her against him. Kiss her. Slowly remove those soft, flowery pajamas. Sean wanted to know what she looked like, head to toe, with nothing to hide an inch of that strong, supple body. He grew hard picturing her, and even though he hadn't moved a muscle Delaney slid her arms around his waist and pressed right up into him, making him groan reflexively.

"Something tells me I'm right." The rasp in her voice purred through her words. It felt like that purr melted from her body into his, rolling through him, vibrating softly. The feeling kept him trapped, unwilling to move, in case he accidentally made it stop.

"Am I wrong?" Her voice was a whisper now, her breath against his neck. Her lips kissed softly over his throat. Sean's eyes closed. Delaney had literally paralyzed him with the soft pressure of her lips, which trailed upward, along his jaw, until he tipped his head down, forcing her to find his mouth. She brushed her lips along his, but denied him the kiss he craved, instead passing over, to the other side of his jaw, where she planted little kisses that were like maddening drops of pure torture.

Sean's hand fisted at the back of her tank top, but he let her have control, resisting the urge to take over the kiss like he'd wanted to the other night. When she finally found his lips with hers, taking him in slowly like a dessert that she savored, it was worth the wait. She wound him up with increasing pressure, her lips, her tongue, teasing and plying against his until it was all he could do to not lift her in his arms and carry her to the couch. She drew back carefully and looked up at him, her irises bloomed with desire. "Well, Detective?" Her voice was low and sweet. "You promised to check out my apartment."

Sean drew a deep, calming breath. "Right." *Damn.* Castillo's words echoed through his mind: *That chick is a badass. Like, a flat-out, serious badass. She will eat you for dinner, Callahan.* Then he shoved that thought away as quickly as possible because he definitely didn't want to be thinking about Castillo while his dick was hard.

Delaney stepped back, her nipples peaked beneath the white tank top and a huge distraction to Sean's attempt to cool down and focus. As soon as he felt like his legs would work, he took steps toward the only other rooms up here. The bathroom smelled the same as her hair. The towels and accents were a soft pink. The bedroom was small, with a queen-size bed in the far corner, next to a double window. A bedside lamp that looked like a glowing pink rock revealed another pink-and-green-patchwork quilt. The closet was neat, had very few clothes and zero intruders. "Everything looks good," Sean said, bumping into her on the way out of the bedroom.

"I'm not surprised," Delaney said. "I have a Glock in my drawer over there. I already checked everything out before I showered."

Sean laughed at her sneaky grin. "Then why'd you let me up here?"

"So you'd kiss me good-night. I'm surprised you didn't figure that out, Detective."

"We didn't have to come up here to do that. You could've kissed me in your shop," Sean said. "You can kiss me anywhere."

Delaney's eyebrows rose. "I'll keep that in mind."

"But I should go now." Whoa. Had he really just said that?

"Should you?" She hooked a finger in his waistband and tugged him a little closer.

Sean let out a soft, low laugh. "Damn, you are making this hard." And now, he was going to make a decision that he couldn't believe he was making. He'd made a complete fool out of himself on more than one occasion chasing after this woman, and now that she'd basically left it open to him whether or not he wanted to stay—for at least a little longer—he wasn't going to. "Look, I have a tendency to..." He searched for words while she crossed her arms over her chest and waited patiently. "To take things too fast. I get an idea in my head and then I just run with it, like a hound. I rushed into the Marine Corps. I rushed into marriage. Even when I dated Sunny—which wasn't long after my separation—I rushed into that. Rushing never works out well for me. I just want to..." He pressed his palms together, hoping he chose the right words. "To be careful with you."

Delaney's smile fell, but the expression left on her face was more like surprise than disappointment. "I don't think any-body has ever said that about me."

Idiot, Sean thought. *What the hell is wrong with you?*

But the smile returned to Delaney's lips. "It's okay. I totally respect your wishes." She stretched her arms over her head and groaned. "I'm whipped, anyway."

Sean didn't think it'd been deliberate, but that stretch made her top tighten enticingly across her chest. Her nipples were no longer hard but he could still see the faintest outline of the darker skin. Sean's urge to lift her top and run his thumbs over that tender skin was almost overwhelming, especially since that might've been an option if he'd taken her up on her offer to stay. Instead, something strange had happened and he was acting like a scared teenager. With no other recourse, Sean headed for the stairs, wishing his blood would go back to all the places it belonged. He probably needed to be completely out of her presence for that to happen. "Hey, I was wonder-ing." Sean paused halfway down the staircase and looked up at her slender figure. "When you said you would date Sunny, were you being facetious? Or would you really date Sunny?"

"Ha," Delaney said. "Wouldn't you like to know."

"I really would."

"I really would, too." She grinned. After a moment, when Sean hadn't moved a muscle, Delaney added, "Sunny reminds me a lot of Leilani. Not in looks," she went on. "They look nothing alike. But they have a similar personality. Kind of girly and sweet, but not spoiled. Leilani was my last serious relationship. When I was stationed in Kaneohe."

Sean took a moment to mull that over. "What happened? To you and Leilani?"

Delaney shrugged. "I moved. As usual."

"She didn't want to go with you?"

"To Camp Leatherneck?"

"Ah."

"We kept in touch for a while. Then things just kind of faded away. That's what happens with all my relationships. I leave—and in the absence of each other, we fade."

Sean gave a dry laugh. "Have you ever thought about staying?"

Delaney shrugged. "We'll see how it goes. So far, I'm not so impressed with permanence."

"Right." Sean could see how, between the stolen bike and the Dudes bashing her shop at every turn, she might not think she'd made the right decision. If Sean's instincts were right—and they usually were—Delaney Monroe was struggling to not hit the road and leave everything behind. Which meant it was time for him to go. At least for now. "'Night, Delaney."

"'Night, Detective."

nineteen

If it hadn't been for the light breeze that played across the grass, Tabitha would've sweated out her tank top before the workout even started. At 0830 it was already eighty-five degrees with 80 percent humidity and that breeze felt like a gift from God, lifting stray hairs from her neck and drying some of the perspiration. As she looked around at her gym mates who littered the grounds of Canine Warriors, Tabitha knew they were thinking the exact same thing. Delaney had her head tilted back, arms open, like she could hug the unexpected wind. Trinity, a few feet away, had settled into the grass and panted gently, but she and Humphrey and about a dozen other dogs had it easy today: they were all in the shade and weren't about to work out for an hour in the dirt and blazing sun.

Rhett was in the middle of the field with Pete, who introduced himself and welcomed everyone, thanked them for coming, and for paying the fees to work out, which were all donations to Canine Warriors. Rhett took over after that, his voice much bigger than Pete's, stretching across the main dog run where everyone had gathered as he explained how today's "battle of the boxes" would work. When Tabitha had signed up last week she'd had no idea that it wasn't just Semper Fit taking part in this fundraiser, that half a dozen gyms would be there, and that the event would be a friendly competition. If she had, she probably wouldn't have come. Already she could feel everybody's ambitious moods in the air. "At least we're outside, right?" she said to Trinity, who'd settled next to Humphrey and seemed to feed off the energy, filling with happiness at all the voices, the human and dog bodies, and her return to Canine Warriors, where she'd become who she was today.

"Not only are we battling gym against gym, we're also going to be battling within our gyms, by pairing off and making this a partner event," Rhett announced, a big grin on his face like he relished dropping bombs on people when they were least expecting it.

Tabitha felt her throat tighten up as the crowd's energy went up another notch. She almost fled. The only thing that kept her in place was the memory of Auntie El, who had run around the kitchen all morning in a bright yellow sundress. The cheerful color had looked like sunshine against her dark brown skin, the brightly jeweled pies in each hand almost enough enticement to get Tabitha to do as Auntie wanted and go to church with her instead of to the fundraiser.

"You paid the money," Auntie said. "Or, I did. So they have what they need for the dogs. They could care less if you actually show up or not. Come to church with me instead. The reverend will be so pleased."

"They *couldn't* care less," Tabitha had corrected under her breath, against her better judgment, but her nerves were worn on Auntie trying to get her back into Sunday services. In fact, the mention of church had darkened her mood to the point where her need to work out, an itchy, edgy trigger that threatened to explode inside her brain, had increased tenfold.

"What's that?"

"Nothing, Auntie El. I just said I have to show up today. I made a commitment."

"Mmm-hmm." Auntie El didn't like her choice but couldn't argue. She'd raised Tabitha all her life that if you made a promise, you kept it.

No, Tabitha couldn't flee, she couldn't be sitting at home when Auntie El got back from church, especially since Trinity looked like she was enjoying herself. The poor creature never got a day off, was always working so hard.

"Form two lines," Rhett was saying, "and start counting off."

Tabitha wasn't sure what was going on, and when Rhett got to her and pointed, she parted her lips and didn't know what to say. "Seven," Rhett said. "You're seven."

"Seven," Tabitha agreed.

When Rhett was finished he told everyone to go find their partners—whoever had the same number from the opposite line. Delaney was a six, because she'd been standing right next to Tabitha. Clementine wasn't there, as she had to work, though she'd made a donation to the rescue. The only other people Tabitha knew were Constance, who was already paired up with Duke, and Detective Callahan, who wasn't present today, either.

"Lucky number seven!" a boisterous voice shouted.

Tabitha flinched. She turned around and saw Hobbs, standing a few feet away, hands on his hips while he scanned the group. He wore a pair of aviator sunglasses, a rescue dog

T-shirt and bright pink shorts. "Lucky number seven!" he shouted again. "Come get some!"

"I'm seven," Tabitha said, uncertain if Hobbs would even hear her. She was kind of hoping he didn't, that way she could approach Martha, a lady in her seventies, to see if she could swap numbers. Martha was wearing some kind of shiny pink number reminiscent of an '80s infomercial for a thigh-toning gadget.

Hobbs's grin softened beneath his mirrored shades. "Of course you are."

"We can find someone to switch with," Tabitha said. "If you want to work out with someone more your speed."

"You're exactly my speed."

"I don't want to hold you back."

"No switching," Rhett shouted, even though he was a couple yards away and couldn't possibly have heard them. "Part of this effort is everyone's ability to adapt and overcome. Maybe you have a partner you've never met. Maybe you have a partner with a vastly different fitness level. Maybe you have a partner you don't get along with. I don't care. Get together. Create a strategy that plays to your individual strengths. Make it work."

"Come on, Tabby." Hobbs nodded toward an empty patch of ground. "Let's get our equipment together and figure out our strategy."

Tabitha was fully on board with figuring out a strategy that played to their strengths. Problem was, whereas Hobbs had a lot of strengths, she didn't really have any. The workout, once unveiled, revealed med ball tosses, dumbbell snatches, med ball partner sit-ups, synchronized burpees, double unders and partner carries.

Partner carries? Tabitha's palms grew sweaty, and it wasn't because of the heat.

She didn't have much time to worry about it, as Rhett had

already called everyone in to demonstrate all the movements. As he went through each one, Tabitha's tension eased a little. They were going to be jumping rope, and out of everything in the gym, that was her jam. Growing up, jump rope had been a favorite pastime, was often all she and her girlfriends had to do on a hot summer day outside, nothing but them and the pavement and the alternative of getting into trouble. Double Dutch was the best because it required three people, two ropes, rhythm and street rhymes. When it came to jumping rope, Tabitha's youth came in handy and she often found herself singing in her head. *Cinderella, dressed in yella...*

"And that brings us to partner carries," Rhett was saying. "Hobbs." He pointed at the spot in front of him, where Zoe had just finished demonstrating double unders. "Grab your partner and bring it in."

Tabitha's heart thudded in her chest as she followed Hobbs to the patch of grass in front of Rhett. He regarded the two of them for a second too long, then loosed what could've been considered a sneaky smirk, gone too fast to tell. "I don't care how you carry your partner today," Rhett said. "But I'll show you the easiest ways. First, a simple piggyback."

Hobbs bent his knees a little and stuck his arms behind him. "Jump on," he said.

Tabitha gave a little hop and landed on Hobbs's back, knees around his waist and hands on his shoulders. His body was warm and smelled like sheets drying in the breeze on the line outside. He trotted in a circle, making the crowd laugh.

"Great job, guys," Rhett said as Tabitha slid to the ground. "Your second option is as follows. Hobbs is going to step one foot between Tabitha's. He's going to take her by the wrist and slide her onto his shoulders, his free arm behind one of her legs."

Hobbs turned to her and said, "That sound alright?"

"Sure." Tabitha felt herself flush a little.

Hobbs dipped, grasped her wrist, slid her around his shoulders and stood, hooking his arm around her thigh. His other hand gripped her forearm. As before, he walked around, easily moving her weight and going at a steady trot. People cheered, which quickly dissolved into laughter and pointing.

Tabitha wondered if her butt crack was showing, or something equally embarrassing to get the crowd going so hard, but then her gaze connected with Trinity. The little pittie trotted after Hobbs, matching his steps with her own. She rose to her haunches and pointed her nose, like she was demanding, *Put my person down!*

"Ladies and gentlemen," Rhett said, gesturing to Trinity, "Canine Warriors in action."

The crowd cheered and clapped. Pete removed his baseball cap and took a bow. Hobbs gently slid Tabitha to the ground and steadied her to her feet. "She's okay, I promise," he said to Trinity, without touching her.

"At ease, Trinity," Tabitha said. "I'm okay."

The pittie settled back on all paws and waited.

The clapping and cheering grew even louder.

"Good girl. Come." Tabitha led her back to her spot in the shade, next to Humphrey. She smiled and stroked the dog's ears, slipped a treat from her pack and gave it to her. Trinity quickly reverted to relaxed mode. "Stay," Tabitha commanded, then headed back over to Hobbs. "She'll stay with Humphrey now," Tabitha promised.

"She's welcome to work out with us." Hobbs smiled in the dog's direction. He turned back to Tabitha. "Did that feel okay?" It seemed like he might be studying her face, but it was impossible to tell with the sunglasses. "The carry?"

Tabitha ignored the little flutters that were building in her stomach, remembering the way Hobbs had gently set her down and then what appeared to be genuine concern for how she felt. "Yeah, it was fine. But we need to practice me carrying you."

"You can split the carries any way you want," Rhett was saying. "I realize some of you may be paired off with a big person and a little person. If one person does all the carrying, that's okay, though I encourage everyone to at least try. We're not going to differentiate between a conscious and an unconscious carry today, so don't even ask," Rhett added. "If your partner is unconscious, stop working out and call 9-1-1."

Laughter rippled through the crowd.

"Alright." Rhett clapped his massive hands together. "Let's make this happen!"

Hobbs and Tabitha moved back to their equipment and faced each other. "How about I do all the carrying?" Hobbs tilted his head, like he was sizing her up.

"I can do more double unders," Tabitha offered. "I can jump rope all day."

"Alright." Hobbs stuck out his fist. "Looks like we might make a good pair."

Tabitha bumped his knuckles with hers. From the corner of her eye, she caught Delaney sneaking glances as she warmed up with Duke. On her other side was Trinity, lolling in the shade with Humphrey. *I have two protectors*, Tabitha thought, which erased some of the darkness that had been building since this morning.

After Rhett shouted, *"Three, two one, go!"* everyone got down to business and Tabitha's mind was emptied of worry over Auntie El being disappointed in her, worry over whether or not she would let Hobbs down during this workout, worry that he might've noticed that ever since the Fourth of July he kind of made her knees weak—despite the fact that he flirted with every woman he saw and he was probably too old for her anyway—worry over the past, worry over the world being so big and so small all at the same time, worry over worrying. Between the heat, the music—Rhett had Daddy Yankee's "Con Calma" booming from a set of speakers in the grass—and the sweat, Tabitha didn't have time to worry. They worked methodically through their partner tosses, the heaviness of the men's ball, which Tabitha had insisted they use because she saw Delaney with the twenty pounder, making her stumble only a few times. Every stumble Hobbs would smile beneath his shades and say, "That's okay, Tabby, get a grip. Keep going."

When they got to the dumbbell snatches, Hobbs knocked out ten at the speed of light, sweat barely glistening on his brow while Tabitha struggled to drop under for the catch. "Keep the dumbbell close to your body," Hobbs said. "The more you swing out, the heavier it's going to feel. Good. That's better."

Once they made it to the sit-ups, Tabitha regretted her macho decision to use the men's med ball, but she gutted it out, her abs screaming, her torso struggling as she bent to meet her knees. Hobbs would smile, and she'd keep going, determined to make him sweat, at least a little.

"Let's go one-to-one on the burpees," Hobbs suggested, once Tabitha had struggled through her final sit-up and threw the ball, slick with her sweat, sideways in the dirt. He dropped down, pushed up, jumped to his feet and finished his first burpee in a flash.

Tabitha went next, landing in a patch of dirt and grass. She struggled up much slower, her lungs and heart screaming from the work and the heat. After completing the rep she swiped some dirt from her chin, a blade of grass stuck in her saliva and sweat. Hobbs did another burpee, then stripped his shirt over his head and laid it down in front of Tabitha. This tiny, and mostly useless, strip of protection from the ground gave her energy a boost, and she dropped quickly. The shirt was damp with Hobbs's sweat and still had that fresh-from-the-clothesline smell. She jumped up and avoided stepping on it, clapping overhead with renewed vigor.

They went back and forth like that unbroken, Tabitha pushing through the pain solely on the gesture of that shirt. It was like having a gentleman drape his cape over the proverbial puddle.

When they were done with burpees, Hobbs left his shirt in the dirt and grabbed his rope. His double unders turned out to be flawless, despite the fact that he probably didn't play much double Dutch when he was growing up. He kept his legs and arms straight and moved easily through the agreed-upon split, which was fifty for Hobbs and a hundred for Tabitha. When it was her turn for the rope she dug deep and hoped for an unbroken set, but her shoulders were too sore from the burpees and snatches and she felt the burn at fifty. She tripped and stood there, a dirty, puddly mess, trying to catch her breath.

"Let me get twenty-five while you rest," Hobbs offered.

Tabitha went to protest, but saw that Duke and Delaney were already almost done with the partner carries, Delaney slung across Duke's shoulders as he easily jogged down the field toward the turnaround marker. By the time she tore her eyes away, Hobbs was done and waiting on her to finish the last twenty-five doubles. Tabitha drew a deep breath and knocked them out without tripping.

"Alright." Hobbs stepped closer and grasped her wrist. "Ready?"

Tabitha nodded and he slipped her easily to his bare shoulders. She hung on to keep the bouncing to a minimum as Hobbs started his trek. The ground went at a downward slope so he moved with good speed. Just as he hit the turnaround marker and headed back, going slightly uphill this time, Tabitha watched Delaney finish the last hundred meters of their second carry. Delaney was slightly taller than average, at around five feet and eight inches, with a muscular build that was on the athletic, rather than bulky side. Duke, on the other hand, was over six feet of solid muscle, yet there Delaney was, hauling his giant ass over the starting marker for the last time, completing their workout. She sank to her knees, Duke spilled off her shoulders and they both collapsed in the grass.

Hobbs and Tabitha had just made one full trip down and back, where he paused to yell, "Good work, overachievers!" to the pair who were gasping in the dirt. On his second trip down, Hobbs picked up a little speed as the ground sloped down, but he went much slower than he had the first time around. Tabitha knew that her body weight was nothing to him, but even lightweight gets heavy when you're carrying it too long. As soon as they reached the turnaround marker for the second time Tabitha tapped him on the shoulder.

Hobbs, now plenty sweaty, his skin slick under Tabitha's body, paused. "You okay?"

"Hobbs," she said. "What's your name? Your first name?"

Hobbs was quiet a second. "Chris," he said finally.

"Set me down, Chris."

He obeyed, waited until she was steady before he repeated, "You okay?"

Tabitha had been able to recoup quite a bit of energy while Hobbs had done three-quarters of the carries. The memory of Delaney struggling across the finish with Duke the Giant on her shoulders fresh in her mind, Tabitha didn't even answer, just stepped between his feet and grasped his wrist. Hobbs's eyebrows raised above his sunglasses.

Tabitha nodded, then leaned in and let him fall across her shoulders. At first, her knees buckled. Hobbs wasn't overly tall but he was built. But then she caught and steadied herself, and using her legs and glutes she pushed herself to standing. Hobbs dug in, making himself small and tight as Tabitha took her first steps. To her surprise, she could move. She could actually move pretty good. Two steps. Three. Four. Yeah, she was struggling, and no, she didn't have the best posture, but she could do this. She could carry him.

She *was* carrying him.

"You got this, Tabby," Hobbs said, somewhere near her ear. "One foot in front of the other. Come on."

Tabitha made it halfway across the field before she realized she'd chosen to carry Hobbs on the incline. So now she had 180-odd pounds of muscle on her back *going up*. She paused, her head drooping under the strain, her muscles burning.

"C'mon!" somebody yelled. A stranger. Nobody she knew. Then another chimed in. And another. Clapping followed. Whistles and shouts.

"Move it or lose it, Tabby," Hobbs commanded. "You can do this. C'mon. I'm too tired to carry your fat ass any farther."

Tabitha laughed, despite the fact she was struggling to breathe. But it worked. She started up again, one foot, another foot, slowing climbing the incline, the finish line in her sights. Standing up and much recovered were Delaney and Duke, their hands cupped around their mouths while they shouted out to her.

Tabitha didn't exactly remember the last fifty meters of her carry. She was pretty sure she blacked out on her feet. Her last solid thought was *you have to get this man over that line. Period.* When she came to, she and Hobbs were on the other side of the flag marker, both on their backs in the grass.

"That's right, Steele," Delaney was saying, her voice sounding muffled through the blood that rushed in Tabitha's ears. "That's how we do it."

Something heavy covered Tabitha's chest. She knew right

away it was Trinity. Her fur smelled like grass and Auntie El's pies. She smiled, said, "Off, Trinity," with what voice she had left. "I'm okay."

Trinity scooted away and sat nearby. After a while, Tabitha sat up, too. Hobbs stood over her, hand outstretched to help her up. He smiled big, his shiny sunglasses pushed up on top of his head, revealing his bright eyes and red marks on the sides of his nose. Tabitha accepted his strong grip and rose to her feet like a newborn deer.

"Hot damn," Hobbs said, squirting some water into his mouth from a plastic sports bottle that had a faded sticker that read Murph across the front. "You're stronger than you look, am I right?"

Hobbs had dirt and grass stuck to his sweaty chest, his shirt in a ball on the ground where they'd left it. Tabitha didn't care. Her throat tight, eyes burning, she sank into him, her arms going around his back. Her eyes closed, to keep anyone from seeing her tears. Hobbs's body went rigid. After a few seconds, one hand settled tentatively between her shoulder blades. "Alright, Tabby," he said, when she didn't let go. "Alright."

twenty

"Okay, Buddy. Come tell me what you think of this." Delaney had the '33 in the center of the floor. She gave the bike a good polish with a shop rag and admired the shine on the fuel tank. "It's supposed to be a ride-in contest," she explained, as Wyatt trotted over and circled the bike. "So it doesn't have to look amazing. Just be as classic as possible." He sat near the rear wheel and gave a short bark.

This, Delaney had learned, was something he did when he was interested. It was almost like he was trying to talk to her.

"You think it has a shot?"

Wyatt gave another short bark.

"Me, too."

He hadn't been as chatty about his dog bed, on the other hand. It took Delaney two weeks to get the bed over near the foot of the staircase. Well, not so much the bed, as Wyatt himself. Delaney had found out quickly that she could move the bed all she liked, Wyatt just wouldn't follow it. For three nights he'd slept on the concrete in the storeroom instead of on the dog bed that Delaney had moved to just inside the doorway. Undeterred, she'd started over and put the dog bed back in its original place. The next night, she'd moved the bed only a couple of feet.

Pete's acclimation plan eventually worked. It just took a lot longer than Delaney thought, as she had to move the bed in much smaller increments. Now Wyatt snoozed in his dog bed by the foot of the stairs and never went near the back room. So far, Delaney had been too afraid to take that last step of moving his bed up to the apartment. That was a huge leap. Wyatt never followed her up there and it wasn't like she could move the bed in small increments up a staircase.

She tried every day, though. Wyatt would follow her command to come just to the foot of the stairs and there he'd stop. He'd sit at the bottom, shift his paws and whine while she climbed. That's when the commands became useless and Delaney was unwilling to force his will. Who knows what trauma he'd suffered around these steps. Clearly the Dudes banned him from the apartment at some cost.

He didn't like being alone, either. Every time Delaney went to the gym or out for groceries, she'd come home to ripped up trash, claw marks at the base of the front door and, once, a low shelf emptied of its contents, strewn about. Now the trash got emptied before she left and nothing lived on the low shelves. Plus, Wyatt always got a rawhide stick to chew on.

"By next month, I'm going to be itching to open that door, Wyatt." Delaney looked at the closed bay. She'd kept it closed ever since Wyatt had come home with her, practicing Pete's commands while they went for walks. Despite knowing that that training was good for Wyatt, Delaney always heard her father's voice in the back of her head if she got frustrated at his pulling or his urges to run: *You gotta let people be who they're supposed to be, Pippie.*

Anytime Wyatt seemed anxious and started tugging on the leash or when he wasn't listening to her commands, Delaney had taken up the habit of singing to him. It happened by accident, really. She'd been busy working on Sean's bike one afternoon and had started singing, like she and Dad used to do. It was a thing they had where, if the shop got too quiet, one of them would burst into song and the other would join in. Joining in was mandatory, whether you liked the song or not. Most of the time she and Dad liked the same music but sometimes they would irritate each other on purpose for humor's sake and Dad would start belting out "Free Bird" or Delaney would do "Stairway to Heaven."

"Who the hell doesn't like 'Free Bird'?" Dad had demanded the day he found out she hated it, somewhere around the age of twelve.

"Exactly the point," Delaney had said. "It's so overdone. There are way better Lynyrd Skynyrd songs."

"Like what?"

"Like 'Tuesday's Gone.'"

"Alright. Alright. Can't argue. And yet you like that sappy 'Stairway to Heaven,'" he'd said in rebuttal. "There are way better Led Zeppelin songs."

"Name one."

"'Bron-Y-Aur Stomp.'"

"I hate when you're right."

Delaney hadn't sung since Dad died. But the morning after Wyatt's fostering he was mooning around the shop, acting skittery near the front door, like if it was open he'd go running back to Sunny's. Delaney let him pace awhile, kept using Pete's commands, and sometimes he'd listen, sometimes he wouldn't. Delaney started working on Sean's bike and struck up "Take It Easy" with as much gusto as she could muster. She hadn't planned it. She just remembered how good singing with Dad used to make her feel, no matter what was going on in her life, if school sucked or her mother wanted to visit or hormones were raging.

Delaney hadn't expected it to work. But Wyatt's ears had perked up and he'd stopped pacing. He came over by the Willy G, watched Delaney work on the carburetor as she sang.

As of yet, though, Delaney had been too afraid to try out either the commands or the singing with an open bay door. Those final pieces—up the staircase and opening the bay door—would be true tests. That is, unless someone adopted Wyatt before then. Sometimes Delaney forgot that she was only fostering him. The thought of someone else taking him home made her heart feel heavy.

She took a picture of the '33 and sent it in a group text to Boom, Sal, Donny and Zip, just like she had when the motorcycle had been mysteriously returned.

She's ready to be judged, was the caption.

The replies came in quickly, one after the other. Delaney glanced at her watch, calculated time difference and figured they'd all be at Gunny's eating lunch right now.

Boom: Get 'er done Pippie.

Donny: Nobody stands a chance.

Sal: Sweet. Get pics of the Harleys while you're there.

Zip: Make sure there's carbon in the pipes, Squeaky.

Delaney smiled to herself. Zip was a judge at the classic bike show in Omaha and when he found out she'd be entering the

'33 he'd provided tips galore, all of which centered around
the bike being truly classic. So basically, his advice was like
Dad's, saying everybody should just be allowed to be themselves. "I'm going to ride it over tomorrow, so there will definitely be carbon in the pipes," Delaney spoke her text aloud
as she typed, so that Wyatt could be part of the conversation.
"You'll stay here and be a good boy, right? Remember, you
can go upstairs if you get bored down here."

Wyatt lay down on the tile and stretched out. He'd been
good all morning, greeting guests with a fair amount of di-
plomacy. He didn't approach anyone, but if someone wanted
to pet him, he was always game. Basically, he was a hit with
her crowd. Only one woman had whined about having dog
allergies, but she wasn't here for anything, had only come
along with her niece who liked old bikes and had popped in
to see what was here.

"You're not allergic to dogs, Aunt Gertrude," the niece had
said, rolling her eyes. "And if you are, go wait by the car."

"It's too hot."

"So either sweat or itch. I don't care."

Another customer had decided Wyatt looked like the shop
dog on a popular vintage car television show, and things sort
of fell into place in Delaney's mind. Those Dude brothers really had thought Wyatt was a prop to sell their bikes.

Delaney slapped the rag over the fuel tank a few more times
and decided the bike was as good as it was going to get.

Sean was going to meet her at the fairgrounds early. For
the past couple of weeks, their interactions had been mostly
business. Sean let Delaney know that the camera footage from
Prince Boulevard hadn't revealed anything better than her
eyewitness account. The rider was fully clothed and wore a
helmet, leaving no clue as to identity. Dusting the bike had
revealed nothing but Delaney's fingerprints. So they'd gotten

exactly nowhere in figuring out who had taken '33. Considering it'd been returned, and nothing unusual or threatening had happened since, Sean wasn't sure where that left the case. In any event, Delaney had assured him that she'd installed a camera at the back of the shop and she was ready to catch anyone who planned on sneaking around or smoking cigarettes under her eaves.

Something subtle had changed in Sean, though, since that kiss. Ever since his speech about taking things slow, Sean had eased up a little. It wasn't a retreat so much as a settling into the groove the two of them had created. Like they were testing the depths of their friendship before they addressed the sizzling undercurrent that was always there. Maybe they were testing each other's past habits: Delaney was trying to see if Sean had any chase left, and Sean was waiting to make sure Delaney didn't bolt.

Delaney eyed the '33, and, despite everything that had happened, was happy with her chances tomorrow. Good thing, because she would need the prize money for next month's rent. She looked up at the picture of Dad on the wall and gave him the thumbs-up. The shop was suddenly too quiet. Even though Wyatt was snoring softly in his bed and not at all antsy, Delaney started singing, *"If I leave here tomorrow... would you still remember me?"*

Otherwise perfectly still, Wyatt thumped his tail.

Sean had been to the county fairgrounds a million times over, ever since he was a little kid. They hosted an annual fair, which, over the years, as the area had become less and less rural, had become less and less about showing off prized hogs and giant vegetables and more and more about cheap carnival rides. There were also gun shows, car shows, quilt shows, craft fairs—you name it, the fairgrounds had hosted it.

An attendant in a reflective vest waved him to a long line of cars parked in the grass and dirt outside the gates. Sean angled the minivan next to a Harley Fat Boy and stepped out into the blazing July sun. It was going to be a hot one today, but at least rain wasn't forecast. Delaney had been so excited to get the '33 back in time for the show it would've been a blow to have the event rained out, though the flyer said that would only happen if there was an electrical storm.

Inside the grounds, there were motorcycles everywhere. Vendor stalls that rimmed the area were a hodgepodge of bike shops, parts shops, gear shops, riding groups—anything at all related to motorcycles had been jammed into spaces that ranged from small to large, depending on who had the most money. Sean's feet crunched on popcorn from the fair, which had ended last weekend, as he headed toward the opposite side, where Delaney had said the concours would be. That's what he loved most about the fairgrounds: one weekend there could be guns and ammo and the next an antique doll show, but anything and everything in between was welcome and seemed to fit in here. The grounds and the parking and the wooden buildings that housed some of the vendors never changed, but what was inside the gates could be as different as night and day, depending on the week. Connecting every event were threads of shows past, so that popcorn from the fair could end up stuck in your boots when you arrived to check out the Classic Motorcycle Show. Everything was a part of everything else, the ghosts of shows past all around, on the ground and even in the air—stale cotton candy, sweetening the wind.

The crowd, like the events that took pace at the fairgrounds, was eclectic, but leaned heavily toward leather and tattoos. Sean figured he would blend in at least a little, wearing jeans, boots and a Capitals T-shirt sporting the championship victory in 2018. A good handful of people had dogs.

He reached the opposite end of the fairgrounds just in time to see Delaney drive in on her dad's recovered motorcycle. She maneuvered the bike out to where she was directed by the organizer, then stripped her helmet and shook out her short, dark hair. Sean enjoyed watching her as she pulled off her gloves, tucked them in the back pocket of her jeans and raked her fingers through her hair, checking herself out in the motorcycle's single round mirror. When she was satisfied, she left the bike in the lineup for judging and looked around. When she spotted Sean, she headed his way.

"Guess what," Delaney said, as soon as their boots were toe to toe, her smile big.

"You won already. They took one look at her and fell in love."

"No," she laughed.

Sean let the heartbeat of silence register and wondered if he'd just voiced something really, really stupid.

"They allow dogs," Delaney said. "As long as they're well-behaved and on a leash."

Sean quickly connected the dots. They allowed well-behaved dogs here. Wyatt was a well-behaved dog. Delaney had ridden her motorcycle here. Wyatt, the well-behaved dog, wouldn't fit on her motorcycle. "You want me to go get Wyatt."

"Oh, wow, would you?" She leaped on it. "He would have so much fun. Get him outside, away from the shop and the neighborhood. You know he has a vagabond soul. He needs to get out and see the world."

"A vagabond soul?" Sean shook his head. "Wow, you're good."

"Well." Delaney shrugged in mocked innocence. She dug

her keys out of her pocket and slipped one off the ring. "This is to the front door. His leash is hanging on a hook right next to it. He's trained on basic commands, like come, stay, sit, down."

"It's like we're an old married couple." The words slipped out before Sean could stop himself. "And we haven't even slept together."

"Well, that can change."

Sean reached for the key in her outstretched fingers and closed his hand around hers. "How do you expect me to enjoy the motorcycle show now that there's only one thing I'm going to be thinking about the whole time?"

"Is that what you're here for? The motorcycles?"

"Damn straight," Sean joked. "Getting ideas for my Willie G. Maybe I can ride him in next year. How's that going, by the way?"

"It's going." Delaney got a sneaky little grin on her lips. "I can tell a lot about a man by working on his Willie."

"Oh, yeah?" Sean was suddenly aware of the warming sun burning down on him. "Like what?"

"Like how well he took care of it. How hard he rode it. If he's worthy of it." She slowly slid her hand away.

For a moment, Sean was paralyzed. How the hell was he going to take things slowly if she was going to keep talking like that? "I better go get Wyatt." Just like that night at her apartment, distance was probably the only solution right now.

"We don't want him to miss the judging," Delaney agreed, the faintest of smiles on her lips. "Besides, I have to go register my bike." She pointed toward a table that had people filling out forms.

Sean got his hand stamped on the way out, then drove fifteen minutes to Delaney's shop, his mind on her lithe body in her jeans and tank top and the way her eyes looked gold in the sun. He briefly wondered what color combination had created hers: green and brown, maybe? Then he wondered whose eyes were green and whose were brown. Green for the vagabond dad, he decided, the color of mystery, magic and new beginnings—because Delaney wasn't fooling anyone about why she loved this dog that Sean was going out of his way to collect.

He unlocked the shop and stepped inside. It smelled of motor oil and coffee. There was a standard drip coffee maker to the left of the counter, on a little table with cups and packets of sugar and creamer. There was a white coffee mug by the register with a vintage motorcycle printed on it and the name Pipsqueak above, like it had been personalized. It was a quarter full of coffee, black. Sean wondered if Delaney was Pipsqueak, and if that had been her father's nickname for her. The thought made him smile. The mug was otherwise clean, no ring of bright pink lipstick on the rim like Kim's. Sean didn't think he'd ever seen Delaney wear lipstick, now that he thought about it.

He was about to check the storeroom when he saw that Wyatt was on his dog bed, at the foot of the staircase. Delaney had been somewhat successful in moving the bed, but obviously hadn't made the final leap to upstairs. Wyatt perked up at the sound of Sean approaching, his face curious. "Woof." It was a unique bark—almost like the sound of a person saying *woof*.

"Hey, boy." Sean collected the leash and gave the dog a wave.

Wyatt rose to his feet, his curious look ceding to something more apprehensive.

"I know," Sean said. "I'd be disappointed, too, if I was expecting Delaney and I walked in the room instead."

Wyatt backed up, moving away from Sean until his butt hit the edge of the staircase.

"Hey, it's okay." Sean held up both his hands, like one of his suspects, under arrest. "I'm a friend. She asked me to come get you."

"Woof."

"What does that mean?" Sean was starting to feel increasingly foolish. First, he'd waved at the dog. Then he'd held up his hands, like he'd been caught during a robbery. Now he was asking the dog what he meant by *woof.*

Wyatt leaned harder into the staircase, physically rearing back, even though Sean had not approached any farther.

"C'mon, Wyatt." Sean dropped to one knee. "I know this will surprise you, being a cop and all, but I'm a cat person. I don't know what to do with this." He gestured to Wyatt's flinching body. "I take it you don't like men very much. It can't be me, right? Because I'm pretty cool. I may not look it, but I'm one seriously cool dude. So maybe just let me..." Sean leaned forward, extending the leash.

Wyatt bolted up the stairs. In a flash of white fur and scrambling paws, he was gone, around the corner and into the apartment.

And this day just kept getting better. "We're going to miss the judging!" he called up the stairway. "Delaney's counting on us!" The sound of paws scrambling over the apartment followed, then silence. Wyatt had settled in somewhere to hide. Sean sighed. He really didn't want to go up to the apartment without permission but Delaney wanted Wyatt and that left Sean little choice. He headed upstairs and found the apartment completely silent. The living space was tidy, the pink-and-green quilt draped neatly over the back of the couch, the television off.

No dog.

"Wyatt? Where'd you go?" Sean called out, but nothing. His only saving grace was there weren't a lot of places to hide in a studio apartment. He put himself in Wyatt's head. If Sean were hiding from a large man—and he didn't like large men—he'd probably go wherever it smelled the most like a sweet woman. Sean poked his head in Delaney's bedroom, which was also tidy and quiet. Wyatt was not on the bed, where Sean thought he might go, nor in the bathroom. The small closet was also devoid of canines.

"What the hell...?" Sean mused aloud. His gaze settled on a laundry basket in the corner. It was full of white linens and towels, like Delaney had just changed the bed sheets. The mound of linens shifted.

"Wyatt." Sean spoke softly as he neared the basket. "Are you hiding in the laundry?" Once Sean was right on top of the basket he could see that part of the white mound was Wyatt's rump. The dog wasn't just in the basket, he was deep in the laundry, too. The sight was cute enough to make Sean chuckle but it also made his heart ache. Wyatt was scared.

The pittie was found, but what now? Sean wasn't about to reach in and haul out a frightened dog. He stared at the ceiling and thought about all the ways he'd used to get Callie to come out of hiding—she always knew when it was time to go to the vet—but Sean didn't think putting out an empty box or building a tent with blankets would entice the dog.

While he was thinking, something about the drop ceiling caught his eye. One of the panels in the far corner was slightly pushed in, like someone had popped it open and neglected to nestle it back in the runner. The ceiling had not been like that the night '33 was returned and Sean cased Delaney's apartment. He would've noticed. Sean fetched a stool from the kitchen, brought it back to the bedroom, stood on it and poked his hand through the dislodged panel. He felt around inside the ceiling space, but came up with nothing.

Sean carefully replaced the panel and returned the stool to

the kitchen, his brain puzzling. Maybe it was nothing. Maybe the ceiling had always been that way. He suddenly felt guilty for poking around in Delaney's bedroom so decided he'd check to make sure all the doors were locked before he left, and if so, he'd just not mention this.

Meantime, Wyatt still hadn't come out of the laundry.

Sean headed back downstairs and spied Wyatt's empty food bowl on the floor near his bed. Well, that was one thing that worked universally on all species. He searched behind the counter and came up with a box of dog biscuits. On a whim, he shook it. Silence. He shook it again.

A moment later, the sound of paws over the ceiling came faint but certain. One more shake of the box and Sean was rewarded by the sound of paws lumbering down the stairs.

"The good news is," Sean said, when he arrived over an hour later, Wyatt trotting at his side and Sean looking a little too sweaty for having simply collected the pit bull, "I know how to get Wyatt to go upstairs to your apartment."

Wyatt strained against the leash when he spotted Delaney, so she jogged the last couple of yards between them and greeted him by petting his ears. She slipped the leash from Sean as they walked, and Delaney listened to Sean explain his trials of the past hour, with way more humor in his voice than irritation. Wyatt trotted along happily, his head turning this way and that, admiring the crowd and the motorcycles and the smells of greasy food truck fare on the wind. Sean used broad arm gestures while he talked about Wyatt being frightened, running upstairs, the dog biscuit trick and then the gentle struggle to get him into the minivan without being traumatized. A trail of biscuits like the candy pieces in *E.T.*, leading from the shop to Sean's van had been a slow but successful strategy.

"Those Dudes really did a job on him," Delaney said, her heart squeezing up at the thought.

They walked as Sean talked, and Wyatt came alive like Delaney had never seen him, that last little bit of desperate loneliness he clung to vanishing with the breeze as he loped around the motorcycles and the bikers and gobbled up the stray popcorn pieces in his path. Then, in one unexpected moment, something funny happened inside her, way down deep, in a place she kept tucked away tight, safe and protected. She hadn't felt this way since Chunk crossed the threshold, that warm Omaha night. Since that day in Boom's shop when she and Dad first battled it out over "Free Bird" and "Stairway to Heaven." Since she'd changed out her first clutch, nothing but a skinny kid in braids and miniature motorcycle boots.

Delaney didn't realize she'd frozen in her tracks until Sean asked her what was wrong. He and Wyatt were both staring at her with concern.

"What? Oh." Delaney shook herself free. "It's nothing," she said. "I just...just..." She glanced at the stall she was facing—a vendor called Hell's Bells that sold protective bells for motorcycles. "I just want to look at the bells," she lied.

"Oh, my heavens, isn't he the cutest thing on God's green earth?" The vendor, a tall woman with bright red hair, wearing a Harley vest and a full sleeve of tattoos, shoved through her tables, straight toward Wyatt.

Glad for the save, Delaney smiled as the woman bent to pet him.

"What's his name?"

"Wyatt."

"Like Wyatt Earp," the woman said, kissing Wyatt right on his muzzle. Wyatt took the kiss in stride, not even flinching.

"You've got an amazing assortment here," Delaney said, pressing into the stall to get a look at the goods. At a quick glance, Hell's Bells seemed to have every kind of bell a person could want. The perfect size to affix to the back of one's motorcycle, the little bells were decorated with roses, gremlins in cages, Jesus and the cross, guns, cats, skulls, roses, words—like *lady rider*—angels and dragons. Delaney could spend an hour here and not get bored.

"Thanks." She gave Wyatt one last kiss on the top of his head then stood up and stuck out her hand. "Lydia," she said. "Feel free to ring my bells."

"Delaney," she said, as they all laughed at her joke. "I just opened a shop on Three Rebels Street. Triple M Classics? We sell, repair and rebuild vintage bikes, parts, apparel." She handed Lydia a business card. "I was too late to get a vendor space this year."

Lydia took the card and looked it over. "I've heard of your place," she said. "All the women riders I know are saying good things. I'll definitely check it out. Any interest in carrying bells?" She handed over her own business card.

"Definitely." Delaney checked out the card before slipping it in her back pocket. "These would be amazing for behind the register. I have a glass case with nothing of note to put there. Your bells are definitely something people will see on the way out and just have to buy."

"They're not just any old bells, either," Lydia said. She lifted one from the table, nestled atop a black velvet pouch. "My old man designs most of these himself." The pewter bell was about an inch and a half tall and had a skull carved on the front, along with the words *ride it like you stole it* around the bottom of the bell. The skull's eyes were gleaming red jewels. "Not real jewels, of course," Lydia said. "That would be stupid, seeing as how it'll be dangling over the open road all day. Every bell comes with one of these." She showed Delaney the little paper inside the velvet pouch, which explained the legend of the Evil Road Spirits that latched on to motorcycles and brought their riders bad luck. To defeat them, motorcyclists attached the protective bells to their bikes, where the road spirits would get trapped and go insane by the constant ringing of the bells and would fall to the ground, defeated.

"These are great," Delaney said. "I'll definitely get in touch."

"Awesome. Thanks."

Delaney waved goodbye just as a young woman asked to ring up one of the bells with a rose carved on it.

Wyatt loped along after them, his nose either in the air or on the ground, that little smile on his face as he admired the big, wide world of motorcycles and the fairgrounds.

They stopped at the food trucks and while Sean ordered himself a gyro Delaney searched for vegetarian fare. She knew where to look in places like this, where the highlights were always smoked meat or meat on sticks or giant meat you could clutch in one hand. Off in a corner, hiding behind all the smoke curling into the blue sky, was a smoothie truck, which was popular due to the heat. Delaney was surprised that Groovy Smoothie listed an impressive array of tantalizing options, as she often had to make do with overly sweet lemonade or snow cones with five different artificial flavor options. Sean shared his gyro meat with Wyatt while Delaney sipped on a banana strawberry matcha smoothie with spinach. Both of them wrinkled their noses at each other's lunches but Sean wasn't above taking a sip and admitting how good the smoothie was.

When they were done, they hit the rest of the vendors before Delaney glanced at her watch and got butterflies in her stomach. "We better get to the concours. Judging will begin soon."

Delaney was surprised at how many bikes were waiting to

be judged by the time they made it back to the other side of
the fairgrounds. When she'd driven in this morning she'd seen
only a couple dozen motorcycles but now the space boasted
over a hundred bikes for the concours alone. Delaney pointed
out the different categories for Japanese, European, American
and British bikes. "Within each category there are subcatego-
ries based on Veteran, Vintage and Classic, as well as Custom,
Racers, Choppers, Standard, Lightweight, etcetera," she said.
"Dad's bike is only in the concours competition. It's technically a classic and an antique. We're hoping for Best in Show."

"Of course we are," Sean agreed. He eyed the field, which
was literally a field, with all the bikes parked directly on a
swath of green grass that seemed to go on forever. "I see a lot
of amazing bikes but none that compare. Only because your
bike is so unique. And well taken care of." Sean nodded toward a '64 Triumph polished to the gills, its black-and-silver-
striped fuel tank gleaming in the sun. "That looks like your
strongest competition."

Delaney was reading the specs on the entry card, which
rested on the grass, against the motorcycle—"superflow head,
800cc routt cyl., trw pistons"—when a big voice came booming over her shoulder.

"That's ours."

Delaney turned to find Dude and Dick standing only a few
feet away, like they'd been watching her. They wore matching black leather vests, boots and sunglasses pushed up on the
tops of their heads.

"Nice ride," Sean said. "I see you guys are back into motorcycles."

"Nice dog," Dick countered, his eyes narrowing at Wyatt.
"And we never stopped riding."

"Oh," Sean said, keeping his voice mild. "Thought you
guys gave it up after your shop failed."

"We moved to our father's place," Dude chimed in. "We'll be opening up a new shop soon. Better location."

"The location has been good to me so far," Delaney said. "Despite the lies you two are spreading around about me." She felt Wyatt's body tighten through the leash, even though her grip was loose.

"No idea what you're talking about." Dick's steely gaze shifted downward. "Hey, Sinbad." His voice rose in pitch. "There you are. Hey, boy." He stepped toward him, arm outstretched.

Wyatt backed up, pressing into Delaney's side. "His name is Wyatt now," she said.

"The hell it is." Dude snorted as Dick retracted his hand. "His name is Sinbad and he's my dog. And now I've got space for him. Twenty-acre farm for him to run around."

A pang of guilt ran through Delaney, even as Dick's words fueled her anger. She thought back to how many times Wyatt had escaped Sunny's doggie heaven, risking the woods and getting stuck in slippery ditches in thunderstorms just to satiate his need to explore. The only way anyone had been able to contain him so far was with strict training and commands. Dad wouldn't have approved, yet he wouldn't have wanted to turn Wyatt over to Dude and Dick, either.

"I'm happy for you," she said. "But you gave up on Wyatt. And you didn't treat him well when you had him."

"You don't know anything about us," Dude said.

"Right." Dick's deadpan face was enhanced by his soulless eyes. "She doesn't. But she'll learn."

"What do you mean by that, exactly?" Sean stepped up, slightly in front of Delaney.

Dick flicked his gaze at Sean, then quickly back to Delaney. "This is the last time I'm going to ask you to give my brother's dog back."

Delaney wanted to fill in the blank. *Or...?*

But Dick took her silence as refusal. "That's that, then," he said.

Wyatt whined.

"You two can shove off." Sean's voice came cool and controlled. His hand rested on her shoulder. "And if I were you, I'd be careful about the things you're spreading around town about Delaney and her shop."

"Don't know what you're talking about," Dick repeated.

"Uh-huh." Sean guided her away, closer to the judging and well away from the Dudes. Wyatt followed, the happy back on his face and a bounce to his step.

"Thanks for that," Delaney muttered, once they were out of earshot. Much of her joy about the bike show had evaporated, leaving her feeling sick and strained.

"I've got your back. Don't worry."

"I know, but..." Delaney paused, pushing her hair back from her sweaty forehead. "Those guys are really trying to mess with me now." She closed her mouth and shook her head, ashamed at herself. Was she really letting these guys get to her? So many years of dealing with the loneliness of being a female marine, of dealing with sexism and stalkers and being underestimated, and she'd taken them all on, pushing her way through and smacking them down. *Suck it up, Squeaky,* Dad would say. Or, if it were Boom, *No weakness.* Sal's version: Que verguenza! *Don't let anyone take up space in your head for free,* pequita.

"Hey." Sean took her gently by the arms, both of his hands on her biceps.

Delaney looked up at him, waiting for the usual platitudes. *I understand how you feel.* Which he didn't. *You're bigger than them.* Delaney was tired of having to be bigger. *Ignore them.* Which solved nothing.

Sean glanced down at Wyatt, who was smiling up at them, wagging his tail against the grass. "I'm not going to let those guys mess with you," he said.

Delaney tried to smile, too, but it wouldn't come. She wasn't used to being the one who needed protecting. She wanted to lean on Sean, but leaning too often led to falling.

"C'mon," Sean said. "Let's go near the stage. Looks like they're about to announce the winners."

They did just that as over the next half hour the winners of the various categories got ribbons tied to their bikes and the emcee—an older man in jeans and a faded Ride for Kids T-shirt—announced them over a microphone. Best in Show was last, and as the judge wove through the bikes, inspecting each one and writing on his clipboard, Delaney passed on to Sean what she knew. "He's looking for stock pipes, stock paint, carbon in the pipes. My uncle Zip judges these kind of events and he says that by the time he's checked the plates, pipes and paint he's eliminated nearly three-fourths of the field."

"Your uncle Zip must really know his shit." Sean's brow narrowed as he eyed the motorcycles. "Some of them are really flashy."

"A lot of times the flashy ones don't make it because they're trailer queens," Delaney said. "Or what I call divas." She grinned. "Which would be fine for a show event, but this isn't that. This is all about how classic is your classic. So once Zip gets past the plates and pipes and paint he's literally down to the nuts and bolts. Gauges. Front forks."

Sean's face fell as the judge hung a ribbon on the Dudes' Triumph.

"It's okay," Delaney said. "He's just marking all the finalists." She pointed as the judge walked past several other bikes to hang an identical ribbon on the '65 Ducati Mach 1 that Delaney had admired on her way in this morning. The judge then walked near Dad's '33. He would either walk on by or stop and hang a ribbon. Unless she was seeing things, Sean crossed his fingers and hid his hand behind his back.

The judge stopped and hung a ribbon on the '33.

"Yesss!" Sean hissed, pumping his fist at his side.

"I think you're more excited than I am," Delaney laughed. Her humor died away as she watched Dick walk up to the judge and pull him aside. Dick pointed at '33 and said something to the judge, who nodded and said something back. Dick made a few gestures and spoke again. The judge nodded, then knelt down and inspected Delaney's bike.

"Sean, what are they doing?" Delaney said, her voice almost a whisper.

"I don't know," Sean said, even though both the question and the answer had been rhetorical.

"'33 is prime for the show," she insisted. "What's going on?"

This time, Sean stayed silent.

Dick, who was still standing behind the judge, glanced up at that moment. His gaze connected with Delaney's.

Dick smiled.

It felt like Delaney's heart stopped.

The judge finished his perusal, rose, wrote on his clipboard, then handed his list over to the emcee.

Dick turned away, collected Dude, who was standing a few feet behind, and the two of them headed back toward the stage for the final results.

Delaney drew a deep, steadying breath and looked up at Sean.

Sean returned the look, but said nothing, his face set in hard lines, his jaw grinding.

Delaney swallowed the tightness in her throat, then knelt and poured her water bottle over Wyatt's lapping pink tongue. He was panting now, as the searing sun was directly overhead and beating down. "We're almost done, boy," she said. "Then we can go back to the shop where your dog bed is. Trust me, I want to go home, too."

Wyatt lapped up the stream of water and seemed to enjoy the drops that landed on his face.

"Alright, folks." The emcee had a big Southern twang to his voice. "We're down to the last trophy of the day—the Dogwood Classic Motorcycle Award. This is also considered Best in Show. We've seen a lot of amazing bikes today and we want to thank everyone who participated. This is a great field of motorcycles. Okay, here we go." The emcee slipped on his glasses and peered at the sheet he'd been handed by the judge. "In third place we have Ginny Wilson with her beautiful '65 Ducati Mach 1."

The crowd cheered and applauded as Ginny, a petite woman with dark brown skin and a head full of silver hair climbed the stage. She wore a motorcycle vest that had Black Magic Woman Bikers emblazoned on the back. A pack of older ladies near the front of the stage who wore similar vests called out, "Go, Ginny!" as she accepted her bag of prizes.

"Thank you, Ginny," the emcee said as she exited the stage. "Gorgeous bike. Okay. We'll announce the second place and the first place winners at the same time."

"This is it." Delaney's heart was beating so hard she felt sick. Sean was beside her in complete silence, like he sensed a storm coming. Wyatt rose to his feet and wagged his tail.

The Dudes, up front near the stairs, were laughing and chatting with each other. Dick glanced her way. Delaney quickly averted her gaze, her legs now shaking.

"In second place...we have Delaney Monroe, with her '33 Indian Four! And in first, winner of the Dogwood Classic Motorcycle Award, is Richard Worley, with his '64 Triumph! Come on up, y'all!"

The Dudes high-fived each other and climbed the stairs to the stage. Sean placed his hand on Delaney's shoulder and squeezed. Delaney stood there a moment, the jangle of her nerves settling into disappointment and confusion. After a while of just standing there, frozen, unsure if she could move, the emcee repeated Delaney's name. Sean gave her a little nudge, so Delaney put one foot in front of the other and discovered that her legs worked, even though they felt like concrete. She climbed the stairs as the crowd clapped and cheered, and stood next to the emcee. The Dudes were on his other side, smiling. Dude held a trophy in his hands and Dick had an envelope, which presumably contained his cash winnings.

"Congratulations, Richard and Delaney! Good job today, everyone. Thank you. Please enjoy the rest of the day. Show is open until four."

The emcee and judge both shook Delaney's hand as she accepted her second place ribbon and a bag of swag. "Good job, Ms. Monroe."

"Yes, sir," she said, her voice sounding thin. "Thank you."

The judge, an older man with a bushy white beard and long, white hair to match, smiled at Delaney. "That's a fine piece of machinery you got there, miss. You've taken good care of it."

"Thank you, sir." Delaney's palms were sweaty and a headache was forming at her temples. "It was my father's. He passed away this year." She bit down on her lower lip. TMI. Nobody wanted to know her sob story. She'd taken second place to what was admittedly a beautiful bike. It was her own fault for banking so much on winning that cash prize and advertising. And all of that would've been fine, if it weren't for the Dudes, standing there, looking like the fat cats that had eaten an entire flock of canaries. She desperately wanted to ask the judge what Dick had said to him, but that wouldn't be appropriate and she would come off like a poor loser.

"I'm sorry for the loss of your dad," the judge said, his voice taking a tender, grandfatherly tone. "But good on him for taking care of that cycle. And for how you've cared for it, too."

"Thank you, sir."

He leaned in close. "You would've won first place, if it weren't for the cadmium-plated rear brake rod. Your bike is a true testament to the classics. I have to admit, you surprised a lot of us today. Word on the street has been, well..." He glanced at the Dudes, then shook his head. "Never mind. You obviously do great work. You made your dad proud. But in the end it came down to you having that brand-new part on the bike."

Delaney heard everything the judge said, but it was all background noise to his first sentence. "Wait. The rear brake rod? What do you mean?"

"It's not a big thing. I almost didn't notice it myself. But it did become the tiebreaker. I'd love to see you enter it again next year, though. And I'm going to check out your shop soon. I'll bring a bunch of my group by, if that's okay."

"Definitely." Delaney tried a smile, even though her brain was still racing. "Thank you."

As Delaney watched the judge exit the stage, she rolled his words around in her head. Was he thinking of a different bike? '33 had an original brake rod—that admittedly needed replacing, but Delaney hadn't gotten around to that yet. She caught Sean, from the corner of her eye, squinting in the sun with Wyatt by his side, panting with his big, pink tongue out.

She slowly turned to Dick, who was just now exiting the stage. He looked over his shoulder at her, pressed his fingers to his temple and gave her a mock salute. Then he laughed. Dude laughed, too.

Delaney rushed off the stage, barreling past them, over to

'33, where she quickly checked it over. He couldn't be right, could he? She'd checked the whole bike out, multiple times.

Except it was right there, just like the judge had said. Delaney knelt down on the grass to keep steady.

"What's wrong?" Sean and Wyatt were by her side.

"The rear brake rod," Delaney said, running her fingers over it. "Somebody replaced it." She peered closer at the bike and wondered how she could have missed such a thing. "The generator bracket, too. They're cadmium plated. They weren't before."

"Which means...?"

Delaney looked up at Sean and squinted into the sun. It felt like her entire body had been drained of blood. "The Dudes sabotaged my bike."

twenty-one

B ack at the shop, Delaney opened the front bay and drove '33 right into the shop. Later, when she wasn't so frazzled, she wanted to get Dad's bike up on a lift and go over it with a fine-toothed comb. Sean pulled up beside her and let Wyatt out, who raced inside and lapped at his water for about thirty seconds straight, then dove into his bed, curled up and closed his eyes.

"Thanks for hauling him back and forth today." Delaney set her swag bag and ribbon on the counter, which included coupons and little gifts. At a quick peek, she noticed a package from Hell's Bells in there, but couldn't get excited about it. Her brain was still going a thousand miles a minute about what had happened at the motorcycle show.

"No problem." Sean, whose face was tanned from the day spent in the sun, looked over at '33. "I'm going to check out your storeroom again."

"Knock yourself out," Delaney offered. She followed him

into the back and watched as he put his hand on the chain used
to raise and lower the bay door. He imitated the motion, pulling on an invisible chain, then squatted down and examined
the floor, touching the concrete lightly with his fingertips.

"What're you thinking?"

Sean glanced up at her. "I don't know yet."

"This is no mystery, Sean. The Dudes did this. Plain and
simple. They stole '33, then put in new parts to sabotage me
in the show. They knew I was planning on entering because I
told them so at my grand opening. They also are very familiar
with the show and the judging. They waited until the judge
was looking over '33 and then pointed out the new parts."

Sean rose and rolled his shoulders back, like he was working off some stiffness. "But if they went to the trouble of
stealing the bike, why not keep it? I don't think sabotaging
you in the show is the best plan for them. They were already
sabotaging your business by talking shit about you to everyone around town. If they stole the bike, my bet is that they
could've sold it or stripped it for parts. They have those kinds
of connections. But to steal the bike, put in new parts, then
give it back and hope you don't notice... This doesn't seem
like them. They're mean, and probably dangerous, but they're
not particularly clever."

"But they pointed out the new parts," Delaney insisted,
even though Sean's logic was sound. "We both saw them
talking to the judge. This was a way to come at me from behind. Make me look foolish and be able to see my face when
it all went down."

"I agree that the Dudes saw the new parts and pointed them
out to the judge. That's as far as I'll go."

"They saw the new parts because they put them there,"
Delaney insisted.

Sean shook his head. "No. It's personal."

"I know you like solving cases, Sean. But this is no great mystery."

"No," Sean said. "I mean, it's *personal*." He nodded toward the front of the store, where '33 sat.

Delaney felt the hairs on the back of her neck rise. "What are you saying?"

Sean planted his hands on his hips and looked around. "I'm saying what's been bothering me this whole time."

"Which is what?" She watched Sean's expression change as his mind ran through the puzzle. He looked almost like a little kid figuring out how something works for the first time. "Did your rear break rod need replacing?"

"Yes. I just hadn't gotten around to it."

"See? Whoever stole the bike didn't want to chop it up and sell it for parts. That much we know. Whoever stole the bike took care of it. They *fixed* it. Then they gave it back. Why would they give it back?"

Delaney ruffled her hair, working out the wind and sweat from the day. "To mess with me. We already established that."

"But if they wanted to mess with you…" Sean grabbed the chain and raised the door, for real this time, which creaked and groaned. When it was open about two feet, he stopped. "Is this about how much you left the door open that night?"

"Yeah," Delaney said. "I left it propped open in case Wyatt came back to the shop while I was out looking for him. I didn't want him stuck out in the storm."

"You left it open just enough for the dog to fit through. Which meant you had to duck to get in and out." Sean imitated, bending in half to go out, then back in.

Delaney rubbed her forehead with the back of her wrist, her mind scrambling to follow Sean's train of thought. "Alright, Callahan, I'm a grunt mechanic, what're you—"

"The person who stole your bike came upon an open door,"

Sean cut in. "They knew you had gone out. They probably watched you leave." He ducked outside the door, then ducked back in. "That's how they got in. But in order to get the bike out—" Sean grasped the chain and raised the door all the way "—they had to do this." He pointed at the wide-open door. "Is this how you found it? When you came back?"

Delaney thought back to that night. "No. It was just like I left it," she said, her voice low as she pictured the scene. "I would've noticed right away if the bay was wide-open." She closed her eyes and let the memory flesh out. "Yeah." She opened her eyes again. "I had to duck to get back inside."

"Which means," Sean said, lowering the bay door all the way and tamping it down with his foot to lock it, "whoever stole the '33 took the time to put the door back how they found it. Why?"

"Well... I..." Delaney sighed, feeling stupid. "Probably so that when I got back I wouldn't notice right away that the bike was gone. Like I said, I would've noticed a wide-open bay right off."

"Okay." Sean shrugged. "So how long did it take you after getting inside and drying off Wyatt and settling him in his dog bed to notice the bike was gone?"

"Not long."

"Right. So by not alerting your attention to a wide-open bay, the thief saved himself a couple of minutes, tops. That's not really worth the effort of getting off the bike and messing with the door, especially since he had no idea when you might come back."

Delaney rubbed her temples in slow circles. "None of this makes sense."

"Agreed. That's why I'm not convinced this was the Dudes." Sean crossed his arms over his chest. The gesture highlighted his big pecs and biceps. He looked like a tough, sun-kissed cowboy in his boots and jeans. "I know you dislike them, and for good reason. But I'm not convinced they stole your bike."

"Oh, really?" Delaney crossed her arms over her chest, too. "Then who did? Poor old Walt, the retired shop teacher? C'mon, Sean."

"I don't know yet. But I'm going to find out." This was the first time that Sean's gray eyes looked the tiniest bit blue, like sparks of the sky had shot through the clouds.

Delaney stepped a little closer, rested her hands on Sean's biceps and peered up at him. The blue inside the steely gray intensified. "I think you're wasting your time," she said. "If you focus on the Dude brothers, you'll find the evidence." Though, suddenly, she didn't want to talk about it anymore. The day was over. The bike was safe. The shop was closed and Wyatt was asleep and happy in the next room. Delaney could pick up the threads of this knotted mess tomorrow, when her head was clear.

Sean's arms loosened, inviting her closer. "I don't think I'm wasting my time one bit," he said, though the tone of his voice suggested that he wasn't focused on the Dudes anymore, either. He reached up and rubbed the scar near his eye, then blinked a few times, like he was clearing away some dizziness.

It hit Delaney then just how hard Sean had been working on this case. Just how much time he'd been putting in for her. All for her. He must be exhausted.

She held his gaze for a spell before she tipped up on her toes, leaned in and gently pressed her lips to that scar. Sean's body jolted. He gave a sharp exhale. She lingered there until his arms loosened completely and one of them crooked around her waist.

Delaney drew back slowly. "I wanted to give you something else to think about when you see that scar," she whispered.

Sean's eyes changed, pupils expanding. He watched her

a moment in silence, like he was making a decision. Then
he leaned in, pausing at her lips. Instead of kissing her, Sean
dipped his head down and pressed his lips to her neck, just
below her jaw. The contact rooted and bloomed, sending a
rush of heat through Delaney's weary body, livening her. He
kissed her again, a little lower. Then again, right at the crook
of her neck and shoulder. His lips were soft and suggestive.
Curious. Warm.

Delaney's body had the slightest tremble. She could feel it
all over, like a tremor beneath her boots. She wasn't used to
patient men. Men who didn't leap at the chance to immediately get her naked. Men who touched her like she was delicate and worthy of deliberation.

Sean worked his way back up, his breath sweet with the
mints he kept in his pocket. After a pause, impossibly soft lips
touched hers, brushing against her until her mouth parted.
Delaney's arms went around his neck. One of Sean's hands
was at the small of her back, holding her steady. He suckled
her lower lip, then gave a soft lick of his tongue, just a suggestion, an invitation. Her arms tightened as her legs lost their
strength. Sean responded by pressing her tighter against his
body, offering up his arousal, openly sharing how his body
was responding to hers. His lips and tongue traced and teased
her own, not too much, not too little, just enough, like a wine
tasting, warmth blooming in their shared breath, filling her,
all the way down to her gut, then her toes. Sean's soft groan
finished the ceremony, a verbal offering to show her how
much he wanted her.

Delaney took a moment to regain her senses, to figure out
where she started and ended, before she grasped Sean's hand
and guided him out of the storeroom and upstairs to the apartment. They didn't even bother flicking on the lights. As soon
as they hit the top of the stairs Delaney pulled him against

her. They fumbled their way to the bedroom, locked in each other's arms, their kisses growing more insistent, rougher, desperate. As soon as the backs of Delaney's legs hit the bed, Sean pulled away. His movements slowed, like he was trying to regain control, slow things back down. His fingertips slid beneath the hem of her shirt, his touch burning over her rib cage. He expertly undid the front clasp of her bra and slid her shirt over her head, tossing it to the floor.

His eyes fixed on her bare skin. "I've been dying to know what you looked liked since that last night in your apartment." Sean's voice was raspy. "You had on that white top with no bra. I could see a little bit but not everything. Just enough to drive me crazy."

Little shivers built inside Delaney's body. Sean ran his hand up her spine, soft enough to raise goose bumps, then rounded over her midriff as he traced his thumbs over her nipples, slow and sweet, until they'd hardened to stiff peaks. He tipped his head down and took them into his mouth, one after the other, his tongue rolling them around with just enough pressure to send tremors shooting into Delaney's core.

She realized, somewhere in the back of her fizzy mind, that she probably tasted like sweat. They'd been out in the heat all day, but that didn't seem to faze Sean, who sank to his knees and undid her jeans. He pushed her back onto the bed, and drew off her boots, one by one. There wasn't much that could make Delaney forget to take off her footwear, but kissing Sean was definitely at the top of the list. Her jeans came off next, then Sean's fingers gently slipped beneath the simple cotton of her panties and drew those away, too. Once she was fully naked, Sean's gaze was rapt, his breathing slow and hard.

"Take off your shirt," Delaney said, with what little voice she could muster.

He obeyed, stripping it over his head and dropping it to the floor. He was leaner than he'd been on their last run, a fact she knew because he'd often mopped his face with the hem of his T that day. He'd been muscular then, but now Delaney could clearly see his abs etched above the hem of his jeans. "I've been running more," he said, following her gaze. "You inspired me to pick it back up."

"Well, let's see. I need the whole picture." Delaney sat up and undid the buttons on his jeans, opening him up slowly and pushing them down his hips. Sean naked was a match to his personality: hard, fast and edgy, like a lithe animal ready to give chase. She admired him for a moment before he pushed her back on the bed, forming a protective cage with his arms. Sean kissed her slowly, starting with her lips, moving to her jaw, neck, up toward her ear, and back again. The hollow of her throat. Her breasts. Delaney's eyes closed. She hadn't let go in so long. Always, Delaney was in control, in charge, running the show.

Right now she was glad to forget about everything, just lie there and let Sean do anything he wanted. Sean's lips and tongue worked their way down, all across her body, a mingling of breath and tongue trailing a path of heat until Delaney was nothing but a puddle, melting into herself, her pulse raging. When Sean had wound her up so tight she couldn't go another second without feeling him inside her, she pushed against his shoulders and made him flip over onto his back. She reached into the drawer of her end table and withdrew a condom, rolling it slowly over him before straddling his hips. Sean's hands went to her waist, where he slowly helped guide himself inside. He squeezed her hips, his grip rough, his passion growing, despite how careful he'd been up to this point.

Delaney drew his hands from her waist and pinned them to the mattress. Sean's body pulsed inside hers, hardening even more as she slowly rocked her hips up and down and around, waves of pleasure already rising and crashing inside her. The feeling of his hard body beneath her, the sound of his gasps and moans as she drove against him were too much. Her climaxes came one on top of the other, a new one starting before the first one even finished.

Sean broke free of her grip, his hands grasping her forearms then sliding around her waist, and pulled her beneath him where he drove deeper inside her, reaching, claiming, owning every inch of her body. Delaney's arms circled his shoulders, his face in her neck as he gasped and cursed and praised his religion all at the same time.

The sun had shifted in the sky, the late afternoon rays coming through the half-open slats of the shades over Delaney's bedroom window. She rested in the crook of his arm, her shoulder rising and falling gently in her slumber. Her hair was glossy and ruffled, the back of her neck browned from the sun. A line of tiny black bird tattoos ran from the inside of her shoulder blade, up toward her neck, their wings in different stages of opening and closing, making it seem like they were actually moving. Sean imagined the birds were her soul and her skin was the sky.

She seemed so vulnerable like this. Naked and asleep, her limbs still, the soft curve of her hip peeking out from under the white sheets, her body smelling salty and flowery, like the cup of jasmine tea Sean had once drank at a luncheon where he and Castillo had been undercover.

One of her legs was threaded through his. Her head was tipped forward, into her pillow, highlighting the rounded prominence of her spine. Sean ran his fingertips over the soft skin of her shoulder. Delaney didn't even twitch, her breathing stayed deep.

The enormity of this moment was not lost on Sean. This

was a woman who wouldn't put her back to just anyone, let alone fall into a hard sleep in a man's arms. She was completely open, her weapon only a reach away, the dog she'd been entrusted to protect downstairs, along with the prized motorcycle. Everything Delaney cared about was within Sean's reach. Under Sean's watch.

He nuzzled close to her neck and ran his lips over the birds, one after the other, drinking in the warmth from her skin. She made a soft noise and shifted, pressing closer. A few more kisses and she rolled over in his arms. Delaney blinked, her dark lashes fluttering over her eyes, bright with sleep. "Hey," she said. Then smiled.

"Hey."

They stared at each other a spell before they both laughed. Sean pushed her hair from her face, enjoying the sparkle in her eyes.

Delaney ran her hand over his shoulder and down his back, over his hip, tracing his skin with delicate fingertips. When she reached his abdomen, Sean was ready to tell her that it wasn't going to work. He wasn't eighteen anymore. But then, in fact, it worked.

"You look surprised," she said.

"I am. I can't remember the last time…" He trailed off, his attention suddenly caught by noise in the hall. Something clacked over the wood floor. Delaney sat up in bed and looked in the same direction as Sean.

A second later, Wyatt appeared, carrying his leash in his mouth. He sat down in the doorway and dropped the leash on the floor.

"Wyatt," she gasped. "You came upstairs!" Delaney turned to look at Sean. "You weren't kidding. He finally came upstairs."

"That's quite a trick, with the leash," Sean said. "Pete taught him all kinds of things."

"Pete didn't teach him that." Delaney pushed back the covers and stepped out of bed. "At least, I've never seen him do it." She reached for her T-shirt, which lay on the floor, dropped it again and grabbed a robe that hung from the top of the door.

Sean watched her move around, carrying herself with confidence, completely comfortable being naked in front of him. She slipped her arms into the silky pink robe and closed it, hiding away her creamy skin and all the dips and shadows of her muscles and curves. "You need to go outside, don't you, boy? Good boy!" Delaney lifted the leash but didn't attach it to Wyatt's collar. "Come." She patted her thigh and the dog followed her out of the room. Sean listened as they headed downstairs, but he didn't get up.

Not right away. He stayed in bed a few minutes, enjoying Delaney's lingering scent and warmth all over his body and in the sheets. He'd gotten hard again and needed to let his body wind back down before he rose.

After a few more minutes, Sean reluctantly left Delaney's warm, sweet bed behind and stuffed himself into his sweaty, dirty clothes. A shower was going to feel like heaven. As he jammed his feet into his boots his gaze connected with the ceiling tile that had been crooked earlier. At the time, he'd decided it was nothing, but now, in light of how the Dudes had behaved at the motorcycle show, Sean wasn't so sure.

By the time he made it downstairs, Delaney was headed back inside, Wyatt in tow, on his leash. "He wasn't too interested in his walk today," she said with a grin. "We wore him out at the fairgrounds. Just did his business and wanted to come back inside."

"He's a big boy," Sean said. "He'll need lots of exercise."

Delaney's smile fell as she watched Wyatt rush to his water

dish and lap up the contents. "Do you think the Dudes were right? About him needing more space?"

Sean followed her gaze. "They weren't right about anything. People have dogs everywhere. Long as his needs are met, he'll be fine. He doesn't need a thousand acres to run around in."

"I know, but—" Delaney hugged herself "—what if they are right? What if Wyatt would be better off with—"

"With who?" Sean cut in. He grabbed a bottled water from the case Delaney had near the register. The sign on the glass listed them at a dollar fifty. He slipped two bucks out of his wallet and set them on the counter. "Those guys who thought he'd be a cool shop toy and terrified him into favoring a cold, concrete workshop? You know what it must feel like in there in the winter?" Sean twisted the cap off the water and took a long drink, not realizing just how thirsty he was until he drained the entire thing in one go.

Delaney's face crumpled, and Sean regretted putting that image in her head. Sometimes he forgot that the ugly things he saw on a daily basis while doing his job were things the average citizen wouldn't want to know about. Not that Delaney was an average citizen, but Sean hated how sad she looked. He honestly just wanted to wrap up her body, silky robe and all, into his arms, bury his nose in her jasmine hair and tell her it'd all be okay.

"Not the Dudes." Delaney waved a hand. "But maybe Wyatt would be better off with some nice family that has a big yard and a few kids for him to play with. Not stuck in a motorcycle shop with a biker chick who finds it hard to sit still on a good day. He hates when I leave. He's always trying to get out."

Finished with his water, Wyatt padded over to the Willie G, which Delaney had on one of her lifts, and did circles around the motorcycle.

"He looks happy to me. You just have to give him time." Sean eyed the motorcycle as much as he did the dog. He wondered what she was doing to the bike, getting a small surge of excitement picturing Delaney's hands on his motorcycle, making it better, like she had with his body. "Hey." He tore his gaze from the Willie G and the happy dog and strode over to where Delaney stood, arms wrapped around herself in her worried hug.

She tilted her head up to face him as his hands lit on her shoulders. Delaney Monroe's eyes were a clear, bright amber—the color of irony, since ancient things had met their demise being trapped in the lifeblood of an extinct forest. "You only promised to foster him, right?" Sean reminded her. "If you really think Wyatt would be better off with a nice family with kids and a yard, then you can hold on to him until that happens. Right?"

"Right," she agreed, her mouth turning down at the corners.

"Hey, I need to ask you something." Sean hated to bring up the Dudes, but since Delaney already had, he went with it. "Earlier, when I came back to get Wyatt, and I had to go upstairs... I noticed a ceiling tile in the corner of your bedroom, by your window, that was popped out of the track. Just kind of stuck out to me as odd. Has it always been like that?"

Delaney's eyebrows rose. "I... No. I don't think so. I would've noticed that."

"I felt around up there and came up with nothing," Sean admitted. "And then I slipped the tile back in the rail. I didn't think much of it at the time, but..."

Delaney was quiet, her bottom lip tucked in at the corner. After a moment she grabbed her phone off the counter and pushed some buttons. "I'm checking the cameras," she said. "Just in case." Another long moment went by, then her jaw dropped. "Sean, look at this."

Sean peered over her shoulder as she backed up the footage. One second the screen showed the back of Delaney's shop, and the next something large and blurry came flying fast, right at the lens. Then everything went black.

They looked at each other, then they both bolted for the back room.

Delaney got to the bay first, which she raised as quickly as her arms would go. Sean dove outside as soon as he had enough space, with Delaney close behind. She gasped.

The camera lay on the concrete patio that rimmed the shop, smashed and dented.

As Delaney rushed over to pick it up, Sean grabbed her by the elbow and reined her back in. "Leave it," he said. "I'll call it in. And get pictures."

Delaney froze, her face a mask of anger and fear. Sean spied the weapon, a few feet away. A large rock, out of place on the patio, some mud and dirt still clinging to the bottom, like it'd been freshly dug up to serve as a missile. He pulled out his cell and started taking pictures.

"This was Dude and Dick." Delaney's voice was cold, her words measured. "I know it. They came here while I was at the fairgrounds. After I left and before you came to get Wyatt."

Sean rolled the clues around in his mind, and, though he tended to agree with her this time, he said nothing.

"Clearly they were after whatever was in the ceiling." Delaney's eyes widened.

Sean had just parted his lips to speak when the sound of multiple engines came roaring up the hill, toward the shop.

Delaney and Sean both rushed around to the front, to see

who was coming. Delaney shielded her eyes against the setting sun and peered into the distance. "Holy hell."

Sean followed her gaze but only saw a mass of bikers headed this way. "What's going on?"

"My uncles are here," she said, her voice barely loud enough to ride over the engine sounds as the motorcycles, bearing some seriously rough-looking dudes, whipped into the lot and angled near Delaney's truck. "My uncles drove out from Omaha!"

twenty-two

Sean spent the rest of the evening meeting Delaney's "uncles" in between taking photos and an official report about the vandalized camera for Delaney's case. They were a hard-nosed bunch who clearly would do anything to protect their buddy's daughter, and who clearly didn't love cops. Sean took it all in stride. After introductions he kept mostly to himself while he gathered clues and reaffirmed his opinion that the uncles had nothing to do with the theft of '33.

By the time he made it home for a shower, it was late and Sean just collapsed on his bed, asleep in seconds. He woke to sunshine, Callie wrapped around his back and a head fresh and ready to solve this case once and for all.

At the station, Castillo was already at her desk and gave him side-eye for being late. Sean mumbled hello and buried himself in his notes. He'd done some poking around last night to find other bike shops in the area, and today he called up a dozen or so, starting with those closest and working his way farther out.

Near the end of his list, with a shop called Vintage Rides, he hit pay dirt.

"Dogwood County PD, this is Detective Sean Callahan. I'm just looking to see if you sold a certain part recently. A cadmium-plated rear brake rod that would work on a '33 Indian Four."

The guy at the other end of the line, who had a scratchy, older voice, didn't even hesitate or hem and haw about Sean really being a cop or did he have a warrant or any of the other stuff Sean had been getting all morning. "Yep. Sold one of those not too long ago."

Sean waited, trying not to get too excited. When nothing else came he added, "Do you keep records? Know who bought it?"

"Yep," the guy said again. "I'd have to pull it up."

Silence passed. "Okay, that'd be great. Do you happen to remember, while you're pulling it up, what the customer looked like? Young guy or pair of guys? Or an older guy with gray braids, maybe?"

"Nope. A woman bought it. Don't have to pull up the record to remember that."

Sean sat back in his chair and let that tidbit wash over him a second. Castillo glanced his way, obviously curious at his stunned expression. "I see," Sean finally said, clearing his throat. "Can you pull up that record, then?"

"Yep. I'll call you back. I got a few customers right now." *Click.*

The guy hung up.

Sean sat there a second, momentarily lost. A woman? He started to get a sinking feeling in his stomach. This could very well be a different brake rod, not the one that was bought for

Delaney's bike. It was also possible the old man at Vintage Rides hadn't heard him correctly, and this brake rod wasn't for the same kind of bike.

Sean sat there, staring into space. He turned back to his notes. He'd studied Delaney's social media at the start of the Great Case of the Missing Motorcycle, but now that he'd vowed to find whoever was behind the theft, the return, and apparently the repair of the bike, it was time for a revisit.

Personally, Delaney didn't do much. There were some old Christmas pictures on her Facebook and Insta accounts. Professionally, for Triple M Classics, she had a website, a Facebook business page and an Insta business account. He spent an hour scrolling, eyes sharp for anything out of the ordinary and anything in association with the motorcycle.

He'd just given up and closed out all tabs when he spotted something in his notes that he'd missed before. Delaney had provided a Facebook page for her father, which he'd glossed over because it was tucked in next to hers and he'd taken it for a repeat. Sean quickly called up the page and chuckled at the sparse contents. Looked like Martin Monroe had used Facebook about as much as Sean did—almost never. From the look of it, Delaney had been logging into her dad's page and using it as a sort of diary, posting things since her father had passed, maybe like she was talking to him, even though she knew he was dead. Sean got a twinge of sadness in his gut.

The most recent posts were of the truck and the motorcycle. There was a photo of '33 on the day it had arrived at Delaney's shop. The photo had one like, from somebody who called herself Lauren Bacall and who also used the old film star's photo as her avatar. Further poking revealed that Martin's only two friends were this Lauren Bacall and Delaney.

Sean clicked on her name. Lauren Bacall had no other

friends and no posts, though she had joined ten years ago.
"Really," Sean said. "Who the hell are you, Lauren Bacall?"

"We had it all!" Castillo's voice, coming from behind burst
into song. Sean jolted in his chair. *"Just like Bogie and Bacall!"*

"Jesus." Sean threw a balled-up piece of paper at her, which
she batted away with the finesse of a cat.

"Here's lookin' at you kid…missing all the things we did…" Castillo planted her hand on her chest and swept out her other
arm in a dramatic gesture.

"What *are* you singing?"

"You know. It's a sappy song from the '80s."

"No. Don't know it."

"Do so."

"No. I'm way cooler than you."

Castillo rolled her eyes, leaned in and poked her face into
Sean's screen. "Whatcha looking at?" After a few seconds she
sighed. "Didn't you get laid? You told me you got laid. So why
are you still on this case that isn't a case anymore?"

"First off." Sean raised a finger. "I never said I got laid."

"I know you went to the motorcycle show. Then you come
in here this morning with the sort of smile on your face that
only means one thing." Castillo shook her head and wagged
a forefinger. "Nuh-uh. Don't even try."

"Second." Sean moved on. "The case is fresh. Somebody
took out Delaney's security camera with a rock yesterday."

Castillo's eyebrows rose. She eyed the monitor again. "So
who's Lauren Bacall?"

"That's the million-dollar question, isn't it?" Sean texted
Delaney, asking her exactly that. Sean wondered which would
come first: Delaney's response or the call from Vintage Rides.

"Alright." Castillo shrugged. "You let me know when you
figure it out."

Sean eyed his messy desk with a sigh. He'd gotten slack on

the whole tidying up thing. He decided to keep busy while he was waiting so he got up, threw away a coffee cup, organized his pens and straightened out his keyboard. He'd just finished pushing in his chair when he froze, hands on the back of it.

"What?" Castillo was waiting in the doorway, fist on her hip.

"How's that song go again?" Sean didn't look up. He was afraid to break the spell, lose the thread of what was unraveling.

"What? Oh." A few seconds passed. *"Wrapped around each other...trying so hard to stay warm...we had it all..."* Castillo hummed a little bit, like she might've forgotten some lyrics. "Why?"

Sean finally looked up. He knew he was smiling, but he didn't realize how big until Castillo mimicked him.

"I know who did it."

"Did what?"

"I know who stole Delaney's bike."

twenty-three

"My mother took '33?" Delaney's voice was small and hard, like it competed with itself. "Are you sure?"

"I went to your dad's Facebook page. I saw the picture of the bike. I saw Lauren Bacall was his only other friend. Then Castillo started singing."

Delaney's eyebrows knitted. They were the only ones in the shop, other than Wyatt, who was lying on the tile, gnawing on a rawhide. When Sean had asked where the uncles were, Delaney said they'd gone out to buy her a new camera to install out back of the shop—this time in a different location, one Sean had suggested because it was hidden but would still capture the grounds. "What do you mean, 'Castillo was singing'?"

"We had it all," Sean sang, his voice low, so as not to reveal just how bad a singer he was. *"Just like Bogie and Bacall."*

The corners of Delaney's lips twitched up.

"Anyway." Sean stopped singing and waved his hand. "It's a love song. It's about old love. And loss. And I thought, maybe

Bacall was an old lover. I mean, she's obviously important to him. Your dad didn't give two fucks about Facebook. His only friend was his daughter. Who was this other extra special person? She had to mean something. Then I was cleaning up my desk. Tidying it up—this thing I've been doing since my divorce. Making sure everything's neat to end my day. And when I first started doing it, it just made me feel sorry for mothers because they're always cleaning up our messes. And as I stood there, tidying up and thinking about mothers, I thought again what we've asked ourselves over and over. Who would do that? Who would steal a bike and fix it? The same person who'd take the time to lower the bay door to how she'd found it. So the rain couldn't get in." Sean gestured with his hand as the thoughts crystallized beyond what he'd realized back at the station. "It all made so much sense, seemed so simple, once I figured it out."

Delaney was quiet for a long time. She kept parting her lips, then closing them again.

"Also," Sean added, when he could see there was still some doubt in Delaney's eyes, "I tracked down the person who bought the brake rod for '33. A shop a couple hours south called Vintage Rides. The woman who bought the part paid cash but the shop owner described her to me. Slender. Small. Dark hair. Raspy voice. Sound familiar?"

Delaney's expression changed, slowly going from doubt to anger. "Are you going to arrest her?" she finally said.

Sean gave a short laugh. "Do you want me to arrest her?"

Delaney jerked back a shoulder. "She stole my bike. And she knew how much that bike meant to me. To my dad."

Sean stepped in and placed his hand on her back. The warmth of her spread from his palm up into the rest of his body. "Maybe that's why she fixed it."

"Nah." Delaney flinched a little under Sean's touch. "She

doesn't care about anyone but herself. She probably hit rock bottom. Lost her job. Stole it to sell. Fixed it up a little and then figured out it wasn't as easy as she thought it would be to move." Delaney stared into space, her eyes glittering with anger. "I was the stupid one who posted a picture. And the name of my store."

Sean slid his hand to Delaney's jaw and grazed his finger under her chin until she looked up at him. "This doesn't feel like that. I said it before. This feels personal. She might've had her own reasons for taking that bike. Your father was still connected to her, Delaney. From what I know of him...everything you've told me..." Sean shrugged. "He doesn't sound like the kind of guy who would keep her in his life if she hadn't been picking herself up. If she didn't still mean something to him."

Delaney swallowed hard, her eyes now glittering. Then she shrugged. "I wouldn't know. I haven't talked to her in years."

Sean shrugged back. "Maybe now is the time."

Delaney sniffed deeply and drew up her shoulders. "No offense, Detective, but that's none of your business."

"Not even a little?"

"I'm not a big fan of people who give up on the ones they're supposed to take care of. You should understand that better than most. Even if my mother is clean, she can't make up for what she did with a few new motorcycle parts."

"Nobody said that. All I'm saying is, talk to her. Give her a call or drive down. She doesn't live far. If you want to know why she did it, just ask her."

"I don't want to know. I don't care. Arrest her if you want. But as far as I'm concerned, that's the only say you have in the matter."

Sean crossed his arms over his chest. "I see. Well, I may not have any say in the matter but I'm giving you my two cents anyway. Don't be so stubborn you lose an opportunity to at least listen to her."

"I appreciate all your help with the case, Detective." She imitated him by crossing her arms over her chest, too. "But you can now officially consider it closed. I don't want your two cents. I can take care of myself."

"Nobody doubts you can take care of yourself. I'm just giving a little advice. I don't have parents anymore. You no longer have a father. But your mom is alive. And from what you told me, she didn't really have parents, either. Maybe show a little compassion. Maybe don't waste that opportunity."

Delaney's whole face turned red. "She's an opportunity now? She stole my bike! And now you're taking her side."

"I'm not taking her side."

"Well, whatever you're doing, I don't like it. I also don't want your advice. Just because we slept together one time doesn't mean you get to tell me how to live my life or deal with my relatives." Her words spilled out in an angry rush.

Sean was quiet awhile. "We slept together one time?" he finally said. "Is that what we did?"

"Isn't it?" Delaney's eyes narrowed, her cheeks on fire, her eyes bright with fury.

"It felt a little different to me," Sean said. "I thought it was to you, too."

"Well, it wasn't." Delaney's voice got tight, sounded a little choked. "We should've known this is how things would go. You like to chase and I like to run. That's all we ever were. All we could ever be. Pretty soon, you'll get bored and I'll get antsy. It'll just be a game of chicken to see who flinches first."

Some silence passed before Sean spoke again. "Maybe that's how you see it. But I thought we were good together. Better together." Sean reached for her, but she stepped back, well out of his reach.

"This shop isn't going to make it, anyway, Sean. I didn't win the money I needed—thanks to the mother you want me to magically reconnect with—and the Dudes have pretty much sunk my chances with all their bad press. I probably won't be here much longer."

"So you're giving up?"

"No, I'm not giving up." Her words snapped out. "I never stood a chance."

"You stand a good chance, if you don't quit." Sean knew which way this was going to go, even as he spoke. But he couldn't stop himself. "No matter what the Dudes said, you've got bikers behind you. Every single woman in this county." Sean loosed a laugh that had no humor. "And if money is the problem, you'll find it. All you have to do is let someone help you for once in your life."

Delaney's jaw dropped.

Sean knew it was time to shut up, but he just kept going. "You think everything is fight or flight. And that's okay. That's how you've been trained to live for a long, long time. Your mistake is thinking you have to fight alone. You have a whole army of people here to help you. So quit making excuses. Quit looking for a reason to bolt."

Her eyes flashed, rivaling a lightning storm in a tornado's yellow sky. "Get out."

"Sounds like I touched a nerve."

"I said *get out*."

"Don't worry." Sean's words came out a hard growl. "I'm leaving."

He paused as he reached the door, his gaze settling on Wyatt. The pittie was perched near the Willie G, up on a lift. His ears were pinned back, his eyes anxious. The dog let out a nervous whine. "You gonna bail on him, too?" Sean's voice came softer than he expected.

Delaney had her face in her hands, and didn't lift it. Her shoulders twitched.

"That's a damn shame."

Then Sean turned and left Delaney Monroe's motorcycle shop.

Maybe for the last time.

twenty-four

Tabitha nearly had her nose pressed to the glass, hiding in the darkness outside the front door. The interior of the shop was brightly lit, and inside she could see a group of large men, all in blue jeans and leather vests, plus Delaney, clustered around one of the motorcycles she had up on a lift. Wyatt was there, too. He was excited, circling the men like he was part of the conversation. Tabitha wondered how long Wyatt had been back.

Trinity had just started whapping her tail with impatience when Delaney looked over, squinting at the glass. Tabitha waved, feeling foolish, like a window peeper.

Delaney jogged over and unlocked the door. As she pushed it open the cool air leaked out into the muggy night. "Hey, girls." She smiled down at Trinity. "C'mon in."

"Sorry to bother you." Tabitha stepped inside. She nodded toward the men. "I didn't know you'd have visitors."

"It's okay. These are just my bum uncles." Delaney raised

her voice on the last two words, making the men burst into smiles and laughter. "They rode all the way from Omaha to check up on me. C'mon over and meet them."

"Don't listen to her!" one of them shouted. "We just wanted to go for a long ride. Pippie just happened to be at the end of it."

Raucous laughter followed.

Tabitha drew closer, Trinity at her side, calm and alert. Wyatt rushed over to greet her, maybe remembering her from before. His entire backside wagged as he pressed his muzzle into Trinity's face. Trinity maintained her composure, tilting her head this way and that to deter his eager greeting.

"Wyatt, come," Delaney said, and the dog went, after some consideration, to her side.

Tabitha assessed the four men who faced her and knew immediately that these were probably not genetic uncles, at least not all of them. Despite the similar clothing, not one guy looked much like the other.

"Tabitha, this is Boom." She pointed to a huge guy with a barrel chest and legs to match, his umber skin highlighted by a white T-shirt and a salt 'n' pepper beard. "Donnie." She patted the potbelly of a slighter shorter guy with a bushy beard and a hoop earring in the left ear. "Zip." Delaney waved a hand at a tall, skinny guy with knobby elbows and thick eyebrows, drawn in at the center, perpetually thoughtful. "And Sal." The last guy was shorter than the rest and had the most tattoos. From what was showing on his forearms it looked like he had two full sleeves, along with a couple on the sides of his neck and even some on his fingers.

"Hi." Tabitha waved, feeling completely at ease with the uncles, even though they might give some people pause if they were clustered outside a bar. "Omaha, that's a long ride."

"Well, if Pippie would stay put for more than a damn day,

we wouldn't have to work so hard to see her." Boom, who obviously got his nickname from his voice, clapped a hand on Delaney's back like she was just another big dude in the lineup.

She lurched with the impact. "With uncles like these, who can blame me for leaving home first chance I got?"

The laughter went up a notch, filling the room with male rumbles, finger-pointing, curses and testosterone. Tabitha didn't know if she should be scared or jealous. Her quiet life of churchgoing and crossword puzzles, all under the watchful eye of Auntie El, was clearly an entirely different world from what Delaney had grown up in.

"How long are y'all staying?" Tabitha didn't know if the usual small talk was appropriate for this bunch, but it was all she knew. She couldn't talk motorcycles and had no idea how to deal with father figures. They were like this strange, foreign, scary and yet desirable entity that sent her running and yearning at the same time.

"We've been here a few days," the one with tattoos said. Tabitha was pretty sure it was Sal. He had a gentle lilt to his voice. "We're headed back tonight. Just a quick visit."

"Had to check on our girl," Donnie added. "See how she's doing. See with my own two eyes." His voice softened.

"Awww, you guys." Delaney pretended to sock him in the gut. He caught her wrist and pulled her into a bear hug. The other three closed in, like a giant football huddle. Wyatt came alive and ran around them, rising on his hind legs and barking.

Trinity took it all in with quiet patience. Tabitha tried not to laugh, but when Delaney emerged from the circle, looking like a girl bursting through the surface of water, out of breath, she couldn't help loosing a smile.

"You ride with Pipsqueak, here?" Sal looped his arm around Delaney's waist and drew her to his side.

"Um, no." Tabitha had come out here feeling down and a

little lost, her need to glom on to some of Delaney's strength like a desperate pull. She'd never expected to discover the *pipsqueak* side of hard-ass Sergeant Monroe. "I've never ridden a motorcycle. Not even on the back."

All of the big uncle men exchanged horrified looks. Delaney followed this with a grin. "You're in trouble, Steele," she said. "You're going to be on the back of a bike before the night is over."

The next half hour was filled with conversation, most of which Tabitha couldn't follow, despite the herculean efforts of everyone to make her feel part of the family. They sipped coffee from paper cups, brewed in the pot beside the register, and ate mini chocolate bars from the bowl next to the coffeepot, until Boom decided he was way too hungry to keep eating "baby chocolate" and needed real food before they got on the road.

"It's All You Can Eat Pasta Night at Nonni's, across the street," Delaney said. "I go every Wednesday."

"Let's do it," Boom agreed, which is when Tabitha tried to mind her manners and head home.

"No way." Delaney squeezed her shoulder. "You're coming along."

Tabitha almost protested, not wanting to interfere, but Auntie El was at book club tonight and the choice between sitting at home alone with a sandwich and sitting in a warm Italian restaurant, eating pasta with friends, was an easy one.

Everybody geared up and headed for the door, which was when Wyatt tipped his head back, ears flopping, and let out a long, low howl.

"You sure he's not a hound?" Donnie joked.

In reply, Wyatt sat back on his haunches, tapped his front paws and howled again, this time like he was facing down a full moon on a smoggy night.

"What the...?" Delaney crossed over to him, knelt down and rubbed his shoulders. "What's up, Wyatt? Don't be sad. You can't go to Nonni's, but we'll be back quick."

"He sees that Trinity gets to go," Tabitha suggested.

Sal tapped his temple and pointed at Tabitha. "She's right. You're a smart girl."

"He tears up the place when I leave," Delaney said. "He's a wild spirit and hates to be left behind. That's why I worry about him here. I don't have as much space to offer as other people."

"Yeah, he might need a big place to run," Zip agreed.

"Bunch of kids," Sal added.

"You're just fostering him, right? He'll find a family," Boom chimed in.

Delaney's face, which had been plastered with a smile that just seemed a little too big since Tabitha had arrived, crumpled as the uncles fired their suggestions. Tabitha felt the dark cloud to her core. Delaney's soul had been on fire all night, her insides coming alive inside this group of men she obviously loved and trusted with her life. Now she was drying up inside. Something was eating away at her. Maybe it was just Wyatt, but Tabitha sensed it was more.

"You should get him a sidecar," Tabitha said, her small voice just an undercurrent to the cacophony of male opinions. She was pretty sure nobody heard her, except maybe Trinity, and she wasn't going to repeat herself. It hadn't been Tabitha's place to speak in the first place.

"What was that?" Delaney held up her hand to the men and closed it in a fist. The men went silent.

"Nothing." Tabitha shook her head. "It was—" she eyed the restless pit bull who had calmed a little bit since nobody had actually walked out the front door "—stupid."

"Stop doubting yourself, Steele." Delaney's words were strong, but her voice was soft, encouraging. "What'd you say?"

Tabitha shrugged. "Well, it's just that...well, it's pretty obvious to me that you and Wyatt are the same. You just said he's a wild spirit. He loves motorcycles. And he's always running off. Why would he belong with anyone but you? You're perfect for each other. So, my suggestion was...get a sidecar. For Wyatt." The room got even quieter, if that was possible. "That's a thing, right? I've seen it on TV. Dogs who ride with their people. They get them some goggles and a sidecar. I've seen little ones ride inside people's jackets, but," she said, stifling a giggle, "that wouldn't work for Wyatt, obviously. But if he had a sidecar, he could go with you lots of places."

The men cast glances between Wyatt and Delaney and Tabitha, each of them raising their eyebrows or murmuring approval. "That'd be easy for you," Sal finally said. "You could put a sidecar on your Rebel, no sweat."

"There's no question he loves motorcycles," Boom added. "I've only been here a few days and have never seen a dog act like that. When she takes him out—" he turned to Tabitha "—he runs circles around all our bikes out there, lined up in a row. Poor Pippie tries to keep up with him, flying behind with the leash in her hand." He loosed a belly laugh that filled the whole store.

Everybody laughed now, except Delaney. She wasn't quite smiling, but Tabitha could tell that her spirit had filled her back up, at least a little bit.

"You know what, Steele? That's not half-bad. I think I might actually do it." Delaney's eyes held Tabitha's for a long moment. "Thanks, girl."

Tabitha shrugged, her cheeks suddenly warm. "No problem."

★ ★ ★

Their strategy when departing, to avoid another howling incident, was to leave in stages. Tabitha and Trinity left first, followed by the uncles in pairs, and finally, Delaney, who handed Wyatt a chew stick before she locked up behind her.

It seemed to work, and everybody settled into the soft lighting and garlicky smells of Nonni's in high spirits. Once the food was underway, Delaney turned to Tabitha, a forkful of eggplant parmesan poised in front of her lips, and said, "Thanks for that, back at the shop."

Tabitha poked her fork around her salad and shrugged. "It was nothing."

"That's not what I'm thanking you for." Delaney gave her a knowing look. "You were the only one who saw how I was feeling. About Wyatt. All these lunkheads were trying to make things easy for me." She tilted her head toward the four men down the length of the table, but they were deep into a debate about the greatest basketball player of all time. "Only you saw what I really needed to hear, which was a solution to keeping him, not giving him away."

Tabitha sighed and looked down at Trinity, who was settled on the floor next to her chair. Just looking at the dog made her feel better sometimes. "I could feel it," she admitted. "You don't want to give up on him, like everyone else has. More than that, you don't want to be someone who takes the easy way out. Bails when things get hard. That's not who you are."

Delaney's chewing slowed. Her eyes misted up. She looked away. Tabitha got the sense once again that there was more going on here than the issue with Wyatt. "You're good at what you do," Delaney said, after some time had passed. "You still in the spiritual guidance field?"

Tabitha's pulse picked up a little. "Not since the navy. I don't do anything. I'm…nothing right now."

"Don't say that. You're not nothing. You're just…re-becoming."

Tabitha smiled. "I like that." She nibbled at her garlic bread. "I do have an interview tomorrow. It's with Clementine, from the gym. To work at her running store."

"Well, there you go. Good next step. And if you don't want to work there, I'm going to need someone to run my register soon, if business keeps up."

"Maybe I'll do both."

"Now we're talking. Hey. I've been wondering." Delaney lowered her voice. "About the captain. I looked him up, you know. I know he died a couple years ago."

The room started to squeeze in on her, like the ceiling was getting shorter and shorter. Tabitha drew air into her lungs slowly, held it a few seconds, then let it out for the same count. Then she made a decision. It was time. And Delaney was the right person. She knew that. She'd always known that, from that first moment in Afghanistan when Delaney had come rolling in with her crew to haul them out of the aftermath of that explosion. She'd been so confident. Fearless. Tabitha might've lost her mind without Delaney. "Yeah, the chaplain died," Tabitha said. "My auntie heard about it. Complications from the injuries finally got to him. Auntie sat me down, thinking I'd be upset. I was, of course. But not for the reasons she thought."

Delaney's eyes held a sharp glint against the candlelight. "You'd be upset because he died, and it was your job to protect him." Her words were slow, measured. "That's what everybody thought."

"Obviously, I was upset by what happened. But." Tabitha did some more of her box breathing, then pushed on. "That man made my life a living hell."

The waitress appeared to refill their water glasses. Delaney waited until she'd passed on to the men to speak. "In what way?" Her voice was soft, but not surprised.

"He didn't think women belonged in the military, let alone in Afghanistan. And he certainly didn't think I belonged in Religious Service. I guess, in his mind, all the places in the world are for men...except one."

"I met plenty of those." Delaney lifted her fresh water and took a long drink. "Not the religious part, because I'm not into that stuff. But the rest? Yeah. Been there. Did he harass you verbally, physically or both?"

Tabitha choked on her water. Some dribbled out on her chin. "How'd you know that?"

Delaney leveled her with a stare. "Let me guess. He made a lot of remarks about women and their place. He made remarks about your body, your hair, your smile. He'd brush by you. Bump into you. As time went on, these things got worse as he got more aggressive. You didn't like it, but you never said anything. You didn't want to be called weak. Or not a team player. Or prove him right, that, you know...you didn't belong there. You didn't want to speak out against an officer. A man. A chaplain."

"It happened to you, too?"

Delaney shrugged. "Same story, different details. Nobody in Motor T, though. My guys were legit. I never made use of the chaplain."

"It was so much worse to me because he was supposed to be a man of God," Tabitha admitted. "I tolerated that stuff more from others. But him? He wasn't supposed to be like that. He was supposed to be better than that."

Delaney tucked the side of her mouth into a wry half smile that stopped just short of being chiding. "Yeah."

"But I could handle that," Tabitha rushed on, before she lost her courage. "It wasn't right, but I could handle his comments, his criticism, his 'accidental' brushes. Then one morning, right before we rolled out, I…I said something." Tabitha felt her voice getting thinner, losing its power.

Delaney faced her, silent, waiting.

"I told him that God sees all things. And that he would be judged one day for the way he was treating me."

Silence passed. Delaney laid her fork down on her clean plate, folded her hands together, elbows on the table, and fixed Tabitha with a long look. "Is that the day you hit the IED?"

Tabitha didn't even have to nod. She felt the unwanted warmth and wetness fill her eyes. "I remember sitting there, after the explosion, just sort of out of my mind. It was like my words had come true, before my very eyes. But I didn't want it like that." She shook her head, tears leaking down her face. "Not like that. My only saving grace was that he lived. And then…" Her words choked off. "He died. So much time had passed, but everything came back. Just came rushing back."

Delaney slid an arm around her waist and drew her in, until her head was against her shoulder. She patted her back and said nothing. For some reason, that was perfect. People were always trying to say things. Say things that they knew nothing about. Tabitha closed her eyes and listened to Delaney's heartbeat, and the chatter of the uncles, still going on about basketball, and the clink of forks on plates, and her heart slowed. Her breathing slowed. The world slowed.

"I meant what I said." Delaney drew back and watched Tabitha swipe at her eyes and cheeks. "You're really good at the spiritual stuff." She made a gesture with her hand near her heart. "I mean, I don't know about all the religious things, but, you can see people. You can see what's inside, what's eating them up, how to really help them. Don't give up on that, Steele. Promise me." Delaney lifted her glass and held it out, suggesting they were going to seal a promise with a water toast.

Tabitha hesitated, but only for a second. Her eyes locked on Trinity, who'd sat up, body rigid, waiting with concern to see if she was needed or not. "I'm alright, Trinity." Tabitha stroked her head. "Had a little human help this time." Then she lifted her glass and clinked it to Delaney's.

The uncles kept talking sports and bikes while Delaney and Tabitha continued their private conversation well past the time the waitress grew impatient to turn over the table to hungry customers pressing against Nonni's crowded seams. When none of them could sit any longer, they moved to the parking lot to part ways.

"Alright, Pip." Boom drew her in against his massive chest and crushed her there. "Shop looks great. Your dad's bike is back. New camera is up and running and you let us know immediately if anybody hassles you again."

"Got it." Delaney's voice came muffled from the folds of Boom's jacket.

All the men took turns hugging her goodbye and telling Tabitha it was nice to meet her. Then they hopped on their bikes, fired them up and took off, one after the other, disappearing into the night. Tabitha could hear their engines roaring long after they were out of sight.

"Shouldn't they wait until morning?"

Delaney laughed. "They prefer night riding when they can get it. Less idiots on the road."

Tabitha felt wrung out but also lighter, like a two-ton weight had been lifted from her shoulders. Delaney, though, still looked troubled.

"You feel better, Steele?" She patted Tabitha's shoulder.

"I actually do," Tabitha said. "But how about you? You seem like something's eating away at you."

Surprise flickered over Delaney's face. "Damn, you're good," she muttered. Then she shook her head. "I've got some stuff going on. Personal stuff. Relationship stuff. Mom stuff. But I'll be okay."

Ah, Mom Stuff. Tabitha didn't know Delaney's situation with that, but if there was one thing Tabitha did know it was that Mom Stuff could rip you to the core. "Did you talk to your uncles about it?"

Delaney sniffed a sad kind of laugh. "No. They worry about me enough. I definitely wasn't going to bring up my mother during their brief stay. Then they'd never leave." Delaney tried another laugh, but didn't pull it off.

"You sure you don't want to talk? I've got time. God knows, I owe you."

"You don't owe me anything." Delaney's smile fell and her voice was serious. "And I'm going to be fine."

"You sure?" Tabitha repeated. Delaney's mouth said one thing and every other part of her body and soul seemed to be saying another.

"Yep." Delaney nodded, just a little too emphatically. "You go ahead and get home, Steele, and don't give me another thought. I'll always be fine."

twenty-five

B y the time Delaney made it back to the shop, it was late. She was ready for a hot shower and a warm bed. She'd just close her eyes and let all the sadness and worry disappear with her slumber. Come morning, she'd take stock of her life and go from there.

As soon as Delaney unlocked the door and flipped on the lights, she knew something was wrong. The shop felt cold, somehow, which was to be expected when you walked into air-conditioning on a muggy July night, but this wasn't like that. This was an empty kind of coldness. A vacancy that shouldn't be there.

"Wyatt?" It was the first word out of her mouth. Always, every time she came home, the restless pittie ran up to greet her, like he'd been waiting with high anticipation for her return. Tonight, there was no greeting. Delaney whistled and called his name again.

Silence.

Delaney's lungs squeezed tight, like she'd been hit in the gut. She tore through the shop, into the back room, even though the door was shut, then upstairs to the apartment. Surely, he was up here, fast asleep. He just hadn't heard her come home.

A quick rummage through the studio, heart pounding, revealed an empty apartment. He wasn't even in the laundry basket, where Sean had found him during the motorcycle show. *How?*

Everything had been locked. She'd used her key to get in. No doors had been left open this time. Delaney stood in the middle of her quiet apartment, remembering what Sean had said about the loose ceiling tile. If somebody really had gotten into her apartment after they'd knocked out her security camera, come upstairs and rooted through her ceiling for something, how had they gotten inside?

Delaney drew her phone from her pocket so she could text Sunny, just to see if Wyatt was there. In the silence, her heart loud in her ears, Delaney noticed the room felt thicker than it should. Humid. Her fingers paused on her phone and her gaze went to the window over the dining table that she never ate at. Through the sheer curtains, she could see the window was raised about one inch. The window that was always stuck. The window that never quite latched properly.

She rushed over and threw the window open, poked her head out into the hot night. It was too dark to see, but she knew the ground was far below.

Delaney grabbed her phone again and pulled up the footage from the hidden security camera that her uncles had installed. She cycled back, over an hour of stillness, until finally, she froze. "There," she hissed aloud to herself.

The silence was punctuated by peepers and crickets coming from the open window. Two men hoisted a ladder from a truck and laid it against the back of the shop, leading up to Delaney's apartment window. The smaller of the two climbed the ladder while the big one footed it. The smaller guy fiddled with the window, then climbed in.

Dick. He was unmistakable now. Dude put the ladder back in his truck, then went around front. Moments later, Dick came out the front door, Wyatt in tow, attached to a leash. The pittie sat down on the pavement and wouldn't budge, even when Dick tugged on it. Dick got in Wyatt's face and shouted at him. Wyatt pinned his ears back. Dick jammed his boot under Wyatt's rump and shoved him. The pittie fell over. A little gasp escaped Delaney's throat. Her hand covered her mouth as both men closed in on the dog, lifted him and shoved the struggling pittie into the back of their truck. Then they drove away.

Delaney's heart was seized by an icy grip. She might've been wrong about who stole '33, but she'd been right about the Dudes casing her shop. Tonight, they'd kidnapped Wyatt, and now she had no idea where they'd taken him.

Her body started to shake. She closed her eyes and rubbed her temples. *Get a grip, Delaney. They've got Wyatt and he's terrified of them. Think!*

Her eyes flew open. At the fairgrounds, the Dudes had bragged about inheriting their father's farm. Their name was Worley.

She closed out the video of the Dudes stealing Wyatt and did a search for Worley in the local white pages. Within seconds, she had it. The only Worley near her zip code, just one town over.

Delaney ran it all over in her mind as she barreled down the freeway in her truck. She ate at Nonni's every Wednesday. The Dudes had likely been staking her out and knew her routine. They also would be the only ones to know about the window latch that didn't fasten right. Dude's words from the motorcycle show came back to her, which she'd found odd at the time but made perfect sense now: *Sinbad! There you are!*

Like Wyatt had been missing. Or, rather, like Wyatt had been hidden when the Dudes had broken in and rummaged through Delaney's ceiling. Odds were, if Wyatt hadn't hidden from them—probably in the same laundry basket where he'd hidden from Sean—the Dudes would have taken him that day. Since they couldn't take him then, the Dudes had come back to finish the job, thinking that her security camera was still broken and unaware of the new one, placed out of sight.

Within twenty minutes, Delaney's GPS indicated that the Worley farm was coming up on her right. She hooked a sharp turn down a long, gravel road that was thickened with trees. The truck bumped and bucked over the old, pothole-riddled drive until the tree line receded and the road opened up to reveal an old farmhouse with a wraparound porch. Lights shone from the front windows. Parked out front were two older Harleys.

Delaney drew up beside them and sat in her truck, pondering her next move. She knew the Dudes had Wyatt and it was clear they were here. For a brief moment, it crossed Delaney's mind that maybe she was in over her head. She should've called the police, but calling the police meant probable interaction with Sean, and Sean was the last person Delaney wanted to see right now. The image of Wyatt, being knocked over by Dick, then thrown into the back of his truck, flooded her mind.

She leaped out of the truck and stormed the front door, banging as loudly as possible with the outside of her fist. She could take down Dick. Hell, she could take Dude. She just wasn't sure she could take on Dick and Dude at once. But there was no way she was backing out now. Delaney didn't stop pounding until the door swung open and she nearly clobbered Dick in the face.

He didn't even speak. He just stood there, hands stuffed in the front pockets of his jeans and a big smirk on his face.

"Give me back my dog," Delaney demanded. "Now."

Dick shrugged. "I don't know what you're talking about."

"You don't even want him." Delaney's voice shook, but she couldn't calm herself. "You said it yourself, he's just a goofy dog who wants to play. He's not a guard dog. He's not a *dangerous breed*. So give him back and go find yourselves a snake for a pet." Even as she said it, Delaney regretted her words. She wouldn't wish any living creature on these two.

Dick's smug smile fell. He took two steps toward Delaney and got right in her face. "You're right," he said, words barely escaping his clenched teeth. "That stupid dog isn't a dangerous breed. But I am. And you better get the hell off my porch before I prove it."

A chill ran down Delaney's spine. She drew a deep breath and steeled herself. She'd faced down way worse than Dick Worley. She shifted her stance, making sure her weight was equal on both feet. Time to get Wyatt back the old-fashioned way. Just as she'd braced herself to throw a fake punch, then sweep Dick's feet, Dude stepped up behind Dick, a rifle in his hand. "Is there a problem, brother?"

Dick's eyes didn't leave Delaney. "I don't think so. Miss Monroe was just leaving. Weren't you, Miss Monroe?"

Delaney quickly assessed the situation. The odds of taking both brothers were about fifty-fifty, without a weapon. The rifle wouldn't just be for show—Dude had probably been hunting all his life. He'd know how to use the weapon and wouldn't hesitate. Delaney was on his property. Yes, they'd broken into her shop and stolen her dog, but she should've called the police. Instead, she'd high-tailed it out here on adrenaline and anger—leaving her Glock at home because anger and guns don't mix—and now she had no recourse but to back out and regroup.

"This isn't over," she said.

Back behind the wheel of her truck, Delaney watched the Dudes finally close the front door. Once they disappeared she sat there, tears in her eyes, unsure what to do. She knew they had Wyatt. She couldn't leave him. But she couldn't get him out, either.

Without thinking, Delaney drew out her phone and texted Boom the Worley address, along with the words, They got Wyatt. After she'd done it, she realized her folly. Her uncles had been gone awhile and they were on their bikes. By the time they saw the text, it could be hours from now.

Delaney dropped her phone to her lap and her face to her palms. She cried quietly for a few seconds then raised her head and sniffed deeply.

Right before she started her engine, she heard it.

Coming faintly on the breeze, through the open window of her truck.

Wyatt's howl.

It was a lonely, sad, pleading cry.

He was somewhere nearby. Locked up. Desperate to get out.

Without another thought, Delaney lifted her phone again, hit Recents and clicked Sean's name. She linked the Worley address to the message, then just beneath it she typed three words.

I need you.

Sean stood inside the storage unit, dim light from the overhead bulb shining down on him as he stood amid a sea of boxes, one of Kim's Hummel figurines gripped in each hand. There had been many times over the course of his life that he'd asked himself the question, *What the hell are you doing?* And this was definitely one of them.

His answer to that question was lacking. Rather than watch some television, have a couple of beers, or even turn in early, Sean had made the decision to drive out to the storage unit in the middle of the night and throw out Kim's things once and for all. He'd told himself he was doing this to make sure that there was space in the unit to store the Willie G, which he planned to go pick up from Delaney tomorrow, in whatever stage of repair the bike existed. He'd give her some money, thank her for her time and haul that stupid bike back here, where it belonged.

The truth was, though, Sean already had plenty of space in the unit for the Willie G. So why was he standing here, angrily tearing through Kim's old crap?

His phone vibrated in his pocket. Sean set one of the rosy-cheeked figures down and drew the phone out. When he saw a message from Delaney, his heart felt like it might explode from his chest. He opened the text, ready for anything.

He dropped the remaining Hummel to the ground, listening to it shatter as he rushed out of the storage unit, not even bothering to lock it behind him.

Delaney didn't get very far down the Dudes' gravel road. She drove just until she was out of sight, then parked and headed through the trees, back toward the farmhouse. She wasn't sure what she was going to do, but she knew she couldn't leave Wyatt here. What if Sean was asleep and didn't see her text until morning? The Dudes didn't want Wyatt. They just didn't want Delaney to have him. They'd already hurt him by stealing him. There was nothing to stop them from hurting him more.

Delaney wound through the woods until she reached the back of the house, hoping to hear Wyatt howl again. A porch light offered enough illumination for her to see but was far enough away she was hidden in shadows. She stood there, next to an old shed, wondering what she was going to do next, when a whimpering sound came from close by. Delaney froze.

The whimpering sound came again.

Delaney rushed to the shed and grappled with the double doors, which had been chained and locked. "Wyatt?"

A scrambling sound came from behind the door. The whimpering turned to quick, sharp barks.

"Wyatt! I'm here." Delaney sank down and peered through a gap in the warped doors. A white muzzle poked through. "Wyatt!"

The pittie's barks turned to excited yelps. He licked at the hand Delaney offered.

"Don't worry, boy. I'm going to get you out." Delaney rose, brushing the tears from her cheeks as she scanned the shed. There was an old dirty window to the left of the door. "You two aren't the only ones who can throw rocks at things," Delaney growled as she spied a pile of bricks not far from the shed. She hefted one and tossed it at the window, which shattered easily.

Knowing she probably didn't have much time, Delaney stripped off her shirt and punched through the rest of the glass and rotted wood, then climbed through the window in nothing but her bra, her shirt slung over any remaining shards. Wyatt rushed into her arms as she squatted. His fur was lathered up, like a horse that had been ridden too hard. His tongue was hot with fear and agitation as he lapped at her face. "C'mon, boy. We have to go."

Delaney deadlifted him up to the window and pushed him through. She had just crawled out after him when shouts came from the direction of the house. Two figures were headed her way, one large and one small, both moving quickly.

Wyatt lifted his nose to the air, then darted for the woods.

Delaney turned to go after him, but the Dudes surrounded her. Apparently not thinking her a threat, they hadn't brought their rifle. Dick lunged for her, but Delaney blocked his arm and swept his feet. Dick went down on his back so hard he made a noise like the wind went out of him. Dude grabbed her from behind, his monstrous arms wrapping around her and lifting her off the ground. Dick had just risen to his feet, his face in a snarl, when the sound of a siren wailed in the distance.

The Dudes' heads whipped in the direction of the sound, which was soon followed by blue and red flashing lights that spread out over the grounds.

"Sean!" Delaney screamed, just before Dick reared back and popped her in the face.

"Freeze!"

Only one of them did as Sean commanded. The big one. The subservient one. The one who had Delaney in his grubby squeeze when Sean rushed to the sound of her voice. Dude dropped Delaney—who wore nothing but a pair of blue jeans and a bra—to her knees and stuck his hands in the air.

Dick ran.

"Dammit," Sean cursed, as he threw a pair of cuffs on Dude and watched Dick sprint into the woods. His gaze connected with Delaney. Not only was she half-naked, she had a red, swollen eye. "You alright, Delaney?"

She nodded rapidly. "Wyatt took off in the woods. They broke into my apartment and stole him." She pointed in the same direction Dick had gone.

Sean took off after Dick like a jackrabbit.

Dick clearly already knew how things were going to go down. Sean didn't care that this was the Worleys' property. He didn't care about the details of what happened here. All he knew was that Delaney was in their backyard, half-dressed, sporting the beginnings of a shiner. Rage fueled his speed.

Sean's feet pounded hard, one after the other. He didn't yell *Stop*. Sean wasn't in cop mode. He was something else entirely. Something that called on all his recent running training to kick in full throttle.

Dick was small and spry and knew the grounds, but Sean hauled after him in the pale moonlight. Dick's shadow moved quickly, but Sean kicked it into fifth gear.

He wasn't losing the race this time.

Just before Dick reached a break in the trees, Sean leaped. His chest slammed into Dick's back and they both went down, face-first in the dirt. Dick coughed and moaned. Sean drew Dick's arms behind his back and yanked him to his feet. "You're under arrest," Sean gasped, his lungs burning with exertion. "I'll let you know for what as soon as I figure it out."

twenty-six

Wyatt was curled in a ball at the foot of the bed, wrapped in such a tight coil it was like he was trying to disappear in on himself. His breaths came in deep, sharp gasps. Sean had felt like that a few times over the course of his life and empathized with that poor dog.

Delaney sat on the edge of the bed next to the exhausted pittie, who they'd found hiding under her truck after Sean had called for backup and the Worleys had been arrested. Her hand was on Wyatt's back as it rose and fell in his sleep. She looked up at Sean, her eye swollen and bruised. "Thank you," she said, her voice hoarse.

"None needed," Sean said.

"They're in trouble, right? Please tell me they're in trouble."

Sean nodded. "We have your footage of them breaking and entering. They had no idea that new camera was there. Plus, my guess is that the Dudes had drugs hidden in your bedroom ceiling. Based on the footage of them stealing Wyatt,

I'm getting a warrant to search their house. I'm sure we'll find something."

"Am I in trouble, too?" Delaney's voice sounded small and helpless.

"No." Sean didn't think he'd ever seen her so vulnerable. It was all he could do not to wrap his arms around her and draw her close. But he remembered her words, and kept his hands to himself. Just because she'd called him for help didn't mean she wanted his affection.

"Thank you," Delaney said again. She stroked Wyatt some more, her face so sad it broke Sean's heart.

"You already said that."

"I'm saying it again. I don't know what I would've done without you."

"Well, I'm...that's what I'm..." Sean drew a breath and sighed, steeling himself. "It's my job."

"Right." She turned back to the pittie, her strokes slowing.

"Listen." Sean cleared his throat. "Get some sleep. The Dudes are locked up. Nobody's going to bother you tonight."

"Okay. Thank you."

"Good night."

"Sean?"

He made it to the doorway before he turned back. Delaney looked small and sweet next to her sacked-out pit bull. "Um...Wyatt thanks you, too," she said.

Sean smiled. "Well. When he wakes up, tell him...anytime."

Delaney lay at the foot of the bed, curled around Wyatt, her body shaking, for a long time. She hadn't cried since Dad died, and before that, she couldn't even remember. Probably the day Chunk passed away. Tonight, she'd been crying so much her face felt like a swollen mass. The salt in her wound from Dick wasn't pleasant, either.

She must've dozed off, because when she woke the clock read 0333. Her eyes and nose were swollen and her throat scratchy. She pulled herself away from the snoozing dog and slipped downstairs. The security lights lit up the picture of Dad, sitting on '33. "I don't know what to do," she whispered.

After a round of silence she went to the Willie G, still up on the lift, and ran her hand over it. Her eyes filled up fast as she thought about Sean. All she'd had to do was text him tonight and he'd come running. He probably hadn't even thought about it. Even after the things she'd said during their argument.

Delaney grabbed a wrench and picked up where she'd left off on the bike, enjoying this moment, despite her turmoil and her black eye: the quiet of the shop, out on Three Rebels Street; her dog snoozing safely upstairs, not stuck in some ditch during a thunderstorm or in the Dudes' shitty shed. She started whistling, and as the sadness drained away and a new feeling started to fill her up, the whistling slowly morphed into "Tuesday's Gone," and in that moment, she remembered.

Her whistling stopped.

"Name one Lynyrd Skynyrd song that's better than 'Free Bird,'" Dad said.

"'Tuesday's Gone.'"

Dad smiled. "That's because your mother always sang it to you when you were a baby. That song always got you to sleep when you were fussy."

Delaney stayed frozen awhile longer, wondering how she'd pushed that memory away, or how it had morphed into something else, over time. It was clear as day now. She slowly put the wrench down, then found her cell phone on the counter. She held it for a few seconds before unlocking the screen and pulling up the number from her contacts. Her thumb hovered over the call button.

Finally, she pushed.

The line rang five times before a deep male voice, familiar somehow, said, "H'lo?"

"Hi, uh…" Delaney cleared her throat. "Is this Nora's phone? I know it's late. Or early. But…this is her daughter and I…"

"Delaney?" The man's voice sounded immediately awake.

"Yes. Do I know you?"

Brief silence. "Yeah," he said. "It's Walt. You okay, hon?"

Delaney thought maybe she'd fallen asleep and this was all a dream. But she found her voice. "Walt. Fat Boy Harley Walt?"

"Yeah. That Walt."

"Oh, my God." Delaney had to squat down to keep her knees from buckling.

"Listen, hon, I can explain—"

A rustling sound came, like someone snatching the phone, followed by a woman's voice, laced with sleep and guilt. "You figured out I took it, didn't you?"

Delaney's eyes closed. She was quiet a second, absorbing her mother's voice. "Well, hello to you, too, Nora."

Nora sighed heavily. "I didn't plan on taking it, if that means anything to you."

Delaney drew a deep breath. "Why did you?"

The flick of a lighter filled the temporary silence. "After you posted the picture on Facebook, I looked up your shop." The sounds of Nora sucking her cigarette to life came around her words. "Walt knew that store from before. Dude's Bikes. He said they were bad news and I got worried. Thought maybe you were caught up with them or… I don't know. I know a thing or two about the drug scene, y'know? I got scared. I know how close you were to your dad and I thought…well,

I thought you might need me. I know you won't believe me, but I was worried so I had Walt ride up to check out your shop. Make sure everything was okay. And after he came back and told me how good you were doing, he convinced me I should come up, too, and see for myself."

Delaney resisted the urge to interrupt her. Resisted the anger that tried to fill her back up. She thought of Sean's words, suggesting that she at least listen. She even thought of Tabitha, who seemed to be able to see right through her, and would probably tell her that listening to her mother wasn't what Delaney wanted, but it was likely what she needed.

"So Walt and I rode up to see you. All day long I couldn't get the courage. Just sat in the hotel and watched TV, thinking up all the reasons I should leave you alone. That night, I went out alone and had a few drinks. I don't know. Call it liquid courage. I realized your shop was just across the street. A quick walk away. I knew it was late but I thought, now or never. I was almost to your shop when the sky just opened up. That storm came up so fast I couldn't even blink." Nora paused, took a drag of her cigarette and blew out, long and slow. "I'd come that far. Despite the storm looking like some kind of sign, I kept going. By the time I got to your shop I was soaked to the bone. I was going to knock when I saw you outside, running around with a flashlight. And *that* is when I lost my nerve. When I actually saw you. So I ducked beneath the eaves to hide. And you took off in the woods, chasing down whatever you were chasing."

Delaney sank to the bottom step that led up to her loft and swallowed hard against her constricted throat. Still, she said nothing.

"I hid there, chain smoking for a while, unsure what to do. Then I saw the open bay door. I went inside. I stood there, dripping, tipsy, foolish…and that's when I saw Marty's bike."

A little blip ran through Delaney's gut. She'd never heard anyone call Dad Marty and anyone who tried got shut down, quick. *It's Martin*, he would say. Even the uncles called him Martin.

"I wasn't going to take it, Lanie." Nora gave a loud exhale, like she was at the end of her cigarette. "Then I saw the key was in it. And then the rain. It just…stopped."

Nora's voice whispered over *stopped*, like the ending of the rain had been magical. And, thinking back to that night, standing in the woods and the sudden silence allowing Delaney to hear Wyatt whimpering in the ditch, it had been.

"It was like a sign. And I thought, what if I ride it just one more time? For old time's sake. We had such wild times on that bike. Back when Marty and me were kids. Back before…" Nora trailed off, her thick voice choked. She sniffed deeply and continued. "Once I'd done it, I didn't know how to undo it. So I stayed in town quite a bit longer than I'd planned. Walt popped in on you and found out you wanted to enter the bike in that show. So I made some parking lot fixes to the old girl before I brought her back. I didn't want you riding around unsafe."

Delaney was quiet for a long time. She wanted to make sure the anger didn't rise back up before she spoke but once she decided to say something, she realized that the anger had never come back. It its place was something else. Something Delaney wasn't used to feeling. Something that could only be described as a *tucked in* feeling, like somebody had pulled that old pink-and-green quilt up to her neck after she'd fallen asleep on the couch. Somebody who would look out for her.

Somebody like Sean.

Walt.

Tabitha.

And yes—maybe even her mother.

It wouldn't be an instant fix. But it could be something. Maybe.

If Delaney gave it a chance.

"I know I've fucked up in so many ways it'd take you all night to list them, but I just wanted to tell you that—"

"I'm going to come down for a visit."

There weren't enough pin drops in the world to fill up the silence that followed.

"What did you just say?"

"I'm going to come visit you, Nora. Soon."

twenty-seven

Delaney's uncles, who didn't receive her text message until they stopped at a hotel that night, drove all the way back to her shop the next morning. The first thing Boom said when he saw Delaney's black eye, was, "Who do I have to kill?"

She filled them in on the night's adventures, particularly the part about the brothers being in jail. After some coffee and doughnuts, Delaney calmed them down by letting them help work on Sean's bike for a while.

Zip stood back and appraised the cycle as Delaney rolled the Willie G off the lift. He'd helped her put in a new clutch and restore the sissy bar and rear stash bag, which had been lost long ago. Delaney had found the parts by scouring on-line, cashing in a few favor chips and paying a little extra on expedited shipping. "Can't get over that oxblood color," Zip said, offering the bike a sweet, low whistle.

"I know, right?"

"Your copper is going to love it."

"He's not mine," Delaney said, her voice stilted. "I kind of fucked that up, even though he helped me get Wyatt back last night."

Wyatt perked his ears up and whapped his tail at the mention of his name. He'd made an amazing recovery the next morning, when he'd discovered he was back in the shop, surrounded by motorcycles. He'd run around like a toddler, tearing into everything, spinning, chasing his tail. Delaney wasn't a dog expert, but that sure looked like happiness.

"Bullshit," Zip said, chuckling as he admired Sean's restored bike. "Nobody does this good a job unless they're in love."

"Mmm-hmm!" Boom, perched at the counter, raised his coffee mug in a toast to that comment. "Don't even try to hide it, Squeaky. I'm happy for you. Even if he is a cop."

"Every inch of that hog screams love," Sal agreed, swirling his hips around in a gesture Delaney wished she could un-see.

"I'm good at what I do," Delaney protested. "Restoring bikes is my passion."

"That cop is your passion," Donnie piped up, eliciting laughter all around the shop.

"Oh, my sweet love," Sal raised his voice an octave and rested his cheek against his hands, palms pressed together. "I don't know how to tell you this, but my heart has been *arrested* by you."

The laughter rolled through the shop.

"As a token of my love," Boom chimed in, far less successful at making his voice sound like a woman's, "I want to offer this cherried-out Willie."

The laughter swelled and exploded, making Wyatt tilt his head back to bark.

"Don't you guys have to get going?" Delaney spoke above the din, glanced at her watch, then grabbed a handful of pens from the counter and started pinging the men one by

one to a chorus of protests. "Hour's getting late. Omaha is a
loooooong drive."

The laughter intensified, but died off as Delaney drew the
little guardian bell from Hell's Bells from her pocket and attached it to the back of the Willie G. In what could only be
explained as a wild coincidence, the bell included in Delaney's
winnings had Celtic knot work carved on it, something called
a *triskele*, when Delaney had looked it up, which seemed perfect for Sean Callahan.

"Seriously, Pip." Boom set his coffee mug down and came
over by her side. "What am I missing? He comes out to save
you in the middle of the night. And now you're hanging a
sweet little bell on his bike. You're not fooling anyone but
yourself."

Delaney drew a deep breath and gave her uncles the answer
they deserved. "My mom is what caused the fight." And then
she filled them all in on the story about '33.

"You told us you didn't know who took '33 or gave her
back," Sal said.

"Well, I wasn't really sure then."

Everybody was quiet awhile, exchanging glances, until
Boom spoke up in his confident bass. "Nora had a hold on
your dad all his life. She had something inside that he knew
was worth saving. And she did finally get clean. Long time
ago. By then, you wanted nothing to do with her and your
dad respected that." Boom shrugged. "She was the love of
your dad's life. Like it or not."

"She came out after your dad died." Sal glanced at the other
men as he spoke, obviously spilling a secret. "She waited until
she knew you were gone, but once you were, she went out
to the grave. She stayed in Omaha a few days. Was a mess. A
complete mess. She loved that man. Regretted all the years
she wasted."

Delaney considered that for a long time. It felt like the ceiling of the shop was bearing down on her, making her world too small to breathe.

Sal was there, holding her hands in his. He was the most sensitive of them all, despite all the tattoos that tried to suggest otherwise. "Nobody's telling you what to do. We're only saying that your mom is a new person. Or, who she was meant to be before life got real mean to her. And your cop boyfriend isn't so bad, either. Coming from us, that means something."

Slowly, the ceiling lifted. Delaney smiled, despite the burning behind her eyes. Soon, they were one big circle, all kinds of man sweat and leather and motor oil crushing in on her.

Smelled like home.

twenty-eight

"I don't know where you're at." Rhett's voice came over his shoulder. "But your snatches sucked today."

"I didn't get much sleep last night, but...yeah, you're right." Sean wasn't going to lie. His heart hadn't been in the weight lifting. The conditioning portion of the workout probably wouldn't go much better. But, he told himself as he eyed the stack of boxes people were grabbing, at least he wouldn't be able to think for twenty minutes. His mind would be cleared of everything but physical pain, which was so much better than all the other kinds of pain. Besides, Tabitha was here, and she needed a good role model, not a moody excuse-maker.

Sean had just slid his hands into the slots on the sides of the box he chose for his jumps when a soft whiskey voice spilled near his ear. "You think you could get mine for me? I could use a pair of strong arms."

Sean froze for a second, his body stiff but his insides thawing, which was an odd competition. He turned, and there she stood. Delaney hadn't been there for the barbell work, so she'd obviously just walked in. She wore jeans and a leather jacket and motorcycle gloves. "You aren't wearing workout clothes," Sean said, playing along, his voice cautious.

She shrugged. "Guess I don't need the box, then." She took a small step closer and tilted her head at an angle. Her eyes sparkled, beautiful, even with the shiner. "Just the strong arms, maybe?"

Sean offered a soft laugh. There was no point in acting standoffish. He'd already showed his hand when he literally dropped everything to rush out and run down the Dudes. He reached for her, already thinking about how good she was going to feel in his arms. Delaney's hand slid into his, the leather gloves warm from the sun. She pressed up against him, snaked her arms around his waist and peeked up. "I'm sorry I was such a jerk. Said the things I said. I just—" She broke off, thought for a moment. "My mom is a trigger. Which should tell me something. I've spent so much of my life on my own. So much of my life making everything temporary. So much of my life building up my defenses. But you were right. I can't give up on my dad's dream shop. *My* dream shop. I can't give up on…" she looked him up and down "…all kinds of things here."

"So what're you saying?" Sean suppressed a smile.

"I can make it up to you. I have some really good ways to make it up to you." She squeezed closer.

"Take it outside," Rhett grunted as he walked past.

"Oh, hush," Red scolded, also walking past, and swatted Rhett on the ass. "Leave them alone."

Sean jerked Delaney against his chest and she squeezed back, hard. He remembered Wyatt, when he'd curled himself into a tight ball on the foot of Delaney's bed and she'd comforted him. Except now, Delaney was the one in the center of that coil, and Sean was the one doing the protecting. Despite her brave face, he could feel the tremor that came from deep in her core. "Hey, you don't always have to stay put," Sean said, over the top of her head, nestled under his chin. "I'm a pretty good wanderer, too."

Delaney pulled back and peeked up at him, a glint in her eye. "I'm glad you said that. I was wondering if you'd like to take a little trip with me."

"A trip?" Sean was vaguely aware of the workout beginning without him, of Rhett calling out "Three, two, one, go!" and the music jacking up inside the speakers and booming around them. "Like a motorcycle trip?"

"Yeah. Exactly like that." Delaney raised her voice over the music. "Just a couple hours south. To Williamsburg. Someone I need to visit down there."

"Ah, I see." Sean's insides felt lighter than they had only minutes ago. "Sounds good. But I don't have a motorcycle."

Delaney grinned. "Yeah, you do."

twenty-nine

"Alright," Delaney said. "This is it. This is the test." She unhooked Wyatt's leash and pointed at the newly affixed sidecar attached to her Honda Rebel. "Place, Wyatt."

The pittie bounded inside so fast he probably hadn't even needed the command. He sat up tall in the seat, full of pride. Tabitha giggled and Sean burst into laugher. "Okay." Delaney slipped the dog goggles from her pocket. "Here's the real test." She offered the doggles, letting Wyatt sniff all over them before she carefully slid them over his eyes and attached them at the back of his head and under his chin. Delaney waited to see if he would shake his head or paw at the goggles, but he sat proudly, waiting.

"Last piece. The harness." Delaney strapped him in, and still Wyatt didn't struggle.

"I think he's ready," Tabitha said. "Fire it up and see what he does."

Sean slid onto his Willie G and gave a nod. "I'm all set. Ready whenever you are."

"Sure you don't want to get on the back?" Delaney looked at Tabitha and nodded at the seat behind her. "You can put Trinity in the shop and come along for the ride."

Tabitha shook her head. "I promised I'd watch the shop while you're gone and that's what I'm going to do."

Delaney smiled before she slipped on her helmet. "Good for you, Steele. I'm glad to hear that. Keep it up on re-becoming. You're doing a great job."

"You know what, Sergeant? So are you."

"Ha. Cheeky. I like it." Delaney gave the thumbs-up, then turned to Wyatt and said, "Wyatt, I want you to listen carefully. There's only one thing you have to do while on this ride." She held up a finger. *"Stay."*

Wyatt woofed.

"Alright, then. Let's go."

Sean called out, "I'll be right behind you, in case something happens!"

Delaney blew him a kiss, then fired up the Rebel. Wyatt didn't budge. She rolled out, and Wyatt smiled. The wind ruffled his ears back and danced through his fur. A mile down the road, and he was still smiling. "That's it, boy!" Delaney called out. "I knew you could do it!"

Once she was confident Wyatt was going to be okay, she clicked on her music and hit Shuffle. The song that poured through her earbuds made her laugh out loud. "Oh, Dad." She laughed and shook a fist at the sky. "How'd you get 'Bron-Y-Aur Stomp' on my ride playlist?"

Sean rode up next to her at a stoplight and shouted something. Delaney couldn't hear him but could read his lips. *How is he?*

"He's fine!" Delaney called back. "He's the finest dog I

knew, so fine!" Sean's confused expression told her he wasn't privy to the inside joke between her and Dad and Led Zeppelin. Didn't matter. Just as the light turned green Delaney shouted, "Guess what?" The next three words she just mouthed, deliberately slow, no sound at all. *I...love...you!*

And then she took off, the stun on Sean's face the perfect match to Wyatt's big motorcycle grin. Delaney saw in her mirror that Sean idled there a few seconds, apparently unsure what to do with that information as people started to honk at him.

Then he popped the clutch, restarted and came roaring after her.

"What do you think, boy?" Delaney called down to Wyatt. "Should I let him catch me?"

Wyatt's ears blew in the wind.

"Yeah. I thought so."

Then she gunned it.

★ ★ ★ ★ ★

acknowledgments

Many thanks to everyone who helped bring this story to life:

To Literary Agent Extraordinaire Sara Megibow, and everyone at KT Literary.

To everyone at MIRA/HarperCollins, especially Margot Mallinson, an amazing editor who sees the forest *and* the trees and can magically distill my novels into two-word titles.

To Chris Boswell, the best beta reader who ever lived.

To Detective Garry Mendoza, for helping make my police detective a true hero.

To Major Tristan Murray, USMC, for helping authenticate my badass heroine. Thanks to you and all the servicewomen who provide examples of strength and courage to our girls.

To Magdalena—my girlie, my first reader, my Biker Chick Hero. You amaze me daily.

To my entire family, for all your support and encouragement.

And to all my readers. You guys are the best.